The Donor

by

Nathan Wright

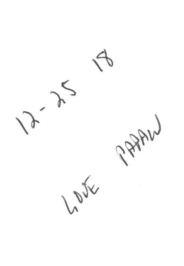

This is a work of fiction. All of the characters, organizations, and events portrayed in this novel are either products of the author's imagination or are used fictitiously.

ISBN: 978-1-7246-2236-5

The Donor

Autumn arrived early this year. The tree just outside the window possessed only a few leaves here and there and these lacked the deep green color of summer. The harsh winds of fall hadn't stripped the limbs completely bare, at least not yet. Colors of gold, brown, crimson, and even some light shades of green still decorated the tree as if dressing it up for the season.

The old woman who sat just inside that same window watched as a light breeze made the remaining foliage dance and sway. The few leaves that remained rocked back and forth, as if they were waving goodbye before letting go to make their final journey back to the earth from which they came.

The old lady watching this wonder of fall was the resident of a nursing home. Her name was Helen Montgomery and she was eighty-two years old. The last few days had been precious to Helen. It was as if she had just awakened from a long dreary sleep. Each day now brought back memories of events that, up until recently, had long since been forgotten. Things like leaves and a fall breeze were not to be wasted or ignored. They were to be observed and enjoyed with what little time remained to her.

She didn't know how long she had slept but it felt as though it had been years. Helen sat with her face only inches from the cold window pane, her mind deep in thoughts and memories from long, long ago. The smile on her face might have been similar to the one she had worn for months, the blank smile presented by a mind that had let go of so much. Today's smile was different; it was one of hope and joy, not the old one of confusion and darkness.

As Helen sat and enjoyed the moment, a nurse entered the room with a chart on an aluminum clipboard and a blood pressure cuff in her right hand. Around her neck hung a stethoscope which the old lady knew would be used, along with the blood pressure cuff, to check her feeble blood pressure. Helen hadn't spoken to the nurse in days due to the sleepy confusion that now seemed to be leaving her. This morning would be different; she could even remember the nurse's name.

"Good morning Mrs. Montgomery, how are we feeling today?" The nurse never expected to get an answer; Helen hadn't uttered a word in several weeks. The sounds she did make were not words at all, just noise made by someone who had lost their mental faculties many months, if not years, before.

Helen looked away from the window and thought about the 'we' the nurse had put in the question.

"I am fine thank you. You look so lovely today Nurse Sally, as you always do," Helen said before looking back toward the window.

The nurse smiled and continued about her duties as if she hadn't heard the compliment, and she probably had not. Nurse Sally, as the old lady liked to call her since back when she had first been admitted to the nursing home, had a true case of the 'speaking without listening' syndrome which seemed to plague all Hospice nurses. Don't get too attached to your patients. It was a defense mechanism used by caregivers who saw to the needs of the terminally ill. In some ways Sally considered herself a Hospice nurse although she really wasn't. Hospice nurses took care of end of life patients. Most of the patients at the nursing home weren't near the end of life, but they were heading in that direction.

Sally suddenly stopped what she was doing and gave Helen a surprised look. "Why Mrs. Montgomery, it is so nice to hear you say something this morning. You haven't uttered a word to anyone in such a long time." Sally only stood and looked at her smiling patient, not quite sure what to make of her. The smile was familiar; Helen had worn it for months. The voice this morning though was new.

After a moment she gently put the cuff around Helen's thin upper arm and positioned the stethoscope at the inside bend of her elbow. As she pumped the bulb that filled the cuff with air she noticed the nearly empty breakfast plate that sat on the roll-around table by the bed.

"Why Mrs. Montgomery, that is the most you have eaten in the past week." Helen only looked at Nurse Sally and continued to smile. The pressure cuff grew tight on Helen's upper arm but the old lady continued to smile without a hint of discomfort. Sally began releasing the air in the cuff and listened. The tightness slowly went away as the air escaped. A slight smile came across Sally's face as she gently took the device off Helen's arm.

"One-ten over seventy," Sally said as she rolled up the cuff.

"First you eat nearly all your breakfast and now I find that your blood pressure is the best it's been in many weeks, I am so proud of you." Sally finished rolling up the cuff and then noted the pressure on the chart held by the clipboard.

"Can I get you anything this morning Mrs. Montgomery?"

The old lady looked back to the window.

"No Nurse Sally. I think I may take a stroll down the corridor in a little while. Might even go out on the terrace and take in some sun."

Nurse Sally looked out the window at the rolling clouds and overcast sky. She then looked back at her patient. In her many years as a nurse Sally had seen a few dementia patients rally and experience a slight improvement. It could only be described as momentary though, lasting a few hours at most, maybe even a day, which was rare. But still she had never seen such alertness in a last stage dementia patient as she was experiencing now.

"I don't think that would be a very good idea Mrs. Montgomery. It is so cool out there and it seems the sun doesn't want to shine today."

"My memory of the sun is all I need Nurse Sally. In my mind the sun shines every day." Helen turned her gaze back to the nurse.

"Has any of my family called or stopped by in the last few days? My memory seems to be coming back to me now and I don't recall any visitors or phone calls in such a long time."

It was true that Helen Montgomery hadn't seen or heard from very many people since being admitted to the nursing home. One of Helen's ailments was dementia, described in Webster's Dictionary as 'The loss or impairment of mental powers due to organic causes.' But anyone associated with the disease, whether it be family or friend, knew it was much more than that.

It destroyed the ability of a person to maintain any semblance of independence or normality in their life. As the disease progressed the mind became locked in its own 'cell of solitary confinement' so to speak. No thoughts or ideas could escape. Nothing of the outside world could invade. The mind became a castle's keep. Dementia became the wall and moat. The drawbridge to the outside world would slowly close until nothing could either enter or escape.

Helen's case had been diagnosed four years prior. Very slowly at first the disease made its appearance. A forgotten name or a misspoken word became more commonplace. A lost thought that could never be recovered made conversation difficult and frustrating for Helen. Before long, the weeks turned into months and the months into years and Helen spent more and more time alone as friends and family started to visit less often. Some even began to stay away altogether.

This isolation seemed to accelerate the disease. It was as if it fed on silence and loneliness, which in turn broadened the gap between her and the family she loved and needed so desperately during this tragic time in her life. It was as if a torrent of loneliness had suddenly overwhelmed her mind and in its weakened state it succumbed altogether.

This rapid advancement of the disease was not uncommon. The easy diagnosis was that Helen must have experienced a small stroke or a 'Mini Stroke" as they have been known to be called.

The truth though was that Helen's mind had finally given way. As much blame could be attributed to the lack of family and friends, as to the disease itself.

But this morning Helen was alert and inquisitive. Frail as she was, the thought of a walk outside inspired her and gave color to her pale cheeks and lips. Her smile was warm and her eyes sparkled with enthusiasm. It was both a happy and a sad moment for Nurse Sally. Happy because, although she was a hardened Hospice nurse who kept an emotional distance from her patients, she was glad to see such improvement in a patient who, in reality, was beyond improvement. She was also sad because she knew the improvement was a temporary situation, soon to be replaced by an aimless blank stare without focus or future.

As Sally prepared to leave the room she stopped and turned to say she would be back in a little while to check on Helen. Helen was sitting very upright and firm in a chair beside her bed and next to the window. She was looking right at Sally.

"It was nice to talk with you this morning Helen. I will check on you shortly to see if you need anything." Sally stood a moment longer, not expecting a reply.

"Thank you Nurse Sally. I want to apologize if I am repeating myself but have there been any calls or visitors for me?"

Sally was caught off guard, and a little embarrassed. In her astonishment of Helen's remarkable turnaround this morning she had totally forgotten to answer Helen's previous question. The answer was no. No one had stopped by or called in at least four days but Sally couldn't bear to give Helen such news.

"I will check at the nurses' station for you. This is my first day back in three so I am not quite sure." Nurse Sally gave Helen a pleasant smile as she turned and walked from the room.

Helen turned back to the window just as a golden red leaf waved its last and released the grip it had held for so long on the very object which had given it life. As it fell from sight below the window sill and continued its journey back to earth Helen wondered just how long before she too would loosen her grip on life and drift back to the earth from which she came.

Helen thought of her big long-haired cat which was being kept by a neighbor who lived more than a hundred miles away in a small town in Floyd County, Kentucky. Blackie had been a very large part of Helen's life for more than nine years. As soon as she spoke to anyone in her family she was going to insist that someone bring Blackie to the nursing home for a visit. This in itself brought another smile to Helen's face.

The old lady slowly stood and made her way to the bathroom. Suddenly Helen stopped and noticed she hadn't reached for her walker. As she stood there she fully expected to topple over and break her arm, or even worse, a hip. But she stood straight and firm. No tic or wobble, no weakness or dizziness. This was truly the best she had felt in many a moon.

As she entered the bathroom her gaze fell upon the wall mirror. The reflection that stared back at her was of a woman ten years younger than she last remembered. The image took on a smile and then began to laugh softly. Helen was suddenly mesmerized with what she saw. Her skin was of a smooth even texture and color which hadn't looked this way in many years. She raised her right hand and touched it to her cheek. She then ran her fingers across her forehead and through her hair. The hair was soft and thick, the color seemed less gray and even a little less coarse, or was she just imagining it. Helen grabbed for her brush and pulled it through her hair. The brush felt good pulling her hair back from her face. She then took the brush and held it in front of her face. No loose hair, not a single strand. Helen continued to brush and fix her hair with all the joy of a young child. This must truly be a dream. For Helen it was a dream, one she hoped would never end.

Dr. Neil J. Slade pulled his Audi into the physician-only parking area at Beaumont Regional Medical Center in Lexington, Kentucky. It was already past 10:00 AM and he felt a little mischievous for showing up at such a late hour. His usual arrival time at the office was somewhere between 5:00 and 6:00 AM. This morning was different because today was his tenth wedding anniversary. He was proud of the fact that in his super busy schedule he had remembered a month prior to write the date in his Daytimer. Last year he had forgotten altogether and paid the price when he arrived home that evening at a very elderly hour, having worked late at the hospital.

Mrs. Sheila Slade, also an M.D., was showing up a few hours late for work herself at a private clinic which she and another female M.D., one she had roomed with in college, owned and operated five days a week on the outskirts of town. Both Mr. and Mrs. Slade, or Doctor and Doctor as Neil liked to tease his wife, had cleared their morning calendars weeks in advance so they could enjoy each other's company during a slow breakfast. It was the most time either was willing to spare from their busy practices. It was also the most time they had spent together on a weekday morning in many years.

As Dr. Slade grabbed his briefcase and slid out of the car his cell-phone began to vibrate. He flipped it open and recognized the number of the nursing home where a few of his patients were residents. Dr. Slade had a smart phone that he carried in his briefcase but found a flip phone to be more convenient to carry in his pocket. Anytime he failed to answer the smart phone after three rings the flip phone would then ring.

"Hello. This is Dr. Slade," he said as he headed toward the staff elevator.

"Good Morning Dr. Slade, this is Sally Jenson. Will you be swinging by the nursing home anytime today?"

"Good Morning Sally. Is there a problem?"

Nurse Sally hesitated for a moment. "Not really Doctor. I just thought you might want to visit Helen Montgomery and possibly do a quick examination."

"Has there been a change in her condition that would warrant a visit from me? My schedule today is pretty full, not sure I can spare the time."

"Her condition has changed Doctor. As a matter of fact she is eating and talking. Her vital signs show remarkable improvement this morning." Sally told the doctor.

"That is good news, but I must say in her condition it is highly unusual." Dr. Slade thought for a moment. "I have seen a few patients rally briefly and regain cognitive and verbal skills but not in the last stages of dementia. How articulate is she on a scale of one to ten, with one being the worst and ten being, let's say, as well as you and I are talking right now?"

Sally without hesitation answered "She would be a ten doctor."

"Are you sure this is Helen Montgomery we are talking about?"

At this Sally took a slight offense. A licensed registered nurse didn't make mistakes, especially when relaying confidential patient information.

"Dr. Slade, I am sure that the patient we are talking about is none other than Helen Montgomery."

Dr. Slade could tell by the tone that he had questioned a highly trained professional at the wrong time.

"Nurse, I am sorry if I have offended you. It was not my intention. Please understand that what you have just told me is quite out of the ordinary. As soon as I make a few quick rounds I will be straight over. In the meantime if there are any other changes please don't hesitate to call my cell again."

"No offense taken Doctor; please come by as soon as your schedule permits."

Dr. Slade closed his phone as he stepped into the elevator and pressed "G." As soon as the elevator doors opened he almost sprinted to his office. Once at his desk he quickly pulled up the chart on Helen Montgomery.

One of the great things about Beaumont Regional was that the information on any of his patients, including the ones at the nursing home, was uploaded to a main server at the end of every shift. With the clerical staff on eight hour shifts rather than twelve, which was the case for doctors and nurses, the information would never be more than eight hours old.

Dr. Slade scanned through the voluminous files back as far as four years prior, which was when he had first met Mrs. Montgomery and accepted her as a patient. The story was the same as with so many others he had seen over the years. Onset of the disease, slow progression with a steep decline toward the last and then the death watch! Mrs. Montgomery was in the last stages and beyond hope. That was yesterday! Now he had been informed that she was suddenly cognitive. Impossible!

Dr. Slade closed the program and leaned back in his chair, deep in thought. He knew that a trip to the nursing home would not be possible for at least three hours, if he hurried through his rounds, possibly two and a half. No good, he wanted to go right now. He had to see for himself. He had to know what was going on. His job was healing. That was the short of it; his job was to create healing. Now he had been informed of someone who was experiencing healing and he wanted to go and see for himself.

A doctor's life is more or less filled with the stress of watching their best work wasted by the relentless drive and energy of one disease or another. And if that were not enough of a deal breaker, throw in the abuse that most patients heap on their own bodies along with the fact that they rarely take the advice given by said doctor. Dr. Slade pondered these thoughts and decided he would leave for the nursing home within the hour. He would allow the nursing staff to cover for him during his absence. A smile consumed his thoughts as he anticipated his visit to the nursing home.

Fear can be described as either a word or an emotion. If you are talking about the word fear, it doesn't really mean much. 'I fear I have left my coat at the restaurant, or I fear the weather today will interfere with our plans.' Just a word used to put emphasis on a statement, nothing more, and nothing less.

The emotion 'Fear' can also fit into any number of situations, some very slight while others can be quite severe.

John J. Oden sat in the waiting room of his family physician's office and thought of the fear that had been his unwanted companion, both day and night, for the past six months. When he lay down at night he was accompanied by fear. When he woke up in the morning he woke up with fear, assuming he had slept any that night to begin with. Fear of the unknown, fear of pain, fear of dying. He was emotionally drained, physically exhausted and almost ready to give up.

His wife of almost twenty five years sat there beside him patting his hand. Nancy Oden was a very strong woman who had seen her share of heartache over the years. But this was without a doubt the most painful of them all. Her Husband was her life. They had no children at home or even nearby. Both the kids, John Jr. and Nellie lived away, one in Ohio and the other in Tennessee, and could only come in about once a month during the last six months. The children called every night though, to check on their dad and see how mom was holding up.

The prognosis six months earlier had not been very encouraging. The medical path he had staggered through during those same six months had been both physically painful and utterly without hope. John J. Oden had cancer.

It all started at work one morning in May. John considered that May morning as the comma in his life. He had been hurrying along at full go up until then. After that he had spent most of his time contemplating what the future held, or the end of it as it may be. The comma is the pause or slight separation in a sentence. In this case it was the separation in a man's life between the time when he was healthy and the time when he is sick.

Back before the comma John had been a successful farmer in Wayne County, Kentucky. He worked ten to twelve hour days and loved every minute of it. His spread consisted of two hundred acres of rich fertile farmland. He raised all crops, no livestock to mention other than his bird dog Clyde. He and his big John Deere six-wheel tractor pulled earth for ten acres of tobacco and eighty acres of corn every year. John only planted enough tobacco to even out the cash at the end of the season. Tobacco was getting a bad reputation as of late so each year he planted just a little bit less. The smaller tobacco crop suited him just fine. Tobacco not only destroyed a man's health, it also wore out the ground.

That had all been before the comma. Now John's life was filled with doctors' appointments and treatments. He had been diagnosed with lung cancer, well progressed. He had felt fine the morning of the comma. His wife fixed him his usual breakfast of country ham with biscuits and fried eggs. He ate heartily and finished his meal with a cigarette, something he had done for at least thirty years. After a second cup of coffee he kissed his wife goodbye and headed for the barn. He told her he would be back around 1:00 for lunch. As he pulled on the heavy barn door one of the rollers that supported it came off the track and the edge of the door bit into the ground. John grabbed his ladder and leaned it against the top of the track and up he went, hammer in hand. As he beat and banged on the track he was suddenly taken with a severe cough. The cough persisted. He eased down the ladder and sat on a stool that was by the door. Five minutes later he was still coughing, and hard. It was as if he couldn't catch any breath at all.

Finally the cough eased up a little. John sat on the stool and rested, completely exhausted and covered in sweat. He took out his handkerchief again and dabbed it across his forehead. Then he wiped his face and mouth. When he finished he looked at the handkerchief, it was covered in blood, bright red and frothy. He quickly touched his bare hand to his mouth and looked again. He was even more startled to discover that his hand was covered in blood. His chest heaved as he sat there and tried to rest and catch his breath before heading back to the house. Finally he stood and steadied himself on the edge of the barn door. He was slightly dizzy and very tired. He knew he wouldn't be doing any work today. A little rest and he would be fine. He must have just coughed so hard he made his throat raw, that was it that was where the blood was coming from he told himself. Very slowly he turned and began making his way back to the house.

His wife had been in the kitchen at the sink when she noticed John on the ladder and then a minute later on the stool with his white hand-kerchief to his mouth. After a while she put down the dish she had been washing and headed for the back door. As she came off the back porch and down the steps she watched him get up on wobbly legs and steady himself against the barn.

As he started for the house she headed toward him. That was when she noticed the bloody handkerchief. What had happened? Had he hit himself with the hammer while he was up there working on the door? John had, on any number of occasions over the years, injured himself in one way or another, nothing ever very serious. This looked worse. Then she saw his face. Blood was everywhere, even down the front of his shirt. When she was almost to him he went to the ground. She screamed and ran as hard as she could in her house shoes and apron. When she got to him he was on his back breathing heavily. His chest rose and fell at an alarming rate as if he was trying to grab a breath but couldn't make it stay.

Nancy took her apron and wiped away the blood from his chin and mouth. His eyes were glassy and unfocused. She spoke to him softly, not trying to make the moment worse than it already was.

"John what happened, what have you done to yourself?"

He didn't speak, didn't even move other than his labored breathing. Nancy put her hand on his cheek and asked again, more forceful this time.

"John what is wrong? Please speak to me?"

There was still no response. Nancy knew what she had to do, but she couldn't just leave him here alone on the ground. It took only a second for her to realize that she would have to abandon him here while she went inside to dial 911. She hurried home and ran up the back porch steps and opened the screen door. As soon as the door came open, Sadie, her little Jack Russell Terrier, ran out and straight for John. The two month old shelter pup was never allowed out of the house for fear that some larger animal might make a meal of her. Clyde, John's bird dog, came running from the woods and joined Sadie who was now sitting beside the ailing man. Nancy took a small amount of comfort knowing that her husband wasn't actually alone now; Sadie and Clyde were with him.

It took almost twenty minutes for the ambulance to arrive. In that time John had managed to speak a few words and tell his wife that he felt like he was drowning. He kept coughing up blood and in the process he would get choked all over again. With Nancy's help he was placed on his side, a couch pillow from the living room sofa under his head. This seemed to ease the cough, but not by much.

Finally the ambulance arrived. It drove past the mailbox and all the way to the spot where John had fallen. The paramedic did a full body assessment but didn't find any external injuries. No lacerations, no broken bones or anything that would indicate a fall from the ladder which John had been standing on when the attack started. The mouth and nasal cavity contained blood but again no sign of injury. The pulse was rapid now and shallow. The blood pressure was weak. John was going into shock. The paramedic and the EMT with him put John on a wheeled stretcher and strapped him in. After they loaded him into the ambulance the paramedic hooked him up to oxygen and set the gauge to a high flow.

All this time Nancy had been by her husband's side holding his hand and trying to look stronger than she actually was. The paramedic and the EMT asked her to stop at the back of the ambulance as they rolled him in and locked the gurney's wheels in place.

As the EMT began to close the double back doors Nancy asked if she could go with her husband. The EMT, whose name was Gerald, told her that it would be best if she followed them to the hospital in her own car, not much room in the back of an ambulance. Nancy stepped back and asked where they would be taking him. Protocol for any emergency dictated that the patient had to first be taken to the nearest medical facility. The nearest to Monticello was a small hospital in Somerset, about fifteen miles away.

"We'll be taking him to Somerset Regional. You can follow in your car but please don't try to keep up. I wouldn't want you in an accident on the way to the hospital."

Nancy stood back as the EMT closed the back doors to the ambulance. He then raced around the side and into the driver's seat. She watched as the ambulance went around the house and down the driveway toward the main road. As soon as it made the blacktop at the end of the gravel drive the emergency lights came on. The sound of the siren startled her back into the real world. Her husband was on his way to the emergency room in the back of an ambulance and she needed to be in her car headed in the same direction. She turned and went inside to get her purse and car keys. As she passed by a mirror in the living room the full horror of the situation became apparent. Her apron was covered in blood. She also had it on her hands and the side of her face where she had apparently put her hand over her mouth.

Nancy quickly went into the bathroom and cleaned the blood off her skin. She put the apron in the tub and ran a little water over it. She quickly brushed her hair and then grabbed a sweater from the closet. She grabbed her keys and purse and was out the door no less than five minutes after the ambulance had left. Before she got in the car she remembered Sadie. She turned to call the dog but before she uttered a word she noticed her on the front porch sitting by the door. Nancy ran up the steps, unlocked the front door and put the little terrier inside. There was a red swipe on the dogs' coat. John must have put his hand there while she had gone to call the ambulance. She took some comfort knowing that her husband had reached for the dog when no one else was there for him.

As she backed the car out of the driveway and started down the road she kept hearing the words of the paramedic telling her to not drive fast. She felt that under the circumstances ten miles over the speed limit was acceptable, and certainly necessary.

The drive to Somerset took thirty-five minutes. It was probably the longest thirty-five minutes of her life. As she pulled into the parking lot of the hospital she noticed the ambulance that had transported her husband was now backed up to the emergency room entrance. The back doors were closed so she assumed her husband was already inside and receiving care. She parked and hurried to the door. The hospital was a small affair but even so she still had to ask directions to the emergency department waiting room. Once there she went directly to the reception window and inquired about her husband. Instead of an explanation on her husband's condition and care, she was given a clipboard that held a questionnaire with questions about any pre-existing medical conditions and insurance information.

"Please, can you tell me anything about my husband? His name is John Oden. He was just brought in here by an ambulance and I am worried. I am so worried, almost out of my mind with worry". Nancy stood there holding the aluminum clipboard and waiting for an answer. The lady on the other side of the window didn't look away from her computer monitor. Nancy waited patiently for an answer. Finally, the emergency room receptionist looked up from her work.

"I'm sorry, may I help you?"

Nancy realized now that the receptionist hadn't been listening, or for that matter even paying attention.

"I was asking about my husband, he was just brought in by ambulance only a few minutes ago."

The receptionist reached over and picked up an aluminum clipboard and reached it through the window. "Please fill out this paper work and I will check for you."

Nancy held up the clipboard in her hand and said. "You already gave me a clipboard dear. If you don't mind I'll take a seat over there and when you find out anything please come over and let me know." Without a word the receptionist stood and left the window. Nancy was astonished by the total lack of empathy and unprofessional behavior she had just witnessed. As concerned and worried as she was about her husband, Nancy couldn't help what she did next, she eased closer to the window and leaned in to see what was on the computer monitor that had the receptionist so entranced.

Facebook!!!!!!!!!!!!!!!!!!

Nancy leaned back from the window and went to a seat in the reception area. She picked a spot against the wall next to a table that was covered with very tattered and outdated magazines. Digging through her purse until a black fountain pen caught her eye she wondered how a person who worked in an emergency room, where both life and death existed side by side, could be so uncaring, so out of touch with the very people that require her help. Nancy tried to put the thought out of her head as she began to fill out the forms. As she wrote in the information she felt sure that if anything bad happened at least someone knew she was in the ER waiting room. After a few minutes she looked up to see the receptionist back at her post, engrossed in her computer monitor, undoubtedly Facebook again. That little bleach blond anorexic bitch. Why was it that young women didn't feel attractive unless they were half starved? With that thought Nancy lowered her head and asked for forgiveness.

Nancy quickly finished with the forms and headed back to the reception window. She put the metal clipboard down a little harder than was necessary and waited for a response. The loud clap got the attention of almost everyone in the room. The receptionist looked up into the scowling eyes of Nancy Oden.

"May I help you?"

"I doubt it, but since you asked, what did you find out about my husband?"

"What was your husband's name?"

"Is my dear, please don't say was, was sounds so post mortem. Try to show a little respect and stay off Facebook if you don't mind while you're working. I have been here twenty minutes and my husband has been here for thirty. You have been nothing but irritating. My husband's name is John Oden and I want to know where he is and how he is doing and I want to know it right now." Nancy had spent eighteen years teaching high school English to smart mouth teenagers and she knew she could hold her own with this little bitch.

To Nancy's total surprise the receptionist was not offended. She didn't show the least bit of surprise to the way she had just been spoken to. Apparently in her position, with her attitude and poor work ethic, she had received quite a bit of verbal abuse, most of it deserved. She looked at her monitor and punched a few keys on the keyboard, snapping gum all the while which made a very irritating noise.

"Let me see here. John Oden is being transferred to a hospital in Lexington. A helicopter has been requested and should be here in about an hour."

Nancy did not speak. She did not move. For the longest time she only stood and let the moments consume her. Slowly she turned from the reception window and found her way back to the chair by the wall where she had filled out the forms. It was as if time had slowed but her mind raced. Visions from the past came to her and it was as if she were transported back in time. The first date, the first kiss, the first everything she and her husband had ever experienced flashed by, and then, just as fast as it had appeared, it was gone.

Big Van Goodwin sat on his front porch in the early morning mist. He puffed the last of his Camel and then flipped the butt into the bushes beside the steps. Sunrise was still more than an hour away and Van had already been up for an hour. Sleep these days was always brief and troubled.

It was a Wednesday and Van had a seven o'clock appointment at the Dialysis Center. In fact Van had had a seven o'clock every Monday, Wednesday and Friday for nearly the last three years at the Dialysis Center and he was about to get tired of it. Van was sixty-seven years old and in declining health. He seemed to suffer from a never ending list of ailments. The most concerning of these was heart disease, diabetes, poor circulation and now due to his sugar, as he liked to refer to his diabetes, his kidneys were failing.

The kidney problems had started when he was sixty-four. At first the symptoms were handled with medication such as Lasix. This wonder-drug took fluids off a patient in torrents. But as the diabetes progressed and began to weaken his kidneys even more he was forced to begin the dialysis.

Now anyone who has ever been on dialysis will tell you that it is extremely hard on the body. The veins are poked and the blood withdrawn and cleansed by a machine that removes excess fluid and then puts the blood back in. The process can take several hours and leave the patient completely exhausted. Van was tired of the whole thing. For the last few months he had considered not going back, just quitting the dialysis altogether. Another patient he had known and had been on dialysis for more than five years had finally given up, he just stopped going. Van later heard the man had lived for nearly two weeks before he passed away.

Now Van loved living as much as anyone, but he hated the feeling he got while he was on the machine. He also hated the feeling he got when they took him off the machine. He finally decided that he hated everything about it and he had just about had enough. He once read that happiness in life required only three things, something to do, something to look forward to and someone to love. Van was retired and didn't have much to do. The only thing to look forward to was dialysis, Yuk. And since his wife had died nearly two years ago he had no one to love. Three strikes you're out.

Van got up and went inside to get his car keys. He was weak and a little wobbly. His head hurt from the Lasix, which was still prescribed, although he really didn't know why. He moved slowly and kind of shuffled his feet as he went instead of taking normal steps.

"Life sucks." He said out loud once he made it to the kitchen.

Why he had said this out loud didn't really matter, he just wanted to hear it with his own two ears instead of only thinking it. He reached for the keys on the counter where he had left them the night before. After a fumble and a toss he dropped them on the kitchen floor. As he bent down to pick them up he bumped his head on the counter, lost his balance and luckily for him landed perfectly in a kitchen chair that had been left out from the kitchen table where he had eaten his Corn Flakes earlier. At that very moment while sitting in the chair and rubbing his forehead Van made a life changing decision, this was going to be his last trip to the Dialysis Center. He would use the occasion to say goodbye to the other patients he knew and to thank the center's staff who had shown such kindness to him during his treatments. As he drove to the center he became aware of a calmness that now replaced the daily dread, and he liked it.

Van parked his car, locked the door, and walked to the front entrance. It was a little before six-thirty in the morning. As he walked through the Dialysis Center's double front doors he thought about how he would tell his friends that this was going to be his last visit. They would invariably try to talk him out of it. The staff would give him a pep talk on not giving up, if not for himself then at least for the other patients who would be devastated over his decision. He still had time before he had to share his news with anyone; his procedure took more than two and a half hours. Or maybe he could wait and tell them as he prepared to leave, break the news and then make his exit. No, that would be too abrupt. It would also be too cold and unfeeling. He just couldn't be that mean to people who were suffering with many of the same health problems he had.

As he stood and deliberated, he was suddenly brought back into the here and now by a voice coming from the sign-in window.

"Good morning Mr. Goodwin. If you will sign this I will have Lucy take you on back."

Van shuffled over to the window and gave her a big smile as he reached for a pen.

"Good morning to you. Is my usual bed ready?"

The receptionist took the signed form and said, "It most certainly is."

Lucy Carter entered the reception area with a wheelchair and a big smile. Van always wondered how everyone who worked at the Center could always be so cheerful. Never in the three years he had been coming here had he ever saw one of the staff in a foul mood. Maybe they were just glad they weren't the ones being hooked up to the machines. In any case he still had the problem of how to break it to these people that he wouldn't be back; this would be his last visit, he was sure of it. He decided to use the two hours he was hooked up to the machine to figure out his exit plan.

Doctor Slade made his morning rounds in record time, one hour and ten minutes. It wasn't the hour he had promised himself but hey, it was still pretty damn good. He had to continually caution himself not to seem rushed in front of his patients. His mind had been elsewhere the entire morning. After his last patient visit he returned to his office and called Sally Jenson at the nursing home.

"Good afternoon Ms. Jenson. This is Dr. Slade, how is Helen holding up?" He almost expected to hear that she had slipped back into the dementia that had held such a tight grip on her for so long.

"Oh Hi Doctor. She's out on the terrace talking to some of the other patients. Are you going to be able to stop by?"

Doctor Slade was again surprised.

"Did you say she is outside and talking? Is she just jabbering or actually carrying on a conversation?" He was both shocked and excited at the same time.

"She has been on the terrace for over an hour. As word got around that she is feeling so much better, more and more of our residents have gone outside to say hello and congratulate her on her recovery. They don't know that this is probably only temporary, and no one is going to tell them any different. So many of her friends have gone outside to be with her that the kitchen staff has decided to make an event of it and serve lunch on the terrace, sort of a picnic if you will. "

"I can't get over this. Is she feeling overwhelmed? Be very careful, too much excitement might send her back into her shell." Slade said.

"We have asked her several times if she wanted to go back to her room for a little while to rest. Each time she has said she is fine and wants to stay outside to catch up with her friends. The last time I asked she even questioned me about when lunch would be ready."

There was a short pause as Dr. Slade thought about his course of action.

"Are you there doctor?"

"Yes Ms. Jenson. I was just thinking that a few tests need to be run. Pull blood samples and have them ready for a courier I am sending over from the hospital now."

As Sally was writing down the instructions in Mrs. Montgomery's chart the Doctor added.

"Tell you what, I will finish up with a few loose ends here at the hospital and then be straight on over. I should be out the door in five minutes and be there in less than an hour."

"Oh thank you Dr. Slade. I think you should see this first hand."

They both said their goodbyes and hung up. Dr. Slade dialed the lab and told them to expect some bloodwork on a Helen Montgomery and he wanted it worked up as soon as possible and then E-Mail the results back to Nurse Sally Jenson at River Terrace Nursing Home. He would most likely be at the Nursing Home and would review the results there if they could get them to him in time. He then dialed the front desk and gave them instructions to dispatch the courier.

Before he left his office he again pulled up the digital file on Helen Montgomery. It went back almost four years. Dr. Slade started at the beginning and quickly reviewed the information up until the last entry made on the previous day. The original diagnosis was Vascular Dementia. Her symptoms occurred in steps more so than a constant gradual decline. She had symptoms of a stroke early on, maybe more than one. The strokes were probably a result of high cholesterol which she battled throughout her entire adult life. Even with medication and diet her cholesterol levels were never really under control. Her family had a history of high cholesterol and this had been passed on to her.

The stroke, or strokes, damaged the blood vessels that supply blood to the brain. If the reason for the dementia had truly been a stroke it should have been prevented with a more rigorous cholesterol lowering regimen, but that was before she had been his patient. Some people put off going to the doctor for too long. Others stop taking their prescriptions because they think they don't need them anymore. In any case that was the past. At the moment she was showing signs of significant improvement and he wanted to know why.

Dr. Slade stopped by the front desk on his way out of the hospital. "I will be heading over to River Terrace for a couple of hours. If I should need a patient there transported to the hospital and admitted for a few days, could she be given a private room."

The admittance nurse looked at her monitor. "Yes Doctor, I actually have three private rooms available."

"Would one of them be on the second floor?"

"Yes, as a matter of fact two are on the second floor. Any particular reason for the second floor, I can note it on the schedule and hold it for the remainder of the day?"

"Two reasons actually. First, it is nearer to the lab, I intend to do an extensive battery of tests. Second, it is the same level as the staff break area out on the shaded veranda. If I do transfer this particular patient I think she would like to have access to a little fresh air."

The admissions nurse looked up at the doctor. "You do realize the veranda is off limits to patients!"

Dr. Slade anticipated this and already had a response. "Yes, I will clear it through Dr. Osborne; he has granted me patient veranda privileges before."

The nurse looked at the doctor in total defeat; Dr. Osborne was the hospitals head administrator. If it was okay with Dr. Osborne then who was she to complain?

"Sure thing Dr. Slade, I will see to it that the room is held until you say otherwise."

Slade thanked her, turned and headed for the parking garage. He could not quite understand why the hospital's staff was so reluctant to allow a single patient out onto the veranda. It wasn't like he was putting them at risk by rolling a contagious patient into their space.

Once he made it to his Audi he navigated his way out onto the street. He used his hands free to call Dr. Osborne.

"Hi Jack, this is Neil."

"Hello Doctor, what can I do for you?"

"I might need to have a patient brought over from River Terrace this evening and have her checked into a private room on the second floor. I want her to have veranda privileges, if you will allow it." Without a moment's hesitation Dr. Osborne gave his answer.

"Sure thing Neil, what's up?"

"I have a Hospice patient from the nursing home that is suffering from late stage dementia. As of a few hours ago she is showing signs of significant improvement. I'm going over there now. I want to do a preliminary examination and possibly have her transferred to the hospital for a more extensive battery of tests."

"Not a problem at all Neil. I'll notify the floor and shift supervisors. Good luck with your visit. Dementia has a nasty history of false hope."

"I keep hoping for a breakthrough. Everything we learn puts us one step closer."

With that both doctors hung up. Neil drove the speed limit, although he wanted to go much faster, and pulled into the parking lot of River Terrace after about thirty-five minutes. He was always impressed with the neat appearance presented by the well-kept lawns and buildings.

Most nursing homes were underfunded and understaffed. Not this one. It was well managed and, if anything, over staffed. One look and you could see that this facility was a cut above the rest.

Neil pulled into one of the parking spots reserved for physicians and put the Audi in park. He grabbed some files he had brought from the office, along with his laptop, and got out. As he headed for the front entrance he could hear the automatic door locks of his car engage. He entered the building and went immediately to the nurse's station. A young woman was on the phone as he approached. As he waited he heard footsteps and then a familiar voice.

"Good afternoon Doctor Slade."

He turned and saw the familiar face of Sally Jenson.

"Hello, how is Mrs. Montgomery doing? Please don't tell me she has deteriorated since we last talked." Dr. Slade noticed he was talking more rapidly than usual.

"No doctor, not at all. She is still on the terrace. As a matter of fact over half the residents are out there now."

Neil smiled and said, "Please, lead the way."

Sally turned and headed down a long corridor with the doctor close behind, neither spoke. Sally wanted to let the doctor have a look with his own eyes and Neil was afraid to ask any more questions because he didn't want to hear any answers that might dash his hopes. When they reached the double doors Sally hit the handicap button and both doors swung out slowly.

Both Sally and Doctor Slade stepped out onto the wide covered terrace from which the nursing home got its name. The scene outside could be mistaken for a very reserved cocktail party. Everyone was smiling and talking in small groups. Some were standing while others were sitting either on the wicker furniture or in a wheelchair. All seemed happy to be out of doors even though the sky was overcast and the air was just a bit chilly. There were several members of the staff present keeping a watchful eye on the patients, or residents as they liked to be called. A long table had been arranged by pushing several smaller tables together and covering the whole thing with white tablecloths from the dining room. These particular tablecloths were generally used for holidays, such as Thanksgiving or Christmas, but the kitchen staff decided to spare no effort on this day, a day in which a resident had shown such remarkable improvement.

Sally had to stop for a moment to look for Helen. She spotted her at the edge of the terrace surrounded by several women.

"This way Doctor, I see her over there with that group of women near the railing."

"Can we wait here for a moment? I want to observe her interaction with her friends before we go over. She may act differently if she knows we're watching so I want to see her without her knowledge of us being here."

"Sure doctor. But I doubt if we can go unnoticed for very long."

The doctor didn't respond, he just watched. Helen was sitting with a very erect posture on a wicker love seat. She talked, listened, smiled and laughed. She was the picture of health, and at the moment, the center of attention. Suddenly she turned from the lady she was talking to and looked directly at Sally and Dr. Slade. Caught off guard by Helen's sudden awareness of their presence neither the doctor, nor the nurse, moved. Helen excused herself from her friends, got up without the least hesitation and came over to the two startled observers.

"Why, good morning Dr. Slade? I noticed you and Nurse Sally and wanted to say hello. It has been such a long time. Are you here to see a patient of yours?"

Sally smiled and looked at the doctor. Neil reached out his hand and Helen reached out hers. Apparently the doctor was at a momentary loss for words. Whether by the condition of his patient, or from being caught observing her form a distance, Sally couldn't tell.

"Hello Mrs. Montgomery. Sally here told me that you were feeling much better today so I wanted to come over and see for myself."

Helen looked at Nurse Sally and smiled.

"I do feel so very good today. The weather is just great and all my friends have come out here for a picnic the nursing home is having today."

Neil looked at the overcast sky. It was dark and gloomy and the breeze had a slight chill to it. He wondered if Helen couldn't tell good weather from bad and if her condition wasn't as good as he was led to believe.

Helen saw him look at the sky and before he could respond she added, "Don't you just love dreary fall days Dr. Slade? I have always looked so forward to the holidays and the dreary days are just part of the season, don't you agree?"

"I do enjoy this season very much. And you're right; the clouds suit the occasion." Slade found he was stammering as he tried to grasp the condition of his patient and also carry on a conversation with her.

Before releasing Helen's hand he reached over and patted her shoulder with his other hand. "Mrs. Montgomery, I would like to do a brief examination if that would be alright?"

Helen looked at the doctor for a moment before looking back at Nurse Sally.

"But doctor, they are about to serve lunch. It would be so rude of me if I left my friends and went inside now. Can't we put the examination off for a little while?"

"Well, I do understand but I don't have a lot of time. The exam will only take thirty minutes or so and I really do need to get back to the hospital."

"Oh, but Dr. Slade, you do work so hard. Why don't you stay and have lunch and then we can do the examination afterwards?"

Dr. Slade looked over at Sally who was smiling to the point of a laugh and knew he was defeated. He felt torn at the moment between wanting to do what was needed and doing what his remarkable patient asked. Then it dawned on him, this would be an excellent opportunity to observe Helen interacting with her friends during lunch. It was actually a very good idea.

"Why Mrs. Montgomery, I would love to stay and have lunch, but I do have one condition."

"That is wonderful doctor, now what is the condition?"

"That you see to your friends and enjoy yourself. I will find a place over to the side, out of the way, and when lunch is over we can talk. I need to make a few calls anyway."

"Why Dr. Slade, that will work just fine, and thank you so much for staying."

With that Helen turned and strolled back over to where she had left her friends. Dr. Slade smiled as he watched her go and wondered what had happened to create such a drastic change of events in the life of Helen Montgomery.

He turned to Sally and said, "Well nurse, it looks like I will be staying for lunch after all."

He stood for a moment and observed Helen. She was smiling and carrying on what looked like two conversations at once with at least three other ladies.

"Sally, if you could inform the kitchen staff that I will be staying for lunch then I will step back inside and call the hospital. I want to have Mrs. Montgomery transferred to Beaumont where I can do a more extensive battery of tests. And by the way, you were correct in calling me this morning."

Sally smiled and then headed for the kitchen. She felt better knowing that the doctor had approved of her actions. She had known she was right from the beginning but it is always nice to be acknowledged by another professional in her field.

The dark blue Ford Sedan was back. It was parked down the street on the opposite side in almost the same spot it had been in on Tuesday. This time though there were two men inside, one white and the other possibly Hispanic. The driver seemed focused on a newspaper but still managed to glance over the top of the steering wheel at times. The other one sipped coffee from a tall white cup and tried to seem interested in a magazine. Each man, and the unknown car, looked terribly out of place. It just seemed odd for two men to drive to this street and set by the curb in their car reading. Why would anyone do that?

The Donor

Samuel Edgemont had lived on May's Branch in Prestonsburg for a little over five years. He didn't associate with his neighbors very much due to his busy schedule, but he knew many of them and also knew what most of them drove. The car now sitting four houses down had first been noticed by Sam a few days back.

It had been a sunny October day and he'd been home working on a leaky gutter over his back porch when his phone rang. It was Mrs. Potter who lived three doors down. She asked if he knew who owned the dark blue car that was parked in front of her house. He told her to hang on and he would get his cordless phone and go to the front window and have a look. Once at the window he could see the car she was talking about. It was a late model Ford, the same type that a lot of the rental car companies use. He told her he had never seen that particular car in the neighborhood before. She thanked him and said it was probably just someone visiting a friend and let it go at that. There wasn't anyone inside the car at the time.

Sam noticed the car again the next day and then again the day after that. Usually the car was empty but today it was not. He made sure the lights were out in his living room before going to his den and getting his Nikon binoculars. He went back to the front window and raised the Nikons to his eyes. He carefully adjusted them in and took a long careful look at the car and its two occupants. There were no plates on the front which meant the car was probably from Kentucky. Front plates were not required in this state. He noticed a small tag hanging from the rear view mirror but couldn't make out what it said. He did know that in the past when he had rented a car from one of those rental places at the airport there usually was a small tag of some sort hanging from the rear view mirror.

He then observed the driver. He could make out the face each time the newspaper eased down so the driver could observe his house. He wasn't sure of that but it certainly looked like the man was looking straight at his house. He hoped the slightly darkened room would not allow either of the two men to notice him inside with his binos. The driver was white and had a neat close cut haircut. He had dark hair, maybe black or possibly dark brown, and a mustache. Not old and then again not young either.

Sam then switched his gaze to the passenger. What he thought to be a Hispanic turned out to be an Asian. Slightly dark complexion and short cropped black hair. He noticed a white foam coffee cup sitting on the dashboard. These two had been here for a while and had come prepared. Both looked like cops, but why would they be watching his house? Sam lowered the Nikons and took in the situation with his bare eyes. Nothing else on his street seemed out of the ordinary except for the blue Ford and the two men inside.

Sam sat the Nikons on the coffee table and went to the kitchen. He looked out the back door at his tiny back yard and scanned for anything out of the ordinary. All seemed perfectly fine. He then went back to the living room and picked up the binoculars again. When he scanned out the front window the blue Ford was gone. Had they seen him looking at them through his front window? He didn't think so. The reflection from the street on such a bright sunny day should have made it almost impossible for anyone to see inside his house from that far away. He returned the binoculars to the coffee table and went to his bathroom to shower.

He had a 1:00 appointment at the Blood Center to donate platelets. His normal donation time was 10:00 in the morning but some sort of scheduling problem at the Blood Center prevented it today. On a normal donation day he would just drive over from his teaching job at Pikeville College, but today with such a late appointment he decided to take a half day off from work to do a few chores around his house. As he showered and shaved he thought about the mysterious blue car and its two even more mysterious occupants.

The drive to the Blood Center took forty-five minutes. On the way Sam stopped at a drive thru and ordered a grilled chicken sandwich with lettuce only and a bottle of water. For the last few years he had been very health conscious, not that he needed to be. His blood pressure and cholesterol had always been perfect. He wasn't a diabetic but these traits did run in his family.

His father died of heart disease at the age of seventy-two. His mother was a diabetic but had managed to keep it under control with medication and a somewhat proper diet. She had passed away two years after his father. Both had died before his move to Kentucky. That was only a little over five years ago but for some reason it seemed much longer. Sam had no other family, only the fading memories of his parents.

In the years since his parents died he looked back at the memory, that was all he had left of them, memories. The more he thought about his parents the more he felt he had never really known them. It was such a strange way to think of one's parents.

Sam listened to his favorite country radio station as he drove and munched on his sandwich. He only sipped his water though. On donation days it was always best to be a little thirsty than to need to use the bathroom during the procedure. You can't just unhook and go to the john any time you want at the Blood Center.

The parking lot was a little more full than usual today. Several of the cars still had people inside. He found a spot and put his Bronco in park. After finishing the last few bites of his snack he searched in the bottom of the bag for a napkin. Nothing! If he only had a dollar for every time they forgot something at a drive thru window he was sure he could pay off his house. No problem, he always kept extras in the glovebox. He gathered up the trash and grabbed his newspaper and magazine. If you are going to be hooked up to a machine for the better part of two hours you better have something to read.

Sam walked to the front door and entered expecting to find the place full. It was not. Only one donation bed was in use and it was a regular blood donation bed. All three of the platelet beds were empty. The girls at the registration counter were in a serious conversation about some movie that was all the rage at the time, Fifty Shades of something or other that Sam had never heard of. It sounded like they had seen it a year or two prior and were now comparing notes, the few words he caught made him aware that it was a conversation he should stay away from. He never heard anything that bad really, the staff was far too professional for anything like that.

The sign-in clipboard was on top of the counter along with a black Bic Pen. Sam signed in before any of the women on the other side of the counter even noticed he was there.

"Good morning Sam, how are you today?" One of them finally said.

"Just fine, thanks. What's with all the cars in the parking lot? You got training going on in the back again?"

"No. About an hour ago four or five cars parked out there and so far no one has gotten out of a single one of them. You know the story; they use our parking lot for a park-and-drive all the time, been doing it for years. They figure we won't have anyone towed. One of these days though, they are going to figure wrong."

The phlebotomist finished some paperwork and then started toward one of the small rooms that they used to take a blood sample and also to check his blood pressure and iron count. If all that checked out then he would be given a two page questionnaire to fill out. The questions on this form could make a preacher blush, but after years of donations Sam was immune to embarrassment. He could just about fill out the form without reading it. This would make his one-hundred and twenty-fifth donation, which meant he would be answering the same questions for the one-hundred and twenty-fifth time. He could bubble in the answers blindfolded, that is assuming they didn't change the forms.

As Sam followed the tech to the blood pressure room he glanced out the window at the parking lot. He stopped dead in his tracks. Sitting three spaces over from where he had parked his big green Bronco was the blue Ford Sedan with the same two men inside. He hadn't seen it when he pulled in because it was parked beside a box van the Blood Center used to haul supplies. Neither of the men in the car was attempting to conceal the fact that they were there. Both were looking straight at the Blood Center building. The driver was on a cell phone. Apparently they didn't think Sam would notice them once he was inside.

This was too much. Sam turned and headed for the front door. Once outside he walked straight for the blue sedan. As he crossed the parking lot the two in the car straightened up and looked straight at Sam. Neither the driver nor his passenger tried to conceal the fact that they were there.

They were caught and they knew it. As Sam approached the driver's side window the man behind the wheel started the car and put it in gear. Sam had anticipated this and decided to do something foolish; he stepped in front of the car. He then pointed at the driver.

"Hey buddy, I would like to have a word with you if you don't mind."

The driver rolled down his window and leaned his head out.

"Well I do mind. If you don't get out from in front of my car I am going to call the cops."

"I just saved you the trouble. I had one of the nurses' dial 911 just before I walked out here." Sam lied.

The driver looked at his companion and then back at Sam.

"You can't just block the road and hold us here, in some states that might be called false imprisonment."

"I think we will just let the cops decide," Sam replied.

Sam had already noticed that the parking spot behind the Ford was empty and hoped the two in the car were not aware of this. His hopes were in vain. Just as he feared the driver dropped the car into reverse and sped backward. It was very fortunate that no other traffic or someone on foot hadn't stepped out, because the driver would have caused a very tragic accident. Once in the clear the driver put the car in drive and sped away. Sam could only watch in amazement. There was no way to get a license number, by the time he was away from the other parked cars the blue sedan had turned onto another street. Sam turned and headed back to the lobby of the Blood Center.

Upon entering Sam noticed the crowd of Blood Center employees standing in front of the big lobby window, undoubtedly watching the excitement outside? He could only smile as he waited for someone to ask him a question.

"What was that all about Sam?" One of the techs asked.

Sam didn't feel like explaining all the details of the morning. He just said he thought he had seen that car in his neighborhood a couple of times and wanted to ask the man behind the wheel a few questions, that was all. The employees looked at each other for a second and then back at Sam.

"Did you say those guys have been near your house Sam? Don't you live all the way over in Prestonsburg?"

"That's right, seen them not more than two hours ago parked across the street from where I live. Seen the car they were driving a few days ago too. That makes three or four times and it's starting to spook the neighbors, so when I saw them outside I thought I would ask a few questions. Apparently they didn't want to talk; you saw how they sped away."

Sam could tell by the looks he was getting that the four women probably had something to add to the story.

"Have any of you seen them before?" Sam asked.

"As a matter of fact the one who was driving, you know the one you were talking to, came in one day last week. He wanted to know about becoming a donor and asked for some brochures. We happily obliged, you know the center is always in the need of new donors. Thing is, when he left one of the girls mentioned that she noticed he had shirt sleeve tattoos on both arms. He was wearing a long sleeve shirt but she could see them through the cuffs of his sleeves. Tattoos are not a reason to be denied as a donor if you haven't had a new one applied in the last six months. But none of us can remember ever having a donor with shirt sleeve tattoos. He also seemed to be a little too inquisitive, kind of like he really didn't want to donate but was just pumping us for information."

Sam thought this over for a second.

"What was he asking for?"

"He just asked a lot of questions about the other donors. Who donates, how old the average donor is, male or female and what percentage.

"What was so unusual about that? As I remember I asked a lot of questions my first time here five years ago."

"Yes, that is true, you did ask a lot of questions, but this guy had a swivel for a neck, he just kept looking the place over. And before he left he asked to use the restroom. A few minutes later Lorrie found him in the back, which is off limits to patients, he said he got confused and went toward the back of the building thinking he was actually going toward the front door. After he left she told us when she found him he had his phone out and was taking pictures of the file room and the back entrance. Ever since that happened we have been extra vigilant to keep everyone out of the back."

"That is so strange. What do you make of it?" Sam asked.

Lorrie looked at the other three women and then back at Sam. "Corporate has told us to not mention this to anyone and as you have just heard we have already said too much. I can tell you this much though, we were told to call the police if that man ever came back into this building, just as a precaution."

Lorrie and Sam went into the interview room. Lorrie pulled a sheet of paper from a file and laid it on top of the small desk. "Alright Sam, you know the drill, answer all the questions and when you are finished push the door open and I will come back in." With that said Lorrie went out and pulled the door shut behind her.

Sam quickly answered the questionnaire and then pushed the door open. Within a minute or two Lorrie came back in and took a seat. She quickly glanced over the bubbled in answers and when she was sure that none of the answers represented a problem she quickly put the paper down and continued. She swabbed one of Sam's fingers and then, using a small device that punctured the skin, drew a small amount of blood and then covered the wound with a small piece of gauze. This blood was then used to determine the iron level. Too much red meat and your iron would be elevated. As usual Sam's was alright.

"I doubt if you will be able to donate today Sam." Lorrie said as she grabbed the blood pressure cuff.

"Why is that?" Sam asked.

"With all the excitement out in the parking lot a few minutes ago I would imagine your blood pressure is elevated. If the bottom number is over a hundred then you will be denied." Lorrie put the blood pressure cuff on Sam's arm; she then pumped the bulb to increase the pressure. With a stethoscope she listened to the familiar sounds as the air was slowly released and blood again began to flow.

"One-twenty over eighty, aren't you a healthy critter today." Lorrie said.

Sam smiled. In all his years of donating his blood pressure had always been around those numbers that Lorrie had just mentioned. They never varied more than a point or two in either direction. He had been concerned when she had first mentioned he might not be able to donate and this in itself should have also been a reason to elevate his blood pressure. He had never been denied a donation in all his years of coming here and he wouldn't be denied today. Maybe he really was a healthy critter.

Sam picked out his favorite donation bed, the one closest to the window, and was soon hooked up to the machine. For a little over an hour he read his magazine and newspaper. When he finished working the Sudoku puzzle he looked out the window and noticed the parking lot. He was nearly finished and wondered about the blue sedan and the two men inside. They were nowhere in sight.

During lunch Helen sat with three other women who were younger but seemed to be less energetic than their eighty-two year old friend. Dr. Slade was seated to the side where he could notice Helen without drawing attention to himself. The noontime meal consisted of spaghetti and garlic bread. A small salad was placed to the side of each plate. Desert was angel food cake, all this was extremely nutritious and healthy, something Slade admired about the nursing home. Drinks consisted of coffee, tea or water with lemon. Slade knew the food would be very good, he was always impressed at the care of preparation and variety the nursing home offered its patients, even something as everyday as spaghetti was prepared as well as what you would find in a fancy restaurant. A full time dietitian was employed and on previous occasions when he had visited a patient he always made a point to notice the meals they served on those days. After one visit he had sent a note to the staff complimenting them on the care they gave and the professionalism he had observed.

Slade took a few notes without being too obvious about it. The lunch took nearly forty-five minutes and by the time plates were collected he had filled three complete pages. He checked earlier and found the blood samples had been taken by nurse Jenson and then sent by the courier to the hospital. With any luck he would know the results as soon as he returned to his office, they might even be sent to him while he was here. As he was writing he was unaware that Helen had walked over.

"As I said earlier Dr. Slade, you do work so hard. You have hardly touched your lunch."

It was true, Slade had been so preoccupied with his notetaking he had only finished the salad and barely touched the spaghetti. He looked up at Helen. "Oh, it was very good; I usually eat very little at lunch," he told her. And it was true; Slade only snacked each day at his desk. "Are you up to a brief examination?" He asked her.

"Certainly, I hope it won't take very long. I want to be out here this afternoon and enjoy some more of this lovely weather." As she said this she looked at the rolling clouds and smiled. "Those fast moving clouds remind me a little of you Dr. Slade, always so busy."

Slade looked at the sky and realized he had never heard an analogy quite like that before. He realized Helen's statement made perfect sense. It seemed he was always busy and she had just pointed that out again. The doctor quickly gathered his notes and stood. He and Helen walked across the terrace toward the automatic doors. He noticed her walk was brisk and without the least sign of a limp or a wobble. Most all patients in their eighties had trouble with arthritis and in Helen's file he read that she was afflicted by it as well. Her walk could have been that of someone in their thirties.

Sally Jenson assisted with the examination. Once complete Dr. Slade sat on a stool and finished his notes. "Mrs. Montgomery, I would like to send you to Beaumont General for a couple of days. There are a few tests I would like to run. Would that be acceptable to you?"

Suddenly Helen thought something was wrong. "I really don't know doctor. Is something wrong, I mean I feel so good right now? Please tell me if you suspect anything."

Dr. Slade realized he could have done a better job of preparing his patient for the news about additional tests. "I assure you Mrs. Montgomery everything is fine. I am going to be completely honest with you." He tried to think of a way to say what he thought. "Up until this morning your condition was stable. You had been in pretty much the same state for months. You didn't recognize anyone from your family when they visited or any of the staff who saw you every day. You were suffering from dementia.

"Now though you seem to be completely capable of carrying on a conversation and it seems you recognize most everyone you see. I would like to have a better understanding of what has happened for two reasons. One is if we can figure out what has happened then maybe we can keep you active and alert, like you are now. Secondly if there is anything we can learn then it will be helpful to other patients who suffer from dementia."

Helen's face changed from one of worry to one of happiness. "I feel so good today doctor. If you think what has happened is only temporary then I would rather spend my time here with my friends. If on the other hand I might be able to help others, even if it is only one, then I will go to the hospital for the tests."

What Helen said moved both the doctor and the nurse. Even if she only had a day or two left to enjoy her recovery she was willing to allow that to be taken away in order to possibly help others. Dr. Slade wondered if he were told that he had one day left before his memories were taken away forever, would he give that day to be prodded and poked by a bunch of doctors and nurses.

"Thank you Mrs. Montgomery. I promise the tests will be done as quickly as possible. If you want to gather any of your things then I'm sure some of the staff will assist you. I'll call for an ambulance to be sent."

Slade stood to leave but was stopped by Helen. "Did you say an ambulance, why would I need to travel in an ambulance Dr. Slade?"

Now this was a good question, but he had the answer. "It is just policy Mrs. Montgomery. We always use an ambulance when a patient is transported from one medical facility to another."

Helen stood, the worried look was back. "If I am to share what few hours I have then I would rather ride in a car instead of an ambulance."

She made a good point. "I see what you mean," he said apologetically. "Let me check on a few things first and in the mean time you can enjoy spending some more time with your friends on the terrace."

Once Helen left, Slade went to the front desk. "Is the administrator in?"

A slight built woman in her forties looked up from her work. "I believe so Dr. Slade."

"I need a word with him if that is alright?"

The lady picked up the phone and punched in a three digit number. "Mr. Bevins, I have Dr. Slade here from Beaumont General and he would like to see you."

She hung the phone up and said, "You can go right in doctor, it is the third door on the left down this corridor."

As Slade started to head in that direction he turned to Sally and said, "I would like you to join me."

Sally followed Slade and both entered the administrator's office. Slade was met at the door by a man who apparently spent too much time in his tidy office and not enough time walking the halls of the facility. He was at least fifty pounds overweight. This fact wasn't helped by his height, Slade himself was a little over six feet tall, and by all appearances Mr. Bevins would need elevated shoes to reach five foot six. Slade knew to never judge a person by their physical appearance, but being a doctor he couldn't help but notice those things about a person that were a product of lifestyle.

The two men shook hands. "Please have a seat." Bevins motioned at the two chairs that sat in front of his desk. Slade and Sally each sat down.

"What is it I can help you with this afternoon?" Bevins asked.

"You have a resident here by the name of Helen Montgomery. I would like to have her transferred to Beaumont General this afternoon."

This was no problem for Bevins, moving patients was always at the physician's discretion. "That won't be a problem. Just notify the front desk and they will see that the paperwork is ready by the time the ambulance arrives."

"That is the problem Mr. Bevins. Mrs. Montgomery insists to be taken in an automobile. She is showing remarkable improvement in the last twenty-four hours and says she doesn't want to spend any of her time in an ambulance when she could just as easily go in a car."

Bevins thought about this. "Our protocol requires all transfers between medical facilities be done by ambulance." This was all he said as he looked at Slade.

"Yes, I realize that. Is there any way around this?"

Bevins smiled. "I'm afraid not. If the patient were to take sick during the trip this facility would be open to a lawsuit."

Slade frowned. Again he was being forced to comply with rules that were in place just to protect against lawyers.

Slade looked at Sally, he was defeated. "Well if the patient doesn't agree to the ambulance then there is nothing we can do."

"Let me have a talk with her Dr. Slade. You head on back and I'll give you a call as to her decision either way." Sally said.

As Slade rose to leave the administrators office Bevins picked up a note pad and then dialed a number. He had gone back to work without acknowledging the meeting with Slade was over.

As the two left the administrator's office Sally spoke to the doctor again. "I must apologize for Mr. Bevin's behavior. He is a very good administrator but as you can see he is lacking in basic social skills."

"Oh, no need to apologize for him nurse, I have actually spoken to Mr. Bevins before and know of his quirks."

Dr. Slade left the nursing home and headed back into town. As Slade neared the hospital thirty minutes later, his cell phone rang. The caller I.D. said it was the nursing home. "Hello this is Dr. Slade."

"Hi doctor, this is Sally Jenson, I've been talking to Helen and she has agreed to ride over in an ambulance."

"That is good news. I'm just getting back to the hospital. As soon as I get inside I'll have an ambulance sent over."

Beeler-Jordan is the third largest Pharmaceutical Company in America, fourth largest in the world. The person who oversees operations at Beeler-Jordan is a man by the name of Jason Freemont. When Freemont joined Beeler-Jordan, the company was ranked twenty-seventh in the nation, that was thirty two years ago. Freemont had been the CEO for the last nineteen years and had managed growth that startled the competition and dazzled the stockholders. The move up to third place had been accomplished just the previous spring. This in itself should have been a defining moment for the CEO but it only fueled his massive ego. Freemont wanted his company to be number one in the U.S. and after that he would see about becoming number one in the world.

The two companies that stood in his way in the U.S. market were Allied Chemical at number two and Baird-Pharma at number one. Allied Chemical led Beeler-Jordan by a mere five percentage points which Freemont discounted as fancy bookkeeping. But Baird-Pharma was a behemoth. It held licenses on seven of the top ten selling drugs in the country and also on scores of lesser drugs. It had invested heavily in research and development over the past twenty years, more than its next three competitors combined. It was also rumored to have several new drugs in development that, if the rumors were correct or even partially correct, would propel the leader's revenue past the next four smaller companies combined.

Freemont knew his company's research and development lagged other companies and this was perfectly fine with him. His ability to keep the stock strong was due in part to the high dividend he paid to his investors. What he saved on R&D was ploughed back into the dividend each year and this kept the stock price high. Part of his compensation was in the way of shares in the company and the hefty dividend was making Freemont extremely wealthy in the process.

The problem with accelerated growth at the expense of R&D was that the numbers could only go so far without a new wonder drug or two. Freemont had been warned repeatedly about the lack of funding for new products. Several of the cash cow drugs the company did hold license and patents on were about to hit the open market, license and patents had nearly met their allotted time limit. At that point anyone could produce a generic product and revenue would plummet.

Freemont had managed to keep the dividend up for the last five quarters by way of some fancy bookkeeping himself. The company's accounting department was led by a man who was also being enriched by the company's dividend. His name was Alex Trivett. Trivett and Freemont met daily for lunch. It was Freemont's desire, actually his demand, to know what was happening with revenue and what his Chief Financial Officer was doing to keep the numbers acceptable to the needs at hand.

Trivett was a master at his trade and craft. He could bend accounting rules to the limit but still keep everything in that magical gray area between legal and illegal. A lot of what the CFO had been doing for the last year had passed beyond the gray area and was now entering an area that could be considered thin on legality and thick on jail time if things began to falter. If an extensive audit were taken and the truth was found out then the stock would plummet and someone would go to jail, one of those nice country club type facilities where fences didn't exist. But still, jail is jail.

Both Freemont and Trivett knew this but believed that scenario was a long shot at best. What Freemont needed was a wonder drug of his own. What he had devised was a team of very talented people to monitor not only the two leading drug companies but also several of the smaller ones. If his company wouldn't support the expense of R&D then he would just try and steal it from a competitor.

This was the team that monitored the rumblings of a new drug or a lack of one. Reports had circulated about several people who suffered from different diseases and nearly all weren't expected to survive. In one case it was reported that a patient with fourth stage lung cancer was now in remission. This wasn't just a stabilization, or minor reduction of the disease, but a rapid reversal. Freemont had been updated once a week after the initial discovery, as information was gathered it was decided to invest more and more into the investigations. It was always a possibility that the rumors were just that, rumors, but until that became the case it would be treated as fact. Not only did Freemont meet with the CFO daily but was also in touch with the head of the investigative team.

The Donor

Patterson Tingler or PT as both his friends, and enemies, called him, was the man in charge of this new investigative branch at Beeler-Jordan. After eight months on the job he was still putting together the team of operatives he considered crucial to meet the expectations of Freemont and Trivett. The budget for this branch of the company was steadily growing as more and more people were found and hired, all were either ex-military, ex-CIA, ex-FBI or EX-about anything else you could imagine.

When Freemont put out feelers in search of someone to head his secret department, a list of names was compiled. Five different lists were used with each having a different set of criteria for the best candidate. PT's name was at the top of four of the lists and second on the fifth. Freemont knew this was the person he wanted to fill his new vacancy. Another bonus was the two had known each other prior to the job search, it was part of the reason PT's name had been included.

PT was hired at one-hundred and sixty thousand dollars a year with performance bonuses that more than matched the base pay. PT was single and this mattered to Freemont and Trivett. Both had agreed if the investigation became a problem for Beeler-Jorden then it would be very convenient to have PT disappear, forever. Of course this wasn't part of the package offered to PT when he accepted the job but with his background he suspected if things went south he would need to watch his back, it was just the nature of the business.

The new department was to be known as 'Alterations.' Alterations because if any of the competitors got the heads up on a new drug it was to first be qualified as legitimate and then modified for Beeler-Jordan's use. PT had the offices for Alterations separate from corporate headquarters, by about seven-hundred miles. He had five-thousand square feet on the fourth floor of a small high-rise in Downtown Chicago. The rent was steep but price wasn't really a factor when the results meant so much. PT liked Chicago, he liked it because in his thirty-seven years he had committed two of his killings there and was never a suspect in either. He travelled well in the underworld and knew if he ever needed to disappear on his own in order to not actually 'Disappear,' this was the town to do it in.

If the time ever came to have PT disappear that task in itself might prove difficult. He had joined the Army Ranger program when he was eighteen and spent the next ten years doing some of the dirty work that was required by our nation's military. He was proficient in hand-to-hand combat and also with firearms and explosives. He had extensive training in electronic surveillance and espionage. He was the right man for the job. His staff now included some of the best and brightest in both surveillance and field work.

Right now the problem PT was dealing with was one he suspected would have arrived much sooner. A security company from Lexington, Kentucky, had been retained before PT was hired. This particular company was tasked with field operations within a hundred and fifty mile radius of Lexington. At first this company, known simply as Secure Inc., had done a tolerable job. Their main task was monitoring a few of the suspected patients that were making fabulous recoveries from the hands of death. When a potential surveillance was screwed up to the point that local law enforcement was notified then it was time to terminate the contract with Secure Inc.

With the amount of money at stake, and also the reputation of the third largest drug company in America, PT decided to carry the word terminate to the next level. Secure Inc. was a small operation with five men working in the field and one more manning the offices. When something as basic as unnoticed surveillance had resulted in a description of two of the men, along with the car they were driving, it was decided by PT to have the entire company eliminated. He couldn't just have the two men who were identified to disappear, the rest of the employees at Secure Inc. would go screaming to the Feds and before you know it, everything would be at risk, including Beeler-Jordan.

Within hours, the two men who had been identified were killed in a car crash. The office manager died when there was a gas leak, and subsequent explosion, at the main office. The other three operatives were lured to a potential meeting with a new client and three hours later their bodies were dumped from a boat into Lake Cumberland with a bit of movie drama thrown in. All three had their feet stuck in buckets of very fast drying cement. PT assigned someone to monitor all the local papers to see if a connection was made between the six murders. There were none. Apparently people who worked in the shady world of surveillance never had much in the way of families and therefore no one to raise any suspicions.

The two men in the blue Ford Sedan, the ones that had been spotted outside the blood clinic, were told to take the rental car back to the airport in Lexington but to wait until dark. They were told to meet with an operative at the rest stop in Slade at eleven that night. Once at the rest stop, which was usually vacant at that time of night, they were to get directions on how to proceed with the surveillance in order to make the two think nothing was amiss. At the rest stop they were met by a young Englishman who told them he would brief them on their continued assignment during the drive to the airport in Lexington to drop off the car.

The Englishman had been dropped off at ten-thirty so there would be no car left behind. At two that night there was a report of a car fire on the Mountain Parkway near the Ervine exit. When the local fire department responded they found a Ford Sedan fully involved. After thirty minutes, and the help of a second pumper truck, the fire was finally extinguished. The local coroner was called and by four in the morning it was determined that two men had died in the fire. The engine or the gas tank must have exploded and the two men were unable to get out.

PT was given a summary of the elimination the next morning at nine-o'clock. Six men eliminated in the course of twelve hours. He smiled at his own lack of guilt or empathy. When he was hired he knew some of the things he would be asked to do were the very reason he was hired in the first place. He had never met any of the six men, and for that matter, hadn't talked to any of them either. If the six had any other surveillance jobs and the people they were working for started asking questions it would be an easy task for Alterations to deal with them too. It was all in a day's work for PT.

Even before the Englishman was sent to the meeting at Slade another team was in route to Kentucky. Alterations had determined that most of the medical recovery cases, so far, were located in that state with a few more in West Virginia. It was also suspected that three more cases existed in Tennessee and four in Virginia.

Space was rented on New Circle Road in Lexington under the guise of new law offices. Business signage wasn't allowed, only lettering on the door, and this was one of the reasons Alterations liked the address. Twenty four hours after the lease was signed the door was professionally painted with the letters 'Strum, Harbinger and Follett, Attorneys at Law specializing in Offshore Finance. A phone number was listed which went to an answering machine with a message that announced the attorneys scheduled meetings by appointment only and to leave a message. It wasn't added that a return call would never be received. It was doubtful anyone in Lexington Kentucky that noticed the door would ever dial the number, who in their right mind would know what Offshore Finance meant anyway?

The main appeal with the new address in Lexington was the ample parking out back and two doors that led directly to that parking. It was hidden from the main thoroughfare and would conceal the comings and goings of the men and women who would be working there. One of the main rules of anyone who worked for Alterations was to leave as narrow a trail as possible.

The facility had been rented for six months with an option for five more six month renewals if needed for a total of three years. If anything came up that would require the facility to be evacuated in a hurry there were several safeguards in place. All the computers and monitors had an encrypted crash code that would render their hard drives useless in a matter of seconds. Even the best hacks in the business wouldn't be able to pull any information from any of the devices after the crash code was enabled.

Each desk was also furnished with a cross-chipping shredder. All notes were to be loaded into the computers and the hard evidence was then fed into the shredders for disposal. Paperwork was frowned upon anyway but it was inevitable that some would be generated. Anyone who has ever dealt with a cross-chipping shredder will tell you that no amount of work can ever put Humpty-Dumpty back together again after being ran through that little device.

The building would be staffed twenty four hours a day, seven days a week. All employees and operatives would enter through the rear of the building to make it look as if the offices seen from the front of the building weren't staffed yet. A false front was built twelve feet back from the front doors and windows. Anyone looking in would see nothing but empty desks and chairs while behind the false walls work would be going on at a furious pace.

PT hadn't been to the facility in Lexington yet and, barring a disaster, he never would. The world was becoming a place where almost anything you did, or anywhere you went, your face would be picked up by any of a multitude of surveillance cameras. If you read any news concerning a crime in a metropolitan area you would almost always hear that the police were still reviewing footage from three, four or even five different cameras. By never going to Lexington, PT would never have his face on a camera in that city.

The head of IT for the new offices off New Circle Road was a man by the name of Stewart Hannah, or Stu, as he was called. Stu was an interesting case study. He had a Bachelor's Degree from Michigan and two Masters from Arizona. Now there are quite a few people with three degrees out there but still Stu stood apart, he was nineteen years old.

He acquired his Bachelor's by the age of sixteen and the only reason it took him nearly four years for the two Masters was those programs wouldn't allow less than two years of study each. Still, with a little fudging, he managed to finish the two degrees in less than the required four years. The extra study it would require to complete two Masters back to back was fine with Stu because he wasn't going to study anyway. He didn't need to; his I.Q. was in the top one percent.

The nearly four years he spent getting his Masters, one in computer sciences and the other in finance, could be described more of waiting than studying. The material seemed so easy that Stu was the most bored student on campus at either school. He spent all his spare time on a bank of computers he had special ordered and then promptly enhanced.

His favorite pastime was developing software that could be piggy-backed onto a corporation's mainframe. He just loved to sit in front of his screens for hours at a time and look at the secrets most of corporate America kept hidden from the rest of the world. One added bonus was that as he snooped around inside different company's computers he found ways to subsidize his income.

His favorite targets were midsize loan institutions, the types that were created by companies in order to self-finance equipment or service sales to its customers. Stu found these companies, although very profitable, neglected to spend the amounts of money needed to safeguard their software. Large companies such as big banks and large industrial corporations would be harder to infiltrate although he could do it with a little extra time. The problem with these larger targets was not the infiltration but the checks and balances they incorporated to make sure everything was on the up and up, they had stockholders to contend with.

The slightly smaller than mid-size companies were more into sales than safeguards. The type of thefts Stu had in mind were incremental in scope and size. He looked for companies that had tens of thousands of transactions a day in several states. What Stu looked for primarily was the spare change a company wouldn't notice. Spare change was anything less than a penny. In his college finance classes he noticed that interest rates applied to varying amounts over varying times created numbers that were never accurate to an even penny, still though, they were close enough.

An example would be the interest rate of a loan and the following payment dates. Let's say your due date for a payment is the fourth of each month. Most of the payments aren't made on the fourth, they are made a day or two early. Now if you are paying interest on a varying rate loan it is calculated by the day because all months are not the same. If you pay a day early Stu noticed you aren't given credit for the time between the early payment and the actual due date. The Corporation just made a few cents or a few dollars more depending on the size of the loan. Stu managed to manipulate the software of the target company into actually posting those early payments on the due date rather than the early payment date and crediting the interest that shouldn't be charged on the amount of the early payment. This excess was then sent to several online accounts as an ACH from the company. The ACH would show up as a legitimate payment to several firms that actually did billing to the Corporation so no red flags would be raised.

Stu wasn't nervous at all the first time he raided a company's files and started skimming cash into the online accounts he controlled. Each account was in the name of a complete stranger he had gotten out of a phone book. Once a week Stu emptied the ACH accounts and had the money sent to a bank in the Bahamas, from there he wired the money somewhere else. Stu never considered this as stealing; most criminals never see themselves for what they are. He considered it taking money from a large company that never had any right to it in the first place.

By the time Stu had his second Masters in hand he had a net worth of slightly more than four million dollars. He knew the reason most people get caught when they have the perfect crime is that they themselves do something stupid. They spend money like crazy and this gets them noticed. They get greedy and run the scam too long and eventually the most stupid Corporation will stumble upon the scheme and notify the authorities.

Stu wasn't going to allow this to happen. He grew up in a middle class environment, the only child of an unhappy marriage. His father had left when he was four and his mother died when he was seventeen. He had no brothers and sisters, no one to notice he had some money and had never worked a day in his life for it. Stu shut down the scam the day he graduated. His car of choice when he finally turned seventeen was a badly used Honda Accord. He had driven that beat up wreck for two and a half years.

Now he was rich, although the money was all in overseas accounts earning less than one percent per year. Stu decided it was time to splurge. He walked into a CarMax and told them he was fresh out of college and wanted to start building his Credit Score. He picked out a three and a half year old Audi A4, solid black, stickered at nineteen thousand nine hundred and ninety eight dollars. He paid five thousand dollars cash, which could be accounted for as his only inheritance from his dear departed mother. His payment was three hundred and forty five dollars a month for five years. He lived in a run-down apartment and his total expenses, including the car payment, were a little over twelve hundred dollars a month. If this were ever questioned due to his lack of employment he was going to use the excuse that he brought in that amount each month by panhandling at different intersections throughout the city. Stu seriously doubted anyone actually took a census of the numerous panhandlers the city was infested with, his plan was foolproof. His largest creditor wasn't the helpful people at CarMax; it was his student loan which was substantial. This he couldn't just pay off, although he could do it many times over. The problem would be in describing where that substantial sum had originated and how a man who said he panhandled for a living had acquired it. The minimum the student loan folks would accept without turning his account over to collections was two-hundred and twelve dollars a month. This amount was gladly taken care of each month before the due date. At the ripe old age of nineteen, almost twenty in a few days, Stu truly had it made, or so he thought.

Most people will tell you that to retire rich would be a dream come true. This was what Stu thought too, that is for about the first two days. After that, boredom hit hard. By the third day Stu was restless and looking for another career. He knew better than to re-ignite the scam he had used throughout college, that's how people get caught. He needed something new and just anything wouldn't do. A level of excitement had to be involved.

By the third day while networking with some of his much older college friends he listened while four members chatted away about IT work in the field of cyber-security. Stu was careful not to add anything to the conversation but he did manage to record everything that was said, in his mind. After a while he signed off. That night Stu decided to investigate some of the opportunities out there for a computer whiz with no work experience. One of the companies he sent his rather thin resume' to was Beeler-Jorden.

Twenty-four hours later Stu was leaving Arizona and heading for a place by the name of Lexington, Kentucky. Stu managed to get all four of his tee-shirts and two pairs of short paints, (he was wearing his third pair of pants and his fifth tee-shirt) into two Wal-Mart bags. Underwear went into a third bag, (he didn't own any socks).

Before leaving Arizona he paid off the remainder of the lease on his crappy apartment. He only did this so as not to be sued by the landlord which would have generated paperwork, something that terrified anyone who might have relieved a few large companies of some cash. He gave a forwarding address of a place in California he had taken from a cheap tour book. Stu hit the road on a Monday morning and didn't rent a motel room during his entire three day trip to Kentucky; he slept at rest stops along the way.

With his credentials and grades from the various colleges and universities he had attended it was pretty much a given that Stewart Hannah was a genius. The quirky personality and poor social skills forced PT to allow the nineteen year old to stay at the New Circle Road facility both day and night. A team of carpenters who agreed to work for cash built a small apartment inside the7500 square feet of rented space. This was the only way Stu would agree to relocate from Arizona to Lexington. He never had any friends in Arizona and didn't plan on finding any in Lexington either. He didn't drink or carouse, didn't even smoke; his only hobbies were video games and computers.

When Stu arrived at the offices he carried in his three Wal-Mart bags and was officially congratulated into the new brotherhood at 'Alterations'. Stu wanted to get right to work but it was suggested he go to his new living quarters and take a shower, three days in a hot car, the air conditioner was never used by Stu because it decreased the mileage his Audi got, and the boy was truly ripe. So ripe that once he was ushered into his new quarters a can of citrus air freshener was sprayed liberally around the offices.

Within two days Jason Freemont was informed by PT that Stu was the right man for the job, other than his lack of proper hygiene he was brilliant with anything that involved computer software, or hardware for that matter. He could break into virtually any smart phone and listen to conversations. He could also read every text and every message. But the most promising, and for that matter the most alarming, was that he could access either the front or back camera of any smartphone. As someone walked he could see the side of their face and with the opposite camera he could watch the surroundings in that direction. With the phones GPS he could tell by default where the owner of the phone was at any time.

Before the demise of all six Secure Inc. employees PT had requested an update. All the information that could be obtained from the surveillance company was to be downloaded onto an external hard drive and delivered by armed courier to the main office in Chicago. PT had used the ruse that he wanted to see firsthand what had been going on at Secure Inc. The office manager thought nothing of the request and had the hard drive loaded up and ready when the two couriers stopped by at fifteen minutes after four o'clock on a Thursday evening. The two hit I-75 ten minutes later and by the time they were two hours past Louisville the office manager was dead and the small offices where he worked were reduced to a charred ruin, natural gas explosions will do that to a building.

The information was too sensitive to travel any other way. PT knew the surveillance company was fairly good but after two of its operatives had been identified he had his doubts. Not knowing if all the files could be sent via E-mail he decided on the armed couriers. After the files were on the way and the building that housed Secure Inc. had exploded PT realized he had just created a thread, a thread that could lead an investigation, if there ever was one, straight to his offices in Chicago. It was decided to divert the couriers to an isolated waterfront location and reduce the chance of exposure significantly.

When the unmarked van pulled to the spot for the drop off the two couriers were on alert, something just didn't seem right about this alternative drop off point. It didn't matter how alert they were. Once the hard drive was in hand two snipers with night vision scopes dispatched the couriers with one head shot each. Again buckets were filled with fast drying cement and the bodies were taken out and dropped in a hundred feet of water. The van was taken to a chop shop and donated, no questions asked.

When someone called the next day to see why the couriers had never checked back in at the home office the people in Alterations were ready. The courier company was notified that the package was never dropped off. The contents of the package, which would forever remain unknown, were nonetheless insured with the courier company for one-hundred and fifty thousand dollars. It was assumed the two men in the van must have fallen prey to some of the senseless violence Chicago was famous for. Four weeks after the disappearance the overworked Chicago Police Department put the file in a room with hundreds of other unsolved crimes. PT found this out through a contact Alterations had in the department. He smiled to himself as he lit a seventy-five dollar cigar.

The courier company was told a claim would be filed for the missing package against the company's insurance carrier. Alterations never intended to file the claim. Through much research it had been found that a company waiting for unwanted news, such as a claim against its insurance carrier, would sit on its hands and do nothing until the bad news arrived. Alterations knew this and every day the courier company did nothing about its missing van, or employees, was another day for the case to grow that much colder. The murder of two innocent couriers was deflected away from anyone at Alterations.

PT now contributed eight murders to a project that was far from producing any solid information. With his focused and very limited conscience he attributed the murders as just another part of everyday Corporate America. PT himself was only given enough information from Freemont and Trivett to keep the project going. It had been agreed by Jason Freemont and Alex Trivett that PT was not to know the true reason for Alterations existence. Alterations sole purpose was to provide information concerning certain individuals, or patients as it were, which had shown a remarkable medical turnaround in a very short period of time.

PT was given names and then required to start a dossier on each. Background information of each name was to be obtained as far back as birth. As could be imagined a lot of information was being compiled. The task was helped immensely by something as everyday as the internet. Once a new name was obtained a member of the team, one who worked out of the New Circle offices, was put to work to compile two sets of files. One would be background, work history, and known addresses throughout that person's life and so on. The second file was the one that fell into that gray area of being legal or illegal.

This second file was strictly medical. Anything that could be obtained online was extremely limited due to patient privacy laws. This was where the abilities of Stu came in. Within three days of his arrival at the New Circle offices he had managed to hack into the systems of seven hospitals throughout Eastern Kentucky. Kentucky was given priority over Tennessee, Virginia and West Virginia due to the number of files started on Kentucky residents. Once this was completed the other three states would soon follow.

Stu felt he could hack any hospital system he wanted with a little work. Hospitals seemed to be a target set that felt they needed only limited security for their voluminous files. Who wanted to hack something that only contained hurt and suffering? This was slowly changing as hospitals realized the information they gathered by the truckload was sensitive, private, and in the hands of a criminal could be used for any number of illegal reasons. The computer security at hospitals was improving, but at a slower pace than in the rest of corporate America.

The hospitals in Central and Eastern Kentucky were now falling victim to Stu and didn't even know it. If someone in the IT department noticed a ghost in the system it would take weeks or even months to find the source. If they did find the source it wouldn't be a correct IP address. Stu had built code into the software that would indicate the source as the hospital itself. Any IT tech, one who was over worked trying to keep printers and fax machines working, would see this as just a fluke and leave it be, no harm done anyway.

No, hospitals were not a problem for Stu. What he did find as a problem was the Blood Centers that collected blood for any number of those hospitals. The ones that had access to reliable internet were as easy as the hospitals systems to hack into. But there were two, one in Southeast, Kentucky, and another in Southwest, West Virginia, that didn't use the internet to transmit information. Sure they gathered and sent throughout the day but it was found that in the evenings when most facilities sent the bulk of their files the limited broadband in the area was being soaked up by all the folks at home streaming movies, music or just surfing the web. This contaminated and slowed down the information being sent by the Blood Centers to their main office, either by partially sending files or leaving out substantial amounts of it altogether.

The two blood centers solved this problem by sending the information by way of the same courier who delivered the blood products to a hospital each day located near the main office in Lexington. The information was sent on a small device called a thumb drive, albeit one with massive storage abilities. After the hospital got the Styrofoam containers of blood products, the courier dropped the envelope containing the thumb drive in a night deposit box at the main office. Stu laughed to himself as he thought about the impossibilities of hacking a night deposit box, not much wiring there.

This unwanted information was sent to PT. Work still progressed on all the individuals who were patients at the hospitals but now it was determined that a list of all blood and platelet donors in the four states would be needed. There might be a possible correlation between the two groups. PT looked over his options; they were limited at best, non-existent really. He picked up the phone and when he was assured it was safe by Stu, who monitored all lines pertaining to Alterations, he dialed in an eleven digit number. On the other end an answering machine clicked on, when the recorded message played out PT entered a five digit code and then hung up.

At the other end of that call was a man who read the numbers on the display screen. He packed a bag and exited the apartment he lived in. Twenty four hours later he arrived at the offices on New Circle and was briefed on the situation. It was determined that two branch blood collection centers were the targets. He was to enter the buildings after disabling any security they might have. He was to pull the donor log for the last six months and, with the aid of a small but powerful camera, photograph the log. This was to be done at both donor stations with the use of two different cameras.

It was less than a three hour drive to the first location and another hour to the second. By four-thirty the following morning both locations had been broken into and the information obtained. When the doors were unlocked at ten-o'clock the next morning to allow donors to enter the buildings, nothing at either location seemed different than when the staff had closed up the night before. The two cameras were dropped off four hours later at New Circle and the man with no name received verification that sixty thousand dollars had been deposited into his offshore account which, within thirty minutes, he moved again to another account Alterations knew nothing about. It was a job well done and PT expected nothing less from a man he had used several times over the years and would no doubt use again if needed.

The information on the two cameras was immediately processed and fed into a computer which had no internet hookup or outside access of any kind other than the kill code which would render everything on the machine useless in the event of an emergency. This was a unit Stu had put together using two powerful computers linked together to process information and cross check everything that they had on all their investigations.

Once everything was entered the unit processed for fifty-seven seconds, ten to reach a result and forty-seven more to verify the six names that appeared on the screen. Four were soft meaning they stood a thirty percent chance as being the one they wanted. One was slightly better with a fifty percent chance and the last one was considered a hard hit, ninety percent.

Stu took the information to the man who actually ran the facility. When he saw the results he was humored by the fact that the six members of Secure Inc., the ones that were now dead, had actually done something right, they had come up with the exact name that was on the list as a ninety percent chance of being the right one, or the Primary as he would be referred to from now on. The name of the Primary was Samuel Edgemont.

With anything of eighty percent or higher a protocol was already in place. The information was so sensitive and valuable that it wasn't to be sent by fax, E-mail, phone, U.S. Postal Service, or any other way that stood a chance of being intercepted. The message was to be delivered by the Facility Manager, Hellard S. Bell.

PT had served with Bell in the Army Rangers. The men of the Ranger Unit had quickly dropped the 'ard' out of Bells name which left the Hell S. Bell or as he was known in the unit Hells Bells, which he hated. Hells Bells boarded a private jet, one owned by Beeler-Jordan which had been stationed at Bluegrass Airport for the last two days, and within a few hours delivered the names of the six people, along with their respective files, to Jason Freemont at corporate offices in New York. PT was given a coded call which meant for him to board another of the company's jets that was being sent to Chicago at this very moment to pick him up and deliver him to New York also.

Freemont hadn't expected anything of value to come from the inept employees of Secure Inc. Now he had to admit, with grudging envy, that the six men he killed maybe did something right after all, they had identified the Primary. He was still glad they were gone but now he admitted just a little respect for the six. Freemont chuckled at what he had always known about himself, results were far more important than a man's life, or six men's lives as it were.

Alex Trivett was sent for and once there, Freemont pressed a button on one side of his desk. A unit on the far wall lit up indicating it was alright to talk. It was a masking device with the ominous sounding name of 'Resonance Inhibitor' that made the room virtually undetectable to any listening devices that might be planted either in the room itself or on anyone in the room. Freemont had the main offices swept twice a week for bugs by his own in-house security team but went one step further with the R.I. unit. In the viciously competitive world of Pharmaceuticals no expense could be denied to that of security.

"Alex, we have a Primary," was all Freemont said.

Alex looked at Hells Bells and then at PT. "When was this information obtained Jason?" he asked.

"Less than twelve hours ago, I want to proceed as if the Primary is a hundred-percent match." Freemont addressed his next question to PT. "How well staffed are you in Lexington?"

PT had expected the question and knew the exact number, "Twelve in house along with six more in the field."

Freemont looked concerned. "That's not enough. As of now we have our Primary and I have got to assume Allied Chemical and Baird-Pharma have the exact same information."

PT felt this was off the mark. It was a reflection, and a poor one at that, that he and his team were behind the other competition that may or may not be trying to acquire the name of the Primary. "Most of what has gotten us to this point came by way of coincidence, happenstance, and a little blind luck. How can any other company know what we know about the Primary?"

Freemont smiled. "I always assume the competition knows everything we know. It is the only safe bet and that is what has gotten this company where it is today." The other three men reflected on what the president had just said. It didn't take a lot of thought to realize that Freemont was right.

Sam had been hooked up to the machine for a little over an hour when Katie came over and checked the readings and the bag which contained the collected Platelets. She looked at the digital readout that went by the weight of the collection bag to determine time elapsed and time to completion. "Looks like four more minutes Sam." She looked at the bag of platelets and commented, "I believe yours are the prettiest platelets we ever get in here Sam."

Sam had heard this before. The first time he heard it he thought the staff were just making small talk, he assumed they told all the platelet donors the same thing. After two or three donations he asked what they meant.

"Well, look at this." Katie said as she pointed at the bag. The bag was the very light color of a latex glove but much more transparent. "See how clear your platelets are. Some of the donations we get, actually most of them are much darker. The clearer the platelets the better they are."

Sam looked at the bag and noticed he could almost see through it, his were truly clear. "Surely that isn't the only thing that determines a high quality donation?" He asked.

"No, not at all, but it is a good sign. There are other factors I won't bore you with but I can assure you yours are at the top. The platelets you donate are given to some of the most critical recipients. We will never know who exactly gets your donations because of the HIPAA law but word is yours are good, really good." This made Sam feel good, he loved the fact that he was helping others.

A buzzer beeped and Katie began taking him off the machine. After extracting the needle he was told to hold his arm upright while holding the gauze Katie had put over the extraction point. As Sam did this Katie finished with the machine and then filled out some information on a chart.

In this part of the state you were either a University of Kentucky fan or an idiot. With that in mind the Blood Center used Kentucky colors for the elastic bandage they used to protect the extraction point. As Katie put the deep blue bandage on Sam's arm she asked if he felt alright after his donation. He did.

"Well Sam, you can get up but be careful. Have something to drink and a snack before you leave." She told him.

Sam said his goodbyes to the staff as he opened the glass door on the Coke cooler. He chose a real Coke, not a diet. A special treat on donation day was a can of Coke, all one-hundred and forty glorious sweet calories of it. Under the covered front entrance he stood and scanned the parking lot, there was no sign of the Ford Sedan. Unknown to Sam those two men were soon to be on the Mountain Parkway and later that night destined for a fiery fate.

Helen Montgomery tolerated the ride in the ambulance from the nursing home to the hospital. A car would have been more enjoyable but she admitted to herself, everything on this day seemed enjoyable. The cloudy sky and chilly breeze, the ambulance ride, everyone and everything seemed to bring her joy. Helen had always been a happy sort but now it seemed she was happier than at any previous time in her life.

Once at the hospital she was admitted and wheeled to her room within minutes, all the paperwork had been processed in advance thanks to the insistence of Dr. Slade. The doctor was so excited at her much improved condition that he had ordered a dozen yellow roses to be waiting in the room ahead of Helen's arrival. There was also a fruit basket on the roll around table. The fast admission, the roses and the fruit basket were meant to keep Helen's spirits up. When Helen was wheeled in she smiled at the roses and even giggled a little as if she were a little girl. When she realized she had giggled she then started laughing at herself, this was truly a great day.

As all this was taking place Dr. Slade thought he would have a little fun out of his wife. He dialed her cell number and waited. Dr. Sheila Slade was with a patient but when she noticed the call was from her husband she excused herself and went into the hall. After the wonderful morning with her husband she assumed he was calling to tell her he loved her.

"Hi honey, didn't expect to hear from you until later." She said.

"Hi, I just did something I never expected I would ever do and felt so guilty I had to dial your number immediately and beg for your forgiveness," he told her.

Shelia knew her husband better than anyone and could tell by the sound of his voice he was trying to pull a prank, she went along. "Well if it is anything I can't live with then remember I don't just get half in the divorce, I get it all." It was a longstanding joke between the two. One of their best friends was a circuit judge in Fayette County and he had always joked with Sheila that if the two ever got divorced then he would rule in favor of Sheila and make sure Neil lived out of a storage unit for the rest of his days.

"I know dear and am already looking for a climate controlled storage unit here in town." After a short laugh he told her what he had done. "I just had roses, a dozen of them sent to a beautiful lady along with a fruit tray. If you will take me back then I will introduce you to her."

Now Sheila burst out laughing. "Okay, what's the joke?"

Neil went on to describe the events of the day along with the miraculous recovery Helen Montgomery was experiencing. He never included a name or any information that was protected under the HIPAA law.

"Oh, that is such good news and so very interesting. Keep me posted on the patient's progress." She could tell by her husband's tone that he was extremely excited. Now it was time for her to play a little joke of her own, "Oh, and as for the flowers and fruit, I'll have your things sitting out in the driveway when you get home." She never waited for a response she just hung up and started laughing hilariously in the hallway of her clinic. Luckily no one was around or they might have thought Sheila was having a breakdown.

John J. Oden was flown to Beaumont Regional Hospital in Lexington by helicopter. He made it there two hours ahead of his wife. By the time Nancy Oden made it to Lexington and found the hospital her husband was already in surgery. She again was asked to fill out more paperwork but at least this time she was dealing with someone who was a professional. Nancy was told to take a seat while the receptionist found out some news about her husband. A few minutes later Nancy was told that John was in surgery, it was more exploratory than anything else.

After another hour Nancy was escorted to a room and told her husband was in a recovery room at the moment. From there he would be put into a private room. When a doctor came in later Nancy was given the news that John had stage four cancer in both lungs. All the doctors could do was try and stop the hemorrhaging and then close him back up.

Nancy's world had just been crushed. The look of shock was apparent. "How long does he have doctor?"

Doctors don't really want to give projections, but it is part of the job. "Maybe four months, it's really hard to tell. We will give him medication to ease the pain and manage any other problems that arise along the way." Doctor James, the lung specialist who had done the surgery, felt awful at the moment. "We will keep your husband here for three or four days and then release him. I would like to see him again one week after he's released. An appointment will be set up by someone from my office."

Nancy thanked the doctor as he left and then sat alone as she waited for her husband. 'Four months' she kept repeating to herself.

That was four months ago. Now she and John sat in the waiting room waiting to see Dr. James again. John sat straight and read a magazine as his wife patted his knee. They were taken back to an exam room and told the doctor would be in shortly. Nancy smiled and helped her husband to the seat although it wasn't really necessary.

There was a slight knock on the door as it opened. Dr. James walked in and sat down, he was smiling. "I've been looking over the tests that were done day before yesterday. Mr. Oden I have got to say you are definitely a lucky man; you are probably one for the record books. Four months ago when they brought you in here you were in pretty bad shape. You were hemorrhaging from your left lung and I was doubtful when I operated if I could save you."

Dr. James would never talk so bluntly to a patient, that was if the news were negative. This was far from negative, it was unexplainable. He continued, "The results show your cancer to be in remission and that is without the normal treatments such as Chemo or Radiation Therapy. Frankly, when you were here four months ago those two treatments wouldn't have done much of anything other than cause you pain and more sickness. Before and during the operation you lost a lot of blood. We managed to stabilize the bleeding. You were given quite a few units to make up for what you lost."

John smiled at his wife. "I feel fine doc. As a matter of fact I feel as good as I have ever felt in my life. When do you think I can go back to work? As you know I'm a farmer and for the last few months most of the work has been done by my friends and neighbors. I really don't know what I would have done without them."

Doctor James scanned the chart and then looked up at John. "I see nothing here that would keep you from working. Your incision has completely healed and all your bloodwork is normal. Try to take it easy for a few weeks though, don't rush right out in the morning and start working like you're eighteen again."

John and Nancy laughed. "You got a deal doc." John said. With that James stood and stuck out a hand. He shook both Nancy and John's hands and then turned to leave.

"I want to see you again in one week, the receptionist at the front desk will arrange the appointment." James said. He continued down the hall and then took the elevator up one floor. His office was three doors down and when he got there he closed his office door, once seated he pulled up the electronic files on John J. Oden. As he was entering some notes the screen blinked once, nothing more than a split second but it was noticeable. He made a note to have someone from IT have a look at it. As Dr. James entered his notes he was unaware that across town at a suite of offices on New Circle Road a tech was reading what was being written in real time. Stu even watched the doctor by use of the camera on Dr. James own monitor.

This was the first hard evidence of recovery. All the other cases being investigated were heading in the same direction but were not as complete as John Oden's case. As of now fourteen cases were being heavily monitored by the team in Alterations. It had been decided by Jason Freemont the previous day that at the first sign of two complete recoveries by any of the target group of patients the money would be appropriated to set up the next phase of the operation, actual physical evidence that tied the cases to the Primary. John Oden's file was just flagged as 'Reanimate #1' and moved into a new class. It was now imperative to find 'Reanimate #2'.

Big Van Goodwin tolerated his dialysis reasonably well knowing this was his last visit. He talked with the staff and traded a few jokes with some of the other patients. As he talked he realized he was the longest active patient in the room. He wasn't the oldest but he had made more trips to have his blood cleansed than any other patient. Van was reasonably certain but still asked one of the Techs if he was the longest running patient anyway, after checking she informed him he was. This made his decision to quit harder. If some of the newly started dialysis patients found out that Van quit he was afraid they would feel defeated themselves. This was something he couldn't allow to happen. He would suffer through his three treatments a week until he figured out how to quit, he might never figure out that answer.

As he left the Dialysis Center he was given his next appointment. He took the reminder slip and smiled. As he left he almost laughed, when he came in this was going to be his last treatment and now he realized he would probably never quit until it killed him. He got in his car and started the engine. He was hungry and thirsty. The hunger he could do something about but thirst was his constant companion. He drank as little as possible in order to keep his dialysis to a minimum and right now three days a week was the minimum. He pulled into Hardee's and put the car in park. When he was younger he rarely went inside a fast food joint. He didn't like the bright lighting and the bright colors these places were decorated in. Now though he didn't care. All he wanted was a big fat cheeseburger and a small cup of coffee. He found if he drank coffee slowly it usually suppressed his thirst, it never satisfied it but it did ease the desire just a little.

As he sat and enjoyed his burger, Hardee's makes the best as far as he was concerned, he noticed he had forgotten napkins. As he got up to go to the small counter where they were located he noticed the bandage on his left arm that covered the injection sight for his dialysis had a small red dot at the inside of the elbow. This was a bit unusual, actually it was very unusual. In all his treatments he had never had a problem with his veins before. No problem now either, he would just take it a little easy and also wear the bandage to bed tonight. When he finished his burger and coffee and was just about to get up and leave he noticed the red dot on the bandage had grown larger. He sat and thought about this a minute.

They told him when he first started dialysis that if this ever happened to return to the center and they would check it out and then bandage his arm again. Van had long since forgotten that conversation but now it came back to him. No big deal. Van gathered the trash and stood. As he deposited the paper and empty cup in the waste bin he noticed the spot had continued to grow. The center was only a half mile away, maybe he should go back and have them take a look.

Five minutes after leaving Hardee's Van was back inside the Dialysis Center and having his arm looked at.

"I don't think this has ever happened before Van." Stacey, one of the techs, said.

"Not that I can remember." Van told her.

They took off the bandage and redressed the entry point. It bled a little as they changed the bandages but it wasn't anything excessive.

When she was finished Stacey said, "There you go Van. I used a little extra gauze, hopefully that will do the trick. Try leaving the bandage on as late as possible tonight. If it isn't too tight and doesn't hurt you might want to leave it on until tomorrow morning."

Van thanked her and headed back to his car. He was home forty-five minutes later and spent the afternoon napping, for some reason he was extremely tired, maybe the dialysis had hit him harder this time than before. As he dozed off that evening during the six-o'clock news he thought to himself, 'Naps are good for you.'

Van woke up a little after nine and as he sat there he realized he had slept the bigger part of the day and he was still tired. 'Damn dialysis.' He got out of his recliner, slowly, and then turned off the television. After brushing his teeth and putting on his pajama bottoms he climbed into bed. Within minutes he was asleep again.

About two in the morning Van woke up. He was disoriented and sweating. He noticed his breathing was rapid and he couldn't seem to catch his breath. He reached over and turned on the lamp beside the bed. As he reached for the lamp he noticed how wet his arm and chest felt, he must have sweated a lot. Once the light was on he noticed the sheet he slept under had blood on it, a lot of blood on it. For some reason, even as disoriented as he was, he remembered the scene in The Godfather where the movie director woke up with blood all over himself and the horse's head at his feet. Van almost laughed as he thought about the fact that he didn't own a horse.

He held up the top sheet and looked; blood covered his chest and was on the bedsheets. The bandage was soaked and with his arm holding up the sheet he noticed blood dripping from his elbow. Suddenly he felt light headed and ready to lose consciousness. That set in as panic because he knew if he passed out he would bleed to death without ever waking up again. Van reached over and picked up the phone, he punched in 911 and waited as his world began to spin. Before it rang he passed out and dropped the receiver to the floor.

At the 911 Call Center the call was received. "Hello, what is your emergency?" The woman on the line, Phyllis, had been working dispatch for eleven years and had seen it all, from prank calls to children accidently dialing 911 as they played with the phone. Protocol dictated that all 911 calls were to be investigated. At two in the morning it was doubtful if teenagers would be pulling pranks or young children would be up.

The Sheriff's Department was notified and a deputy was dispatched to the address. While the unit was in route Phyllis pulled up the information on the address and found that the home at that address was owned by a man named Van Goodwin. It was also noted that the man was sixty-seven years old and a dialysis patient. As the 911 system had been upgraded each year someone had the foresight to list information to any address that might be helpful in the event of an emergency.

Phyllis dialed the ambulance service that was tasked with the area where Van lived and two minutes later an ambulance was in route with an EMT and a paramedic. They arrived four minutes after the deputy. A quick check found all the doors locked. Through a side window where a light was on the deputy spotted a man slumped over against the night stand beside the bed. The deputy and the two men from the ambulance sprang into action. The back door was immediately kicked in and the deputy went in first with his gun drawn. It was a precaution in case foul play was involved. Trouble wasn't expected and after a quick check of the house the Paramedic began checking Van out as the EMT brought in the gurney.

The deputy called in one of the other two night patrol units that were assigned for this part of the county. The second car was three minutes out, lights and siren engaged, why not wake everybody up he thought. Let the people of Floyd County know they were being protected. The people had elected themselves a good sheriff and he prided himself on the quality of his deputies. This deputy loved his lights and siren.

The Paramedic quickly checked Van's vitals. He was in shock from extreme blood loss. An IV was started and Oxygen was given at a high flow. The bleeding was stopped by a tighter bandage. At this point it was more important to stabilize the patient for transport than worry about cutting off circulation. Eleven minutes after breaking down the back door Van was being loaded into the back of the ambulance. Again with lights and siren the ambulance was moving. On the way the paramedic called in the vitals so the emergency room staff could be prepared.

All in all, Van's life had been saved by the fast thinking and quick response of a 911 operator, two deputies, a Paramedic and an EMT. Five people Van had never met and probably never would.

At the hospital Van was quickly given blood. He was A Negative and the supply was limited due to a bad car accident earlier. More was needed, more was on the way. By morning Van was in a private room and awake. It had been determined that his blood had failed to clot after the dialysis procedure the previous morning and that had nearly led to his death. It was something that happened from time to time although rare.

Depending on medication, illness, fatigue, or any number of reasons, this can happen. It may last a day or just a few hours. In Van's case it was from his blood thinning medication. He had accidently taken a double dose the previous morning when he had hit his head on the counter and then fallen into the chair. In his confusion he had gotten the prescription bottle down again and taken a second pill. It almost cost him his life.

The doctor came in the next morning and told Van he would be alright but they wanted to keep him in one more night for observation. He agreed. He was tired but other than that felt fine. There was a basketball game on at seven that evening and he looked forward to watching it. He would just nap and build his strength until game time. By noon a tray of food was brought in for lunch. Van looked over what he had and was pleasantly surprised. He liked everything on the tray. Before eating he decided to get up and use the bathroom. This wasn't a problem because all the monitors and the IV in his arm were mounted on a rolling stand. Without asking for help Van threw his feet over the side of the bed and stood.

Van stood there to make sure he wasn't weak, after a minute he decided he could make it. He took a small step using the rolling stand as a helper. No problem, he took another step. Again no problem, he was feeling pretty damn good for a man who nearly died the night before.

Van went into the bathroom and two minutes later he exited. Suddenly he stopped dead in his tracks, he had forgotten to flush. As he turned and went back in he realized he had just made water. Not just a little but a lot. As he stood there and looked at the toilet he tried to think how long it had been since he had used the bathroom. Two months seemed to be about right. Oh there had been times he could make a little water with the help of Lasix, a drug which took water off a person in torrents but even that wonder drug had ceased to do the job. As his diabetes progressed the disease had slowly destroyed his two kidneys, and then came the treatments, the dreaded treatments.

The Lasix had stopped working because both his kidneys had stopped working. Now as he stood and looked at the toilet he thought he should summon the nurse. He never flushed, he just turned and went back to his bed and pushed the assistance button. A moment later a nurse walked in. "Hi Mr. Goodwin, is everything alright?" She asked.

Van looked confused as he tried to figure out what to say. He didn't know how to say it except to just go ahead and say it. "Does my chart down there list my illnesses?" Van asked.

The nurse said, "We don't keep charts at the end of the beds anymore Mr. Goodwin, they are at the nurse's station. Is there a reason you want to know what is on your chart?" She asked.

"I was wondering what it said about my dialysis, I know they are keeping me here overnight but I have to be back at the Dialysis Center at seven in the morning." Van told her.

"Well Mr. Goodwin, I checked your chart earlier and you are scheduled to have the procedure done here at the hospital."

Van thought a minute and then said, "Well, I just went to the bathroom and didn't know if they had given me some medicine or something to make my kidneys work but I emptied my bladder and well, all I can say is I emptied it good."

The nurse thought he was kidding. "Your chart says you kidneys are non-functioning due to your diabetes."

"Up until five minutes ago they were non-functioning, but I swear they work now," Van said. He then added, "I never flushed."

Now that last statement might disgust some people but not a seasoned RN. She immediately went in the bathroom and then came right back out. "Has someone been in your room Mr. Goodwin and used your bathroom?"

"No one, just me," Van said with pride. His kidneys and bladder were working for the moment and he was happy with that.

The nurse said she would be back shortly. She went to the nurse's station and looked at a security monitor. She picked out the camera that monitored the corridor where Van's room was. She backed up the play until the last time she had been in the room which was about thirty minutes earlier. She fast-forwarded the footage and it was as Van had said, no one had been in his room in the last twenty minutes but her. Van was telling the truth. This was worth telling the doctor when he made the last rounds of the day. The nurse, a Miss Judy Campton went back into Van's room and asked him how he felt as she took his blood pressure. He told her he felt fine.

His blood pressure was one twenty-two over eighty. This was perfect. Judy wrote in the blood pressure, it was the second time it had been checked by her. He was hooked up to a monitor that was set to check it every ninety minutes. She compared all the numbers and found his blood pressure had improved each time it had been checked except the last two times and that was because both of those were perfect. Puzzling!

"Van, I want you to enjoy your lunch. Your doctor will be in later today to see you again." Judy smiled and left the room.

Minutes later she was back with a bottle that had a handle on one side and numbers on the other. Sam knew what that particular bottle was for. "Here you go Van. If you go back to the bathroom I want you to use this so we can measure how much your kidneys are putting out."

Van agreed and Judy put the bottle in the bathroom on the sink. As she was leaving Van asked, "Would it be alright if I had a bottle of water? I promise to only sip." There was a large brown cup of water on the table beside Van's bed but he didn't like the way it tasted.

"Sure thing Van, it shouldn't take a minute." Judy left the room and headed toward the nurse's station when she was summoned by another nurse to help with a patient down the hall. The one minute she promised Van actually took fifteen. When she came back Van wasn't in his bed. Just as Judy walked in Van came from the bathroom and he was holding the bottle, he had a smile on his face. Judy now knew Van's kidneys were functioning and functioning well. She reached him the bottle of water he had requested and he reached her his.

"Nurse, I know it's a while until supper but not only am I thirsty but I could really use something else to eat. I wouldn't ask but I can't remember when I've been this hungry before." Van said as he twisted the top off the water bottle.

Judy knew Van was a severe diabetic and knew how swings in blood sugar could happen at a moment's notice. "Please get back in bed Van while I go and notify the kitchen staff. I promise to have something here in a few minutes."

Judy didn't leave the room until Van was back in bed. "Now don't get up until I get back in here Van." He smiled and shook his head yes.

Judy went to the nurse's station and picked up the phone. "I need a tray for room 217 and if at all possible I need it in ten minutes or less." She didn't need to say anything about what kind of diet the patient in room 217 was on, that information was all documented in the system the kitchen staff used to prepare all the meals for patients. "Make sure it's brought by the station, I want to do a blood sugar before and after the meal." She said.

Eight minutes after Judy ordered the tray a tall man in scrubs stepped up to the nurse's station and said. "Here is the tray for 217." Judy was startled at first. She had been updating the chart for Van and hadn't realized the time.

"My goodness that was fast." She said.

The man smiled and said, "We in the kitchen know that all the healing that goes on around here is because of what we do. Where would the doctors and you nurses be if not for the superhuman efforts of people like me?"

Judy laughed. "I hadn't really thought if it that way. Thanks for straightening me out Burt."

He winked and said, "Don't mention it."

Judy and Burt walked down the hall and into room 217. Van was sitting up in bed flipping channels on the wall hung television using his remote. "Got you something to eat here Van, let me check your blood sugar first though."

Van stuck out a hand and said, "Got four fingers and a thumb that would just love to see a sharp needle right now, your pick."

Judy frowned at him and said, "Well, as feisty as you're getting I think I might just poke 'em all."

The little device was digital and the results were almost instantaneous. The readout read 98. "Oops Van, I got a bad reading. Let me check another finger." Judy chose another and waited for the reading, again it read 98. Judy was surprised. According to Van's chart his blood sugar never ran below one-sixty and that was with the help of insulin. "Have you taken any insulin today Van?" She asked as she continued to look at the 98 reading.

"Not today, don't know what they did to me last night or this morning, I was kind of out of it. Can I have my food now?"

Judy smiled and told Burt to put the tray on Van's roll around table. Burt fixed the tray and opened a small can of V-8 juice. Once everything was just the way Burt wanted it he adjusted the height and rolled the table around in front of Van.

"Now Van, I want you to eat slowly, don't rush. When you're finished ring for me, I want to check your sugar again and then every ten minutes after that for an hour." Judy said.

Van reached for the can of juice. "Yes mom."

Judy patted him on the knee. "You make sure you eat all those vegetables if you want to go outside and play later." Judy said this and then left the room, Burt right behind her laughing.

Later that day, after a long nap, Van turned the television to Sports-Center and looked over his supper tray. He had stayed in hospitals before and found the food pretty good. Since his wife died a few years back he had mastered the art of the five minute supper. Something heated in the microwave, something out of a can, anything out of the fridge and he was set. He found that if he was doing the cooking he wouldn't complain. At home now, all by himself, he found the food tolerable and the service terrible. At least he could laugh at himself.

As he watched TV and munched on his food he found himself actually enjoying what they had brought him. There was baked chicken with some sort of mushroom gravy and rice under it, not much rice because of his restricted diet. He also had that old staple, sweet peas and cooked carrots. If there was one thing Sam hated about being a diabetic it was the lack of bread in his diet. As hard as it is to believe he was told that bread was worse than candy for most diabetics. He was never a big candy eater but he did like his bread in just about any form it could be made in.

Twenty minutes after he started eating, the tray was empty, and he found he wanted more. He finished his V-8 and sipped his water. He waited ten minutes to ring for Judy to return and re-check his sugar, the same as she had ordered after his lunch earlier. Finally when he felt he had waited long enough he pressed the call button on his remote.

Judy came back in and immediately noticed the empty tray and empty juice glass. "Well you really were hungry Van, did it fill you up?"

"Pretty good I guess. When I was younger and working every day I had a really good appetite," Van said as he dabbed his chin with a napkin. "Lately with the sugar and all, I've taught myself to do without. I've just been nibbling it seems for years. Today though, I could eat a sixteen-inch pizza and drink a six pack of Triple Black all by myself." He looked at Judy and added, "I would share with you though, nurses eat too I suppose."

"Thank you Van. When the pizza and beer gets here just ring the nurse's station and you'll have six dinner guests down here in thirty seconds. Nurses love Triple Black and pizza." Van thought that was hilarious.

Judy checked his blood sugar again; she expected it to be north of two-hundred. It was 102. She looked at Van who was smiling and expecting a high number himself. "102 Van, something must be wrong with this meter." The low reading just after lunch could possibly be explained by the blood Van had been given during the night when he was first brought in. Now though the reading was nearly the same as before.

"Well take your time getting another one, as of right now I'm sticking with 102," Sam told the nurse.

A second meter was brought in and the blood checked again. It was the same, 102. Judy looked at Van and smiled. "And you are certain you haven't had any insulin today Van?" She knew the answer.

"No, I really don't think so. I had my dose yesterday and that was the last dose I can remember taking. As I said, I really don't know what they gave me when I was brought in last night."

It was possible he had been given insulin in the emergency room. "Van I want you to stay in bed until I get back. Until we can figure out what your blood sugar is doing I don't want you up by yourself."

"I'll stay right where I am. If you don't mind though, see if I can get another tray, same as before."

"You got it. Just give me a few minutes." Judy never intended on getting a second tray until she knew what was going on. She went straight to a monitor at the nurse's station and pulled up the file on Van. Everything that had been done the night before in the emergency room was listed; no insulin had been given by any of the ER staff. She picked up the phone and dialed the ambulance service that had brought Van in to see if the paramedic might have given him insulin. She knew this was highly unlikely. She hung up the phone once she had been told what she already knew. The ambulance personnel only treated Van for shock before dropping him off at the ER.

It was now a few minutes before seven-o'clock. Dr. Arvid Yusuf usually started his rounds each evening at seven. He was one of the doctors on staff that liked to keep his schedule. Judy called the kitchen and had them to prepare another tray for room 217 and again made sure it was delivered to the nurse's station. She would just keep that tray away from Van until something could be determined about his blood sugar.

At fifteen minutes after seven Dr. Yusuf arrived. He spoke to the nurses and then looked over some information about his patients. As Judy came down the corridor she spotted him.

"Doctor, I need to speak to you about Van Goodwin." She said.

"Certainly, he is doing better I hope. That was quite a scare he had last night."

"He is doing better. As a matter of fact he is doing great. I just updated his chart." Judy was holding Van's chart.

"That is good news, I really like Van. He makes me laugh."

Dr. Yusuf scanned the chart and then looked up at Judy." Are you sure this is correct? How can his blood sugar be 102?" Yusuf had only gotten down to the blood sugar number and hadn't seen the kidney output.

"I used two different meters doctor. Did you see kidney function?"

Yusuf looked at the chart again, Judy noticed he read slowly. "If I didn't know who this chart belonged too I would say this person was healthy, very healthy. This is Van Goodwin?" He said this more to himself than anyone else. He looked up at Judy, "Let's go have a look," he said as he turned and headed down the corridor.

Dr. Yusuf walked in Van's room followed by Judy. "Good Evening Van, I heard good things about you." Yusuf said.

Van was sitting up in bed watching Jeopardy and waiting on his second tray. "Hello doc. My kidneys are working." He said this with a big smile.

"Yes, I saw it on your chart. Are you still taking the prescription for Sulfonylurea?"

"I am. You do a hell of a lot better job saying the name than I do though; I just call it 'cellphone' for short." Van said.

Yusuf laughed, "Cellphone, I like it. I see here that you took it yesterday morning, is that correct?"

"I took it yesterday morning doc. You think that is what's keeping my sugar in check today, 102 is my best number in years."

Yusuf didn't answer at first, he was in deep thought. "It could be Van. I want to keep you here a couple of days to make sure your numbers stabilize. Is that okay with you?"

"Okay by me doc, but I'm scheduled for dialysis first thing tomorrow morning here at the hospital. You still going to have that done?" Van asked hoping they weren't.

"We will continue to monitor kidney function. If you haven't gone back to the bathroom by morning then it will still be scheduled."

Van smiled. "Don't need to wait till morning; I went again right before you came in. Nurse Judy told me to not get out of bed but I couldn't wait any longer."

Judy went into Van's bathroom and then came right back out holding the second container she had left there. "That's three times in less than six hours Van." She looked at the numbers on the side and then poured the contents into the toilet and flushed. She noted the number on Van's chart and then reached it back to Yusuf.

"Dialysis might be postponed if this continues Van. I'll know more after we do some bloodwork."

Thinking that dialysis might be cancelled lifted Van's spirits immensely. After they left he turned the volume back up so he could hear Jeopardy. Judy walked back in and sat the second tray of food on the roll around table. "I think you earned this." As she left Van smiled to himself. Twenty-four hours earlier he had made up his mind to quit dialysis. Now it looked like he might be quitting it anyway but for different reasons.

By Monday morning Van Goodwin had been designated as Reanimate #2. Now that Alterations had the second proven case it was time to enter phase two of the operation. Information on the two patients, John Oden and Van Goodwin was being cross referenced against anything that might actually explain away the miraculous recoveries. The emphasis during this phase of the operation was to obtain actual blood samples on both men. Ever since the Primary had been identified, plans had been discussed on how to obtain a blood sample. Everything from breaking into the blood centers again to actually kidnapping Edgemont had been considered. All the plans so far had been deemed as anywhere from impossible to downright stupid.

It was Freemont who finally settled upon a course of action. The courier van containing the donated blood products was going to be hijacked. PT was notified and told to make it happen within twenty-four hours of Edgemont's next platelet donation. Edgemont had just donated two days earlier on a Wednesday. He had given every other Wednesday for the last four months. He had skipped that appointment, the reason wasn't noted but even before that one missed appointment he had given solid for six months. It was assumed his next appointment would be Wednesday after next. That gave the team less than two weeks to finalize a plan and have everything ready.

Samuel Edgemont had been rattled by the men sitting in the street and keeping tabs on his house. The parking lot event at the Blood Center added to his worries. He was sure now that he was being followed and his house was being watched. What bothered him more than anything was what he had read in the Lexington Herald Newspaper the Friday after his donation. Two men in a Ford sedan had burned to death near Campton, Kentucky, at a place called Irvine. The fire happened on the same day he had confronted the two men at the Center. It had been so late on that Wednesday night that it didn't make the Thursday paper; it didn't get reported until the Friday edition.

The Donor

Sam didn't know if it was the same car, or the same two men, but he was suspicious. Since Wednesday he hadn't seen the car on his street and this added to the fact that he thought there was a connection, there had to be. He worked both Thursday and Friday and found it hard not to think of the two men or the car fire. He needed a distraction to take his mind off everything. He also didn't feel comfortable staying at home. He found himself looking out his window several times throughout the night.

It didn't take Sam long to figure out what he wanted to do; as soon as he got home Friday evening he started grabbing his camping gear. He hadn't been in the woods since spring and now he felt the urge to get away and do a little camping for several reasons. Where he liked to camp was a remote state park called the Red River Gorge. It was isolated, it was extremely rugged, and it was dangerous for anyone who wasn't familiar with the terrain. Every year at least one person died in the park. The usual reason for this was wandering around lost in the dark and falling from a cliff. Sam always hated it when he read about another fatality but knew accidents happened all the time.

Another source of danger was the number of snakes in the park. A tremendous amount of non-poisonous snakes called the Gorge home. A smaller number, but still substantial, was the copperheads and rattle-snakes that slithered around looking for their next meal.

Sam wasn't worried about falling from a cliff but he did take extra caution with the snakes. He did this because a copperhead or rattlesnake bite hurt and in his case it stung a little too. Sam had been bitten three years back. If he hadn't done something stupid he wouldn't have gotten bitten in the first place. He was hiking through some of the lessor used trails when he came upon a tree that had fallen across the path. It really wasn't a people trail in the first place; it was more of a deer run. Sam had been distracted by a squirrel that was making a racket a few trees over as he was stepping over the fallen tree and that was when he felt the bite.

The snake hit him hard in the calf. At first Sam thought he had been snagged by a broken branch but when he looked down he saw the snake, he was actually standing on it. In most cases a big snake will leave before it bites. If it still bites it will leave after it has sent you the message. But a big snake that can't slither away will continue to bite until it can escape. As quick as Sam saw what was happening he jumped clear but it was too late, he had been bitten more than once, two maybe even three times.

Once free the snake went into the underbrush with amazing speed. Sam saw enough to know it was a big rattlesnake, more deadly than a copperhead, just his luck. Sam looked at the back of his leg. There was a big blue knot rising up and in a slightly lower spot another was beginning to show. Two bites, he hoped at least one was a dry bite meaning the snake saved its venom for prey and only bit for effect. Sam knew though that once it had bitten him and was still pinned by the shoe it bit again and this time the snake would deliver a lethal dose.

The thing to do now was to stay calm and keep his heart rate down as to not spread the venom faster. Sam almost laughed knowing his heart was racing with fear, it was a really big snake. The size of the head looked as big as a man's closed fist. It had hit him hard to, it was like being punched. He was about a half mile from his Bronco. The walk there would spread the venom throughout his body and then he could possibly die. He quickly took off his belt and made a tourniquet above the bite mark and cinched it tight. He would release it every few minutes for fifteen seconds and then retighten it. He had been told by a park ranger once that tourniquets were rarely used unless the bite was severe; they could cause more problems than the snake bite. Sam remembered that little conversation but knew even if a tourniquet wasn't the best thing right now it still made him feel better and gave him confidence.

Sam headed for the Bronco at a steady pace stopping every few minutes to loosen the belt around his leg. By the time he made it to his vehicle he was drenched in sweat and his heart was pounding. He climbed in and put the key in the ignition. His Bronco was more than twenty years old but in good shape. Still he found himself wondering if the engine would turn over. If the Bronco had been brand new he would have still worried. The engine caught and he immediately put it in gear. Within five minutes he was at the two lane blacktop road that led to the Mountain Parkway. As he drove he could feel the sweat running down his face, it was so bad it dripped from his chin onto his shirt.

The Donor

The old Bronco was pushed pretty hard that day. As he descended the long hill that paralleled the parkway he was going seventy-five. A park ranger climbing the hill in one of the green trucks with lights on top was startled when he saw the Bronco. He hit the brakes and flipped on the lights. He made a U-turn right there in the middle of the road and sped off after the Bronco.

Sam never really saw the ranger truck as he came down the hill. He was using all he had just to keep the Bronco on his side of the road. When he made it to the intersection for the Parkway he was suddenly confused. Lexington was over an hour away. He didn't know if a medical facility was closer and if it was he was in no shape to drive there. As he sat at the on ramp trying to clear his head he heard the siren. At first he thought it was an ambulance, any number of which traveled the road bringing sick or injured people from Eastern Kentucky to the bigger hospitals Lexington was known for.

The ranger pulled up behind the Bronco, which was sitting in the road on the on ramp. Rangers have arrest powers and some say they have more authority than even the State Police. Rangers patrol both land and water whereas the State Police only patrol on land.

Officer Turley Burke opened the door to his truck and started easing up to the Bronco. He had unsnapped the strap that held his gun in place and had his hand on top of the weapon. He didn't expect trouble but it was always wise to be prepared for it just in case. As he approached the driver's side of the Bronco he could see from the side mirror that the occupant was a man and he seemed to be either under the influence or in some sort of distress.

When Sam finally looked in his side mirror he saw the green Ranger truck behind him with its emergency lights on. Sam put both hands on top of the steering wheel so they would be visible to the Ranger when he got close. He knew the best way to get shot by a policeman was to have your hands hidden. Even with that thought in mind he was still glad the ranger had stopped, he would know what to do.

Turley approached the vehicle with extreme caution. When he could see inside he saw the man's hands on top of the steering wheel. This lowered the tension by about a thousand percent. He also noticed the condition the man was in, labored breathing and drenched in sweat.

The usual question to ask at a time like this was for license and registration but Turley knew this was different. "Are you alright mister?" He asked as he still held his right hand over the Glock.

Sam leaned toward the window and tried to turn his head as much as possible. "I've been bitten by a snake." This was all he said.

Turley realized it was a medical emergency but needed to make sure. "Can you step out of the vehicle please?"

Sam said he could. He reached for the door handle and opened the door. When the door came open Sam fell out onto the pavement. He then passed out. Turley saw the tourniquet on the man's right leg and he also saw the damage the snake had done.

Now in an area that is infested with snakes who would have thought there would be a snake zoo nearby, but it was true. The adjoining state park was Natural Bridge State Park and at the entrance to that park near the Parkway's only rest stop was a zoo that specialized in snakes. At one time this particular zoo contained, as some of its guests, all four species of Mamba, one of the most dangerous snakes in the world. At the time it was one of only four reptile zoos in the world with all four species of Mamba.

Turley called dispatch and notified them as to what had happened and his location. He was told to stand by. Dispatch notified the administrator at the Reptile Zoo and asked for advice. With a man on the ground then the bite was serious. A helicopter was dispatched from Beaumont General and preparations were made to pick the patient up at the on ramp. Turley was instructed to remove the tourniquet altogether and stand by. Another Ranger along with the nearest State Police Trooper was dispatched to the area. Three county deputies were also sent in order to shut down the west bound lanes of the parkway in order for the helicopter to make the landing and pickup.

The trip to downtown Lexington from Slade was an hour and a half by car, eighteen minutes by chopper. Sam came to while in route but couldn't tell what was happening. All he could feel was a vibration and noise. He immediately fell unconscious again.

A rattlesnake bite is known to be deadly if antivenom isn't given promptly. Promptly means thirty minutes or less and that is if the amount of venom is small to moderate. In Sam's case he had been bitten three times. Usually a rattlesnake will hit a large animal, one that isn't considered food with a dry bite, no venom is injected. A snake won't waste venom; it uses it to obtain its food. The snake that had bitten Sam was over seven feet long and truly had a head the size of a large man's fist. Sam had walked up on the snake fast and when he stepped over the fallen tree he had stepped on its tail leaving full range of motion for its deadly head. The three strikes were fast and powerful, each delivering a lethal dose of venom. No one would ever know just how big the snake was but by the size and separation of each fang it was determined that it was big, really big.

Even without the venom just the strike of such a powerful snake had caused extensive bruising and swelling. Sam was rushed into the ER two minutes after the helicopter touched down. The administrator from the Reptile Zoo had been contacted by the hospital. He said the most likely culprit was a rattlesnake. The venom of a copperhead was much milder than that of a rattlesnake and if the subject was unconscious then it had to be a rattlesnake.

Taking into account the time the Park Ranger spotted Sam flying down the road, which led to the Mountain Parkway, and the time now, one hour and fifty minutes had passed. It was unknown how far Sam had traveled or how long it had been before that. Taking all this into account it was guessed the bite had happened at least three hours before. By the look of the wounds and the amount of swelling involved it was apparent that this man had a good chance of dying.

Antivenom was administered. The doctor in charge wasn't that familiar with procedure in a situation involving this much venom and the amount of time it had been in Sam's system. Most doctors can practice an entire lifetime and never come across a snakebite victim, especially with these time and quantity considerations.

The administrator at the Reptile Zoo was consulted again to see if he could shed any light on proper procedure. He advised the ER staff to administer the older antivenom made from horse serum. This serum was more apt to cause serum sickness but under the circumstances it was considered necessary. There was a new serum for Pit Viper bites made from purified anti-body fragments made from sheep. It was less likely to cause serum sickness but not as well known. The hospital had both versions but with the advice of the Zoo Administrator the second option wasn't considered.

Sam was given doses of the antivenom and kept under observation. He was transferred to a room in a critical care section of the hospital. The Zoo's administrator let it be known that there were less than ten fatalities nationwide each year due to snakebite. There were roughly 45,000 to 50,000 snakebites a year in the US and this made the chances of survival for anyone who had been bitten very high. The administrator sadly added that this particular patient, barring a miracle, would probably fall into the other category.

Sam's condition was listed as critical. It was now five thirty and he had been on the antivenom for a little less than three hours. Throughout the evening his condition slowly deteriorated. By using Sam's driver's license an attempt was made to notify his family. It was learned that Sam had been raised by his mother and she was deceased. Online records were obtained and no listing of a father was found. No brothers, no sisters, no aunts, or uncles. This man was truly alone in the world.

By nine that night it was determined that the amount of venom and the lack of quick medical care had resulted in the fact that this man was going to die. Nothing more could be done. The venom was causing blood vessels to leak. It was also affecting the organs. Sam's skin was turning dark and splotchy. His breathing was growing weak and so was his blood pressure and heart rate. The hospital was advised to not administer any more antivenom; he had passed the safe limit twice over. The monitors hooked up to Sam's body beeped and chirped but could do no more than that, the sound would soon change and verify that he had died.

Around ten that night the blood pressure stabilized. Within an hour the heart rate had returned to sixty four beats per minute. Sam stopped sweating and his body cooled to normal. The three large swollen knots on his calf began to shrink and the discoloration began to leave. By one in the morning the skin tone had returned to normal, the dark splotches completely gone. At three o'clock Sam awoke and asked for a glass of water.

The doctor on duty had noted all the improvements and was truly shocked. Never had he seen someone on their deathbed rally with such swiftness and force. Blood work had been done every three hours, by six the next morning it was nearly perfect. When the previous doctor who had worked the case the day before came in at seven he truly expected to hear that Samuel Edgemont had died during the night. It was such a waste, a man in his prime taken away by an accident of nature.

When the seven o'clock doctor walked in the first thing he asked was what had happened the night before? Everyone knew why he was asking. "Come this way doctor, you should see for yourself."

Dr. Edward Frazier was a Kentucky boy. He grew up near Bowling Green in the western part of the state. He had lived in Kentucky his entire life; having studied at UK in Lexington he now practiced medicine in Lexington. He was one of the physicians on duty when Samuel Edgemont was brought in the previous day. He had done all he could including contacting specialist in several states who had the experience and knowledge that he lacked in a situation like this. Dr. Frazier was a good doctor, no doubt about that. It was just that this case had gotten away from him so quickly. Edgemont had been brought in near death and continued to deteriorate the rest of the day. When Frazier finished his shift at 7:00 PM he didn't expect Edgemont to survive until midnight. He left work sad and dejected. As the old saying goes, 'Just part of the job' wasn't cutting it this time.

When Dr. Frazier walked into the room, followed by the nurse, what he saw shocked him to say the least. Sam was sitting up in bed reading a magazine and also glancing at the TV. His skin had returned to a normal color and he was alert. Frazier hadn't seen Sam awake at all the previous day, he had been unconscious. Frazier stood in the doorway for a few seconds without speaking. Sam looked up and recognized the doctor.

"Hello Dr. Frazier," Sam said.

This was also unexpected. Sam hadn't woken the entire day while Frazier was there, how could he know his name?

"Uh, hello Mr. Edgemont," he tried to regain his composure, "Is it alright if I call you by your first name?" The doctor asked.

Sam smiled. "That's fine and I want to thank you for all you did for me yesterday."

Dr. Frazier took the chart the nurse reached him and looked over the information. A couple of times while reading he looked up at his patient. This just wasn't the same man from yesterday. The man he worked on yesterday was dying; this man had the vitals of a marathon runner. Frazier reached the chart back to the nurse and looked back at Sam.

"What do you remember about yesterday Sam?" He asked.

"Everything," was all he said.

"Do you realize you were unconscious the entire day?"

Sam thought the doctor either had the wrong room or was pulling his leg. "I remember everything doc. You left the room three times to speak to a man who was a specialist on the venom of a Pit Viper. Your name is Edward Frazier and apparently you haven't treated many snakebite victims. You said that four times while in the room with me."

Frazier heard what Sam was saying but was having a hard time believing it. Sam was completely unconscious the previous day. "Were you able to see as well as hear what was happening around you yesterday?"

Sam thought a second and then answered. "Now that you mention it I really don't remember seeing much. It was as if my body was asleep but my mind was completely awake. I never tried to move or speak, I just wanted to rest."

This sort of made sense to the doctor, he had read of people being completely awake mentally but their bodies were asleep. People that experienced this found it to be anything from pleasant to terrifying. The medical term for this was Sleep Paralysis.

"I would like to examine your injuries Sam. Turn on your side so I can see the three wounds please." The three areas on the calf where the rattlesnake had struck had been left without bandages.

Sam turned on his side and held the injured leg straight so the doctor could get a good look. Frazier was astonished. The three points where the snake had struck Sam were nearly healed. No swelling, very little discoloration and the broken skin where the fangs had penetrated the skin were little more than scratches now. Frazier turned to the nurse and asked if pictures had been taken.

"Yes doctor. There are two sets from yesterday and one from this morning." She said.

"Sam, you can turn back over now. I want to keep you here for another day, if you agree then there are a few more tests I want to run to gauge the amount of damage that might have been done by the venom. Also we pumped quite a bit of antivenom into you yesterday and I want to make sure you don't suffer from serum sickness."

Sam agreed. It seemed the only symptom he had was fatigue and he would spend his time here resting. "I do have a question Doc? I left my Bronco back at Slade where the helicopter picked me up. Also I was camping on the Gorge side of the park and wondered if my camping equipment has been found?"

Frazier actually had an answer for this. "The rangers took care of your truck and also they found your campsite. All your stuff is at the ranger station. Those guys were real helpful; the one that found you probably saved your life." Frazier didn't know why he had made that last remark, he really couldn't figure out what or who had saved Sam's life.

Sam wasn't out of the woods yet, so to speak. Severe cases usually develop internal bleeding, also heart and kidney failure are possible. Respiratory failure was another concern. With no immediate symptoms it would take time to determine if any lasting damage would be involved. Sam would be monitored throughout the day and a few tests would be run. If everything continued its present course he would be released the following morning and then follow up appointments would be scheduled. Dr. Frazier entered all the information on the chart which would be added to the electronic files the next day. It was these same files from three years back that PT was now reading so thoroughly.

Sam finished packing his gear and was trying to put the snakebite experience out of his head when the phone rang. It wasn't his cell, it was the home phone. He walked over and grabbed the receiver. Sam didn't have caller ID, never felt the need for it.

"Hello."

"Is this Samuel Edgemont?" A female voice asked.

"It is." Was all Sam said?

"Hi Mr. Edgemont, I'm with a company that pays men in your age group to participate in clinical studies. Would you be interested in some information which will net you five-hundred dollars a week for the next six weeks if you participate in our study?"

Warning bells started going off in Sam's mind. "How did you get this number?" He asked.

"Your name was selected at random from our data base."

"How do you know my age, does your data-base contain that too?" He asked politely.

The woman was working from a script furnished by a group of analysts that worked inside Alterations. "Our lists are compiled through online research. We compile many lists and these are used when subjects are needed for our studies."

Any other time and Sam might not have been suspicious, after the blue sedan and the two deaths on the Parkway, Sam was on high alert. "So you have been doing research on me without my consent or knowledge. I'm not sure how I feel about that."

The lady continued from the script. She was good at what she did and hoped she could convince Edgemont of the legitimacy of the tests. "This goes on all the time Mr. Edgemont. Without the help of concerned citizens like you then many of our finest pharmaceuticals would never make it to market. You can take pride in the fact that you might be saving lives."

This woman was good, very good, but Sam was still suspicious. "Tell you what, give me the name of the company you work for and a phone number so I can call you back in a couple of days. I'm on my way out the door right now for a little camping trip." Sam wanted some information of his own. He doubted he would get either the name or the phone number.

"Due to federal regulations regarding tests and trials we aren't allowed to give out information by phone. This is to protect those who sign up for the trials." This last line was meant to satisfy Sam, it didn't.

"If you can't tell me who you are, and who you're working for, then I feel at a disadvantage. You know my name and phone number and who knows what else. I must decline and also ask that you purge my name from your files." Sam said this but knew nothing would be purged.

"We totally understand Mr. Edgemont. I will give you another call in a couple of days. You may change your mind about the test. Thank you and have a nice day." She hung up.

PT was listening by way of some fancy routing of the phone lines done by Stu. He was impressed by the way Sam had held his ground. It was a long shot in the first place but it had to be tried. Now the heist of the Blood Center truck would go on as planned.

Sam hung up the phone and stood there for a minute. The woman sounded legitimate. He knew of a few men at work that had actually participated in clinical studies and they had made some money doing it. Sam went back to gathering his camping gear and packing some food. He wanted to get out of town where no one knew him or for that matter could even find him.

The mistake Sam made was telling the woman he was going to be out of town for a couple of days. He had told her this to make it sound legitimate, that he needed to think it over and maybe call her back later. He actually realized his mistake as he was saying it. He put very little worry into that slip of the tongue. What were they going to do break into his house while he was gone?

That was exactly what they were going to do. All the new people who would be doing the field work for Alterations were in place as of noon Friday. At the moment there were two teams and they had the resources to conduct surveillance that rivaled the federal government. Two different vehicles would be outfitted every other day and driven in by four different men. In any forty eight hour period there would be different cars or trucks and different men inside those vehicles.

It was also decided to verify where Edgemont was headed this weekend and shadow him. As soon as his Bronco pulled onto the main street a car pulled in behind but stayed a safe distance. Unknown to Sam he would be having a little company on this camping trip.

As soon he was gone a service truck, with AEP on the door, would be parked outside his house while two men went in to install both audio and video equipment. The AEP truck was to arrive just after dark; this would allow a small amount of freedom of movement. Once at the back of the house the two men could enter and quickly mount the cameras and listening devices. Everything was wireless. The inside equipment transmitted to a gathering device installed in Sam's attic. The information was then picked up by a hub on the utility pole out front and that device could be accessed by something as simple as cell service, or in this case piggybacked onto the phone lines.

As Sam traveled the Mountain Parkway he was unaware that his house was about to be broken into and infested with cameras and listening devices. The tail car following Sam's Bronco kept Stu informed on the direction Sam was heading. When it became apparent he was entering the Mountain Parkway it was decided to head two more cars from the offices at New Circle in that direction. They wanted to know where he was going to be camping. Two men were hurriedly sent to a Dick's Sporting Goods, located in Hamburg, to pick up camping gear and supplies. Sam didn't know it but when he finally made camp for the night there would be a couple of other campers in the vicinity monitoring his movements.

As Sam drove he replayed the events of the week, starting with the two men surveilling his house. The same two men he would confront that very same day in the parking lot of the Blood Center. The fire and deaths on the Mountain Parkway later that night, and now the mysterious call wanting him to volunteer for a Clinical Study. Sam couldn't remember another time in his life when he wanted so badly to get far into the woods and away from people.

The Donor

The trip took about an hour and a half. Sam's old Bronco had a cassette player installed in the dash. When he purchased it back in 2012 the sight of a cassette player was almost laughable. He told himself he would replace it with a CD player but never seemed to get around to it. Five years later and he was still using the old cassette player. His selection of music was limited. He had managed to find a few cassettes of artists he liked, mostly country. At the moment he was tapping the steering wheel to the tune of 'That Ain't No Way to Go' by Brooks and Dunn.

Sam pulled off the Mountain Parkway at the same exit the helicopter had used as a landing site three years ago when it picked him up at the beginning of his little rattlesnake adventure. There is a rest stop there and a few other businesses catering to motorist, campers and hikers. From time to time a little kayaking takes place but that sport falls behind the hiking and camping. Sam pulled into his favorite filling station, one that not only sold gas but also firewood and many of the other essentials needed to spend a few nights in the woods. He needed the firewood because it is a crime to chop wood in the parks. You packed in what you needed and when you left you made sure no one could tell you had been there. Campers and hikers, on average, are a neat and tidy bunch.

Sam bought a six pack of Diet Coke and a small bag of ice for his cooler. An eight pack of hot dogs and buns, four bags of Corn Chips and a few other snacks. He paid twelve dollars for a two day camping pass and was all set. After he paid he turned to leave and nearly collided with a man standing behind him, too close behind him, holding two cans of Coke. After getting outside Sam backed out of his parking spot and then had an idea. He didn't need gas but decided to top off his tank anyway. He pulled up to one of the pumps and got out. After pre-paying with a credit card he began fueling the Bronco's tank. As he pumped gas he watched the door. The man who was right behind him in line didn't come out. That was odd, he seemed so anxious to get to the register Sam almost collided with him.

As Sam pumped he realized the tank would be full too soon, he had half a tank when he pulled in. He slowed the nozzle to only a trickle. The extra time he was using to fill up the tank would appear Sam was almost empty when he started. Sam was determined to wait it out and see what the man was driving. The nozzle clicked off. Still no one came out the front doors. Sam suddenly got an idea to see if he could flush the man out.

Sam got his paper receipt from the pump and then got in the Bronco. As soon as he did the front door came open and the man walked out carrying the two cans of soda, nothing else. Sam was pointed away but still saw the man through his side mirror. At that moment he decided the windows on the Bronco needed cleaning. He got back out, got the brush and began scrubbing the dead bugs from the windshield. As he done this he could see the vehicle the man got into. He wasn't alone although Sam couldn't tell if it was another man in there or a woman. It was dark now and the other occupant of the vehicle could have even been a large dog sitting up in the passenger seat.

Sam finished the windshield and hoped the other vehicle, a Chevy Tahoe, would start up and leave, it didn't. Sam made a point to wash every window on the Bronco, even both side mirrors. Hell he would have used the windshield brush to wash the entire vehicle if he thought he could get away with it.

Sam had killed enough time; he put the brush back in the bucket beside the pump and got back in the Bronco. He knew where he was going, it was a spot he had used before and hoped no one else had already taken it. Sam didn't mind setting up his tent and the rest of his gear in the dark, it was actually fun. What he did mind was for the two people in the Tahoe to know which way he was heading and maybe even follow him there. When Sam pulled out he didn't head for the Gorge, he turned right and went under the Mountain Parkway overpass. He was heading into Natural Bridge State Park.

Sam wanted to know if the Tahoe was going to follow him and if they did he didn't want the occupants to know he was on to them. As he drove into the park he watched the station in his rearview. The Tahoe pulled out just as Sam went under the overpass. As he climbed the small hill he saw them again, they were going the same way he was. Sam knew the area well and decided he would lose them. When he rounded the curve about a quarter mile ahead of the Tahoe and lost sight of them he floored the Bronco. One thing he really liked about the big Bronco was its oversized engine. Within seconds he had gone from twenty-five miles an hour to seventy five. He was on a straight and wanted to be past the next curve before the Tahoe came into view. He did it.

There were a couple more short straights and curves and coming out of the second curve there was a T-bone intersection. Sam knew exactly where it was and broke hard without leaving skid marks in the road. As he turned onto the secondary road he killed the Bronco's headlights. There was another right hand turn and he didn't dare use his brakes. The brake lights would show which way he went. He put the Bronco in neutral and let it coast around the right hand curve, it was still fast enough that he thought he might slide into the opposite lane but the big Bronco held. He continued to roll down the side road still watching the highway.

After less than fifteen seconds a vehicle came around the curve and it was going fast. When the driver saw the T-Bone intersection he locked the brakes and slid to a stop. The Bronco was still rolling down the side road. Sam thought they might make the turn and come over to investigate; he didn't think they had seen him though. If they did come this way then he had a problem, this was a dead end road. The only thing down there was a sky-lift that took visitors up to the Natural Bridge.

Sam's mind was racing; he was sure now that the Tahoe was following him. He was also running the possibilities of what to do if the Tahoe came in his direction. The last thing he wanted was to be confronted by whoever was in the Tahoe out here in the boonies. As his vehicle continued to slow he kept his eye on the Tahoe sitting in the highway. After what seemed like ten minutes but was probably only ten seconds the Tahoe accelerated and went around the next curve.

Sam knew this was his chance. He dropped the Bronco in drive and made a U-turn right there on the two lane road. He was quickly back on the main road and heading toward the intersection. He went under the Mountain Parkway and then took a left at the same station where the chase had started. He drove nearly forty minutes on the two lane road that would take him into the Red River Gorge Park doing exactly the speed limit. He was fortunate no park rangers had been around when he made his seventy-five mile an hour getaway earlier.

When he finally put the Bronco in park it was almost ten-o'clock. He had kept a close eye on the rear view mirror as he drove. No one came up behind him and at this hour he met very little traffic in the park. He was well hidden and the Bronco's dark green and tan exterior broke up its outline really well in the dense undergrowth. He was less than two hundred feet from the park road on a grassy leaf strewn path that was used for vehicles and campers. His was the only vehicle in the area. Sam got out and pulled a folding chair from the back.

Sam put the chair right behind the Bronco and then got one of the Cokes and a bag of Corn Chips out of the cab. He really wanted to start setting up camp but decided to put that off for a while. If someone followed him he wanted to be able to make a fast getaway without having to worry about his tent and other gear. He also knew he wouldn't be using the firewood tonight, no need to broadcast where he was.

Sam sat and enjoyed his snack. He hadn't thought about supper tonight. It was his plan to set up camp and then crawl into his sleeping bag and sleep off a hectic and disturbing week. He always started a small fire in order to ward off predators. Even a fire that was dying out put off a smoke smell and he believed most wild animals would stay away. As he sat he listened for the sound of a vehicle coming up the road, nothing. At that moment Sam made a decision, he didn't want to spend the night in a tent. He climbed into the Bronco and turned it around, leaving it parked so it faced outward. He put the empty soda can and bag in the passenger floorboard and threw the folding chair in the back.

He had slept in the Bronco before when he was tired and needed thirty minutes of sleep in order to refresh himself before driving on home. That was only thirty minutes though. Now he knew he would be spending the entire night. He reclined the seat enough to relax but still be able to see over the steering wheel. If anyone approached in a vehicle he would know it. Hopefully his position was well hidden and the Bronco was the perfect color for concealment in the woods.

The two men in the Tahoe went five miles past the intersection they had stopped at and saw nothing of the dark green Bronco. The driver, the one Sam had nearly collided with in the filling station, was a tall thin Canadian with dual citizenship and the perfect papers to prove it. His name was Scott McCray and he was a professional bounty hunter. Recently he had branched out into the lucrative field of surveillance. PT had read, with no small amount of admiration, of the number of felons McCray had apprehended over the last few years. Some of the most high-profile apprehensions had McCray's name attached. He rarely failed and in a profession where everyone you pursue is looking over his or her shoulder the paychecks could be few and far between. Not so with McCray. He routinely captured someone on an outstanding warrant, usually at least once a month. The income from some of the arrests was substantial.

PT realized that a man who was this good at tracking someone down might be handy in surveillance. Alterations might just be able to use the skill set of McCray. With the amount of money Beeler-Jordon was spending on the Alterations Project, PT was farsighted enough to put McCray on retainer the previous month. When the call came in the previous week McCray was in New York looking for a bounty worth fifty-thousand dollars. He dropped that case and took the first plane to Lexington, Kentucky. He had never been in the state before and actually looked forward to a rural setting for a change.

McCray turned the Tahoe and backtracked. He went back to the station and went inside. The clerk who had waited on both Edgemont and McCray was still behind the counter. McCray walked up and spoke to her. "Where does this left hand road lead to?" He was pointing in the direction he was asking about.

The intersection was well lit due to some halogen lights the state had used to illuminate the 'Park and Drive' lot beside the intersection. It was also lit by the lights the station had over its pumps. The lady looked in the direction McCray was pointing. "That road takes you into the Red River Gorge. Lots of people head into the Natural Bridge side of the park and then, when they realize their mistake, turn and come back this way. The man who was here before you must have made the same mistake. I saw that green Bronco come back through here just a few minutes ago."

Now what's the chance McCray could be so lucky. This woman had just told him which way Samuel Edgemont was headed. McCray now had a problem, was Edgemont aware that he was being followed and tried to get away or had he just made a wrong turn, and then upon realizing his mistake, came back in this direction? McCray would doubt the first scenario; it was extremely unlikely Edgemont had made the connection. Maybe he had changed his mind on where he wanted to camp, there was one way to find out.

"I should buy a camping permit for the night; I was in here a few minutes ago and forgot to get one."

"Is it for one night or the weekend?" The teller asked.

McCray thought a second and then said, "I suppose for two nights. Is there a different permit needed for each park." This would answer part of the question about Edgemont going the wrong way by mistake.

"The same permit works in both parks. If you are checked by a ranger you will be fine."

This helped explain why Edgemont had made an abrupt turnaround, his permit was good for both parks, maybe he just changed his mind. McCray had seen the bundle of firewood Edgemont had thrown in his Bronco. "Better give me a bundle of firewood too." He said.

Outside in the Tahoe McCray picked up his cell phone and dialed the number for the New Circle Road offices. Stu answered, McCray figured the little IT guy never had a home life, it seemed he was always at work. Once Stu verified the line was safe McCray filled him in on the events of the last hour. Stu told McCray to call back in fifteen minutes. PT was notified about the wrong turn Edgemont had made and how McCray had been given the slip. PT suspected Edgemont might be on to something. McCray was told to drive back to Lexington, about sixty-five miles, and change vehicles.

New Circle kept six cars there, all of different makes and colors. He was to change vehicles and head back to the park. The Tahoe would be taken back to the rental company. The vehicle exchange should be completed in less than three hours. Edgemont should by then be tucked away in his tent and if he was on the lookout for a big Tahoe he could look all he wanted. The people at the car rental place were going to get a spike in business due to the needs of Alterations. It had been decided to spread the business of renting cars for Alterations around in order to keep suspicions to a minimum, several different rental companies in Lexington would be used.

Sam spent the night reclined in the front seat of his Bronco. He had to admit he had spent worse nights out of doors. The Bronco was extremely comfortable. When he awoke at six-thirty it was still dark but the skies would lighten shortly. The temperature inside the cab this morning was chilly; as a matter of fact it was cold. When he stepped out the air was crisp. There was a considerable fog and this was good.

The first thing Sam realized was just how hungry he was. His can of Coke and bag of Corn Chips the night before was all he had eaten since his noon time lunch at work the previous day. He went to the fire pit and as he stood there, he stretched. He decided to build a fire and cook his breakfast. He hadn't seen a single set of headlights during the night and now that it was getting light he decided his fire wouldn't be noticed. The fog would also obscure the smoke.

Usually when Sam camped out he liked to start his fire using a fire steel. He would put his tender in the fire pit and then strike the fire steel until he sparked a fire in the tender. It usually took five extra minutes to get a fire started this way and he enjoyed the experience. This morning was different. He was hungry and he was thirsty and the quicker the fire was ready the quicker he could eat.

Once the fire was going Sam got his skillet out of the Bronco and then slid out the cooler he had brought from home. Using the tailgate as a countertop Sam got out the package of bacon he had brought from his refrigerator. He had put four eggs in a baggie from his fridge and was glad to see that none of the four had broken. He cracked two eggs and put in six slices of bacon, they kind of mixed together this way but it would be a little faster. The fire was going good by the time Sam put his folding grate out. He sat the skillet on top of the grate and then got out his coffee pot. He poured in two twenty ounce bottles of water and then sat the pot on the grate beside the skillet.

By seven-thirty Sam was relaxing in his lawn chair eating breakfast and drinking strong coffee. It looked like the sun was going to shine today; the fog was quickly separating as the sun burned it off the ridges. A little after eight-o'clock a vehicle could be heard coming up the hill. By the sound it made he could tell it was some sort of pickup truck, not a car. From where the Bronco was parked there was the slightest clearing of fall foliage to see it was a Ranger truck. To Sam's relief it went right on by. Another half mile and the road was a dead end. There was a parking area there and a turn around. It was where people parked if they wanted to hike out to the Sky View Bridge. Ten minutes later the truck came back and never slowed down, it just kept on going. The Rangers made their rounds first thing in the morning and would be back several times during the day.

Helen Montgomery had been picked up at two-thirty from the nursing home. She asked the two ambulance attendants, one male, the other a tall female, if the lights and siren could be left off, she wanted to enjoy her trip to the hospital even if the only view she would have was out the back window. She was told the siren wouldn't be in use but it was necessary for the lights to be on anytime a patient was being transported. Helen said that would be fine, she couldn't see the lights anyway.

The skies had continued to stay cloudy and the breeze was brisk as she was wheeled out to the ambulance. She felt so silly while she was being strapped onto the gurney. The drive took about forty-five minutes and even though she was riding in an ambulance she could still see out the back glass. The front half of the gurney was elevated which helped with the sightseeing. Now anyone who has ever ridden in the back of an ambulance will tell you it is about as uncomfortable a ride as you will ever experience, that is unless you're unconscious. Helen never complained in the least. She was enjoying everything today, even things that were uncomfortable were still better than the few things she could remember of the last few months.

When the ambulance pulled into the covered area where patients were unloaded Helen looked at the paramedic who was riding back there with her and asked if she could walk in.

"I'm sorry but we have to take you inside on the gurney. The hospital staff will decide what to do after we get you inside."

As promised the back doors were opened and the gurney was rolled out. Once the wheels were down the two attendants rolled Helen inside. Dr. Slade had been notified, as per his request, and was waiting just inside.

"Well, hello again Dr. Slade, I didn't expect to see you as soon as I arrived."

"It was the least I could do Mrs. Montgomery. I wanted to thank you for agreeing to come over for the tests. You looked like you were having such a good time with your friends at the nursing home and I know it was a sacrifice for you to come here."

"Oh not at all doctor, I can make new friends here."

"The staff will see you to your room, it is on the second floor and that floor has a veranda. You can go out there anytime you like and enjoy this beautiful weather."

Both Helen and the doctor looked out the glass doors at the gloomy skies. "I do love a cloudy day, especially when it looks as if it might snow." Slade said, as much to himself as to Helen.

Helen found her room to be pleasant. She was extremely happy with the fruit and flowers. In all her years she had never gotten flowers while in a hospital. Once they had her off the gurney and onto her bed she immediately got up and thanked the two ambulance personnel. As they left Helen walked over and peered out her window. She could see most of the front parking lot and the busy road that ran along that side. Across from that were houses, not the everyday type of house that Helen was accustomed to but large multi-story homes. Each looked like it was only a few feet from the next. Helen never understood why they built houses so close to each other. By the looks of things anyone who could afford a house like that could at least afford a little yard to go with it.

"Hello Mrs. Montgomery, I'm Rachel Bevins. I'll be looking in on you from time to time. Is there anything you need at the moment?" Rachel asked as she wrote her name on the chalk board on the opposite wall from the bed.

"Hi Rachel, please call me Helen. When will the tests begin that Dr. Slade mentioned?"

"Soon, I was told you had lunch before they brought you here from the nursing home. We will try to have everything completed before dinner. After that I was told you might want to go out onto the veranda."

Helen looked toward the window as she answered, "Yes, I want to spend the evening outside. The weather is so nice today."

Rachel looked out the window as well. The dark rolling clouds were impressive, not in their good cheer but in the gloom they presented, it seemed to her. "Well as soon as the tests are complete and dinner is over I will show you the way."

Rachel left the room and headed for the nurses station. She had already scanned Helen's chart before she arrived. This new patient was truly extraordinary. As of yesterday Helen was in the last stages of dementia, now she was as coherent as any woman half her age. Rachel wanted to see and talk to her before she made the call to a mysterious man that wanted confidential patient information in return for some serious money.

After finishing up a few details left over from before the lunch break Rachel took a ten and headed for the veranda. Once there she looked up at the cloud cover. Helen must really like cloudy days she thought as she pulled her cellphone from her pocket. She quickly dialed in a local number and waited for a ring.

"Hello," Came the reply from the other end.

"This is Rachel." Was all she said? It was all she needed to say. The male voice on the other end knew some money was about to change hands.

"Hi Rachel, I never expected to hear from you so soon. Have you got something for me?"

Rachel looked around the veranda. The only other people out there were a male nurse and a woman from housekeeping. Both were married but not to each other. The two had been close friends now for three months and the other employees of the hospital had begun to talk, but not too much. Hospitals were notorious for the number of extramarital affairs they spawned. These two were so comfortable on the veranda that more than once other employees had been forced to cut their breaks short just to not witness more than they wanted to.

Rachel was far enough away from the two that she could talk without fear of being overheard. "Yes, I have a file."

The voice hesitated for a moment, "Male or female?"

"Female, just brought over from River Terrace Nursing Home."

"How up to date is the file if she was just brought over?"

"Everything is current as of noon today. I've read over the file and I think your client will want this information."

There was another pause. "When can we have it?"

"My lunch break is in an hour. You can have it then." Rachel said.

"Alright then, the same amount as before, same spot as we used before."

"That won't work this time. What I'm doing could cost me my job and this is a very good file."

Rachel had been contacted three months prior by a man known only to her as Noah. He offered her cash for information pertaining to unexplained recoveries; he used the term, 'Of Biblical Proportions.' Rachel assumed this was why he liked to use the name Noah, obviously not his real name. He offered twenty-five hundred dollars for any files that met these criteria. So far Rachel had supplied two files and pocketed five thousand dollars. These were dollars that would never show up on her tax returns.

Noah had anticipated this and had already worked out what a top offer would garner. Noah worked for Alterations in the offices at New Circle. He and Stu had agreed that twenty-five hundred each for the two files they had already gotten was probably the best money Alterations had spent in its short history.

"What will work?" Was all Noah asked.

"Ten thousand, this file I assure you is worth every penny." Noah almost laughed. He and Stu had already agreed that twenty-five thousand was the limit they could offer without talking to PT. "You got a deal." Was all Noah said before hanging up.

A courier was sent to Rachel's address. The courier was dressed as a postal employee with the only exception being he was driving a solid black Dodge Charger with heavily tented windows. It would have been too much to have stolen an actual mail delivery truck each time they needed to buy information. The Charger would have to do. The courier always parked around back and then walked to the front of the complex where Rachel lived. Anyone who saw him exit the Charger would think it was a Postal Employee who had just gotten off work. When he walked to the front of the building anyone who saw him would assume he was really a Postal Employee, especially when he dropped the thick manila envelope into Rachel's wall mounted box. It had been easy to copy a key to fit Rachel's box.

A different mailman would be back in two hours to retrieve the outgoing mail, particularly one file which contained nothing but medical information. The signal would be when Rachel called Noah back. Once she had retrieved her money she would leave the file and make the call. The second mailman would be there in minutes to retrieve the file. The two parties felt comfortable with the arrangement. Rachel knew she wouldn't try to take the money without giving Noah what he asked for. Noah didn't really care if Rachel stiffed him or not. It was only ten thousand dollars and Alterations had millions. It was the file that meant everything.

Two hours later and the black Dodge Charger pulled around behind the offices on New Circle. Four operatives were ready to take the chart apart and start the gathering process. PT was notified in Chicago. Within two hours the file of Helen Montgomery was given the same priority as those of John J. Oden and Van Goodwin.

Helen was through with her tests by five that afternoon. It seemed to her that she had been given more tests, and of different kinds in those few hours, than she had ever been given before. The hospital staff was so helpful and extremely nice to her, everything went off without a hitch.

After she was wheeled back to her room she sat in bed and watched the local news. Suddenly Helen felt a cold chill run through her.

"Hello Helen, are you ready for your supper?" It was Rachel.

Helen looked at her and for some unknown reason she felt uneasy. It was a feeling you might get if you had just seen a long lost friend but then remembered the reason you hadn't spoken to that friend in so many years.

"Hello Rachel. I believe I am ready for something to eat. Am I allowed to choose what I get?"

Rachel looked at her chart. Part of the reason was to not look Helen directly in the eye. Rachel had just sold Helen's file for ten-thousand dollars and felt a bit guilty, as she should. Rachel knew the guilt would fade tomorrow when she hid the money in her safety deposit box. When she found what she was looking for she said, "It says here you may have anything you want."

Helen smiled. "I think I would like a big hamburger with cheese, maybe some lettuce and tomato on the side. No fries or anything else, just the burger. And I would like to have a milkshake." Helen paused and then smiled, "Yes, a chocolate shake, it was my favorite when I was young." Helen had spent the afternoon thinking about younger days. The memories came to her in torrents.

Rachel wrote down what Helen had ordered. It reminded her of younger days too, when she took orders at an Applebee's she worked at while in college. At least Helen's memories were pleasant, Rachel's certainly were not.

"I'll go and call the kitchen; it shouldn't take more than thirty minutes." When Rachel turned and left the room Helen noticed the cold chill left with her. Helen was never one to judge others but something about this nurse wasn't right. It just wasn't right. Earlier the feeling hadn't been there when she had first met Rachel. What could have happened between that first meeting and now, maybe it was nothing.

Helen didn't know it but her entire medical history was being picked through by members of the Alterations group. By nine-o'clock that night she was designated as 'Reanimate #3.' Helen was now in a special group of people that were being studied by the third largest Pharmaceutical Company in the United States. It was a definition that would have frightened her, it would have frightened anybody.

After Sam finished his bacon and eggs while sitting behind the Bronco he put out the fire. No need to send smoke signals to whomever it was that tried to follow him last night. Something he failed to consider, but now became aware of, was the fact that they must have followed him all the way from his home. How had he missed that? He thought he had monitored all the cars behind him and never really saw the Tahoe until he was at the filling station in Slade. He was sure the big Tahoe wasn't behind him as he drove the Mountain Parkway. So how had they found him at Slade?

As he sat and pondered this he suddenly had the urge to look under the Bronco. The ground was leaf strewn and a good place for snakes. He was under the truck anyway, if there was a snake under there then it would just have to make room for him too. After a good twenty minutes he came out and dusted himself off. He had found nothing although he really didn't know what a tracking device would look like anyway.

Sam decided to drive around a little and see what he could see. There was a really nice lodge in the other park called the Hemlock Lodge. Around noon on Saturday and Sunday they set up a really nice buffet in the restaurant. He had eaten there over the years and found the food to always be good. The reason for this was that Kentucky staffed a chef at each of its larger state parks. That was it then; Sam would clean up and go have his lunch at the Hemlock lodge.

He shaved using one of the side mirrors on the Bronco. He stripped down and gave himself a bath using baby wipes. He discovered this little trick a few years back while camping in the Smokies. There was a trick to it though. His first wipey bath out in the woods was done with the scented wipes. The entire day he could smell the sweet smell of the wipes he had used. The mosquitoes had also taken a liking to the scent. He probably used an entire bottle of bug spray that day. After that little adventure he now carried unscented wipes made just for camping and they worked just fine.

Fresh set of clothes and a little body spray and he looked and felt as if he had just walked out of his own home. Sam made sure the fire was out and then loaded up what little he had gotten out of the Bronco that morning. By nine o'clock he was ready to hit the trail. He climbed in and started the Bronco. Brooks and Dunn was still playing in the cassette deck and that suited Sam just fine. He pulled to the blacktop road and then looked both ways.

Left would take him back toward the Mountain Parkway and the other park. Right was only a half-mile or less to the turn around and parking lot that serviced the Sky-View Natural Bridge. For no other reason than to kill time he turned right. He didn't expect to find another vehicle there, the only traffic the entire night had been the Ranger truck that morning and it had turned around and went back out as fast as it had come in. When the parking lot came into view there was a vehicle there. It was a Ford Taurus. It wasn't parked at the lot, it was to the side where people might park if they intended to camp at one of the three spots that were made available for camping. As Sam drove by the parked Ford he checked to see if anyone was inside. It was empty and that was when he noticed the small sticker on the side glass, Avis.

Sam turned around and headed down the hill toward Slade. He thought about the Avis car and wondered who would rent a car to go camping. It had to have been there the entire night which meant whoever had rented it was at one of the three campsites near the turnaround. It was close enough that Sam should have seen the light of their campfire during the night, he hadn't. Whoever had been there ran a cold camp. Could they have been in the woods watching Sam's Bronco?

Sam hadn't known it but he was right about the Avis car. It was one of the vehicles that was used by the people at the New Circle offices. This was the car the two men had used who had gone to the Dick's Sporting Goods. They purchased the equipment to use if they really needed to look like they were going camping. They were sent to the spot the car occupied and told to stay there until contact was established with the green Bronco. When it was verified Sam was on his way up the hill the two men decided to leave the car and wait in the woods within view of all the camping spots, including the one Sam used. When Sam arrived they were watching. When he turned the Bronco so he could sleep facing the road the two men observed him with night vision binoculars.

The two were in radio contact with Stu throughout the night. It was decided for them to shadow the Bronco rather than set up a camp. The radios the two men used were equipped with headsets so they could talk without being heard. Sam slept the night away in his Bronco and never realized that not more than a hundred feet away two heavily armed men watched him sleep. As bad as that might seem it was probably the safest night's sleep Sam had ever gotten. If anyone had stumbled upon Sam's camp then there were two ex-Army Rangers nearby that would have seen to his safety.

It wasn't only the mission of the people that worked in Alterations to find out everything Sam was doing. It was also their job to make sure that nothing happened to him. If everything continued, as it was expected to, then it was possible that Sam was a walking 'Fountain of Youth.' It was suspected his blood could heal the most serious of diseases. This wasn't confirmed yet by the people at Beeler-Jordan but so far all indications pointed in that direction.

As Sam descended the hill that led back to Slade he thought about the rental car parked so close to where he had camped. With all the strange things that had happened in the last three days he decided to consider this as also connected somehow. As he drove he kept a close eye on his rearview mirror. He also looked for the Tahoe he had seen the night before.

Forty minutes later when Sam went by the filling station he had stopped at the night before, he decided to go in and get a cup of coffee. When he went inside he looked for the same lady that had worked the previous night, she wasn't there. How could she be, no one could be expected to work every hour that a convenient store was open.

Sam pulled a twenty ounce cup from the stack and filled it nearly to the top. The space he left was filled with cream. He lidded the cup and headed for the register. As Sam was paying he noticed the Avis car go racing by, it slowed and took the right hand turn and then headed in the direction of Natural Bridge State Park. Sam got the change for his coffee and then went outside. When he remembered the cooler in the back he went back inside and purchased a bag of ice. He was really just killing time until he figured out what he was going to do next. He knew he couldn't go back to the spot he had used last night. He now even wondered if he wanted to go to the Hemlock Lodge for their lunch buffet.

When he had the ice in the cooler he decided to hit the buffet anyway. It would be busy with the lunch crowd and that couldn't hurt. If someone was still following him then it would give him a chance to look over the crowd. If that was the plan for the moment then he had a good two hours to kill. As he drove under the Mountain Parkway overpass he decided to ride the chairlift that took the less able-bodied visitors up to the Natural Bridge. There was a well-kept trail that the more fit park goers used but he didn't want to be that isolated at the moment. He drove around to the parking lot where the chairlift began and took a seat beside the ticket office. It wouldn't open for fifteen more minutes, perfect. Sam would use the time to look over the other traffic.

At ten-thirty sharp the ticket counter opened and Sam bought a twelve dollar ticket for one. As he headed for the loading area he took one last glance toward the parking lot. The Avis was back. Sam hurried and fell into a seat as it came by and then lowered the bar that would keep him from falling out. Occasionally he turned to look back. There were two men getting out of the Avis and they immediately headed for the ticket office. Now Sam was worried, the last place he wanted to be was on top of the Natural Bridge where anyone could stumble and knock him off. The fall would be fatal. He had to come up with some sort of plan.

There was one place on the way up where the drop wouldn't have been more than ten feet to the ground. If he jumped then he could be back to the Bronco in less than fifteen minutes. As he approached the spot he decided that it would be unwise. He could twist his ankle or break a bone if he didn't hit the ground just right. If he did make it to the ground without hurting himself then he would probably get arrested by the Rangers once he made it back to the parking lot. No, the risks were just too great. As he neared the top he decided on a plan B. It was mandatory that everyone exit the lift at the top, he never really understood that. He would exit the lift and then immediately catch the next one back down. Surely there wasn't a rule against that.

At the top Sam exited at the spot he was supposed to and then walked around to the other side to catch the next chair back down. Funny as it was Sam actually got back into the same chair he had just exited. As he topped the shear rock face and started down he saw the two men from the Avis car coming up the slope. They had been maybe ten chairs behind him. Sam decided to keep his eyes focused on the two to see if he had ever seen them before and also to let them know he was aware. As the two cars got closer the two Avis men didn't return Sam's stare. They alternated looking at the top of the ridge and to the side away from Sam.

After the two cars passed Sam waited until he felt the time was right and then abruptly turned in his seat. Both men were looking back at him as well, busted. As soon as Sam got to the bottom he ran to the Bronco and decided to head on up to the Lodge for lunch. He needed time to think and sort out his options. He never waited to see if the two men followed. He would be well out of sight by the time they made it to their car.

The Donor

The lodge looked to be doing a good business. Sam parked and then strolled inside. The dining room was half full and the patrons were attacking the buffet. Sam was led to a table at the far end where he ordered sweet tea along with the buffet. He quickly grabbed a plate and got in line. He wanted to have his food before the two men came inside, if they did come inside. As Sam sat down he kept his eye on the door. Thirty minutes later he decided they weren't following, at least into the restaurant.

Sam ate slowly as he kept an eye on the door, just in case. After forty minutes the waitress brought the check and Sam reached her a credit card.

The two Avis men had called in that morning when they saw Sam break camp and leave. They were told to follow but to not be noticed. At this they had failed miserably. The prey they sought was on high alert and in such a rural setting it was nearly impossible to keep him in view without being noticed themselves and that is exactly what happened. When they decided to ride the sky lift they didn't realize Sam had identified them. After making it back to their car they radioed New Circle. They were told to head on back to Lexington and turn in the car.

Sam had managed to burn through two teams of surveillance in a little over twelve hours, although he didn't know this. He hoped it was just his wild imagination, surely everything could be explained. He laughed to himself as he thought about this. After he signed the credit card slip he laid a five dollar bill down for the tip and then left the dining room. Outside the sun was high but had little power this time of year. Sam decided to cut his trip short and head on back home, he had had his fill of this 007 crap. Little did he know that while he was in the dining room of the Hemlock Lodge enjoying roast beef and catfish he was still being observed by two other teams. One was seated two tables to his right, a man and woman who looked like husband and wife. They were not. Three tables farther away on the left was another couple, again posing as man and wife.

As Sam first entered the lobby of the Hemlock he was photographed. As he was leaving he was again photographed. These new pictures would be added to the ever growing file at Alterations. Pictures were nice but what PT had demanded was a blood sample within two weeks. All the surveillance over the last few weeks was to try and determine if anything Sam did in his spare time or at work could help explain who he was and what made him so special. PT got a report every six hours and had come to respect the way Samuel Edgemont could spot a tail and then promptly lose it. The people PT had in the field were either ex-military or ex-FBI. They were good but seemed to be unable to keep from being spotted by a college professor that had absolutely no training in how to spot or avoid his pursuers.

PT decided to have his people pull back. It they continued to spook Mr. Edgemont then they might provoke him into doing something stupid. As it was maybe Edgemont would calm down a bit if he didn't see any more people behind him. In a few days he might just think it was all part of his imagination and return to his everyday routine.

Sam had looked for a tracking device under his Bronco while he was at his campsite. This had been observed by the two Avis men using Binoculars. PT decided that since Sam had looked and found nothing that now was the time to install the device. It had been pure luck that the Avis men had picked the spot where they spent the night, only a few hundred feet from where Sam had stayed. Luck was something that PT never counted on, especially twice. It was decided that while Sam was inside the lodge eating that a third team would slip into his Bronco and install the devices. As Sam was being monitored while he had his lunch, the Bronco was broken into and a listening device was installed under the dash. A powerful tracking device was also mounted underneath on the frame. Both had a range of four-hundred yards and could be monitored from another vehicle whether it was in front or behind. The tracking device could also be monitored by satellite. As of now anything Sam said or anywhere he went in the Bronco could, and would, be recorded.

Sam was back in Prestonsburg by 4:30 that evening. As he parked he looked around the neighborhood, nothing seemed any different than it had when he had left the previous evening. He recognized every car parked on the street and knew who it belonged to. He recognized the few people walking on the sidewalks and the children riding skateboards. Everything seemed perfectly fine until he got inside his house. The phone was ringing as he walked in the door and he quickly answered it. It was the lady who had called the previous Wednesday about the dark blue sedan parked on the street, Mrs. Potter.

"Hello Sam, I saw you pull in." Sam was beginning to think Mrs. Potter was a snoop without anything better to do than spy on her neighbors.

"Hi Mrs. Potter. I just got back from camping last night down at the Red River George."

"Did you know some power men were working at your house last night?" She asked.

Sam looked around as she said this, "Well no Mrs. Potter. When I left everything was working fine. Was the power out on the street?"

"No Sam, everyone's power was on including yours. I could see the men through your blinds working. That light you always leave on in your living room was just bright enough so that I could see."

"You mean the power men were inside my house Mrs. Potter?"

"Well yes, I thought you knew?"

It was evident I didn't know or Mrs. Potter wouldn't have called. "No I didn't, I better get off here and see what's going on Mrs. Potter. Thanks for calling." Sam quickly hung up knowing she probably wanted to pry some more.

Sam slowly looked around his house. He was a neat man who left everything the same way every day. He had always been this way; it seemed to make the place look cleaner. Nothing looked out of place. Everything was just the way it had been the day before. Sam went to the back door and checked the lock; it didn't look as if it had been tampered with.

The men and women who worked at New Circle heard everything that was said between Samuel Edgemont and Mrs. Potter. They watched as Sam inspected his house. Stu had a plan in place for just such an event. A lady who worked from a script dialed Sam's number.

When the phone rang, a few minutes after Sam hung up with Mrs. Potter, Sam thought sure it was her calling back. He couldn't just not answer the damn thing, she knew he was there.

"Hello." Sam said reluctantly.

"Is this Samuel Edgemont?" A pleasant sounding woman asked.

"Yes it is."

"Glad to finally reach you Mr. Edgemont. I am with the power company that services your house. We had a hot wire warning on your meter and sent a crew out yesterday evening. We tried to reach you by phone but got no answer. Our Technicians arrived at your house and checked everything outside and found nothing wrong." This part of the explanation was hoped to be enough.

"Is that when you broke into my house?" Sam demanded.

"Sorry Mr. Edgemont but when the Technicians couldn't find anything wrong on the outside they were forced to do an inside inspection."

"How the hell did they get in, both my doors were locked." Sam demanded.

"They used the key you leave on your back porch under the second flowerpot from the door."

It was true; Sam kept a spare key under the flower pot. "How did you know my spare key was there and who gave you permission to enter my house."

"You did Mr. Edgemont." The lady said calmly.

"The hell I did." Was all Sam could think to say.

"Yes Mr. Edgemont. When you signed the agreement five years ago with the power company you signed what we call an Emergency Entrance Form. It states that in the event we detect anything of danger we have your permission to enter your house." She read this directly from the script. It was all a lie.

Sam calmed considerably, he barely remembered that day five years ago when he went into the power company offices and paid a deposit and signed the contracts. "That was five years ago. I don't remember all the papers I signed that day. How did you know I kept a key under that flower pot?"

This part wasn't on the script and suddenly Stu, who had been listening the entire time, held his breath. "You wrote it on page two. You said you lived alone and always kept a spare keep on the back porch and we were allowed to use that key in the event of an emergency." This woman is good, Stu thought.

Sam was convinced except the woman hadn't told him if they found the problem. "After you were inside did you find a problem?"

"Yes, it says here that you had a twenty amp single pole breaker that was overheating due to age, our technicians replaced the breaker and left. It also says there would have been a high probability of a fire within the next twelve hours if our men hadn't entered and fixed the problem."

Sam was satisfied. "Is there a fee for something like this?"

Again the woman read from the script. If it would have been free then they were afraid it would sound too good. "Yes there is, let me check." It had been discovered that a small fee would delight the homeowner rather than cause suspicion. "The bill for the breaker and the service is forty-one dollars." It was hoped this would seem reasonable, after all it did require a truck and two men. "It should show up on your bill within ninety days. Without the service there might have been a fire." The woman said again.

"Well, I guess that sounds fine, anything is better than a fire. Sorry if I was short with you earlier, I have had a really strange week." Sam said and they both hung up.

"Damn right you've had a strange week." Stu thought as he also hung up.

Sam went to his breaker box and opened the front cover. Sure enough there was a brand new breaker whereas all the others looked at least twenty years old. He was satisfied.

It was evident that Sam was no electrician. There is no way the power company can tell if a single breaker in a single house in a service area of thousands of houses could be detected as an overheating danger. There isn't equipment like that installed in residential dwellings. The people at Alterations let out a group sigh of relief. It was also decided to start a file on one Mrs. Potter, aka busybody across the street.

Sam spent the next thirty minutes unloading the Bronco. As he did he thought about the men from the power company and the explanation the lady on the phone had given him. At first it fit in with everything else that had been going on. Now though, he could explain away everything as just an overworked imagination, that is everything except the two men in the dark blue Ford Sedan. He figured that could probably be explained away too if he had all the facts. He made up his mind to dismiss everything as just coincidence. Until something else happened that couldn't be explained away he was just going to enjoy his evening. Plus tomorrow was Sunday.

Sam had a good night's sleep that Saturday night, he could tell the previous night spent in the Bronco had been less comfortably than he had first thought. After church this morning he was going to the grocery and buy himself two of the biggest steaks he could find and that would be his lunch and dinner. Sam wasn't a very good cook but he prided himself on his skill with a barbecue grill. He was convinced he could grill a rock, add some seasoning and make it taste good, if he could only make it tender enough. He laughed at such a silly thought.

The weekend for Sam went by much too fast. He had stayed up late Saturday night, he liked the talk shows. He arose early Sunday morning and had his lawn looking fine by the time he needed to get ready for church. He made it to Sunday School and took his seat. At 10:45 the class broke up and everyone began filling the sanctuary. Sam took his favorite spot in the back on the left. As he sat looking at the building he noticed Mrs. Potter walking in. She knew where Sam sat every Sunday. It seemed that churchgoers are creatures of habit too. Most people sat in the same general spot each week and Sam was no different. When he noticed Mrs. Potter heading his way he hoped she was only going to say hello. She usually sat on the other side of the building with some of her friends.

As she got closer Sam could feel the room getting smaller. "Hello Sam. I saw you sitting here and decided to join you." She said as she plopped down almost in Sam's lap.

"Good morning Mrs. Potter, it is good to see you this morning." He lied and then immediately felt guilty; after all he was sitting in a church.

"We have a few minutes before services start and I wanted to talk to you about a few things." She said.

Oh no, here it comes. "Certainly Mrs. Potter, what would you like to talk about?"

"Well I don't want you to think I'm meddling." She started.

Meddling is exactly what you're doing was what Sam thought.

"I've noticed there isn't a Mrs. Edgemont around. I never see anyone at your house other than you and you always come to church alone."

Meddling just went up a degree Sam thought.

"Anyway I have a grandniece that lives in Ohio and she is coming in this week to visit with the family. She is such a wonderful girl and doesn't know any nice men like you. And she is a pretty girl too Sam, especially on the inside."

Great Sam thought, turn her inside out and I'll meet her. Again he felt guilty.

"If she lives in Ohio how do you know she doesn't know any nice men up there?" Sam asked.

Mrs. Potter smiled and then continued, "She told me so. I call her at least once a week to check up on things."

I bet you do Sam thought.

"Anyway she will be here in a couple of days and I thought you might like to meet her?"

Sam didn't know whether to be flattered or shocked, actually he felt a little of both. The conversation that he was now a part of was becoming sticky really fast. Sticky in the fact that now he needed to answer her request without much information to go on. The main information he needed could be summed up in three words, personality, baggage and last but certainly not least, looks.

"Well Mrs. Potter, I am flattered you would ask but it would be assuming too much to think that a woman who has never met or talked to me would be interested." What he really meant by this was he wasn't interested in meeting a woman he had never met or talked to before. Another very important fact would be age, this woman that he was being forced to meet could be anywhere from eighteen to eighty.

"Oh I've already told her all about you." Mrs. Potter said with a sly smile.

Now Sam really felt at a disadvantage. "Oh, I have to admit, I really don't want to intrude on the time your niece has to visit with family." Sam couldn't think of anything else to say at the moment.

"Oh it won't be an intrusion at all Mr. Edgemont. Part of the reason she is coming in is to meet you. I should have spoken to you about this sooner but with all the strange things going on in our neighborhood lately it has just slipped my mind. Now you think it over during the morning service and I will speak to you as we leave." Mrs. Potter looked at her watch and then put a hand to her mouth. "My goodness, services are about to begin. I better get over to my seat or those other busybodies will think I'm staying over here with you. That's just the way rumors get started you know."

Before Sam could say anything Mrs. Potter was up and heading to the back isle. Sam leaned back against the pew. He couldn't help but exhale, glad the conversation was momentarily over but troubled that it had taken place. When the sermon was over he could safely say he hadn't heard a word the preacher had said. Sam spent the entire time wondering how he had gotten involved in one of Mrs. Potter's schemes. It was well known in the church crowd that the little group of women Mrs. Potter associated with were busybodies. Sam never held an opinion about this one way or the other, at least until now.

As church ended and everyone headed for the exit, Sam decided to get it over with, he would tell Mrs. Potter he wasn't interested, he was just too busy at the moment. This all went according to plan until he was stopped outside by not only Mrs. Potter, but the entire group of women she sat with in church.

"Well Sam, I expect you at my house Tuesday evening around seven. I'm cooking dinner and you are invited. You know my friends here; well they are going to be there too. The four of us are going to fix you the nicest supper you've ever had. My niece will be so anxious to meet you." Before Sam could respond the four ladies patted him on the shoulder in turn and then walked away.

Sam could only stand and watch. Outsmarted by four old ladies from church! He headed for his Bronco, at least he was promised a good meal.

Jillian Ward lived in Columbus Ohio. She had lived there her entire life which wasn't really true; she hadn't lived her entire life yet. Jillian was twenty-nine years old and starting to think she would end up like one of the other women she worked with, alone and dedicated to a job she disliked. Jillian was an attorney. She worked the obligatory sixty hours a week but that was only when she wasn't working eighty hours week.

Jillian's specialty was insurance law. Not the kind where someone has a car wreck and their insurance company gets sued. The small firm she worked for handled corporate insurance, a sub-profession of law which had become increasingly important to big companies trying to limit their exposure to law suits from another sector of the legal profession, lawyers who trolled for clients who had either been legitimately injured by a company's products or in most cases, not injured at all but looking for millions in compensation from cash heavy companies that were unable to defend themselves against slick firms who could convince a jury that a hangnail was life threatening.

Fake claims were expensive for corporations who increasingly had to insure against them. As much as the insurance community railed against the explosion in fake and false claims it was really a boon for them. The more they screamed about the unscrupulous lawyers who would sue for anything, the more they saw their revenue go up. Companies needed to be protected from civil suits with possible judgements in the tens of millions of dollars. That was where Jillian, and the attorneys she worked with, came into the picture.

Jillian spent her days analyzing the insurance coverage of companies who had a lot to lose. The job was actually two fold, make sure the insurance was adequate but not excessive and also go over the coverage to find gaps that could be expensive if exploited. Her days started at seven-thirty and normally didn't end until six-thirty or seven that evening. Throw in a few Saturdays and the hours piled up and the years slipped by.

The firm she worked for was called 'Farnsworth and Troutt.' When Jillian first heard the name, and then actually saw it on the building, she wondered how anyone could end up with the last name of Troutt and how in Hell could it have an extra t at the end. Name a six letter word or name that has T in the spelling three times and you would be hard-pressed to find an answer.

Jillian had worked at Farnsworth and Troutt for nearly three years and found the work boring and tedious. The pay was great but what good is money if you don't have the time to spend it? She drove a nice car and lived in an expensive gated community. She lived by herself. She had a cat throughout college but he was old and passed away a year earlier. It was truly a sad day when she came home late and found Brutus lying beside his water dish. She first thought he was taking a little nap, something a fifteen year old cat will do throughout the day, but he wasn't napping. She had gotten Brutus when she was thirteen. When she went off to college he went too. Every exam she stayed up to study for was always accompanied by Brutus; it was as if he helped her study even if all he did was sleep. He napped on the corner of her desk while she studied and the corner of her bed while she slept.

The morning after she came home and found Brutus by his water dish she skipped work, one of the few times she had ever done that. She took her beloved cat to a business in town that specialized in pet grooming and sitting. One of the lesser known services they offered was burial. The business had its own cemetery where every known species of pet was buried. There were potbellied pigs and hamsters, snakes and iguanas. But mostly there were dogs and cats. The cemetery was segregated believe it or not, segregated at least for the dogs and cats. Some owners just couldn't stand the thought of their beloved cat buried beside their arch nemesis, a dog. For that reason there was a section for cats and another section for dogs.

Jillian was told to come back later that day and the burial would take place. She had to admit, it helped knowing her friend was going to be buried with dignity. There would later be a small headstone installed with his name on the front. Jillian visited the grave at least once each month. She took comfort knowing she and Brutus had fifteen good years together and when he went he didn't suffer. Other than her mother and father, Brutus had been her friend longer than anyone else.

The Donor

As crazy as it might sound there is actually a feeling of loss associated with a pet that is nearly as strong as that of losing a family member or close friend. Studies have been done which suggest that the time of mourning and depth of feeling can be exactly the same. Jillian knew it was true. Her condo was silent and lonesome now. Before Brutus had died she could always expect him to be at the door waiting as she turned the key to let herself in, without fail he was glad to see her.

Now when she turned the key and pushed the door open all she found was an empty home. She left his water dish and food tray just as they were when he was there. The cat toys she bought for him still lay in the corners of the living room. She knew they would always be within sight; it seemed to make her smile.

Now Jillian was dreading her visit to Eastern Kentucky. She had an aunt that lived there; it was actually a great aunt on her father's side of the family. Jillian visited her at least once a year, usually in the summer when the mountains were green. She visited once several years back in winter when the leaves were down. The scars on the mountains that were hidden in summer were there for everyone to see, scars of mining.

Eastern Kentucky had for years been home to every type of mining known to man. Once the easy coal was gone the coal companies just bought bigger equipment and started taking the tops off the mountains. It furnished badly needed jobs and no one really complained. Most of the mountaintop removal resulted in flat land that could be used for housing, or in some cases, industry. Now though, the mining was over, regulation and overproduction had eliminated the possibility of getting at the more difficult coal. Jobs were few and most of the residents that still wanted to work were leaving the area to find jobs elsewhere.

One of the strangest sights now were the multi-million dollar schools that were being built everywhere for a school age population that was shrinking. It wasn't uncommon to see a forty or fifty million dollar high school completed that was built with the intention of housing six hundred and fifty students when there were only four hundred available to attend, a number which declined three or four percent each year. Most of this could be attributed to the new school superintendents that were replacing the ones who either retired or were ran out of town for any number of reasons.

The first thing a new school administrator wanted to do was slip in a few hidden tax increases and then begin building. One administrator in particular couldn't wait to start working on his legacy after he wiggled his way into the top job. He acquired a piece of land for ten times the price the original owner had purchased it for and then started looking for an architect. Before long the bulldozers were moving dirt and the concrete trucks started hauling concrete. Funny thing, that superintendent never lasted long enough to see his new school completed. When that man combined his massive ego with a little infidelity he soon found the need to start his car and find himself another school district to hide in. Apparently his ego was more important than his family because he left them behind. Chances are he'll do it again; people like that never seem to learn.

Jillian left Columbus on a Sunday after church. It was the latter half of October, the sky was clear and the sun shone bright. It was a good day to travel, traffic was heavy in spots but overall not that bad. As she drove she thought about her aunt. She had visited with her in June and stayed for two days. Now she found herself going back and wondering if the fall foliage still covered the scarred mountains. Her aunt had been insisting for weeks that Jillian take time off from work and drive south. Jillian was suspicious and had to nearly demand to be told the reason for this extra trip. When she found out it was to meet a man that lived on the same street as her aunt she at first declined.

That was three weeks ago. After assurances that she wouldn't be disappointed Jillian had reluctantly given in. As she drove south she kept asking herself what on earth was she doing. A single woman doesn't drive over two hundred miles to meet a total stranger. Jillian was also leery of the type of person who lived in Eastern Kentucky. She was from Columbus and the rule of thumb was the farther south you traveled the lower the men's knuckles came to dragging the ground. Jillian wasn't uppity as her aunt was beginning to think. She liked to think of herself as a moderate who could tolerate nearly anything or anyone, but a man from Eastern Kentucky might be stretching it a bit?

Her Aunt Bertha had promised that three of her friends would be at the dinner she was planning for Tuesday evening as chaperones. "Chaperones, really Aunt Bertha," was Jillian's response. Her aunt had replied that her three friends had done some serious investigating of the man she was going to meet. "He is such a nice man, I see him in church almost every Sunday." She had said. Jillian could find hundreds of names of murderers on the internet that went to church every Sunday, if she were so inclined to look.

It would have been easy to go online and search out this person to see what he had accomplished in his life and what he was doing now. The only problem was that her aunt didn't know his last name, or at least that was what she had said. Jillian found it hard to believe her Aunt Bertha and those three bloodhounds she called friends didn't know this man's last name, but that was what they claimed.

Jillian was in a small town called Louisa by four that afternoon. There was an Arby's beside US 23 she liked to stop at, it was extremely clean and the food was healthy, which was a must for her. She loved to get the mid-sized roast beef sandwich and a baked potato, plain. She never ate the bread on her sandwich, only the beef. As she picked at her potato and nibbled on her roast beef she watched the traffic outside. She remembered the coal trucks that in years past traveled the road, even on Sundays. It seemed hundreds of the noisy beasts used the road and roared along at least twenty miles faster than the posted speed limit. Now there were none, natural gas had taken over where coal had once ruled as King.

Her aunt's house was about an hour away in the town of Prestonsburg. Jillian felt guilty by killing time at the restaurant. She wanted to arrive no earlier than six-o'clock. She knew her aunt loved to watch the local news at six and the national news at six-thirty, Jillian liked the news too but seemed to never arrive home in time to watch it. She checked her e-mails on her phone and was ready to leave when she was interrupted, "Excuse me miss, don't I know you from somewhere."

Jillian looked up to see a man in his twenties who apparently worked as a mechanic during the week, his hands were clean but the fingernails were imbedded with what looked like grease. She didn't know why but that was the first thing she noticed, probably because he was holding his tray of food and his hands were right there in front of him. Then she had a funny thought, if he wasn't a mechanic then maybe he was the Superintendent of Schools. It was all she could do to suppress a laugh.

"I don't think so; I'm not from around here," she said.

This must have been taken by the Superintendent as the beginning of a conversation because without asking he sat down across from her. "I could swear I've seen you before, where you from?" He asked as he took a fry from his tray and put it in his mouth.

Jillian stood and picked up her tray, it was the first time anyone at an Arby's had ever been this forward, a bar maybe but this was almost funny. "As I said I'm not from here," she told him as she turned to leave.

The can to dump her trash in was nearby so she deposited the empty wrappers, as she was placing the empty tray on top the man asked, "Well how about a phone number, you might like Louisa more than you think?"

Jillian didn't dignify such a remark with an answer. She smiled and went to her car. As she drove toward Prestonsburg she pictured a man showing up at her aunt's house Tuesday evening and it being the same man from Arby's. That little thought was enough to set her off laughing all alone in her car as she drove toward Prestonsburg for a meeting with a man she had never seen before. How had she let her aunt talk her into this?

Tuesday arrived way too soon. Sam dreaded that day; actually the day was fine, he really only dreaded the evening. Seven o'clock seemed to race at him; if he could he would have stepped aside and let it go right on by. At ten minutes before seven he walked out his front door and headed for the street. His steps fell heavy and forced. When he stepped up to the front door of Mrs. Potter's house he could hear women inside talking and laughing, it sounded like a party. With as much dread as he could ever remember in his life he reached up and pushed the doorbell.

The talk and laughter on the other side of the door immediately stopped. When the front door opened it wasn't Mrs. Potter who opened it. There before Sam stood an attractive woman who might have been in her late twenties. "Hello, you must be Sam?" The woman said. Her voice was pleasant Sam thought. He wondered if this was the woman Mrs. Potter wanted him to meet.

"Yes, I'm Samuel Edgemont from across the street." Sam stopped there, not knowing if he should ask who she was.

The woman stepped back from the door and invited him in. "My aunt is in the kitchen, she along with her friends are hiding from you, they insisted I answer the door." Sam found this refreshing; she spoke what was on her mind.

"Now Jillian, you didn't have to tell him that," a voice said from another room. It was Mrs. Potter coming from the kitchen and she was followed by her three smiling friends. To Sam they reminded him of executioners and he was the one to be executed.

"Sam, I would like you to meet my lovely niece, Jillian Ward," Mrs. Potter said.

Jillian smiled and stuck out a hand. Sam took it and they both shook timidly. Sam noticed her hands were strong but smooth.

"Why don't you two come into the dining room, dinner is almost ready." One of the other ladies said, Sam thought her name was Mabel.

All the women turned and went through a side door into a large dining room. Sam noticed a large number of books in the house. They seemed to be everywhere, in bookcases or just stacked neatly on side tables. It wasn't cluttered at all but seemed to be just right. Sam had always had a great respect for books. He read a lot and owned hundreds himself.

Mabel pointed to a chair at the end of the table and told Sam to have a seat. Sam done as he was told and realized he was placed there so he would be visible to the other ladies once they were all seated. He felt he was on display and being inspected. Mabel took Jillian by the arm and led her to a chair that was to Sam's right. "Now Mabel I wanted to help bring in the food," Jillian told her aunt.

"Nonsense dear, you sit right here and get to know Sam, why if I was thirty years younger I might have tried to get to know him myself." Both Jillian and Sam sat with their mouths gaped open at what had just been said. The four women all went back to the kitchen, giggling as they went.

Sam could tell Jillian was embarrassed, he knew he certainly was. She looked as her aunt and the other three women disappeared into the kitchen. Once they were out of earshot she looked back at Sam and said, "I want to apologize for my aunt, she sometimes doesn't realize how she comes across. When she is with her friends I find her unbearable sometimes."

As Jillian spoke Sam watched her mannerisms. She was very polite and proper. He could tell she wasn't like some of the women he knew around town. He really couldn't tell her what he thought of her aunt so he asked the only question that he could think of. "So you live in Ohio?"

"Yes, actually I was born there. My grandmother, who is Aunt Bertha's sister, moved there a long time ago. I was born in Columbus," She said.

"I could tell you hadn't been raised around here when you greeted me at the door. The accent had a definite Ohio sound to it." Sam hoped what he had just said wasn't rude or improper.

"You don't sound like you are from Prestonsburg either Sam. I mean, it sounds like you might have been here for a while but not always."

"You're right, I moved here about five years ago. I am actually from Virginia, over near Charlottesville," Sam told her.

"Thomas Jefferson's home town," Jillian said with a smile.

This woman seemed to have a sharp mind and conversation with her flowed without any awkward pauses. "Yes, have you been there?"

"No, I do read a lot of histories, always have. I intend to visit Monticello someday. I want to be able to put images to some of the things I have read about his home place."

"It is beautiful there. Some people who visit complain about the house being so small but who are we to judge. Jefferson built it the way he wanted and he was the only one he had to please. If he could ever have seen it finished, as it is now, I wonder what his opinion would be," Sam said.

"I'm sure he would be flattered at the number of visitors that go there every year. But you know, he had quite a few visitors while he lived there. Part of his financial problems was due to the number of visitors he was forced to feed and entertain," Jillian said.

Sam was truly impressed. This woman seemed to be well versed on Jefferson and his home. He wondered if her knowledge extended toward other aspects of history. "I find you are very knowledgeable about our third president. Has history always been a passion of yours?"

Jillian smiled. "Actually, I had to take several political science courses in college. I enjoyed only fiction before that, still do, but now I also include history and biography to my reading list."

Jillian had just told a great deal about herself, Sam knew what kind of professions required political science courses and pretty much knew the answer to his question. "So what did your studies lead you into if I'm not being to forward?" Sam already knew the answer and wasn't sure how he felt about it.

Jillian smiled, "I'm an attorney!" She waited for a response.

Sam could only smile as he thought of a response. Luckily he didn't need to reply as they were interrupted by the four women noisily coming from the kitchen, each carrying plates, napkins, and utensils. They quickly sat six place settings. As they went back into the kitchen Mrs. Potter bumped Jillian with her rump and said, "Jillian, I hope you aren't talking shop at the dinner table."

It was evident to Sam that the women were in the kitchen eavesdropping. When Jillian mentioned she was an attorney they came into the room to interrupt the conversation. Sam didn't mind that she was an attorney; he had a surprise of his own if Jillian asked.

After the women left Jillian said, "I think they are listening to our conversation." She said this with a huge smile.

"That would be my guess. You're aunt seems very protective of you."

"Oh, she is. When I was in college she would call almost every night. I told her if she didn't stop I was going to start failing classes for lack of study. After that she only called once a week."

"How long have you been practicing law?" Sam asked.

"Almost three years. I got hired by a small firm in Columbus. There are four partners and seven associates not to mention the paralegals," Jillian added.

"What type of law does your firm specialize in?"

Now Jillian was impressed. Most people she talked to about her profession just assumed that a lawyer was just a lawyer. Most people wouldn't realize that there are as many branches to the legal profession as there are leaves on a tree. "My specialty is insurance law. I took it because I really didn't want to deal with law breakers or courtrooms." Sam could tell that she wasn't happy with her specialty, it was just the way she had said it.

"Insurance law, do you enjoy it?" Sam asked.

"I thought I did, at first, but now two years later I wonder if I made a mistake. The work is about as stimulating as watching paint dry. The pay is good but the hours and the tedium are starting to take a toll on my sanity." She smiled when she said 'sanity.'

"I can see how that might be difficult day after day but I'm sure there are people who enjoy that kind of work."

"Oh there are a few but I don't think I will ever be one of them." Jillian wondered if she was starting to bore Sam by talking about her job. One reason she never went out was the fact that once men found out she was an attorney they couldn't adjust to a woman who had climbed higher on the ladder of life than they had. The few times she had started to like someone they would break it off once they found they couldn't deal with the fact that they ran a small lawn service or held some other small time job while she worked at a law firm. The ego of a man is a fragile thing and can be crushed easily. Jillian liked the way Sam talked and his mannerisms were pleasant and humble. She didn't want to ask what he did for a living, she would be fine with it but knew he probably already felt mismatched sitting here having a conversation with her.

Sam did enjoy conversation with this stranger he had just met. She was smart and seemed confident. He wondered how she would feel once she found out what he did for a living. The job he had furnished him with excellent benefits but the income was well below that of any attorney. He supposed it really didn't matter anyway, they were only seeing each other for dinner at her aunt's house and then their paths would most likely never cross again.

Just then the four women came back into the room in a rush. They must have heard the lull in the conversation and decided this was the time to announce that dinner was ready.

"Why don't you bring your plates and fill them in the kitchen. Then we can all eat in here and chat a bit," Mrs. Potter said. The other three women stood on either side of her like lieutenants of some army.

Jillian smiled at Sam as she stood and took up her plate. "Well Sam, we have our orders." As she walked by her aunt she winked at her. Bertha winked back and took this to mean that she approved of Sam. Actually Jillian found Sam to be very polite and well mannered. He handled conversation well and she really liked his voice.

Sam picked up his plate and started for the kitchen. Bertha stopped him and whispered like a school girl, "So what do you think?" It's funny how older people think no one can hear what they whisper when in fact everyone can.

Jillian heard and said, "Aunt Bertha, don't embarrass him please, and surely don't embarrass your only great niece either." Sam felt Jillian had rescued him from an awkward situation.

Jillian was smiling as Sam entered the kitchen. "You'll have to pardon my aunt; she is such a great cook but asks too many questions."

The other three women came in laughing at Bertha. Mabel looked at her and said with a laugh," You got busted Bertha." Bertha frowned as the other two women burst out laughing.

Sam looked at the counter; it was filled with different types of food in fancy looking covered dishes with the lids off at the moment. It looked more like Thanksgiving than just an evening meal; there were any number of vegetables and casseroles. The main course was a baked ham with pineapple on top; it looked like it had been cut out of a Better Homes and Gardens magazine. Sam waited until the other women had begun filling their plates before he would fill his. Mabel saw this and reached for his plate. She didn't say anything; she just began putting an assortment of nearly everything on the plate. Sam didn't care, everything looked so good. He was starting to relax, he found he liked the four women and had probably judged them wrong. He still hadn't formed an opinion of Jillian, why should he, he would never see her again.

Jillian saw what Mabel was doing and said, "No one offered to fill my plate." She was only joking.

Mabel looked at her and said, "You are capable of deciding what you want, most men go brain dead in a kitchen and I just thought I would lend Sam a hand." Sam tried to remember the last time, if ever, someone had used the term 'Brain Dead' in reference to himself.

All the women laughed at this and for some unknown reason Sam did too. This was starting to remind him of Thanksgiving back before his mother died. His family was small but there were always friends and acquaintances that his mom would invite from her work. The Edgemont house was always full during the holidays. For some reason these memories always felt like events that never really happened, but the memory was there just the same.

Mabel didn't reach Sam the plate after she filled it with a taste of nearly everything in the kitchen. When she felt she had everything on the plate positioned just the way she wanted she carried it back to the dining room and placed it at the head of the table. Mabel had been the kind of cook that realized that presentation was just as important as taste. When Sam sat back down he couldn't help but admire, not only the look and aroma of his food, but how neatly it was positioned, everything looked great. He had always been the kind of eater that just threw food on the plate and didn't care in the least how it looked. He thought he got this from watching the series 'Mash' on television. One of his favorite parts was when the cook slopped food on everyone's tray with a big ladle, kind of made Sam want to be an Army cook when he grew up.

Sam realized he was sitting at the table all alone. Jillian was still in the kitchen with her aunt and the three other women. He supposed Jillian was being coached and advised, or maybe even warned. Sam could hear the older women trying to talk in hushed tones. When Jillian finally came out of the kitchen she looked at Sam and rolled her eyes. That was all it took to let Sam know his suspicions were right.

When finally seated back at the dining room table Jillian leaned toward Sam and quietly said, "My aunt and her friends are insufferable." Sam took this as a verification that the four older women were whispering in Jillian's ear. They had undoubtedly kept her in there so they could talk so Sam couldn't hear.

Both Sam and Jillian waited until the others were back at the table before taking up their forks. Sam also wondered if Mrs. Potter said a blessing at mealtime. The four noisily came back to the dining room and took their places. Suddenly with five women in the room and Sam sitting at the head of the table he felt uncomfortable. Mrs. Potter looked at Sam and asked if he would do the blessing. Sam agreed and stumbled through the words miserably. He had asked a blessing at meals before but something about this setting made him nervous. When finished he wanted to hide.

Everyone took up a fork and the meal was officially underway. The older women felt compelled to ask Sam questions about what he liked to do in his spare time and what type of television shows he watched. He felt as if he were at an interview for a new job. Finally one of the women asked the question that Sam knew was coming.

"Well Sam, what is it you do for a living?" Mabel asked.

Sam noticed that all the other women grew quiet, kind of like that old stock trading commercial. Jillian dreaded to hear Sam's answer. In the past she had felt sorry for men that she went out with, not that she felt superior because she was an attorney. It was because she knew how most men felt intimidated by a woman who had achieved so much. Her education had been obtained to heighten her station in life and she suspected most men would take that as a challenge. Albeit, a challenge most could hardly compete with. Sam continued to chew his food not wanting to speak with his mouth full. The five women at the table each had a different opinion about the momentary silence. Jillian felt bad for this man she hardly knew, she suspected the worst. Sam could even be unemployed as far as she knew. Her aunt and the other three women barely knew him themselves.

Finally Sam swallowed and then put the cloth napkin to his lips. He took a sip of his tea and then looked at the woman who had asked about his occupation. "I work at the college in Pikeville."

Sam didn't elaborate further. He picked up his fork and continued with his delicious food.

Mrs. Potter then asked with a small degree of concern, "Do you teach at the college?"

Again after Sam chewed and swallowed he answered, "Yes I've taught there for the last five years, it's the reason I moved to Prestonsburg. I didn't want to live anywhere near Pikeville because of my job so I found a place in Floyd County and here I am."

Mabel asked, "If you teach in Pikeville why would you want to live in Prestonsburg?"

"In one of my graduate classes I had a professor who lived near the university I attended. One day during a lecture he gave each of us a piece of advice which I felt was a true nugget. He said that since most of us in the class would at some point in our careers end up in a teaching position he felt compelled to share a personal thought on where one lives and where one works. He said he had found out in his years at the lectern that the best place for faculty was far away from the classroom, especially around exam time. He found that some of his students, the ones that were less focused about their classes of which he hoped none of us were, would panic at exam time and found it permissible to actually knock on his door for advice. He also told us to keep our phone numbers unlisted. Of course that was before the age of cellphones. Now phones are such a part of everyone's lives that it doesn't matter."

Everyone became focused on their food for a moment, it was apparent to Sam the four women were absorbing what he had told them. He wondered what Jillian was thinking.

Finally Mrs. Potter asked, "What do you teach at the college Sam?"

Sam smiled as he took up his napkin again. "I have two classes in history which are my favorite. One of my Masters is in history."

Jillian looked up from her food, "One of your Masters?"

Sam knew he had everyone's attention although that wasn't what he wanted. "Yes I have a Masters in history and one in Psychology."

Jillian smiled now totally involved in the conversation. The next question shouldn't have been asked but Mabel couldn't resist. "Is that all Sam or do you have any other degrees?"

Sam couldn't lie and wouldn't have anyway. The question was asked and he gladly answered. "Besides the double Masters I have a PHD."

Jillian sat her fork down beside her plate. When she looked at Sam she had a weak smile on her face. "What area is your PHD in if I may ask?"

Sam looked at her and smiled, "Political science. In my two other classes I teach those who aspire to be lawyers."

Jillian couldn't hold back. The fact that she was an attorney and the way Sam had phrased that last remark was too much. She burst out laughing and at the same time she put her hand on Sam's arm as to assure him that she wasn't laughing at him. After she calmed a bit she said, "I've taken lots of classes, including political science, and all those instructors, both male and female, were a bit stuffy. I can't picture you as cut from the same mold, you're too nice."

"Well thanks. Actually some of my students think I'm stuffy, I attribute that to generational adaptation. Kids now are twenty years different than when I was in school."

"What prompted you to get a double Masters instead of going straight after your PHD?" Jillian asked.

"I didn't start out to get any of it really. After college I looked at the current job market and let me tell you it was bad. I stayed in and within eighteen months I completed my first Masters, it was in History. I never really studied; the subject was so interesting that all I wanted to do was read. It wasn't hard, it was wonderful actually. After that, due to my grades I got assistance for another year of studies and decided to pursue the Psychology Degree. There was some overlap of classes I had already completed and this allowed me to finish the second Masters in little more than a year.

"I now had two Masters and I was only twenty four years old. One of my professors, it was the one who warned me about living too close to my work, advised me that with the background I had and the grades I had achieved I could work and at the same time complete my PHD in a little over two years. It was an opportunity I couldn't pass up. I was allowed to get my certification to teach at the university and at the same time pursue my PHD. I stayed there four years, finished my studies and then started looking for a place to land. Pikeville offered me a position five years ago and here I am."

Sam told the story no different than a father would tell a nursery rhyme to his children. Once finished he picked up his fork and continued eating. The four older women at the table ate for a while also. Again Mabel looked at Sam and said, "If only I were thirty years younger." Everyone at the table burst out laughing again.

As Jillian ate she realized that for the first time in her life she was the one who should be worried about what the other person thought. Most men felt Jillian was above their station in life. Now Jillian was the one wondering about her station, not that it mattered. Sam had accomplished a lot though, that was for sure.

Finally the meal was over but not before everyone was forced to sample a mud pie. The name might have sounded disgusting but the taste was anything but. It was simply a chocolate pie with bits of brownie in the filling. It was rich, sweet and delicious. As the women carried the plates to the kitchen Sam wondered when he should leave. Jillian put that thought out to pasture when she asked Sam if he would mind sitting on the front porch while the other women put the food away. He gladly agreed. For a man who had dreaded this evening so bad he found he was truly enjoying himself.

Sam had never counted himself a ladies man, far from it. He felt his looks were average at best although he was told otherwise. He did take care of himself and had the advantage of good genes. His health had always been perfect; he could never remember a sickness in his entire life. Never had a problem with his weight, no graying hair and no receding hairline which might be attributed to the fact that he was only thirty-three years old.

Sam had never chased women as some of his friends in college had done. He had gone out from time to time and really enjoyed the company of the opposite sex. Until five years ago he had been so consumed with his studies that he couldn't pursue romance. For the last five years he had spent his time teaching and even though some of the women on campus would like nothing more than to go out with one of their professors Sam felt that was unethical. It was also against school policy, which suited Sam just fine.

Outside of college the prospects seemed very limited. Sam felt he was a fish swimming in a very small pond. A few of the women he found that did interest him carried so much baggage he ran like a rabbit. A woman with two divorces, two ex-husbands and no job seemed like a nightmare without a way to wake up. Sam settled into his life of teaching, working on his house, and a little camping and hiking. He enjoyed UK sports and it was a good thing he did. To live in Eastern Kentucky and root for any other team could be dangerous; UK fans are rabid supporters of their team. His favorite UK sport was basketball but in the last year he began to attend a few football games at Commonwealth Stadium. That name would be changed shortly to Kroger something or other. Sam liked Commonwealth better but understood the economics of corporate sponsorship.

Jillian stood from the table and led the way to the front porch. She sat in a swing and patted the space beside her, intending for Sam to sit there. He gladly done as suggested, as they sat and talked Sam glanced in the direction of his house. The first thing he noticed was a service truck sitting out front and two men with ladders working on the pole in front of his house. They were working on a black box that looked new; at least it hadn't been there before.

Jillian noticed and asked, "Is that your house those men are working in front of?"

Sam answered without taking his eyes off the truck. "Yes it is."

The kitchen window to Mrs. Potter's house faced that direction; it was how she managed to keep such close tabs on everything. Soon the front door opened and Mrs. Potter came out, she was looking in the direction of Sam's house as she spoke, "That looks like the same truck that was at your house Friday night Sam while you were gone. Are you still having electrical problems?"

"I don't think so Mrs. Potter. Maybe I should go over and find out what's going on," Sam told her.

Sam rose from the swing and before leaving he looked at Jillian, "I've really enjoyed my time this evening. It was a pleasure meeting you."

Jillian could have filed a lawsuit on the spot against the two men in the service truck for ending what had been one of the most enjoyable evenings she had experienced in years. She stood and said she enjoyed it as well. With that Sam headed down the front steps and up the sidewalk toward his house. Jillian went back inside and was immediately set upon by her aunt and her three friends, each firing off questions.

Sam noticed everything about the truck as he walked home. It had Ohio plates and no signage on the doors to indicate who the men worked for. It did have a bucket on the back which he knew was used to lift a man up to work on whatever was needed. The two men were not using the bucket; they were using a short ladder to work on the new box that had been recently installed. As Sam walked up one of the two, the one not on the ladder, took a few steps in Sam's direction. Sam found this a bit odd and not the least bit intimidating. It was as if the man who approached didn't want Sam near his co-worker.

"Howdy, nice day don't you think?"

Sam continued walking. "Yes it is. What seems to be the problem?"

"Oh, no problem here, we were sent out to make some adjustments. We should be gone in a few minutes." The box that had been installed Friday night after Sam had headed for Slade, the same night Sam's house had been broken into, had a bad circuit board. The box had worked fine for two days and then stopped sending signals. As the second man finished up he quickly closed the box and then put the small padlock back on the cover, Sam noticed this.

"Why does that box have a padlock installed?" He asked.

The second man climbed down, he was irritated that the lock had been noticed. The first man said, "We lock all these boxes, the circuit boards have quite a bit of silver solder inside and sometimes people that know this will use a ladder and steal the circuits, they just slide in and out."

"Why doesn't your truck have any writing on the side to indicate if you are telephone, power or cable?" Sam asked.

"We're private contractors. We have contracts with different utilities." The man said. The man who had just climbed down from the ladder quickly threw the ladder in the back of the truck.

"Well, we better be going. Got four more service calls before dark, it's been one busy day." The man didn't wait for Sam to ask any more questions. He quickly got in the truck and started the engine. Sam watched them go.

As he went inside he thought about what he had been told, he supposed it was what it was.

The two men in the truck called in what had just happened. Stu told them to bring the truck back to New Circle and switch it for a regular pickup truck. That would take them out of Eastern Kentucky for about six hours. It didn't really matter; there were three other teams in the vicinity.

Jillian stood and laughed at her aunt and her three friends. Each were asking questions and expecting answers. Before she said anything she went into the kitchen to get some coffee. After she filled her cup and added cream she turned to the four and said, "What were you saying."

Mabel got out the first response, "What did you think of him, was he nice?"

"Yes, he was nice. Now why don't you four get a cup of coffee and quit being such busybodies."

Mabel laughed, "Honey, when you get to be our age you live for being a busybody."

Jillian went back to the front porch and sat down in the swing. She forced herself not to look up the street toward Sam's house. If her aunt or any of the other three saw her looking in that direction they would never let her live it down. She was extremely impressed with Sam, he wasn't pushy or uppity. He was truly down to earth for a man with such an extensive education. And he wasn't the man from the Arby's in Louisa either. Thank God for small favors.

Sam went inside his house through the back door. He threw his keys on the counter and went to his desk that shared a spot in the living room with his couch and TV. He had to admit that he liked Jillian. He also had to admit he didn't get her phone number and she hadn't asked for his. As he started working on a book he had neglected for the last few weeks he wondered if she was glad the evening was over. He never expected to hear from her again. Oh well, nothing ventured nothing gained.

Helen Montgomery finished her supper at six o'clock just as the news was coming on; she had really liked the way the burger was prepared. She had eaten slowly, enjoying each bite, the texture of the food, the taste, the smell. Once finished and thoroughly satisfied she pushed the tray back from her chair and stood to look out the window. She was glad her appetite was strong, not that she had to worry about gaining any weight, she was rail thin.

The burger had been delicious, thick and juicy, sitting on a toasted bun. The tomato was bright red and had a pleasant taste; it must have been trucked in from down south, local tomatoes this time of year had to come from a hothouse and were disappointing at best. The lettuce was also crisp and dark green, it must have arrived on the same truck. She had to admit the kitchen staff at Beaumont General knew how to make a burger. She wondered if breakfast the next morning would be just as delicious. Helen turned back toward the bed and took off her house shoes; she rummaged around in the overnight bag she brought from the nursing home to find the pair of warmer shoes she would need before going out onto the veranda.

As she pulled on a sweater and began to button the front Rachel came back into the room. Again Helen had that uneasy feeling, what was it about Rachel that made her feel this way?

"Well Mrs. Montgomery, how was the burger?"

"It was fine dear. I'm almost ashamed to admit I ate the entire thing, that was such a big burger."

"It looks like you're ready for the terrace. Do you want to walk or shall I get a wheelchair?"

"Oh I think I can make it. I feel so good today," Helen said. She continued to button the sweater, as she did she noticed her arthritis seemed better, actually it felt as if it was gone altogether.

Rachel took Helen down the corridor past the nurse's station. She walked slowly as to not rush her elderly patient although it wasn't necessary. The exit for the terrace was another door down on the left. Helen walked out and was very pleased to see flowers and plants in either pots or hanging baskets. She knew these must be artificial; the weather was past the time when you could leave live flowers outside. Rachel led Helen to a table with an umbrella that had been cranked up. It wasn't sunny and would be dark in less than an hour so the umbrella wasn't needed but Helen liked the way it looked anyway. There were a few nurses on the veranda smoking. Helen wondered why people who were in the profession of healing would do such a bad thing to their own bodies.

Rachel asked if Helen needed anything before she left. Helen indicated she didn't. She said she just wanted to sit and watch as night fell.

Rachel looked at the sky, "That shouldn't be long; I'll come back in a little while to check on you." As Rachel turned to leave she remembered one last thing. "Dr. Slade has already gone home for the evening but he said he'll see you first thing in the morning. All the tests today should be finished by then and he can discuss them with you." With that Rachel was gone.

Helen sat and enjoyed the cool breeze and the cloudy skies. She could remember everything that had happened that day. There was a huge blank space in her memories though; anything prior to today and going back several months just wasn't there. It seemed that for so long she had lived as if in slow motion, seeing and hearing everything but remembering little to nothing. As hard as she tried she could only remember bits and pieces here and there. She knew that several years back she had been told her memory was fading, it really had she realized. But now everything seemed fine, she could remember so much of her past, it was almost as if she could relive it all sitting right here in this chair, all except for those months when she was dreaming away the days and nothing seemed to make sense.

Later, as Samuel Edgemont was working at his desk his phone rang. He answered it and was surprised to hear Jillian on the other end. "I hope I'm not bothering you," She said.

"Not at all, I'm just going over a few papers for tomorrow," he told her.

"I wasn't sure I would see you before I leave day after tomorrow and wanted to give you my Cell number if maybe you wanted to call and talk some time."

Sam was delighted. "I would like that," he said. After each exchanged numbers they talked for nearly an hour. Jillian's aunt, or the other women for that matter, couldn't figure out why two young people would talk that long on the phone when they were only three houses apart. They grew up in a different age, one where telephone conversations were a luxury. Before hanging up both also exchanged E-Mail addresses and then said their goodbyes. Sam put the cordless receiver back in its cradle and stood there smiling. It had truly been an enjoyable afternoon.

The men who earlier had repaired the box, which was known as a 'Trap,' in front of Sam's house had done so just in time. The long conversation between Sam and Jillian had been recorded in its entirety. The recording was digitized and sent to PT who listened to it only thirty minutes after Sam and Jillian hung up. Within two hours a file was started on one Jillian Ward from Columbus Ohio. One of the investigators who worked at the New Circle offices was assigned to dig up everything online concerning her. Information such as school and work history was to be gathered. Also it was decided to gather any dirt that could be found on Ms. Jillian Ward. If it became apparent she needed to keep her distance from the Primary then it would be easier if they knew of anything bad she had ever done in her life. Dirty tricks were just another part of the job.

PT wanted a three page summary within twenty four hours. Within a week the file would contain scores of pages of information. The initial report on anyone associated with Alterations was always a three page summary. After that PT would receive one paragraph summaries each day on everyone that mattered to the operation. Beeler-Jordan was getting nervous. There had been some rumblings that at least one other Pharmaceutical Company had started investigating what was becoming known as the 'Ponce de Leon Effect.'

PT was being pushed for results. In turn he was pushing his people at New Circle. Stu didn't mind a little pressure, as a matter of fact he seemed to thrive on it. He sat at his rack of terminals and monitors fifteen hours a day. PT knew Stu would benefit if some of his daily tasks were placed in the hands of someone else. The operations were becoming so large that things needed to be streamlined. Hells Bells had been in charge of the operations at new Circle since right after the offices were set up but spent most of his time in Chicago at the offices PT worked out of. PT made the decision for Hells Bells to move to Lexington and use a hands on approach. Hells Bells, or HB for short, packed what he needed and was then sent south on one of Beeler-Jordan's corporate jets.

Before leaving PT let it be known that failure wouldn't be an option. He was still trying to verify who the other Pharmaceutical Company was and when he found out he would let Hells Bells know. HB said he would work on finding the identity of the other company from his end. Both men would be in touch several times a day.

When HB landed at Bluegrass Field a leased Range Rover was at his disposal, along with a Condo located in a gated community not more than five minutes from the New Circle Offices. HB liked to work but he also liked to enjoy himself. No way was he going to live like the in-house hermit Stu. Life was just too short.

Within forty eight hours it was determined that Jillian Ward was an attorney with a small firm in Columbus Ohio. She had been there approximately three years and was an associate. Her specialty was insurance law. She had at first leaned toward criminal law in her studies but decided she didn't want to spent life working with the type of people that needed a defense attorney. Apparently she fit in well with the firm; her salary was ninety-two thousand dollars a year of which her student loan debt ate a substantial portion. Other than that she was debt free and still driving the same car she had driven in college.

The fact she had studied criminal law worried PT. If a romance blossomed Sam might get some advice that would interfere with the operations of the Alterations Division. He couldn't just assume that this newcomer to the scene would become a problem but he couldn't just assume she wouldn't either. Information would continue to be gathered, just in case.

The main thing now was acquiring blood samples from the Primary and the three Reanimate designates, John Oden, Van Goodwin, and Helen Montgomery. A plan was in place for the following Wednesday to hi-jack the Blood Center truck at Slade. A team had been monitoring the courier delivery that left the Pikeville Blood Center each day and then made the trip to the main offices in Lexington. On four out of five days it was found that the courier stopped at a filling station in Slade. On these stops he always parked the van near the side of the building and went inside. His average stay was eleven minutes. Most always he came out with a twenty ounce paper cup of coffee and a snack.

The van had electronic locks which also activated a security system. The wireless code transmitted by the Key Fob the driver carried had been acquired by way of a fancy little device Stu had purchased from some of his less than honest friends from back in his college days. When the driver came out of the convenience store two days prior the electronic sniffer had easily picked up the code and then it was a minor task to load that code into another Key Fob.

The team knew it worked because they had parked beside the van the very next night and after the driver went inside they unlocked and then relocked the door without even getting out of their own vehicle. They wouldn't have an actual key for the van but a similar make and model van was rented and the member of the team tasked with actually stealing the van had practiced every day for a week until he could enter and start the engine in slightly more time than it could be started with a key. Unless they switched the van then the plan would work.

The plan was to have the team in place on the day Samuel Edgemont donated platelets. Once the van driver made his usual stop at the Slade station and entered the building one of the team would enter the van and drive away. Even if the theft was noticed it was doubtful if any police could respond quickly in such a rural setting. Once the van was stolen and away from the station it was necessary to get it disguised quickly, the signage on the sides made it like driving a moving billboard. The plan was to take it to a spot which had been selected days before that was remote and hidden. There, a box truck would be waiting with the back doors open and a set of ramps ready to drive the van inside. Once loaded the van would be transported from the area without a trace.

It had first been decided to simply unload the van after it had been stolen but this plan had many disadvantages. The worst one being that if a Blood Center van was stolen and the only thing taken was its packages of blood products then it was feared that federal authorities might get involved. Homeland Security had a branch that dealt with possible biological weapons development and a blood product theft would certainly fall under that umbrella.

In order to make it look like just a car theft it was decided to take the van back to a remote warehouse New Circle rented and remove the contents. The van would then be dropped at a spot with the keys in the ignition and a chop shop would be notified of its location. Three hours after the theft, the van would be in hundreds of pieces never to be seen again.

Now all the team had to do was wait. If the theft of the van was successful then the blood would be sent by a Beeler-Jordan jet to Hartford Connecticut where it would undergo extensive testing in the corporate labs. Jason Freemont and Alex Trivett were running out of time. If a new cash cow wasn't identified soon then their house of cards might come crashing down around their ears. They knew from previous corporate downfalls that shaky financials were easily hidden once profits resumed. If they didn't become profitable soon then investigations would begin and the scheme would come to light. Both Freemont and Trivett knew what they had been doing would net both extensive jail time and fines. This wasn't going to happen. Freemont had worked too many years building Beeler-Jordan into the company it was to now possibly go to prison.

The pressure was mounting on PT. He in turn pushed Hells Bells and Stu to get the job done. The plans to obtain the blood samples for the primary were in place. Now the challenge fell to obtaining the samples for the three Reanimates. The source at Beaumont General had been instrumental in finding the recovering patients but now it seemed her conscience was starting to kick in, she had been reluctant to go further than supplying the files. PT wanted to force her to acquire the blood samples. He had one of his operatives from New Circle to arrange a meeting with her at a restaurant in Lexington. It was decided to send a woman, if a man were involved it might seem intimidating. The woman selected would be more intimidating than any man but Rachel didn't know this.

The meet was set for a Thursday afternoon at a place where the tables weren't bunched together. This was important in order to allow some level of privacy so a conversation could take place. The particular restaurant to be used was selected because it usually had a good crowd and the chatter of a busy restaurant was important, sounds would become muffled and hopefully nothing could be picked up by any of the other patrons.

Rachel first declined to meet with anyone but was later persuaded. She was told that what she had done by giving confidential patient information to a third party for money was a felony. If this came to light she would face the charges alone. She had no idea who was involved, other than herself, and could be looking at a five year prison sentence. She was told that if she would cooperate there would be substantial compensation in the form of cash and once they had everything they needed then they would disappear. Rachel wished they would disappear now. She had already been told the alternative if she didn't cooperate. Rachel agreed to meet, PT knew she would.

Rachel Bevins walked into the restaurant five minutes early. It was called the Roadstead and had made a name for itself by serving some of the finest cuts of beef in the state. The service was excellent and the meals were slow. Rachel didn't want a slow meal; she didn't want to be here at all. As she sat and waited she wondered how she had gotten involved in such a scheme. At first she did it for the excitement and also the money. The files she supplied were of people who were at one time considered terminal and then somehow made a recovery. She knew what she was doing was wrong but felt she really wasn't hurting anyone. The people she gave the files to said they were using them for research and the information would actually help others with similar ailments. She believed them at first but now wondered what they were really up to.

As Rachel pondered where she was and how she had gotten involved a slender woman in her late thirties or early forty's approached the table. "Mrs. Bevins?" She asked as she held out a hand.

Rachel stood and they both shook. "Yes, and you would be?"

They both sat as Rachel waited for an answer, none would come.

"Has anyone come by yet?" The woman asked.

"If you're referring to a waiter or waitress, no they haven't. I didn't get your name," Rachel said.

"My name isn't really important but for the sake of conversation you can call me Cal."

Rachel found this both rude and mysterious. "You must be a UK fan," she said.

"I wasn't before I started working in Lexington but soon found out its almost mandatory," Cal said.

A waitress came by and put two menus on the table and then took the drink orders, Rachel took unsweetened tea and Cal ordered coffee. Rachel wanted to leave but knew that wasn't possible. "What is it you and your friends expect me to do?"

Cal looked up from her menu. "You get right to the point don't you Mrs. Bevins."

"Yes I do and by the way it's Miss not Mrs.," she said.

Cal smiled. "Let's figure out what we're having and then we can talk shop."

Both women scanned the menu and as most women will do they looked at what was good and at the same time tried to estimate calories.

Rachel settled on a Caesar Salad while Cal ordered scallops and steamed veggies. Rachel might have worried about her weight more; she rarely found time to work out. Cal on the other hand had already put in thirty minutes that morning on an elliptical machine and planned to do free weights at a local gym that evening. Cal cross-trained as much as possible and managed mixed martial arts classes four evenings a month, her background was military police and she took her fitness seriously.

There was a silence as the two waited on their food. Finally Cal decided to get started. "What we need is blood samples for three of the files you have supplied us with. Not just a smear but a vial. Our timetable has just been advanced for reasons that I haven't been made aware of." As she spoke the food arrived.

"How do you propose I go about getting samples without raising suspicions? Only one of the patients is still in the hospital, the other two are home."

Cal nibbled on a scallop. "How you get the samples is none of our concern. What is important is that they be acquired within the next four days." What Rachel didn't know was it would allow the three samples to be added to the stolen Blood Center donations by Wednesday of the next week. All four samples would then be sent to the Beeler-Jordan's lab for testing.

Rachel put down her fork. "Four days, I don't know how it can be done."

Hells Bells had anticipated this, although Cal had indicated that she didn't care how the samples were obtained it wasn't the truth. HB and Stu had brainstormed until a suitable plan was formulated and Cal had been briefed on the details.

"The patient in the hospital won't be a problem, you just tell her anything you want as you take the sample. The two that have been discharged are a bit trickier. You will contact both and tell them a follow up sample is required. You drive out Saturday to each address and take the samples. Your patient that is still in the hospital knows you but will assume nothing about the blood sample; hospitals take blood by the gallon. John Oden and Van Goodwin shouldn't mind and why should they? They both think the good folks at Beaumont General are the reason for their miraculous recoveries. You take the samples at their homes and leave; neither should recognize you because you never took care of them during their stays at the hospital. Wear your hair differently and change the way you wear your makeup. If either had ever seen you before at the hospital then the change in appearance should help. You'll also be in street clothes whereas at the hospital you were wearing scrubs."

Rachel liked what she had just heard, it would work. "How do you know I never took care of either of the men while they were hospitalized?"

"We have your work schedule and cross referenced it to the two men. You were only on duty three times during either man's stay and you weren't near the wing where they were," Cal said.

Rachel felt weak, "How do you know my work schedule and where I was stationed on those days in the hospital?"

"We know everything Rachel." This remark was an understatement. The people in Alterations knew who her roommate was in college. They knew she stopped at a Starbucks every morning on her way to work.

Rachel felt the plan would work, she knew it would. "What if the two house visits require identification. I wouldn't want anyone to know I was the one taking unauthorized blood samples?"

Cal reached into her purse and pulled out two fake driver's licenses with different names, Rachel's face was on each. She then produced two Beaumont General I.D. badges, one to match each fake driver's licenses. "Use these; make sure you use a different one at each address. After the two blood samples are acquired then shred the fake license and badges, don't just throw them away, someone might find them." Cal then slid over another set with different names. "Here is a third set just in case you feel one of the first two can't be used."

Rachel looked at all six; they looked like they would pass anywhere. She slid all of them into her pocket and then looked at Cal. "Who do you work for?"

Cal was munching on another scallop. After she swallowed she looked at Rachel and smiled. "You know I can't tell you."

Rachel managed to put her pride and professional ethics aside for the next question. "I only agreed to meet for lunch and discuss this. What will I get if I agree?"

"You'll agree, you have already been told what will happen if you don't. But we don't want you to take the risk without compensation." Cal reached back into her purse and pulled out a thick manila envelope. As she slid it across the table to Rachel she looked around to make sure no one was watching or listening. "Here is ten thousand dollars. There will be twenty-five thousand more once you hand over what it is we are asking for. Put this away before someone notices it." With that Cal cut a scallop in half and picked it up with her fork.

Rachel quickly put the envelope into her purse. It was thick and felt heavy. Without actually counting it she was certain it contained ten thousand dollars. She leaned toward Cal, "Thirty-five for three blood samples?"

"That's right. After that you won't see or hear from us again."

Now Rachel wondered if she had just shot the goose that lays the golden egg. "If further information is needed will I be notified?"

Cal knew the power of greed; most people are born with that character weakness. "Certainly. You come through for us on this assignment and I'm sure there will be others, but only if you want." She only said this to make sure the current assignment was carried out. As far as the threat of Rachel being turned over to the authorities for her misdeeds, that was never going to happen. Alterations couldn't afford to let that little cat out of the bag but Rachel didn't need to know this.

Rachel picked up on the word 'Assignment' and for a moment hoped she was actually helping out an agency of the Federal Government. That thought also soothed her injured conscious. Now though she had to think of the assignment at hand. "Once I've acquired the three blood samples how will I get them to you? Blood samples are a bit finicky, if not handled properly they will deteriorate to a point where they are useless."

Cal reached over a cell phone. "This phone will never ring; it has been modified to only call out and only to one number. As soon as a sample is procured use the phone. The person who answers will give you directions on where to meet and he will take the sample from you. When the third sample is delivered you will turn the phone over with the last sample."

Rachel looked at the phone; it was one of the military spec phones that were all the rage a few years ago. Now with the advent of smart phones no one would be caught with such a simple device. She slid the phone into her purse and suddenly felt like someone she had read about in a spy novel. "Will the last payment be delivered when I supply the last sample?" Now Rachel felt like she was part of a spy novel.

"It will. As I mentioned this has got to be done within the time frame of four days. You have until five o'clock next Tuesday to finish."

With the fake I.D.s and the promise of more cash Rachel knew she would have it done on time. Even if she couldn't supply blood from the three targets she would still turn over someone's blood, even if she had to use her own. What Cal said next made Rachel shiver.

"Also, let me warn you against playing any games. We will know if you have actually acquired the correct samples. If the blood isn't from the three people you and I are talking about we will know it even before you turn it over," Cal said.

It was as if Cal had been reading Rachel's mind. "You won't need to worry about that. You'll receive what you want." No more thoughts of trying to fake her way out of acquiring the correct samples.

Cal picked up the check and left a fifty dollar tip on the table. The two women parted in the parking lot, Cal going back to New Circle to write a report on the meeting and Rachel going to her lock box to hide her loot. Both women were pleased with the meeting but for different reasons. Cal was happy to report to HB that the meeting had gone as hoped. Rachel was happy for the unexpected money and how easy it was going to be to carry out her part of the deal.

Cognitive Reasoning is a wonderful thing. When someone does something that is wrong they can think of ways to make it seem right to themselves. The prisons are full of people that convinced themselves, one way or another, that they had done something wrong, but it was required, or deserved, or just the right thing to do. Rachel had gone over the reasons she had stolen the files and once duplicated; given them to someone she didn't know. She convinced herself that what she was doing was for the greater good. The files were important for research, research that might even save lives. Hadn't that been why she went into nursing in the first place, to help people and possibly save lives. The pay had always been good but she felt nurses as a whole were underpaid; she was only subsidizing her income now wasn't she? She kept telling herself this as she put the money into her private lockbox.

HB was thrilled that the three blood samples would be available by the following Tuesday. All the plans were now finalized for the theft of the Blood Center van. A lot could still go wrong. For any number of reasons Samuel Edgemont might not donate on the Wednesday the plan was set to go into effect. This wasn't expected because Edgemont took great pride in donating every two weeks on a Wednesday. Stu had access to the schedules at the college Edgemont taught at and it was known that he had no classes, or office hours, during that particular timeframe on the appointed Wednesday.

The driver of the van might decide to bypass the convenient store on his drive back to Lexington. This too was highly unlikely. That stop had been monitored for nearly two weeks and the driver had never failed to exit the parkway to use the facilities and refill his coffee cup.

Even with the variables HB felt comfortable that everything would go as planned. One thing that hadn't been discussed yet was what to do about Rachel Bevins once she was no longer needed as a mole inside the hospital. It might be dangerous to have her around once everything was finished. Not that she could implicate anyone at Alterations, she couldn't. The only person she had met in person was Cal, which wasn't her real name. Cal had even worn a different color wig and different glasses. Cal was safe. Still though, with the money involved and the reputation of the third largest Pharmaceutical Company in the United States on the line, Rachel Bevins could be a dangerous variable. PT was waiting on Jason Freemont and Alex Trivett to give him the go ahead. As much as HB disliked this part of his job he went ahead and made plans for her elimination. If it were ordered, it would be carried out quickly and her body would never be found, unless finding it somehow furthered the plans, just another person who snapped and left town for a new life.

Samuel Edgemont kept his office hours and classes for the remainder of the week. He was always cautious to clear his schedule for the half day every other Wednesday when he donated platelets at the Blood Center. One of the benefits of working at a college was the ability to alter his schedule. Other than his donations he never really missed any time. A lot of what he missed on Wednesday could be made up at night from his computer at home. Sam was a light sleeper and never seemed to need more than six hours a night which left him with a lot of waking hours to fill. He really hated television, what he did watch tended to fall under the headings of news, sports, or documentaries. If anyone thought the life of a college professor was exciting or stimulating then they were sadly mistaken. After five years in Pikeville Sam felt he had settled into a rut that he may never be able to climb out of.

He occasionally thought of Jillian, a woman he had met only once. Sam had a good memory; he could replay the events of that Tuesday evening in his mind over and over. Sam always had a safety mechanism he fell back on which was one reason he had never married. He could keep an emotional distance as he analyzed all the information at hand. More than one promising romance had been thwarted by the 'Safety Mechanism.' Sam had to admit that one of two things was taking place, either the 'Safety Mechanism' was broken or Jillian was different than the other women he had met.

Jillian wasn't a woman who could walk down a New York runway, at first glance she wasn't strikingly beautiful, it was something different. Sam had always considered three things when it came to beauty. It's true, most men were attracted to a slim waist and a beautiful face but Sam was different. He had been out a few times with women who really knew how to put on makeup. What Sam found attractive was voice, mannerisms, intelligence, and finally, looks. Sam knew his down fall was that any three of these without the fourth wasn't going to work. He would never share his views with anyone for fear of being judged too critically himself and that was alright with him.

What had always gotten Sam's attention first was a woman's voice. Some women tried to go through life with that squeaky voice of a teenager, why he could never figure out. Jillian had the type of voice that could hold a man's attention for hours. It was deep but not gravelly, strong but not overbearing, sweet but not drippy.

He found her mannerisms to be captivating. Something about the way she carried herself, not just in walking but also in her facial expressions. It was as if every motion was thought out, no wasted movements. The way she smiled, the way she looked away when she described something as if she were actually seeing it as she talked.

Jillian was intelligent there was no doubt, after all she was an attorney. Sam knew a thing or two about attorneys, he taught students who wanted to go into that profession every day. As a group they were arrogant and egotistical, overly competitive to the point of pain. Sam considered all attorneys, both male and female, to be alphas. Jillian never fell into that category although Sam hadn't seen her at work. He suspected the Jillian he had dinner with at her aunt's house was probably the real thing.

Lastly was appearance. Sam had always been able to spot beauty as most men can. His worst nightmare was to be going with a woman who turned every head in the room, not that he couldn't handle competition, it was just that why would anyone want to constantly be expecting the worst. The woman who could stop traffic in the street usually knew it. Most women like that wouldn't admit it but they used their looks as a weapon. 'He's with me and he's damn lucky,' seemed to be the message they were sending. Sam had dated a few that fell into that category, it wasn't fun at all. The woman who knows how to work the makeup is usually not trying to hide her face as much as she is trying to hide her weak personality.

Jillian wore very little makeup. Her skin was clear and bright. Her smile seemed genuine and her laughter was reserved. She was thin but not too thin, something that really didn't matter to Sam and this he liked.

Sam had only been around her for two hours during dinner Tuesday evening but he found his mind at times drifting in her direction. He wondered if his 'Safety Mechanism' was going to kick in, if it didn't that was okay too.

After Jillian had gone back to Columbus Sam waited to see if she would contact him first, either by phone or e-mail, she had made sure they each shared the numbers. According to what she had said she was heading back to Columbus on Thursday morning, he wondered if she would call or message him that day. His doubts were put to rest Thursday afternoon, during his afternoon office hours he found an e-mail from Jillian. Sam expected it to say thanks for the visit Tuesday and if she were ever in the area again maybe Aunt Bertha could fix them another meal. She had the perfect safety net; Columbus was two-hundred miles away. If she did visit her aunt again and didn't want Sam to know she could dare her aunt to interfere.

Sam actually had his fingers crossed when he opened the message. *'Hi Sam, I hope this message finds you well. Again I wanted to thank you for coming to Aunt Bertha's little dinner party the other night. I hope my aunt and her three friends didn't embarrass you in any way.'* She closed the message with *'Write me anytime, hope to hear from you soon, Jillian.'*

Sam just sat in his office chair and looked at the monitor. What a nice message compared with what he expected, which was something completely opposite. Sam also noticed the message was written in perfect text, no abbreviations, no silly emoji's, none of the short hand such as U for you. Another feather in her hat he thought.

Sam clicked reply and then composed a response.

Hello Jillian,

Got your message, hope your drive home was pleasant. I want to thank you and your aunt again for such an enjoyable evening. I enjoyed talking with you and hope to speak again soon.

Sam

Sam hit the send button and then wondered if he had said enough or too much. He never had a problem answering e-mails before and wondered why he worried this time. It was three-thirty in the afternoon and he figured she answered her personal messages in the evenings. He was surprised when she answered him right back.

Hi Sam,

I must have caught you during your office hours. I envy you that your days aren't spent entirely at your desk as mine are, you have the luxury of going to a class room and teaching to a bunch of would be lawyers. I know all about those classes, I used to sit through them myself. I can't remember a professor that would have fallen into your category though; most were extremely boring and stuffy. You, I am happy to say, are not. Maybe we can talk tonight, hope so.

Jillian

Sam read the message and was extremely pleased. When he read her name he noticed that she had underlined her it, he wondered why. He would need to ask around to see if it was something he had never caught on to before. At any rate she wanted to talk again this evening, maybe even by phone. Sam leaned back in his office chair and burst out laughing, he was acting like he was back in high school. Sam felt he should respond otherwise she might get the impression he didn't want to talk.

Hello again,

Talking tonight sounds great, until then.

Sam

Sam reread his note and then hit send. He didn't underline his name as she had and again wondered what it meant. He would have to spend a little time researching that. He finished up a few other things in his office and then headed for his last class of the day.

Helen Montgomery finished up her day at Beaumont Regional by watching TV in her room. She had stayed on the terrace until after dark. The air had grown cool and the breeze had picked up. The last thing she wanted was to catch a cold. 'If you're going to catch a cold what better place than a hospital,' she thought. When she stood to go back inside Rachel was on her way back outside. When Helen saw her she wondered if the cold she had felt earlier might have been a premonition. Every time she saw the nurse her blood seemed to chill.

"Helen, I think we should go back inside. It is just too cool out here for you," the nurse said.

Helen agreed with her and they both headed for the glass door. Rachel walked Helen all the way back to her room and then took the last blood pressure of the day; it was 122 over 78, perfect. "Well Helen I'm going home in a few minutes but will be back tomorrow. Nurse Lexie will be on duty tonight, she will take good care of you. Is there anything else you need before I go?"

Helen sat down in the chair beside her bed and picked up the remote that controlled her television. She still wondered what it was about Rachel that made her feel so uncomfortable. Maybe she just needed to try and forget her silly feelings, as of now Helen would try to only think about the positives of the nurse.

"I'm fine Rachel. I want to thank you for taking such good care of me today. I feel as if I have been in very good hands," Helen said.

Rachel hadn't expected such a compliment. Most of the patients would say thanks if they even said that. Now she felt troubled at what she had done. Up until now the handing over of files to some unknown entity had, at most, caused Rachel a momentary feeling of regret. These feelings usually went away when she put the thick wad of cash into her lockbox. Now though, this feeble old woman, a woman who had only so many days left, had complimented her.

Rachel walked over and patted Helen's shoulder. "It has truly been my pleasure. I hope you have a good night." Rachel then turned and left the room. When she finally made it to the hallway she needed a tissue.

Helen hadn't responded when the nurse said what she said and then patted her shoulder. It was the pat that stopped anything else from being said. Helen felt she had just been touched by someone who had done her some sort of harm. She didn't really know why she felt this but it was there just the same. In her entire life she had never known anyone that had made her feel this way. Helen felt guilty; she was a good Christian and a God fearing woman. She didn't believe in holding bad thoughts against her fellow man. This thing with Rachel was just her mind playing tricks on her. She would work harder to keep those thoughts at bay.

Helen watched the news for a while on one of those twenty-four hour news channels. So many things had happened in the months since she could last remember. Why they had even taken Brian Williams off the six-thirty news she found out. What a pity, he had always been her favorite. She was certain Williams had been treated unfairly. She was also astonished to hear that Bill O'Riley had lost his show too. Helen heard the reasons for both their downfalls and sympathized with those that would feel hurt by what they had done. She also knew that people would feel hurt for any number of reasons, some of which could be so trivial. Men will be men and boys will be boys she always said.

Give Williams five minutes in the bad boy chair and start putting salt-peter in O'Riley's coffee, both problems would have taken care of themselves. Helen sniggered to herself. She was raised in a different time and knew most of her thoughts were now politically incorrect. When her husband Charlie had been alive he used to shout at the television news when something didn't suit him. He would argue and rage until the news ended and then pop a wash pan full of popcorn to have while he watched John Wayne beat up some bad guy.

It was late but Helen didn't feel tired, she actually felt refreshed and full of energy. As she stood she felt her strength was coming back to her. She walked to her bathroom and looked in the mirror, again she marveled at the face that smiled back at her. The skin was smooth and had a healthy color to it. The spots that so many women get on their skin seemed to be vanishing. Again Helen picked up her brush and pulled it through her hair. The hair was soft and smooth, not course like she remembered it to be for so many years. As with this morning Helen brushed her hair and couldn't help but giggle like a young girl. Was this all a dream, if so then it truly is a wonderful dream she thought.

Helen brushed her hair and then brushed her teeth. She changed into her pajamas and then went to bed. As she lay there she prayed that tomorrow would be as good as today. For the longest time she was almost afraid to fall asleep. What if it really was a dream and tomorrow would be back to the fuzzy memories and idle stare she knew she had been in for months. She didn't know how she knew this but it was there, she was sure of it.

The next morning Dr. Neil Slade parked his Audi in the staff parking section of Beaumont General. He hurried in and went immediately to his office. After turning on the monitor to his computer he pulled up the files on Helen Montgomery. He had thought of his patient several times since yesterday, much more than any other. The files were updated and all the information from the previous day's tests was there. As he read he wondered if he was looking at the correct file. Once he verified the name was correct he wondered if the wrong information had been posted but knew that was highly unlikely.

Helen's bloodwork and scans looked as if they belonged to an athlete. Dr. Slade stood and then thought about something else. He sat back down and sent a message to a colleague, a Dr. Stanley Hager who not only worked at Beaumont general but was considered by Slade to be a friend. He wanted to tell him about what he just read. The two often conferred about each other's patients. It helped keep them sharp and probably was another reason that both were considered excellent doctors. Once the message was sent Slade headed for the second floor. He had a remarkable patient to visit.

Dr. Stanley Hager had worked at Beaumont General for eleven years. He was fifty-six years old and looking to retire the very next year. He had become frustrated by the premiums he was paying for malpractice insurance and if that wasn't enough the new president had managed to alienate himself from congress over his campaign promise to repeal and replace The Affordable Care Act. No one knew where the next dollar was coming from. The fear was that Insurance Companies were now going to be shackled with more regulations while receiving less revenue. Most people, along with most politicians, failed to grasp the fact that insurance was a business and business's required a profit to operate. At the moment everything was a question and no one had the answer.

Dr. Hager was fortunate in the fact that his wife of thirty-two years had taken finance in college and graduated with an MBA. She worked the first ten years of their marriage until her husband offered her the chance to retire, which she agreed to on the spot in order to raise their two kids. She gladly accepted, but rather than just being a stay at home mom she took over her husband's finances, becoming his financial advisor so to speak. She kept the household on budget and put everything else to work making money. She wouldn't invest in anything risky, just good solid companies that paid a dividend. This was another reason Dr. Hager wanted to retire. Thanks to his hard work and his wife's frugal ways he had a substantial nest egg that would guarantee both a comfortable way of life.

Dr. Hager usually arrived at work around the same time as Dr. Slade. He had a patient of his own that was showing remarkable progress that couldn't really be explained. His patient was John J. Oden. Oden had several doctors at Beaumont General of which Dr. Hager was one. When Oden was brought in by helicopter he was diagnosed with stage four lung cancer. That was four months ago. Now his cancer was in remission and that was without the aid of either chemo or radiation therapy, those treatments had been stopped months earlier. When he was checking his messages before making his rounds he saw one from Dr. Slade. When he read it he realized that they both had an exceptional patient. This was good timing, Hager had another topic he needed to discuss with someone and Slade would be perfect. It was a matter that had been bothering Hager for some weeks now.

He decided to head up to the second floor and have a chat with the doctor. As he exited the elevator he spotted Slade standing at the nurse's station. He approached just as Slade was turning away from the nurse he had been talking to.

Slade saw him and spoke first. "Good morning Hager, I just left you a message a few minutes ago."

Hager walked up and put a hand on Slade's shoulder. "I got your message, that's why I came up. Can I talk to you in private about a patient?"

Slade could tell there was a bit of urgency in Hager's tone. "Sure, when do you want to talk?"

Hager released Slade's shoulder. "Soon, I wonder if maybe around noon you can spare some time. We could possibly have lunch on the veranda away from everyone else." Hager was talking in hushed tones so no one could hear what he was saying.

This was beginning to sound ominous. "That will be fine. I usually try to get lunch around eleven-thirty, does that work for you?"

"Yes certainly. If you are going to see this remarkable patient you talked about in your message I would like to tag along, with your permission of course."

Slade noticed a bit of nervousness with his friend. "I'm heading that way now." As the two walked Slade filled Hager in on the events of the last two days. "Mrs. Helen Montgomery has been a resident at River Terrace nursing home for the last few years. She is eighty-two years old and suffers, or should I say she did suffer from any number of ailments that someone of her age might have, the most severe though is dementia. She has been in the final stages of the disease for several months." The two had now made it to Helen's room, "Here we go," Slade said as he pointed at the door. Slade waited to allow his friend to enter first.

Helen was standing by the window looking out over the city. Hager assumed this to be a relative or friend of the patient. Slade recognized her but noticed she looked in better health this morning that she had yesterday. Helen heard someone enter and turned from the window.

"Good morning Dr. Slade," she said.

The voice was vibrant and smooth, the diction perfect. "Good morning Mrs. Montgomery, I trust you slept well?"

"Oh yes, it was the most restful night I have had in forever."

"This is Dr. Hager, I asked him to accompany me this morning on my rounds. He agreed and here we are."

Dr. Hager stepped forward and stuck out a hand. Helen gladly took it and they both shook. Hager noticed the strong grip along with the warm touch. Most patients of eighty two have cold hands from poor circulation, Helen did not. "It's a pleasure to meet you Mrs. Montgomery."

Dr. Slade watched the exchange between the two; Helen looked as if she were here to visit someone, rather than being a patient. "I've looked over your charts this morning Mrs. Montgomery. Everything looks fine, how do you feel?" Slade asked.

Helen looked back toward the window. "I actually feel like taking a walk, outside preferably if it's allowed?"

When Slade came to work he noticed how unseasonably cool it had become. He wondered how Helen would feel if she were only allowed to walk the corridors of the hospital. "A walk outside does sound nice, it is a little cool this morning though. Maybe if you wandered the corridor here for a while. There is a visitor's lounge at the end and on the right. If it warms a little later maybe you could go back to the veranda for lunch."

"That sounds fine with me doctor. If the tests are finished will I be going back to River Terrace this morning. I'm sure my friends there are worried about me." Helen said with a voice that sounded youthful and energetic.

Dr. Slade hadn't considered a discharge so soon. He hoped to keep her here at least one more day to monitor her progress. By the way she had asked though he could tell she would be happier back at the nursing home. He knew he could visit her there and there wasn't really a need to keep her at Beaumont General. All relevant tests that needed to be run were done yesterday.

"Well I suppose I could release you this morning. How about you stay with us until after lunch, I want to come back and check on you in a few hours. The nurses will already have the paperwork finished and then an ambulance can take you back." He wondered if Helen might protest about the ambulance again?

Helen smiled and said, "That sounds fine doctor. That will give me a chance to catch up on the news, so much has happened in the world in the last few months."

Slade and Hager left Helen's room. Slade was talking as they went down the corridor but Hager never heard a word he said. "Stanley, are you alright this morning?" Slade asked after he noticed Hager wasn't paying attention.

Slade had stopped walking and Stanley only stopped when he noticed he was walking alone. He turned back to see Slade looking at him as if he was puzzled. "I'm sorry Neil, did you say something?"

Slade caught up with his friend and asked in a lower voice. "What's going on Stanley, I've never seen you so distracted." Slade thought he must have a patient that is not responding to treatment and that is why he is acting so preoccupied."

"Actually after seeing your patient I am more bewildered than ever. I mentioned that I have a recovery that I need to talk to you about. There are some other things that are going on and I really don't think it is time to go with it to administration. I need to sort out a few things and maybe you can be of help," Hager said.

Slade could tell that something had Hager troubled. He also sensed anxiety, an emotion Slade had never seen in his friend. "Why don't you meet me in my office instead of on the terrace for lunch? We can both grab something from the cafeteria and shut the door and talk." Slade told his friend.

Hager looked up and down the corridor they stood in. He also looked at the nurse's station for the longest time. He never took his eyes off the nurses as he nervously said, "Your office is no good and neither is mine. We need to talk where we can't be heard. I'll meet you at the terrace at eleven-thirty sharp." With that he walked away.

Slade stood and watched him go. Had he really been talking to the same Stanley Hager he had known for so long? It sure seemed like he hadn't. And what did he mean about talking where no one could hear? The way he said it led Slade to believe both the offices were bugged. That was just crazy.

Slade went to the nurse's station and made the arrangements to have Helen Montgomery dismissed that day shortly after noon. She was to have anything she requested for lunch and a nurse was to document all she said and did between now and her discharge. An ambulance was to do the transfer with absolutely no sirens, just lights.

Slade went through his morning routine much like a robot; his motions were on auto while his mind was thinking about the things Dr. Hager had said. Finally it was near the time for the meeting on the terrace so Slade went to the cafeteria and grabbed a pre-packaged salad with fat free ranch dressing. He also bought a twenty ounce Diet Coke, as he paid he knew if his wife were here she would fuss about the Diet Coke. Stop putting those chemicals in your body, she would say. He always told her he liked the chemicals and they gave him a needed mid-day boost.

Slade took the tray to the elevator and went up to the second floor. On the terrace was Dr. Hager sitting at a table and noticing everything. He was holding his cell phone but didn't appear to be talking or texting anybody. He also had a tray from the cafeteria but it only contained an empty barbecue sandwich wrapper and an open can of soda.

"Well Hager, looks like you beat me here and already finished your lunch," Slade said.

Hager threw Slade a nervous smile. "I thought I would talk while you ate and listened."

Slade wondered what on earth had happened to have his friend acting this way. Hager had always been a laid-back and jovial kind of guy, what he was seeing today was anything but. "Sure Stanley, I'm curious about what's bothering you today so anytime you like, start talking, I'm ready to listen."

Hager slid his tray to the side and then put both elbows on the table. Before he spoke he looked around and then craned his head down which made him look not unlike a tortoise wearing horn-rimmed glasses. "What I've got to tell, you must promise you won't share with anyone else." Hager said this in a low tone and as he spoke he continued to scan his surroundings.

"Sure Stanley. I promise not to say a word." The tension just got cranked up another notch Slade thought.

"Have you noticed anything about your office computer out of the or-dinary?"

Slade thought a minute. "Well, yesterday while I was reading some pa-tient files there was a flicker, kind of like the power went out for a split second."

"Does your computer have a battery back-up?"

Again Slade thought, "Yes it does, I.T. had to replace the old one a few months ago."

"Then I can tell you right now it wasn't anything to do with the electricity. The battery back-up is there for just such an event. Anything else going on; for example while you're reading files?"

Slade thought hard. "Now that you mention it, yesterday while I was updating records my file page scrolled down one page without a prompt, it did that twice. What are you getting at Stanley?"

Stanley did the turtle trick again. "In your message this morning you indicated you had a patient who was experiencing a remarkable recovery. I have a patient that four months ago was in fourth stage lung cancer. How he lived with it for so long, without symptoms, I will never know. The cancer made itself evident all at once; he was within days of death by the time he came to the hospital." Stanley stopped talking as an orderly walked a little too close to their table with his lunch on a tray. He watched until the man had gone by and was out of earshot.

Slade took the opportunity to ask a question. "How is your patient now?"

"That's the point I'm getting at. He was in such bad shape when I first saw him that there wasn't a course of treatment available other than pain management. Chemo and radiation should have been out of the question but his family wanted us to try anything to save his life. We did a few treatments later on but the results were negative.

"When he was first brought in we managed to stabilize the hemorrhaging in his right lung and then basically sent him home to die. We had Hospice care for him, which I thought would be two or three weeks at the most after we stopped the chemo." Again Stanley looked around as if spies were watching from every rooftop.

"So again Stanley, how is the patient now?" Slade asked.

"He's fine. Within a week of his last treatment I was notified that he was doing better by the folks with Hospice. That seemed logical, end of life patients usually have a few more good days, I attribute it to God's will. A week after that, I was notified that his improvement continued and I should schedule an appointment to see what was going on, which I did. I had him come in the very next day."

Slade chewed on a slice of tomato, "And!"

"When I saw him I could hardly believe it was the same man. His vitals were strong, his color was good and he had some energy back. I ordered some tests and then sent him home. I had him come in once a week for a month after that and did all the tests that could be done without actually admitting him to the hospital. Now four months later he is cancer free. Not remission mind you, cancer free." Hager said those last two words with a strong emphasis.

Slade put down his fork. He thought about what he had just heard. He wondered if Stanley's patient and Helen Montgomery had something in common, their recoveries certainly were dramatic. His next question might sting a bit but he had to ask it, "Could you have misdiagnosed your patient four months ago?"

Stanley had expected the question; he had asked himself that several times. "No, I thought so at first, it was the simplest explanation. Just like you, that was one of my concerns but I've gone back over the evidence several times and the diagnosis was correct, he was dying of cancer. Doctor James, the lung specialist, actually performed the initial surgery and I have consulted with him, our original diagnosis was correct."

Slade looked at his watch and quickly started eating again. He didn't know where Stanley was going with this and didn't know how much more time he could spare. "So, how does this pertain to me and my computer?"

Again Stanley looked around as if spies with guns were lurking behind every potted plant. "I don't know yet. The reason I asked you about your office computer was that a few months ago, shortly after I had taken John Oden as a patient I started getting a weird feeling. Things were going on and I couldn't figure it out. The phone in my office started making a clicking sound when I used it. Two or three seconds after someone answers my call there is a click. Very slight and only one but it is a click and it happens every time I use that phone."

Slade wondered if his friend was losing it. "So your computer screen and your phone have a glitch Stanley, have someone from I.T. take a look."

"I did, the computer problem was somehow linked into housekeeping. He isolated it and said not to worry, the problem was all in-house, no outside interference and if he got some extra time he would look further into it. The tech couldn't figure it out on the spot and said it wasn't really a big deal anyway. I had another systems guy check my phone and he said the click seemed to have something to do with the outside lines, nothing he could fix from his end.

"Now this is where it gets good. I had two of our guys look at my phone and my computer, both came up empty handed. Now this is the part where you must swear to me you won't tell a soul."

Slade looked at his watch again and knew he had to be going. "I promise Stanley."

"You know my daughter Donna and her husband Todd?" Slade shook his head yes and then Stanley continued. "Well, my son-in-law is in the military, he's a systems analyst, computers and all that cyber stuff. You know he graduated from MIT with a degree in computer sciences. Well they were in a week ago and I asked him a few questions about computers and phones. He told me if either problem had happened one at a time then probably not to worry. But if both happened nearly at the same time he suspected that someone outside the hospital had breached the security firewall of all our systems and was monitoring the hospital's current files or mining the database in order to get sensitive information, maybe even both."

Now Slade knew he really needed to go. "Can we wrap this up Stanley; I've got rounds to make."

"Okay Neil, I'm about to get to the best part, or maybe it's the worst part. Todd has been doing a little research while he's at work, not something he would want his supervisors to know about. He has access to some pretty powerful hardware and software. He found a few anomalies in our systems. Whoever broke into Beaumont's computers and phones is good and has some pretty sophisticated equipment of their own. To be more specific my name and Dr. Ahern's were targeted to acquire all the files we have back as far as 2013. He could only identify bits and pieces to this but he did find out that whoever it is wants information that can be used pertaining to a 'Ponce de Leon' Project."

Now Slade was all ears. "Ponce de Leon, the Spanish explorer who was looking for the fountain of youth?"

"That right. I have already talked to Ahern and since your message this morning I am talking to you also," Hager said.

Slade was too stunned to respond at first, he was thinking about Helen Montgomery. "The patient Ahern has, are the facts similar to our patients?"

"Yes, a man who had been on dialysis for nearly five years and had all sorts of other medical problems is now completely healed. No diabetes, no kidney failure, everything that was bad is now good. He was in the last stages of dialysis treatment. It just wasn't going to help him that much longer, you know what it does to the body."

Slade did know. A five year dialysis patient was nearing the end of usefulness for the treatment. That is a long time to endure something as hard on the body as dialysis. "What did she attribute this too; you don't just heal from diabetes and kidney failure."

"She doesn't know, and I'll tell you something else. That man's eyesight was failing. Within six months he was going to be unable to drive. Now his vision is twenty-twenty."

Slade pushed his tray aside. "Twenty-twenty, that is something to consider. Do you and Dr. Ahern think you are being spied on because of your patients?"

"I would bet on it and now I think you are going to join us."

Slade suddenly felt weak. He had never been in a position like this before, what would Sheila think? "What are you suggesting we do about this Stanley?"

"We can't go to administration, we can't be certain they aren't involved in some way. We can't go to the police; it would take them a year to understand the problem much less try to find out who is doing it. I doubt any police department in the world would be equipped to investigate a crime in the realm of medical and computer sciences."

Slade agreed. "Do we want whoever is doing this to know that we know?"

"Todd said not to go down that road yet. He told me to let him do some more checking. Some of his buddies in the service take on stuff like this for kicks, no different than you or I going bowling. They do it for the thrill of it. It is their knowledge against an unknown. You know those military types, all gung-ho. He said to not send anything sensitive until he lets me know. Now I think you might be included just by that e-mail this morning, but I would say they would have included you anyway. They found me and they found Reza Ahern, only a matter of time until they started watching you and your patients."

Slade stood and picked up his tray. He was both troubled and angry. "I want to see you here tomorrow for lunch, same time. If there is any new developments you can fill me in then."

Dr. Hager also stood. "There is one more thing Neil and I saved this for last. Todd thinks there is a person working here in the hospital that is helping to coordinate things on the inside."

Slade thought he was beyond shock but was wrong. "Someone inside, who does he think it is?"

"He said it would probably be someone who has access to both records and patients. Just one without the other wouldn't work."

Slade thought a minute and then said, "A nurse or a doctor?"

Hager nodded his approval. "You can rule out a doctor, the three of us are the ones being researched, or at least two of us are, and within a day or two I suspect you will be included.

Slade looked at his watch again. "I really must go now. In the meantime why don't you see if anything might point to a nurse as a suspect? I'll put some thought into it myself and we'll meet here again tomorrow." Both doctors agreed and then headed back inside. Slade went straight to his office and pulled up the file on Helen Montgomery, he sat there for a few minutes and waited, nothing happened. If his computer was being monitored he wondered if it was constant and realized that probably wasn't possible. Who would have the time to sit and look at his computer waiting to see if anything was entered, that gave him an idea?

Slade pulled out the sliding shelf that held his keyboard. He hit the timer on his Tag watch and then typed in one unnecessary sentence on Helen Montgomery's file. 'Patient will be discharged this afternoon.' He then waited with his watch at the ready and his eyes glued to the screen. Fifteen seconds after he had activated the timer on his watch his monitor blinked once. It was quick but it had happened. Slade wasn't sure what had just happened, maybe it was nothing. Maybe it was everything.

At the offices on New Circle, Stu had been alerted that Slade had entered something into a patient file. The program he had installed into the main server at Beaumont General notified him anytime something was entered pertaining to John J. Oden, Van Goodwin and as of yesterday, Helen Montgomery. He read what had just been entered and looked at the file name, it was Helen Montgomery. She was scheduled to be discharged this afternoon. Stu didn't need to know who had entered the information but he thought he would look anyway. After a few key strokes the camera on Neil Slade's computer flashed the face of the doctor onto one of Stu's monitors. Slade didn't know it at the time but he was being watched in real time by a man he would never meet.

Dr. Slade sat at his desk wondering what had just happened. He had lots of work to do and decided to get to it. He stood and exited his office, Stu watched him go.

Stu now had noticed a little snag in the plan. The three blood samples had to be gathered no later than the following Tuesday. There was a plan in place for the two discharged patients, John Oden and Van Goodwin. The one for Helen Montgomery was to be taken while she was in the hospital but now she was being discharged and he suspected his contact in the hospital hadn't acquired the sample yet. He sent a text to a small phone that had been given to Rachel Bevins just for such an occasion. Stu knew all text messages, even ones sent to phones that would be destroyed in a day or two, could be pulled up from any provider by using a little thing known as a court order signed by any number of judges. On his end the messages were bounced off three different destinations, the last being from Panama, and were completely untraceable. The content could be read but the source couldn't be found. The phone Rachel Bevins carried was a different story though.

Her messages could be traced to the phone she carried. Stu planned to switch that phone every seventy-two hours by means of a drop box near Rachel's house. Still though, even if the phone were never acquired by a competing company trying to get information on what was now called 'The Ponce de Leon Project' there was always the possibility of law enforcement being contacted. This was unlikely because the only way that would happen was if someone from Beaumont General or the Blood Center found something suspicious and contacted any number of agencies with the expertise to investigate. It was doubtful if the Lexington Police Department had the technical know how to do anything. As for the Pikeville and Williamson, West Virginia, Police Departments, there was no concern at all. What worried Stu and Hells Bells was if either department contacted the FBI. This was an organization that had the staff and knowledge to investigate the matter thoroughly.

Stu sent a message to the small phone Rachel carried. It read, 'Re. #3, has sample been acquired?'

Rachel felt the phone she carried vibrate. She had been home since she left the hospital that morning. She had always enjoyed the night shift; it seemed she could survive on a lot less sleep. After four hours she had woken up and was sitting on the small balcony of her condo reading the newspaper and sipping on an expresso. She pulled the phone from her pocket and read the message. She had assumed Helen Montgomery would be at the hospital for at least one more day. Actually it was in her file that discharge wouldn't be until tomorrow. She would get the sample this evening after she was back on duty. Her Friday shift ended at 3:00 in the morning and she intended to get the other two samples first thing Saturday morning.

Rachel had been told to use the phone only to answer a request and to be as brief as possible. She thought about her response and then typed, 'Today in P.M., deliver tomorrow.' After she thought about her response and was satisfied that it would be impossible for anyone reading, other than her contact to figure out, she hit send.

Stu read the response and knew the discharge must have been moved up a day and Rachel wasn't aware until now. Now the sample would need to be pulled at the Nursing Home, this he thought could be done but the risk of being detected was much higher. Stu never responded to the message, he knew Rachel would find out for sure once her shift started that evening. He would work on a plan to acquire the sample, if Rachel came up with a better plan in the meantime then so be it.

As Rachel read her paper and sipped her expresso she wondered why they had asked about the sample. Something must have changed. If it was important she would get a second message or at least find out something at work, 'No need to worry if a worry hasn't presented itself,' she thought.

Helen finished her lunch; it was a salad of tomatoes and lettuce with honey mustard dressing. As she ate she thought of the lettuce and tomato on her burger the previous night. This was just as fresh and crisp she thought, or maybe she just appreciated it as much. As with everything else that had happened she noticed her senses seemed sharper. As she ate she didn't just chew and swallow. She first enjoyed the aroma of each bite. She chewed slowly enjoying not only the taste of the food but also the texture. She laughed at the thought of having so much pleasure out of eating something as simple as a salad while most everyone else took large bites, chewed twice, and then swallowed.

After coming out of her sleepy dream, which felt as if it had lasted for years, Helen wanted to get the most out of everything. Even the simple act of breathing, which was something to be taken for granted, was something she wanted to experience more deeply. She sat and breathed deeply and slowly. She wanted to fill her lungs and then exhale slowly as if ridding her body of every bad thought and ailment she ever had. Her senses were alive and she wanted to enjoy what everyone else took for granted. In all her life she had never felt more alive and in control of her happiness than she did right now.

Later that day when Rachel Bevins clocked in for her shift at Beaumont General she had every intention of acquiring the blood sample from Helen Montgomery. When she checked in at the nurse's station on the second floor she immediately saw that Mrs. Montgomery had been released and sent back by ambulance to River Terrace at two-fifteen in the afternoon. This was unexpected; yesterday she was led to believe Helen would remain at the hospital for at least one more day for observation. This had happened on occasion in the past, a patient will improve to a point where discharge is allowed, or at times patients will check themselves out against the doctor's wishes. Rachel assumed the former had happened rather than the latter.

She was very cautious not to show the least amount of surprise, she never revealed any emotion at all. As she continued to look at the monitor she wondered how she would get the blood sample now that her patient had been released. She had plans to visit the two male patients at their homes on Saturday and acquire the two samples using her fake I.Ds. The nursing home was a different story; Helen knew her and would wonder why she was there. After more thought, Rachel decided that she would drive over to the nursing home immediately after she had taken the first two blood samples. Helen Montgomery was old and wouldn't suspect a thing. By dark Saturday evening she would make arrangements to drop off the three samples and get her bonus. That would be the end of it.

Rachel pulled into the driveway of John J. Oden's house at a quarter past nine on Saturday morning. As she got out of her car she could hear a tractor running off in the distance. The drive from Lexington to Wayne County had taken nearly two hours. She left town at seven sharp, after filling her car with gas and getting a cup of coffee she had driven straight there. As she walked up the sidewalk and then the steps she wondered about her looks. She had done as Cal suggested and worn her hair much different than normal and applied less makeup in order to look as plain as possible. If she had been seen at Beaumont General she doubted she would be recognized now.

Rachel pressed the doorbell and waited. She heard barking on the other side of the door and by the noise it sounded like a small dog. When the door opened she was met by a woman wearing an apron and wiping her hands on a towel.

Nancy Oden had been finishing up the breakfast dishes when she heard the doorbell. John had finished eating about an hour before and wanted to get out his big John Deere Tractor, he had put the set of tilling disc on the previous evening so he could get an early start. The tractor Rachel heard was the one John was using out in the field. He loved the big green beast and would rather drive it around on his property than drive his truck on the highway. It had a full cab with heat and air. As he was tilling down cornstalks he listened to George Jones on the stereo.

Nancy heard a knock and hurried from the kitchen to answer the door. There was a woman standing on the front porch wearing the kind of clothes nurses wore in a hospital. The name tag the woman was wearing read 'Beaumont General, Bess Stillman.' Rachel had been told by Cal to wear street clothes to help with her disguise but felt if she was going to get away with stealing blood samples from unsuspecting patients she needed to at least look the part of a nurse.

"Good morning, can I help you?" Nancy asked.

"Hi, I'm from Beaumont General. I was sent over to take a follow-up blood sample from a John Oden. Are you his wife?" Rachel asked.

Nancy looked a little shocked. "Yes I'm his wife Nancy. Is there something wrong?" Nancy asked nervously.

Rachel had rehearsed in the car on the way down; she had anticipated this very question. "Oh no Mrs. Oden, everything is fine. It's just that the lab mishandled the last blood sample and it wasn't suitable for tests. I was sent out to acquire new ones. These things happen on occasion but I can assure you that everything with your husband is just fine." Rachel hoped she had delivered the explanation in a manner to seem sincere.

"Oh, I see. Well things do happen I suppose. Would you come in and I will call my husband," Nancy said.

Rachel followed her inside. Nancy picked up the phone by the table and dialed a number, two rings later John answered. Nancy could hear the rumble of the big tractor's engine but the noise wasn't bad, the cab John always bragged about made it quite enough that she could hear every word he said. Louder than the engine was the wailing of George Jones on the tractor's stereo.

"John, there is a lady here from the hospital who says she needs a blood sample from you."

There was a pause as John asked her a question.

Nancy answered. "Oh no dear, nothing like that. She said the lab messed up your last sample and they sent her out to get a new one."

Again there was a pause as Nancy listened to her husband.

"Okay dear, we'll be here. Try to hurry so as to not keep her waiting." With that Nancy hung up the phone.

"I always call him on his cell phone when we need to talk. You know just yesterday the phone rang and when I answered it John told me he loved me more than he loved his old tractor. He was laughing when he hung up. Don't you think that was sweet?"

Rachel though that was about as sweet a story as she had ever heard, she wondered if she would ever have that kind of love, she truly doubted it. "That was. You two must have a great life here."

They both sat on the sofa and to help pass the time until John got there Nancy told Rachel, actually she told Bess Stillman about the morning John had been stricken. Rachel sat and listened intently, she thought she would be uninterested in the story until she realized she was hearing the first steps of what had led John J. Oden to be designated Reanimate #1. It was a reference both Stu and HB had argued about sharing with Rachel, but in the end it was decided the reference was so ambiguous that Rachel probably couldn't figure it out. It did add another level of mystery to the task Rachel was doing.

Before long the sound of a tractor could be heard outside, shortly after the sound died and the back door could be heard opening. "That would be John now," Nancy said.

A man dressed in a plaid shirt and coveralls walked into the living room. Nancy got up and walked over to steal a kiss from her husband. "This lady is here to get a blood sample for the hospital John. Wasn't it so nice of her to drive all the way down?"

John dug his handkerchief from one of his front pockets and wiped his forehead. "Why did you need to drive all the way down for that, they took samples last week when I was there for my appointment? I was told everything was fine by my doctor before I left."

Rachel had thought in all likelihood at least one of the two men she was to acquire blood samples from had been to the hospital within the last week and would have had lab work done while they were there. She hoped her reply would be sufficient, before she could answer the question, Nancy said, "Oh John, she said the lab messed up on that sample and she is here to get a new one."

John was suspicious, he had been told before he left the hospital that his blood work was fine, he was told this by none other than his doctor. "I don't understand. If the blood sample they took was ruined by the lab then why did Dr. Hager say everything was fine?"

Rachel had one lie she hoped would work. "Well, that is true Mr. Oden but there are more extensive tests that are done after you leave. It is these tests that can't be completed until we get a fresh sample. I can assure you that everything is fine but we always like to run the extra tests anyway."

John thought that might sound true. "Well okay I guess. When will I hear back about the new tests they are going to do?"

"Well if everything checks out, as I'm sure it will, then you won't hear anything from the hospital," Rachel said.

"And if something is wrong when will I hear anything?" John asked.

"Oh, if something is wrong you will get a call immediately but that is highly unlikely, all your tests so far have been nearly perfect."

John began rolling up his sleeve. He wanted to get back to his tractor and his fields. It wasn't that long until lunch and he liked to get a certain amount of work done before then. Rachel quickly took the sample and thanked both John and Nancy as she left. Once she was back in her car and on the road she breathed a sigh of relief. John Oden had asked some good questions. At one point she was afraid he was going to refuse to donate. Her worst nightmare was if he had dialed the hospital to see what this was all about. At that point she would have had to run from the house and drive away, luckily that never happened. She patted the case which contained the blood sample and reassured herself that she was one more patient closer to being finished and that much closer to her bonus.

John watched her rush down the steps and get into her car. As she turned in the driveway and sped down the road he had an uneasy feeling. "Something doesn't make sense, why would the hospital send someone all this way for a blood sample?" As he spoke he rubbed the dark blue elastic bandage that held the gauze over the spot where Bess had poked him. "That name tag she was wearing Nancy, did you get a good look at it?"

"I really never paid that much attention John, I do know her name was Bess though, she told me."

John watched as the car drove out of sight. "Bess Stillman, the tag said Bess Stillman. I was in the service with a man who had the last name Stillman. Did she seem a bit nervous to you?"

"Maybe, now that you mention it, but that could be caused by any number of things. She said she left early this morning and it is my guess she has had a lot of coffee on her way down here. Too much coffee will put someone on edge you know."

John wasn't convinced. "Have you ever heard of a hospital sending someone this far on a Saturday to get a new blood sample?" Nancy thought a moment but before she could speak again John added, "No you haven't and for that matter I haven't either. I'm going to call the hospital and get some answers." John looked at his watch, "How about you and I having us an early lunch out on the patio. I wouldn't no more get back in the field until I would have to come back anyway."

Nancy smiled, "Why John that is a wonderful idea, lunch on the patio." She patted him on the shoulder as she headed for the kitchen. "You romantic old hound dog you." She walked on by laughing, John laughed too.

John picked up the cordless phone and the phone book that had all the important numbers written on the back and went to the front porch. He sat in his favorite rocking chair and dialed the number for Beaumont General.

"Hello, Beaumont General," A friendly voice said on the other end.

"Hi, this is John Oden. I live down in Wayne County. I would like to talk to whoever it is that sends out the nurses that collect blood samples."

The receptionist that answered the phone was accustomed to answering questions from people that knew little to nothing about hospitals. She had never had this question asked before though. "The hospital doesn't have anyone that goes out to collect blood samples Mr. Oden. If you have been asked to come in to give a sample by your doctor then that is only done here, at the hospital." She wondered if she had made her answer understandable.

"No, I wasn't asked to come in to give a sample; the lady was just here and has already left," John said politely.

The receptionist was sure there was a reason for what she had just heard. "Can you hold on for a minute Mr. Oden while I check on it for you?"

"Yes, I can hold."

The receptionist put John on hold and then dialed her supervisor. After briefly explaining to the supervisor what John Oden had just said the supervisor decided to get involved. "Hello, this is Cheryl, may I help you Mr. Oden?"

John asked the same question to Cheryl as he had asked the receptionist.

"Sir, I don't believe we send people out to collect blood samples. Are you sure a lady is on her way there?"

"No, she just left, she took my blood and now she is gone. She was wearing a name badge that read Beaumont General."

Cheryl was now troubled. Who would go to a patient's home and take a blood sample. Furthermore any number of things could go wrong with an invasive procedure like that. "Was there anything else on the name badge, all hospital name badges have the employee's name written on them."

"Yes, it said Beaumont General at the top and the name under it was Bess Stillman," John said.

"Give me your full name and a phone number where I can call you back. Also give me the name of your doctor," Cheryl said.

John gave her his full name and who his doctor was. He gave her his home and cell numbers. After he hung up he went back inside. He could smell ham frying and it was like a magnet to his nose. When he went back into the kitchen Nancy turned and said, "Did you find anything out dear?"

"Not much. The lady said they don't send people out to get blood samples. They are going to call me back if they can figure anything out," John told her.

"Well I'm sure it's nothing dear. Why would anyone drive this far if the hospital hadn't sent them?"

John thought about what his wife had just said. He knew Nancy was right, she usually was. "It smells good in here, what are we having for lunch."

"Ham and cheese sandwiches and iced tea, you can have some baked chips with yours. I had planned on fixing something else but it looks like our plans got changed," Nancy told her husband.

"This sounds really good to me." As they carried their lunch out onto the patio John grabbed the portable phone from the kitchen counter. "If they call me back I don't want to have to run back in for the phone," he said as they went out the back door.

John and Nancy loved to eat on their patio, especially this time of year. The foliage had started to change color and the leaves had started to fall, it made everything around the farm look like one of those thousand piece picture puzzles that most people never seem to finish. Just as they were finishing up with lunch John placed a kiss on his wife's cheek. "I better get back to that tractor; it can't drive itself you know."

"What time will you finish playing for the day, you know it's Saturday and you promised me a movie tonight." Anytime John drove his tractor on Saturday Nancy accused him of playing.

John turned back toward his wife. "A promise is a promise, by the way will I enjoy the movie or is it a woman's movie? You know a chick flick."

"Well, I'll enjoy the movie, isn't that what's important."

John laughed, before he could speak the phone started ringing. He looked at his wife as he walked back over to pick it up. "Hello," was all he said?

"Hello, is this John Oden?"

"Yes, this is John."

"Hi, this is Cheryl from Beaumont General calling you back. I've checked with personnel and we don't have anyone here by the name of Bess Stillman. Your doctor isn't in this morning but I did check with someone who is familiar with your file. There wasn't an order for any-more lab work and if there was you would have been requested to come to the hospital."

"Who was here then, she said she was with your hospital and was wearing a nametag?" John asked as he and Nancy looked at each other.

"I really don't know Mr. Oden, but it wasn't the hospital," Cheryl said.

"What do I do now; I don't like this one bit." John was starting to wor-ry.

"We are continuing to check this out Mr. Oden. I promise to call you back in a couple of hours. Will you be near your phone?" Cheryl asked.

"I guess I will now, thanks for calling me back." John hung up.

Dr. Stanley Hager was scheduled to come in at noon on Saturday. At a little after ten-o'clock one of the nurses called from the hospital and asked about the blood sample that was taken from John Oden at his house in Wayne County.

"Are you saying that someone went to his house and took blood?" Hager asked. "Do we know who done this?"

"We are checking doctor. The patient was a little suspicious and gave us a call after the woman left."

Hager felt his chest tighten. "I'm on my way now. As soon as I get there I want to know everything you've found out." The nurse agreed and they both hung up.

Hager dialed the number for Neil Slade. Slade was at home this Saturday morning, a rare event. He heard the phone and when he checked he recognized the number of Stanley Hager and answered. "Hello Dr. Hager," he said.

"Neil, I need to talk to you, can you spare some time this morning?" Hager asked.

Slade looked at his watch; it was fifteen minutes before eleven. He could tell by Hager's voice that something was up. "What's happened Stanley?"

"I don't want to talk over the phone. Meet me in an hour at the hospital." With that Hager hung up.

Neil put down the phone and wondered if his friend was suffering from some sort of mental condition. Sheila wasn't going to like the fact that he was going to the hospital this morning. They had planned to do some things around the house and then have a night out, movie and dinner. Hager had just managed to change all that.

Slade jumped in the shower and then headed off to work, leaving a very disappointed wife behind. He promised he would be home as soon as possible and Sheila seemed to understand. Neil decided to play along with Hager's conspiracy theory for a little while longer. He needed more evidence than a temperamental computer monitor to convince him that something was really going on.

When Slade pulled his Audi into the staff only portion of the parking garage Hager was standing by the elevator waiting for him. When he saw him there he knew something must be terribly wrong to have his friend so worked up this morning. "Stanley what's up?"

Dr. Hager walked half way to where Neil parked and whispered. "Something has happened this morning; meet me on the second floor veranda in fifteen minutes. Don't use the phone until we talk. We shouldn't say anything else here." Hager turned and walked back to the elevator. As Neil entered Stanley held a finger in front of his lips as if to say, 'Don't speak.' All this cloak and dagger stuff was starting to be unsettling for Dr. Slade.

Neil found the veranda to be busy this morning, it was lunch time and the weather was pleasant, just a little cool. The table he and Hager had used before was occupied so Neil found one that was not as good but it would have to do. Just as he sat down Hager came through the door and headed his way, he was in a hurry.

"What's going on Stanley, I left a mad wife at home in order to come down here on a Saturday."

"I got a call at home just before I called you. You know I have a patient that has made a miraculous recovery," Hager said.

"Yes, you told me about that a day or two ago, I have one myself," Slade said.

Hager cut his eyes from left to right as if someone was listening to every word. "My Patient was here last week and I had a complete set of lab work ran on him. Everything checked out fine, it's as if the man is thirty years old instead of in his late fifties. I saw him and told him the good news; he went home a happy man. I have another follow up appointment with him in six weeks."

Slade cut in, "You didn't run me down here to tell me that Stanley?"

"No Neil, there's more. This morning someone showed up at his house wearing a Beaumont General name tag and said she was there to take another blood sample, said the one from the hospital was contaminated or something to that effect. The tag said her name was Bess Stillman. Do you know anyone by that name?"

Neil thought a moment but knew he had never heard that name before. "I don't know anyone by that name. Does the hospital ever send someone out for a blood sample?"

"Never, we don't do invasive procedures outside the hospital, I checked."

Now Neil was the one looking around. "What does this mean Stanley? Who would want to take a blood sample from one of your patients?"

"I don't know, and another thing, my patient lives nearly two hours from here. Whoever is doing this is very determined."

"Has this got anything to do with the phones and the computers you told me about?" Neil asked.

"I would say it has everything to do with what we talked about. Where does your patient live, the one who suffers, or should I say did suffer from dementia?" Stanley asked.

"She lives at the nursing home, River Terrace," Neil said.

Stanley reached over and grabbed Neil's arm. "You have got to contact the nursing home; my guess is that whoever is doing this will probably try to get a blood sample from your patient as well."

Neil thought a minute. "You told me there was a third patient; I believe you said it was one of Dr. Ahern's?"

"That's right; I made her aware of my suspicions after I talked to you the other day." Stanley thought a minute. "I think we should both go and talk to her right now."

"Do you know how to get in touch with her?" Slade asked.

"She's here at the hospital now. I saw her in the corridor before I came out here."

"Let's go," Neil said as both stood and headed for the door.

Dr. Reza Ahern was in her office after making her rounds. She was looking at her computer monitor when both Stanley Hager and Neil Slade walked in. She always worked with her door open and the two never felt the need to knock. When she saw Hager and Slade she knew something was up.

"Dr. Ahern, would it be alright if we talked to you?" Hager asked.

"Sure, please come in and close the door," she said.

"Maybe we could go out on the terrace and talk; it's such a beautiful day," Hager said as he held an index finger to his lips indicating not to talk anymore.

The three headed for the terrace. Once they were there and Stanley felt it was safe to talk he quickly informed Ahern of what had happened. The news shocked her. It was a little after one o'clock by the time Ahern got the full story of what had happened. She told the two doctors her patient lived in Prestonsburg, Kentucky. Ahern looked at Stanley and asked, "Do you think I should give him a call. I don't want to startle a patient but if you think I should then I will."

Stanley looked at Neil who gave him a nod. "Yes, I think you should but you can't use your office phone." To Neil's surprise Stanley reached into his jacket pocket and pulled out a brand new flip phone. As he reached it to Ahern he said, "I bought this on the way to work this morning. I used a prepaid card and plan on tossing the phone in the trash in a couple of days. No one knows about this phone."

Ahern took the phone and opened the cover; it was a very basic model without the fancy screen. She took out her own phone and looked up the number. She dialed as both Stanley and Neil looked around. Neil looked at his watch, one-twenty.

Rachel Bevins was glad to be back on the road after acquiring the blood sample from John Oden. She hated to admit it but she was scared to death while she was there. All had gone well though and she started to look forward to getting the next sample. She had used the GPS on her phone to find the Oden home and she was doing the same to find the home of Van Goodwin. He lived in Prestonsburg, almost a three hour drive. She settled in for the drive, it was nine forty-five.

Rachel drove slightly more than the speed limit which was posted at fifty-five. She made it to Prestonsburg a little before one o'clock after making one stop at a nice looking filling station in London to use the facilities and grab a Diet Coke. She hadn't made a wrong turn the entire day, 'Thank goodness for GPS,' she thought as she parked on the street in front of the house.

Rachel made sure to change the name tag; the second one read 'Beaumont General' on top and right under that was her new name 'Beverly Rush.' She climbed the front steps and pressed the doorbell. Seconds later the door was answered by a tall man who looked to be in his sixties. She introduced herself and told him why she was there. Van never suspected a thing, he just asked her to come inside. Van went to the dining room and pulled out one of the chairs. Beverly quickly took the blood sample and bandaged his arm.

Van looked at his arm and said, "It was really nice of the hospital to send someone out like this. It's quite a drive from Lexington."

"Well Mr. Goodwin, don't think anything of it. It was a nice day for a drive and I didn't mind at all," Beverly cheerfully said as she quickly put her things away. Van could tell she was in a hurry and he didn't mind at all. This was usually the time of day when he liked to take a little nap.

Beverly headed for the door and Van followed, he stood there as she descended the stairs. This was so much easier than the stop in Wayne County she thought.

"You drive careful now miss," Van said as his phone started to ring. He hurried back inside to answer it.

Beverly, aka Rachel opened her car door and waved to Van. "Thanks," was all she said as she got in and closed her door. She was resetting her GPS when she noticed Van step back out onto the porch. She never paid much attention as her GPS started giving her the first directions out of town.

Van watched her pull out and then went back inside and picked the phone back up. "No I couldn't catch her, she was already pulling out," he said. "Who did you say you were?"

Dr. Ahern hadn't introduced herself when Van answered the phone, she just asked if someone had been there requesting a blood sample from him. Van said yes, and told her to hold on a minute. He put the phone down and tried to catch the lady that had just taken his blood before she pulled out. He was too late.

"This is Dr. Ahern. I am sorry to bother you on a Saturday Mr. Goodwin but could you tell me what kind of car the woman was driving?" She asked.

"I sure can, it was a black Chevrolet," he told her.

"Can you hold on for just a second Mr. Goodwin?" She asked as she cupped her hand over the phone.

"The woman was just there but left a few seconds ago. She is driving a black Chevrolet," Ahern said.

Stanley looked at Neil, "Should we notify the local police and try to have them stop her?"

"I really don't think a description of 'Black Chevrolet' is going to get us anywhere," Neil told him.

Stanley agreed before turning back to Ahern. "Ask if the woman was wearing a name tag and what was on it. Also ask what she looked like."

Ahern put the phone back to her mouth and began asking questions. Before she hung up she assured Van that everything was alright but if anyone else came by asking for anything pertaining to his health to call the hospital and verify it. "Not to worry," was the last thing she said before hanging up.

She reached the phone back to Stanley. "Now what do we do," she asked.

Stanley looked at Neil. "We need to call the nursing home. My guess is she will head there next."

Neil looked at his watch. "It's a two hour drive back to Lexington. We can have the police there and have her arrested the minute she goes toward your patient. She will most likely have the other two samples in her car as evidence."

Stanley smiled, "Now you are starting to get with the program Doctor. Use my phone and make the call."

Neil opened the phone Stanley reached him and punched in the number. He could dial it from memory. After a few seconds he said, "Hello, this is Dr. Neil Slade. Would Sally Jenson be working today?" After a few seconds he said, "May I speak to her please?"

He put his hand over the phone and told Stanley and Ahern that a nurse familiar with his patient was on duty.

After a short time Slade said, "Hello, this is Dr. Slade......," before he could finish he was interrupted. He listened intently.

"Dr. Slade, I was meaning to call you. Why did someone from the hospital come here this morning and take a blood sample from one of our patients?"

Neil could tell the nurse was upset. "I'm sorry but the hospital never sent anyone out, that's why I called. Someone had already taken samples from two of our discharged patients and we were hoping they hadn't been to River Terrace yet. Did anyone get a description of the person?"

"You didn't send anyone. I was told the person wore a Beaumont General name tag. I checked the register when I came in at nine and it was signed by a Sharon Hensley. Is there anyone at your hospital by that name?"

"I will check and see but probably not. The first patient this morning gave us a name that didn't come up in any employee records. I'm sorry about this but please remember the hospital doesn't send anyone out to collect blood samples. Did anyone get a good look at the woman?" Slade was silent as he listened.

"Finding out what she looked like hasn't been a priority until now, I'll check as soon as we hang up, anything else?" Nurse Sally asked.

"What time was she there?" Slade asked.

Sally was at the front desk and looked at the sign in sheet. "It says here six forty-five."

Now Slade asked the question he already knew the answer to. "Nurse, who did this woman take the blood samples from?"

Slade listened and then said he would call back in a little while. He turned to the other two doctors and said, "The patient that the blood sample was taken from was Helen Montgomery." He reached the phone back to Stanley. "We didn't catch this person because the nursing home wasn't the last stop of the day, it was the first."

Ahern thought about a course of action as Stanley and Neil stewed about the fact that they hadn't caught the perpetrator. "Call the nursing home back and see if the patient or any of the staff can give a more complete description of the woman. What she was wearing, how her hair looked, how tall she was. Also ask if she had any kind of accent." The two men looked at the doctor and wondered why either of them hadn't thought of this little idea.

Stanley reached the phone back to Neil, "Here you go, just hit redial."

Neil gave Stanley a look that said he knew how to work a damn cell phone. After Neil looked at it for the briefest time Stanley took it back and hit the redial button. Neil looked embarrassed as he grabbed the phone again. "Hello, this is Dr. Slade again, is Sally Jenson still there?"

Within seconds Sally was back at the phone. "Yes Dr. Slade, you requested me again."

"Sally, did anyone actually talk to this imposter. If so find out if they can describe her. Also see if Helen Montgomery can shed some light on this but be very careful. She cannot, under any circumstances, find out that someone took her blood sample and that same someone wasn't an employee of the hospital."

"I understand doctor. I will check but some of the people I need to talk to have already gone home for the day. I will also check if any of the security cameras might have recorded her. The cameras are not in the rooms due to patient privacy. I know there are cameras in the rec room and on the terrace but not much else," Sally said.

Neil smiled; he hadn't considered the security cameras. "Thanks Sally. Let me know if you find out anything." He hung up and reached the phone back to Stanley.

Rachel Bevins drove the Mountain Parkway back to Lexington that Saturday afternoon. Construction on the road reduced traffic to thirty-five miles an hour in some places and forty-five in others. She really didn't mind, it gave her time to think about her bonus and how she was going to use it. In all she would drive a total of nearly four-hundred miles today.

To have accomplished this without getting caught gave her an immense feeling of relief. She used the cell phone Cal had given her to send a coded message; the package would be at the drop off at the designated time this evening, five-o'clock. The sooner she was rid of the three samples the sooner she got her bonus. Not only that, she felt vulnerable having the samples in her car. It was evidence, she was sure she had broken some laws today and the sooner the evidence was out of her car the safer she would be.

By six-thirty that evening she went to her mailbox and opened it with her key. Inside was a very thick envelope, actually there were five of them, each containing five thick bundles of hundred dollar bills. She stuffed the five envelopes into a shopping bag she had brought just for the occasion and hurried back inside her apartment. Today had been a good day.

Helen Montgomery had spent the day talking with her friends and catching up on months of news that she had missed. A few of her friends had moved back with family or to other facilities. Some had passed away and Helen felt both sad at their passing and also glad that their suffering was now over. After supper that Saturday evening Sally Jenson came into her room and asked if she could have a little talk.

"Why that would be nice Nurse Sally. Please pull that chair over by the window."

Sally did as Helen had asked. The two women were sitting with their knees not more than six inches apart. Rooms at nursing homes were not noted for being spacious.

"What would you like to talk about?" Helen asked.

Sally had tried to figure out a way to broach the subject of the outlaw blood sample without alarming Helen but finally decided to just start talking and then try to work it in. When Sally sat down she noticed the blue bandage on Helen's arm and decided to just dive right in. "I saw in your paperwork today that you gave a blood sample."

Helen held out her arm and looked at the dark blue elastic tape. She gently touched it with her other hand and said, "Yes, early this morning. I always wake up early and I had no more gotten my hair fixed and my teeth brushed when I was told I had a visitor. A nice lady came and said she was with the hospital and needed a blood sample. She was such a nice lady."

Sally watched Helen and noticed when she called the woman who took the blood a nice lady she looked away. She had said 'nice lady' twice and both times she had looked away. "Did the lady that took your blood give you her name?"

"Oh yes, she wore a hospital name tag on her shirt. Her name was Sharon Hensley, such a nice lady." Again Helen lowered her eyes. She had told herself that she wasn't going to judge people again. She had felt the same bad feeling when Sharon had taken her blood as when the nurse at the hospital had come into her room. It was the very same feeling she got from Rachel Bevins. Strangest thing was they both looked similar in some ways. Rachel was much prettier and knew how to fix her hair real nice whereas Sharon Hensley looked as if she had just gotten out of bed and then driven straight to the nursing home.

"Helen, did you recognize this woman, this Sharon Hensley? Had you seen her before, either here at the nursing home or at the hospital while you were there a few days ago?" Sally asked.

Helen thought for a while before answering. It wasn't in her nature to ever lie, it wasn't something she had ever done and she wasn't going to do it now. "I don't think I have ever seen her before Nurse Sally but she does remind me of someone I saw at the hospital. The two are so similar it's almost scary."

Now Sally was getting somewhere. Maybe Helen knew something after all. "Well, who does she remind you of at the hospital Helen, maybe I know her."

"While I was there several days ago the nurse that took care of me, I think she would be called the night nurse, well, the woman this morning looked a lot like her."

"What is her name Helen, the woman that works at the hospital?" Sally asked.

"Her name is Rachel but I don't know her last name, I'm not sure I ever knew. The only name she wrote on the little chalk board was Rachel. Why do you want to know?"

"Oh, I just wanted to know is all? Nothing more than conversation, ever since you've been feeling better I just wanted to spend a little time with you. I wanted to hear you speak Helen. You were silent for so long and now you can talk, you can say what you think. You couldn't do that for such a long time," Sally told her.

"Nurse Sally, I could hear you talking to me while I was dreaming. All those months you said I was unresponsive I could hear everything you said but couldn't answer. It was like I was dreaming but was awake at the same time. You know a dream can be so vivid sometimes but when you wake up you can't remember much."

Helen looked Sally in the eyes and continued, "I remember everything you said Sally and I want to thank you. Some of the nurses would come in and never say a thing. They weren't mean or anything like that, they just never said anything. All those months when you came into my room you never failed to smile and say something nice. I couldn't see your smile but I heard it in your voice. When you were in my room for a while you would speak to me the whole time and I loved you for it. I imagined you were my daughter and you were spending time with your mother. Oh I guess I'm just a foolish old woman for sharing this with you." Helen looked up and saw Sally had tears running down her cheeks.

Sally leaned over and put her arms around Helen. "That is the nicest thing anyone has ever said to me Helen. I am so glad you finally woke up." Both women had tears in their eyes now.

Sally told Helen she would be back to check on her before the end of her shift. As soon as she was back at the Nurse's station she looked up the number for Dr. Slade's cell phone and dialed it. On the second ring Slade answered. He saw it was the nursing home and hoped it was good news.

"Hello, this is Dr. Slade."

"Dr. Slade this is Sally Jenson at the nursing home. I have a clue as to what the woman might look like. Check for a nurse named Rachel. I don't have a last name but she was one of the floor nurses that took care of Helen Montgomery, she worked nights. Helen said the woman who was at the nursing home this morning and took the blood sample looked a lot like this Rachel person."

"Thanks Sally. I don't know if it will help much but I will check into it first thing Monday morning. Did you find anything on any of the security cameras?"

"I checked doctor but none of our cameras were in the corridor where Helen's room is. I plan on going to the administrator first thing Monday and requesting additional cameras be put in all the corridors and one at the check in counter," Sally said.

"That won't help us with our current situation but it may help out in the future," Slade told her. "I'll talk to you Monday."

Slade put away his cell and headed for his car. He wondered how Sheila had spent her Saturday. On the way home he stopped and picked up a yellow rose and a bottle of wine. It was almost seven o'clock when he pulled into the garage and as the door was going down his wife came out of the house with a smile on her face.

"Well I never expected to see that smile this weekend," Neil said.

Sheila put her arms around his neck and asked, "Does your leaving me alone on our Saturday have anything to do with your miracle patient?"

"Actually it does," Neil said as he reached Sheila the rose and wine.

Sheila started laughing. "Well at least I did get a flower. The other woman got flowers and a fruit tray as I recall."

"Well I did bring wine, which has got to count for something," he told her.

"Come inside and tell me what happened today." She took Neil's hand and they both went inside.

It took Neil almost an hour to fill in all the gaps of the day. When finished he got the wine out of the ice and undid the cork. As they sampled the wine Sheila figured out how to proceed.

"The filling station at the corner shares the same entrance as the nursing home. If you look at their camera footage at the same time as this mystery woman was driving in and shortly after driving out you can get a description of the car and maybe even the license number. You know those convenient stores like to get license numbers to match to their drive-offs."

Neil looked at his wife and was speechless. After a minute Sheila began laughing. "You mean you never considered getting the camera footage from the filling station?" She asked.

"Actually it never crossed my mind. Next time I need to go to the office on a Saturday you are going with me," he said.

"Well, another thing you might not have thought of is the convenient store might not want to share the video footage with the nursing home, it might require either a squad car or a judge's signature to see it," Sheila said as she smiled at her husband.

"Did you take a few classes other than medical while you were in school or did you change your major?" He asked her.

"I might have watched Perry Mason a time or two," she said and then burst out laughing again.

"Perry Mason huh? Perry Mason couldn't hold a flashlight for you," Slade told his wife.

Stu got the call around two o'clock on Saturday. Rachel Bevins had acquired all three blood samples for the Reanimates. The courier was notified that the drop would be ready for pick-up sometime after four o'clock that afternoon. The courier grabbed a paper sack of food from a fast food joint and then shadowed the box. At five minutes after four o'clock he saw the drop being made by an attractive woman wearing scrubs. He waited fifteen minutes and as he did he monitored everything within sight of the drop box.

When he felt enough time had passed he used his key and removed the package and left another. As he was pulling into the back lot at New Circle Rachel opened her box and extracted her package. Stu notified Hells Bells, the package had arrived.

A call was made and PT arranged for a corporate jet to be dispatched to Bluegrass Field. The staff at the Hartford laboratories was put on standby and told to expect the package that night around midnight. Eighteen hours after Rachel Bevins had started her day the three blood samples she had, more or less, stolen were delivered to the Hartford lab.

After arrangements had been made for deliveries of the three samples, Jason Freemont and Alex Trivett had a sit down talk about what to do with the mole that worked inside Beaumont Regional Hospital, Rachel Bevins. It was suggested by Trivett that Mrs. Bevins meet with an unfortunate accident. He feared she might be capable of creating a problem, primarily blackmail.

"Blackmail Alex, and just who would she blackmail?"

"This woman is smart Jason. She figured out which patients to pull the files on. She figured out how to get the information out of the hospital and she managed to acquire all three of the Reanimate blood samples without getting caught. If she figures out how much her information is really worth then she might come back for more money."

Jason got up from his desk. It was late and it had been a very long day. He had known about the attempt to acquire the three samples and found himself worried at times throughout the day. It was now seven o'clock and the samples were safely being flown to Hartford on a company jet. It was time for a drink, either to celebrate or to calm his nerves, he didn't care. He went to the credenza and opened a decanter of Scotch. He poured two crystal glasses and carried one back to Trivett. "Have a drink Alex, I think you need it."

"I know what you're thinking Jason; she doesn't know who she acquired the files for. I am a numbers guy, you know this. I look at everything in columns of probability and I'm telling you this woman has the ability to cause us trouble." Alex took a small sip of the Scotch and grimaced, he wasn't much of a drinker.

Jason sat back down and looked across the desk. "What would make you feel better Alex?" He asked as he swirled the Scotch.

Alex leaned forward, "You know what I think Jason. We are on the verge of something spectacular here. If the projections from our analysts in Hartford are even half correct we may be sitting on the goose that laid the golden egg. This is nothing less than Biblical in proportion. It's like the Second Coming of Christ."

Jason enjoyed listening to Alex. Numbers guys always looked at everything in real time. Numbers didn't lie, they were real and the results were always solid. "Tell you what; we don't do anything right now. We keep a close watch and if we see that something might be running amiss then we make the move. If it makes you feel better I'll make the call to Hells Bells and have him put together a couple of plans. If Bevins varies from the center line, even in the slightest, HB will get the call. Does that make you feel any better?"

Alex continued to swirl his Scotch. "You're leaving a potential problem in our wake." He thought about any other options but knew he wouldn't be able to sway Jason. "You are better at things like this Jason than I am. I will defer to your judgement but if a problem presents itself I expect Bevins to be dealt with."

Jason held his glass up in a mock toast and then took a sip. "Agreed," was all he said.

Monday morning dawned overcast and cool, really cool. Neil Slade had to use the heater in his Audi on the way to work. He pulled into the staff parking section and locked his car, it was six-forty. As he was heading for the elevator he noticed Stanley Hager standing in the shadows, he was holding a large coffee in his right hand, Starbucks.

"Is that you Stanley?" Was all Slade said.

Stanley stepped out of the shadows and headed for the elevator with Neil. "Has anything happened since I saw you Saturday Neil?"

Neil noticed Stanley was nervous again, he was clean shaven but his clothes looked as if they had been slept in. "Stanley, what's going on. You look a mess."

They both stepped into the elevator and Neil punched the button for the second floor. As the doors closed Stanley stepped closer. "Has anything happened since I saw you Saturday?"

Neil knew by the way Stanley was acting that something was terribly wrong. "Nothing Stanley, what's happened and why are you acting this way?"

Even though they were in the elevator alone Stanley still cut his eyes left and right. When he saw the ceiling mounted security camera he held a finger in front of his lips. "We can't talk here. Meet me on the terrace in ten minutes." As soon as the doors opened he stepped out and headed down the corridor. Neil was so alarmed by the way Stanley had acted he almost let the elevator doors close on him. He hit the door open button and stepped into the corridor, Stanley was gone.

Neil went straight to his office and hung up his coat and threw his gloves on top of the desk. He sat down and looked at the phone on his desk and then at his computer monitor. As he sat there he looked up, not for any particular reason but just to look up, and there it was.

Neil stood and walked to the door. He closed it and then looked back at the ceiling. There, in the corner behind his desk and to the left, was the smallest of devices. It looked like the end of a felt tipped pen. He wondered if it had been there all along and he had just now noticed it for the first time. As he wondered about the device and how long it had been there, he thought of something. Sheila had been in his office a few weeks ago and while there she had asked to use his cell phone, she said she had left her phone in the car. After she made her call and before she reached the phone back to him she held it up to her face and said, "Smile." As Neil looked up from his desk she took his picture with his cell phone's camera.

As he sat there thinking he looked at his planner. His wife had been there two weeks earlier, it was in his planner because they had plans for lunch and he had written it down so as not to forget. He took out his phone and went into the photo log. He scrolled down a few pictures and there was the shot. She had been seated so the picture got all of his face plus the back wall and part of the ceiling. There in the upper left hand corner was the spot where the device now was, it wasn't in the picture. It had been installed within the last few weeks. It could only be one thing, a camera.

Neil got up from his desk and headed for the terrace. As he walked he realized that Stanley's suspicions were correct, someone was watching and listening. When he made it to the terrace Stanley was sitting at a table sipping on a paper cup of coffee, not Starbucks this time. Neil walked up and sat down.

"What has happened Stanley?"

Again Stanley looked around before looking back at Neil. "My home has been bugged and I believe my car has too. Did you notice anything new in your office this morning?" Stanley asked.

Neil was the one looking around now. "As a matter of fact I did. There is something in a corner of the ceiling, small and inconspicuous."

"It's a video camera. I noticed one in my office late yesterday and Dr. Ahern has one in her office too. As far as I can tell they were installed sometime over the weekend."

"I think it's time we went to administration and got some answers," Neil said.

Stanley shook his no. "We can't do that. I believe administration is involved."

"That can't be Stanley. Why would administration be involved in wiretapping the doctors who work here?"

"They aren't wiretapping all the doctors, just the three of us, the ones who have the extraordinary patients."

"This doesn't make any sense. Why would someone be bugging your home and car and also your office? How do you know all this?" Neil asked.

"My son-in-law called me late Saturday after we left here. He told me to go and buy a new cell phone and to use cash for the purchase. He said once I had the phone to go to a public place and call him back, not to talk while I was in my car. I did what he told me to do and then called him back. He told me he was able to insert some software into the hospital's main server. He did this from his own laptop. He is extremely good at this kind of stuff. Anyway he said the hospital computers are not as secure as they might think and within hours he was able to isolate a software system that didn't belong there. Some of his buddies are helping him; they are calling this a training operation. His commanding officer is a major and he went to him for clearance, it was granted."

"Wait a minute Stanley, you just confused me. Are you telling me the military has hacked into Beaumont General's database? I just can't believe that."

"Neil, would you just hear me out? It isn't the military; it's the Department of Homeland Security. They have a big cybercrimes department and my son-in-law works for a branch of the military that investigates this sort of thing. He works for the military but answers to Homeland Security. Anyway this is bigger than I first thought. Whoever is doing this has resources and the people working for them are extremely talented. Everything points to a foreign entity but Todd said that wasn't unusual. Lots of homegrown cybercrime is routed through foreign countries in order to hide their true identity."

"Who do they think it is?" Neil asked.

"They are working on it. In the meantime I was told to notify you and Ahern about the bugs. Both of you are probably under observation. Don't use the phones in your homes or offices if you intend to talk about this. Watch what you say even if you are in your car."

On Monday morning, October 30th, everyone at New Circle was in high gear. Normally three teams consisting of two men each were rotating in and out of Floyd and Pike counties but for this coming Wednesday that number would be increased by four. Two teams would stake out the Blood Center for the ten-o'clock donation and five more would be used for the operation at Slade where the van carrying the samples would be stolen. The two Pikeville teams and possibly a third would shadow the courier van and set up the time frame for the heist.

If for some reason the van driver bypassed the convenient store where he usually stopped for coffee then a secondary plan was in place. A sniper was stationed one half mile past the Slade turnoff. If it became apparent that the van wasn't going to stop he would be notified via two way radio. He had a scoped Bushmaster .223/.556 with a silencer. Once he got the signal he would wait for the van to approach and take out the passenger side rear tire.

Once the van was beside the road a team would pull up from behind and disable the driver with a stun gun. The blown rear tire could be replaced in two and a half minutes and the van would then be driven to the waiting box truck and loaded for transfer. If it went this far it was decided to dump the driver's body in the river, it would still support the carjacking scenario. The stop at the Slade Convenient Store was one stop the unsuspecting driver had better make.

Stu notified Hells Bells that there was suspicion at Beaumont General concerning the three blood samples acquired Saturday. He had listening devices in three of the offices at the hospital and as of the previous Friday night he now had video. It was apparent that some of the doctors had found out about the blood samples being taken. The only good news about this was the fact that Rachel Bevins hadn't been implicated yet but it was only a matter of time. With an operation of this size and the amounts of money to be made the news didn't bode well for Bevins.

Hells Bells thought over his options and decided to contact PT. "We have movement on the three acquisitions. Our operative is hours away from being revealed." This was all HB said, anyone monitoring the call would just think it was some sort of business deal.

"Give me twenty minutes. Have Stu secure a line for response." PT hung up and dialed Jason Freemont.

Once he was assured the line was secure PT informed his boss about the investigation by some doctors into the three blood samples Rachel had taken two days prior. Jason realized Alex Trivett was right after all. PT was instructed to secure the situation. This was all Freemont said before hanging up.

PT knew at once what had to be done and it needed to be done very fast. He sent a code to HB; it consisted of 10-30 RB immediate. It stood for October 30th Rachel Bevins now. HB knew what to do. In anticipation of such an order three different plans had been devised with a coordinating level of safety. The least advisable plan had only a sixty percent chance of succeeding without problems. The best plan had been run through Stu's computers and had a ninety-three percent chance of success. This was the plan that was set into motion ten minutes after HB got the go ahead from Chicago.

The nursing home contacted the convenient store that shared the entrance to the property. They were more than happy to assist once it was explained that someone, posing as a nurse, had come onto the property and took an unauthorized blood sample from a patient. The station was one of a very large chain and the video equipment they used was some of the latest and most sophisticated on the market. It had just been upgraded two months prior. The local police department was notified and they were the ones who actually picked up the disc from the station that contained the video.

The camera angles from the awning of the station gave a very good view of the street which turned into the nursing home's front entrance. The video was loaded into the computer at the police station and with very little enhancement a license plate number was obtained. The time the car drove by the station and then when it left matched the operational curve they were looking for. There were also no other cars either entering or leaving the nursing home at such an early hour on a Saturday. The license plate number they obtained had to be of the woman's car who had taken the blood.

The plates were run and the match came back as one Rachel Bevins, address Lexington, Kentucky. A call was placed to the nursing home and the information given to the administrator. If they wanted to press charges then a warrant could be obtained in less than an hour for the arrest of Rachel Bevins. Little did the Police Department know but an arrest warrant wouldn't be necessary, Rachel wouldn't live long enough to have it served.

The nursing home said to go ahead and obtain the arrest warrant. They also contacted Neil Slade and Stanley Hager at Beaumont General. The two doctors went straight to personnel with the name they had been given. Rachel Bevins was an employee of the hospital, she was a registered nurse and it was found she had been the floor supervising nurse for Helen Montgomery earlier the previous week.

Back out on the veranda Neil asked if they should go to administration. Again Stanley was afraid. "I still don't know if administration is involved in this or not. I say we wait until she comes in for her shift this evening at six-o'clock. We get her to the side and have us a little chat. She tells us everything she knows and we promise to not go to anyone in Administration." Stanley thought a minute before adding, "I think we should have a couple of the hospital security staff nearby just in case. What do you think?"

"We can't do that Stanley. If we find she was the one that took the three samples then we have to go to the higher-ups. If something comes of this and it is found out that we knew and did nothing then we might be taking on a level of risk ourselves."

"No Neil, that won't happen. If anything comes of this then we are in the clear. Remember we are the ones who discovered the problem and are trying to get to the bottom of it. We talk to Rachel Bevins and we only promise her we won't go to administration, we will go to the police. What she has done is illegal. There are at least four different laws she broke when she took the blood samples," Stanley said.

Now Neil was suspicious, "Four different laws Stanley, how do you know this?"

Stanley smiled, "I Googled it."

Neil had to suppress a laugh. "You and I are doctors; I don't think either of us should presume to know anything about the law."

Stanley grabbed Neil by the shoulder, "I Google stuff all the time." As he said this he realized it added nothing to his side of the argument.

Neil thought a second. "I like it. I'm still not convinced that your Google information is correct but that is beside the point. We get the information from Racheal Bevins by promising to not tell anyone at the hospital but that doesn't mean we aren't going to contact someone else. She might just tell us what is going on, and if she doesn't then the police can give it a try."

Stanley's eyes took on the enthusiasm of a child. He actually rubbed his palms together as he said, "They can take her into one of those small dark rooms with only one light on a table. When they shine that light in her eyes she will confess to everything."

"How do you know stuff like that Stanley?" Neil asked.

"I saw it in a movie; police do stuff like that all the time."

Neil knew Stanley was a good doctor. What Neil hadn't known was that Stanley had very little in the way of common sense. He had known other medical professionals who could work miracles in a lab or an operating room but had trouble putting gas in their cars. He supposed people who spent their entire life reading medical journals were mostly helpless outside their chosen field.

Rachel Bevins felt very secure with her newfound wealth. She spent Sunday night at home watching television and checking cruises on line. She hadn't been on a boat in over seven years and felt now was a good time to start thinking about her next vacation, excess money will do that to a person. She really liked the Alaskan cruises but knew that would be something for summer. What she wanted now was something in the Caribbean, maybe three or four days in all. She would need to coordinate the trip with her boyfriend who was also trying to use up his last week of vacation before the end of the year. The thoughts of a few days in the tropical sun brought a smile to her face.

She had been off both Saturday night and Sunday night and wasn't scheduled to be back at the hospital until six o'clock Monday evening. Rachel slept late Monday morning and was reading the Monday edition of the Lexington Herald Leader when her phone rang. It was Cal wanting to set up a meeting for lunch with regards to some more work. Rachel thought about the bonus she had gotten Saturday and how smoothly everything had gone that day. She agreed to meet and asked where. 'Hall's on the River' was suggested and the two could ride to the restaurant together.

Rachel got ready and waited for Cal to pull up outside. She was told by Cal that she would be driving a five series BMW. At fifteen minutes after noon the car pulled up and parked in front of Rachel's apartment. Rachel saw the car and went outside. As she walked to the curb she noticed the darkly tinted windows. Why was it that people who drove BMWs always hid behind heavily tinted glass? Rachel opened the door and got inside. When she turned toward the driver she saw Cal sitting there with a funny smile on her face. There was movement in the back seat but before Rachel could turn to see who it was she felt the stun gun in her side. That was the last thing Rachel remembered, forever.

The BMW pulled from the curb and proceeded out of town following all the posted speed limits. That night the BMW was in thousands of different pieces going to thirteen different states to be sold as spare parts for use in repairs. There were no spare parts that could have repaired Rachel.

Both Neil Slade and Stanley Hager stayed at the hospital late Monday in hopes of talking to Rachel Bevins. By seven that night it was apparent she wasn't going to show. Human Resources tried her apartment and when she never answered they left a message. They tried her cell phone and when that also failed they left another message and then went about the task of filling her shift for the night. A note was put in her file that only stated 'No Call No Show, 10.30.2017.'

Neil and Stanley both assumed Rachel must have gotten wind of their suspicions and that was the reason she never came in for her shift. They decided to contact the nursing home and let them fill out the police report. After that the warrant would be issued and she would be picked up. The two doctors went home disappointed they hadn't gotten any information from Rachel Bevins themselves. It had been decided that since Neil actually had a patient there and Stanley didn't, the obligation of calling the nursing home would fall to Neil. Hager knew no one there and Neil decided Staley's people skills were somewhat lacking anyway.

"Let the police handle it," Hager said. "When you call the nursing home see if they can keep us updated. If they find out anything tonight you can tell me all about it first thing in the morning."

As the two men left the parking garage Neil thought about calling the nursing home from his car. Then he remembered what Stanley had told him about all the bugs and decided against it. He stopped at a convenience store and bought a disposable phone. He paid with cash and before getting back in the Audi he dialed the nursing home and told them to have the police get the warrant. As he put the phone into his pocket he stood and looked at his shiny Black car. He wondered if it really had listening devices somewhere inside. He had always loved the feel of the German made car but now dreaded getting back inside.

Neil waited at the convenience store long enough for Hager to get home and then pulled out and dialed his fancy little phone that no one knew anything about. "Hager it's me, Neil. Can you talk?"

Hager had just pulled into his garage and was getting out of his car. "Give me a second." He walked through the side door of the garage and into his backyard. "Go ahead."

"You say our cars are bugged. Is there a way we can find out for sure?"

Hager thought a minute. "I can ask Todd tonight. He is supposed to call me on this phone at nine."

Hager looked at the number Neil had used and asked, "Is this a new phone Neil?"

"Yes Stanley, I guess you have finally convinced me to be more cautious. I just bought it and am standing outside a filling station using it because I'm afraid to talk in my car. There has to be a way to have our cars checked."

Hager thought a second and said. "I'll know something soon; just don't take any chances, okay Neil."

"You got it Stanley; I'll see you in the morning." Both men hung up.

At 12:30 A.M, Tuesday morning, the Clark County Sheriff's Department got a call about a possible body in the river out near the rock quarry. Two cars were dispatched and a short time later a search and rescue team from the Winchester Fire Department was called. At 2:45 A.M the coroner was notified. Search and rescue had used boats and found the body about a quarter mile below where it had been spotted by two men fishing for catfish from the bank. They had been using a Coleman Lantern hung from a tree to attract the fish. When the body floated by they at first didn't know what it was, maybe a dead dear or something, maybe even a log. One of the men hurried to his truck and got a flashlight. When he got back to the riverbank and pointed the light into the water he knew at once what it was, deer and logs don't wear sweaters. They had to drive almost a mile before they got service and then used a cellphone to dial 911. The first patrol car got there in less than ten minutes and the second five minutes after that.

The two deputies wanted to see for themselves before notifying the Fire Department, it wouldn't be the first time someone mistook a floating log, or trash, to be that of a body. Within ten minutes one of the deputies used his radio to call it in, there was a body floating in the river.

Two aluminum boats on trailers had been dispatched along with the firefighters that were trained in such things. The boats were put in and ten minutes later the body was recovered. The State Police were notified and immediately took charge. The body would be sent to Frankfort for an autopsy. A detective was assigned to the case, he started his investigation and the body was listed as Jane Doe. It was the fourth alias Rachel Bevins had used since Saturday.

PT made sure the body had been dumped in Clark County, the neighboring county to Fayette where Rachel Bevins lived. It would add a layer of time to any investigation about her disappearance and subsequent murder. He didn't want the body to be positively identified until at least Thursday August 2nd.

Wednesday was going to be a very important day for the people who worked in Alterations and they didn't want the possibility of Rachel Bevins being identified until the next day. Wednesday was the day a sample of Samuel Edgemont's blood would be acquired, the murder of a nurse who worked in Lexington shouldn't pose a problem for the operation but it was still considered a risk. Bevins shouldn't be implicated as having anything to do with a project that few people knew anything about anyway. The trail back to anyone at Alterations would be impossible to trace, at least that was the hope.

If the body of Rachel Bevins wasn't positively identified by Thursday then it was decided to give the police an anonymous tip. By then the hijacking of the Blood Center van would have already taken place and the contents of that van would already be at the labs in Hartford. The murder would then serve its second purpose; it would be a warning to the staff at Beaumont General.

Samuel Edgemont had enjoyed his days since the October 24th dinner at Bertha Potter's house. Jillian had gone back to Columbus on that previous Thursday but she kept in touch. The two hadn't talked on the phone but did exchange e-mails daily. Hers were much more detailed and lengthy than Sam's and this suited both fine. Sam enjoyed reading what she sent, as each day went by he found himself wanting to hear from her. Jillian wrote long messages about her days and the weather. She also waited each afternoon before checking her in-box. His messages were more brief but contained what she wanted, a connection. As she read, she read in his voice, each word was spoken to her as if he were there. Both Jillian and Sam enjoyed the safety in this form of communication, it kept feelings at bay.

Sam told her about his platelet donation scheduled for Wednesday morning at 10:00. She had never donated blood before, much less platelets, it was just something she had never considered but as she read his words she realized it was something that was very important to him.

"How long have you been a donor?" Jillian asked.

"I started when I was eighteen. I actually went on my birthday."

"That's a long time. How many donations does this make for you?" She expected to hear ten or twelve, maybe fifteen at the most.

"I never started counting until five years ago when I moved to Prestonsburg. In that five years I've donated 125 times, this will make 126," Sam wrote. "I'm working on my 16th gallon.

Jillian looked at the screen and was astonished. She couldn't imagine a number this high. She had a friend that was so proud after he had given his first gallon which took eight donations over the span of four years, one hundred and twenty-six times seemed impossible. "I don't know what to think. That is such a large number, why do you do it?"

"I do it for the feeling I get after each donation. Donating has become an addiction for me. I know it is helping people I have never met and will probably never see in my life. I don't know how to explain it other than that."

"I admire you for it, you may never know who is out there walking around with your blood and they will never know you. This is such a noble thing you do," Jillian wrote.

Sam's gift had helped hundreds, if not thousands, of people. One donation doesn't just help one person, it helps several. There had been some miraculous recoveries in the past but these were attributed to other reasons than just receiving blood, plus no one was looking then as they were now. Doctors took credit, hospitals took credit. Until the 'Ponce de Leon' project, initiated by Beeler-Jordan, it was just assumed that some people were destined to heal and others were not. Beeler-Jordan had happened upon the project by sheer coincidence, not because of any real connection to Samuel Edgemont. It was just assumed by Beeler-Jordan that if someone had the proper biological makeup then why couldn't that someone benefit others?

Samuel Edgemont found sleep more difficult lately. He was getting up as much as an hour earlier than usual. After reading the paper and having two strong cups of coffee Sam grabbed his shower and then went to work Wednesday morning a little early. He had office hours from 8:00 until 9:15. He got to his Pikeville office at 7:15 and spent his time organizing for his afternoon classes. After office hours were over he headed to the Blood Center which was only ten minutes away. Since the events of two Wednesdays prior he scanned the parking lot for anything suspicious. He also looked over the lot of the adjacent motel to see if anything caught his eye, nothing looked out of the ordinary. He gathered his new paperback book and two magazines and walked in, the time was 9:50.

Sam would never know but his photo was taken at least fifteen times from the moment he locked his car until he entered the Blood Center. A room had been rented five days prior and in that room was a tripod which held a Nikon D7500 camera with a vibration reduction zoom lens.

The pictures were digital and would be sent to the offices at New Circle within minutes.

Another team posing as cable repairmen was stationed at the front of the building next to a telephone pole. They were in a utility work truck with a hydraulic bucket lift on the back. In the bottom of that bucket was another camera which could be maneuvered and angled remotely from inside the truck. At fifteen feet off the ground the camera could be zoomed in to monitor any of the platelet donation beds. Once it was determined that Sam was donating, the camera, which had a very fast shutter speed, would take a picture once a minute for the entire time he was hooked up to the machine. Once he was unhooked and allowed to leave, the man in the motel would snap more shots of him exiting the Blood Center.

As if this wasn't enough, a third team was stationed at the Dairy Queen to take a few more pictures as Sam left. By the time Sam made it back to his office no fewer than three hundred pictures had been taken and sent digitally to the offices on New Circle. It was doubtful if a runway model would have been photographed more in that short amount of time.

HB and Stu were extremely pleased with the events so far this day. Samuel Edgemont had donated and this could be verified without doubt. Three different teams were set to monitor the pick-up of the blood products later that day. Again a room would be used at the motel next door and another team would use the utility truck to video the driver and cargo. Still shots were going to be taken from the team in the motel but HB wanted actual video of the pickup. It was hoped that as the van pulled in and then turned to leave, a full 360 degree image could be obtained. As the teams arrived and began the wait for the van HB and Stu kept in constant contact, this wasn't the most critical portion of the operation but everyone knew as each piece fell into place there was a higher risk that the next phase might pose a problem.

One of Stu's favorite studies in college was that of statistics. He knew the popular belief was that if a hypothetical operation was broken into ten parts then the chance of a problem occurring could be broken down equally between the ten individual steps. In most studies it was determined that as each step was completed without a problem then ten percent of the chance of a problem occurring was eliminated. Stu never fell into that line of thinking.

He assumed if an operation had a ten percent chance of failure then as each of the ten steps was completed the original chance of failure fell equally to the remaining steps. He considered this as the X-Factor of the equation. Only toward the last few steps did the chance of a problem arising start to fall. He had even developed software to run his equations. It proved that as each of the ten steps was completed the X-Factor didn't fall a comparable ten percent. Using this as a basis he decided, with the approval of HB, to have more teams stationed as the day progressed. HB thought Stu was being overly cautious. This suited HB fine, failure might result in himself being listed as a John Doe floating in a river somewhere.

After Sam donated he went directly to the Dairy Queen near the donation center. He went inside and ordered a chicken salad and diet drink. He didn't know it but as he left he walked within three feet of a man and woman who were there to monitor his movements after leaving the Blood Center. As Sam walked back to his car the two threw their garbage in the bin by the door and headed to their own cars. They followed him as he went back to his office. When he parked he was photographed walking to the building where his office was located. He was easy to spot with the dark blue bandage around his left arm. The two were now tasked with staying there and monitoring whether Sam left early or stayed at work. It was important to know if he might leave early due to the effects of the donation.

As HB and Stu scanned the photos they were receiving Stu noticed something. He punched in some numbers on his keyboard and looked at the data in front of him. The temperature in Pikeville on this first day of November was thirty-six degrees. Stu pointed to the temperature and HB shrugged. "What does it mean Stu?"

Stu then pointed to a few of the photos of Sam as he entered and exited the Blood Center and another as he entered his office. "He is wearing short sleeves. Do you wear short sleeves in November when you know you are going to be outside?"

HB looked at what he and Stu were wearing. Both had long sleeves and they were inside. "I never noticed before but it does seem odd. When did you first notice this?"

"A few days ago, we have had teams getting pictures now for a couple of weeks. I have never seen the Primary wear a coat, a sweater, or a jacket at any time and never long sleeves."

HB thought a second as he scanned the pictures Stu was bringing up. "He doesn't get cold. Either he doesn't feel cold or he just doesn't care. Put together a file of these pictures along with the dates and times they were taken, include the temperature at the time each photo was taken. I'll put together a one page summary and send it along with the pictures to PT. This might be something they need to know. Samuel Edgemont seems to be impervious to cold."

Sam never left early on that Wednesday; in all the years he had donated he had never once experienced any side effects from the procedure. Lots of donors felt weak and some even went home to rest but this had never happened to Sam. He always put in his office and instructional hours on donation day and other than the wearing of the blue armband no one would have known he had donated. He had never experienced fatigue or light headedness. His arm never bled after he took the bandage off later in the day. There was never a bruise and he had never suffered from a blown vein in which the entire forearm might turn a deep purplish color. He always told himself that he was just one healthy puppy. If he only knew!

As Sam parked his car and hurried to his office he was mentally going through everything he had to do today. He had a class at 12:30 and wanted to be there at least ten minutes early. It was now 11:50 and he really hated to rush through the lunch he carried in his right hand. He also wanted to check his e-mail to see if Jillian had messaged him today. As he walked into his office he noticed a single red rose in a long stem vase setting in the center of his desk. There was a small envelope attached which contained a note written by the florist that delivered the flowers no doubt. He opened it and was surprised to see it was from Jillian. "A post donation rose to cheer the day, Jillian," was all the note said, but it was enough.

Sam sat his lunch down and reread the note. In all his time, and in all the women he had known, none had ever sent him a flower. Most of the women he knew were takers, it was apparent Jillian was not. He opened his laptop and went straight to mail, as he devoured his salad he wondered what to write. Finally, with great effort, he decided on what to say. "Dear Jillian, I just got in from my donation. The rose was the first thing I saw and the thought is much appreciated. Can't ever remember such a nice gesture because of a donation! I will message you tonight after class, Sam."

Fifteen minutes after Sam sent the e-mail Jillian read it. She had wanted to do something nice and finally decided on the rose. She found a flower shop in Pikeville and placed the order with instructions to deliver it between 10:00 and 11:00. It was important that it be there when he got back from his donation. Ever since she had read about his donations the previous evening she found it hard to put the thought out of her mind. Donating blood, or in Sam's case platelets, was such a generous thing to do. He got nothing in return except for the satisfaction of donating. She realized that she had found nothing at all about this man that was in the least way negative. Even her Aunt Bertha and the three bloodhounds she associated with knew nothing bad about him and according to Bertha it wasn't from a lack of trying.

Bertha Potter had been extremely pleased at her efforts concerning matchmaking. She was also pleased that not a single one of her friends had been able to dig up any dirt on Sam. It wasn't because they hadn't tried either. The three had contacted everyone in their little network of conspirators trying to see if they might have helped lead Jillian into a doomed friendship. They hadn't. Sam was held in the highest regard at his church and anyone who had ever met him could find only nice things to say. Bertha was very pleased that she had introduced the two. If it went no farther than a long distance friendship she would be happy, if it became more than friendship she would be ecstatic.

Aunt Bertha kept quizzing Jillian when she might be coming back to Kentucky for a visit. It hadn't even been a full week and yet she continued to ask. Bertha had a habit of calling twice a week and had done this for years. Jillian had always enjoyed the calls, her family tree had grown small in the last several years and her Aunt had become more important to her, partly due to the dwindling family and partly because she enjoyed talking to her so much. Bertha was a hoot.

Jillian said she couldn't take any more time from work at the moment. It seemed that as each day went by though she really wanted to get back to Kentucky to visit her aunt and also visit with Sam again. For someone she had only been introduced to a week ago she found herself thinking about him and his messages more and more. She wondered if Sam ever thought of her during the day.

Helen Montgomery spent her days at the nursing home talking with friends and sitting on the terrace. She did get some bad news on Tuesday October 31st. A friend she had known for years and who also lived at the nursing home had passed away. On Wednesday afternoon there was a memorial service held in her memory. Helen and most of the residents attended to say a final farewell. That evening Helen sat on the terrace and pondered this and that, what she mostly thought about was life. Her friend was only seventy-eight, four years younger than herself.

Helen had experienced improving health since coming out of her month's long dream. She even felt a little guilty that she was able to move about with the ease of a teenager while the other residents struggled with canes and walkers; a few were even forced to use wheelchairs. As she thought of the other residents she realized that many wouldn't be there in another year.

Helen wondered about her own circumstances. When she had been admitted to River Terrace a few years ago she, at that time, knew her memory was failing. Small things at first like not remembering to take her medication. Medication was important and she knew forgetting just wasn't acceptable. The event that triggered her admittance to River Terrace was the day she couldn't remember the code to activate her home's security system. As Helen had gotten older she had the security system installed to make her feel safe at night. Not being able to punch in the code left her feeling confused and scared. She had to have her security system.

Helen finally realized that going into the nursing home might be the best; at least she would have others around to take care of her. She just didn't want to be alone anymore. After being accepted she moved in and at first it seemed to slow the progression of her dementia. She strolled the halls and spent hours on the terrace for which the facility had gotten its name.

A few months into her stay her memory again started to fade. The staff kept her as busy as possible. She was put on a schedule that ran with military precision. Breakfast, lunch and dinner were always at the same time of day, never to vary more than a few minutes. Consistency not only kept the patients contented but it was also used to build a routine that hopefully would give a sense of security. No patient, especially the ones that suffered from loss of memory, were ever allowed more than thirty minutes alone. It was feared that isolation could push a dementia patient along at a faster pace. Even on the terrace where Helen loved to sit and watch nature she was always spoken to and asked if she needed anything at least twice an hour. Helen didn't mind the interruptions, she liked the fact that she was cared for.

Besides the terrace Helen spent time in the rec room where most of the other patients liked to watch television, read, or just play simple board games. There was always a thousand piece puzzle on one of the tables. Helen loved the puzzles and worked diligently to finish one no matter the pattern. It was good therapy.

Even with all the activities going on Helen at times missed her home in Floyd County. She missed her long haired cat Blackie the most. She missed so many things about her home that at times she almost wished she could go back. She would have these thoughts, thoughts that maybe she was getting better, that her memory was starting to improve. But then she would forget who she was talking too on the phone or where she had left her glasses. She could even be talking to someone as she worked the big puzzles and suddenly not know their names. She had accepted the move to the nursing home as a necessity; at the time she knew she would never go home again. The nursing home would be her home for the time she had left.

Even if Helen accepted the fact that she would never go home again at least she took comfort in the memories of home. She had been born and raised in Floyd County, Kentucky. Her home was in a small town of that county called Maytown. She and her husband had bought the land and built the house more than fifty years ago.

Now that she had gotten her memory back she was wondered who had taken care of it while she was in the nursing home. She would have preferred to have stayed in one of the nursing homes in Floyd County but she vaguely remembered that if she stayed there they would take her house and land. The property would be sold and the proceeds used for her care at the nursing home. Somehow Lexington would be better was all she could remember being told.

With all the memories now flooding back in Helen yearned to be home, a home her husband had built with his own two hands. Phillip was a coal miner; he worked more than thirty-five years in the mines. He had held many different jobs and titles while working for three different coal companies, the largest being an outfit called Island Creek Coal Company. He spent the last ten years of his working career as a tipple foreman. Helen liked it better for Phillip because he was outside all the time, not underground. Phillip retired at the age of sixty-five and died at the age of seventy-six. He had been gone now for eight years.

The Donor

Phillip and Helen had one child, a son who now lived in California. David had called nightly ever since he was told his mother was doing better and could actually hold a conversation on the phone. He had made arrangements to fly back to Kentucky the day the nursing home contacted him about his mother's remarkable recovery. Both he and his mother counted the days until he would arrive. Since the onset of the disease he had made the trip twice a year. Now he wanted to convince her to fly back to California where she could be nearer to him and her two grandchildren. Both grandchildren lived in California also and had their own families there. Helen had two great-grandchildren she had never met. David and his wife had it all figured out, all that was left to do was convince her to move west.

Helen had listened to her son as he told her all the reasons she would be happier out west. She considered the positives, being near her family and better weather. Being able to see her grandchildren, being able to do so many things she had given up on but now could do. She also considered the negatives, she would be away from the only real home she had ever known, the one she and her husband had built. She would also be losing all her friends who lived in Maytown. Sure it had been four years since she had seen most of them, which was all the more reason to hurry back to Floyd County. And then there was Blackie, her long haired cat. Blackie would now be nearly ten years old and Helen wondered if Blackie would remember her. Maybe cats are a little like elephants and never forget, she thought.

Helen felt the future held all sorts of possibilities for her. She felt the same way she had when she graduated from Maytown High School. She was scheduled to go to college in the fall in Lexington and the excitement was something real, she was ready to take on the world. Now, sixty-four years later she felt as if she wanted to take on the world again. The world she was thinking about was her home in Eastern Kentucky, it meant everything to her. She wanted to visit her husband's grave, decorate it with fresh flowers and touch the headstone. These thoughts brought her no sadness; everything now brought her joy, the joy of living again.

John and Nancy Oden were experiencing a new appreciation for life these days. John's health continued to improve and he was spending more and more time doing the things he liked, namely driving that big tractor around the farm. Once a week now the two drove into Somerset to take in a movie and eat at any of the numerous restaurants that lined the main road. Nancy felt as if her husband's new lease on life was the most wonderful thing. She joked about him looking younger and having more energy than she did. It was true, he got up early and stayed up late. He worked the farm and enjoyed the weekly trips to town for dinner and a movie, he was having fun. He laughed every time he told her that farmers weren't supposed to have fun.

They had gotten a call on Monday after the nurse had visited that Saturday to collect the blood sample from John. John and Nancy told everything that had happened including the time of day and what kind of car the woman was driving. They were given a phone number that could be dialed any time of day or night and be answered by a real person, not an automated message, if anyone else came by and said they were from the hospital. Both were told not to worry but were asked how soon John could come to the hospital for some follow-up tests. Nothing to worry about, but it was necessary. They agreed to come in the next day, Tuesday October 31st.

After they hung up John did what he usually did these days, found something positive to use the trip for.

"I think after we get the tests over with I am going to take you to Red Lobster for dinner. How does that sound. I have wanted that Admiral's Feast for the longest time and this is my chance," John told her.

Nancy was getting over the concern of the call and was happy her husband wasn't worried either. "That sounds nice John; I believe you are getting feisty in your older days," she told him.

"Now what makes you think either of us is getting old?" He winked at her when he said this. She blushed.

The Donor

Van Goodwin had also gotten a call on Monday morning. Someone from Beaumont General needed to talk about the woman who had stopped by Van's house Saturday and taken the blood sample. Again all the same questions that had been asked of John and Nancy Oden were asked of Van, description of the car, description of the woman, anything that might shed some light on who she was.

Finally, after being on the phone for nearly twenty minutes, Van was asked if he could come in for some tests. He would need to drive to Lexington for this.

Van thought a minute and asked, "Is it really necessary. Lexington is such a long drive."

"The tests are important Mr. Goodwin." The nurse conducting the interview had been instructed to not reveal that it was associated with the blood sample that had been taken Saturday. It had been agreed that the hospital might have a degree of exposure if any of the three patients discovered they had been poked and prodded by someone that wasn't a hospital employee. Beaumont General had some very good lawyers on retainer. Even though the three blood samples had been taken by someone who misrepresented their reasons and identity, a jury might still render a substantial verdict against the hospital if a trial ever came about. This was an unlikely event but lawyers are paid to anticipate unlikely events. The three patients were not to be told about the bogus blood samples.

Van asked when he should come in for the tests.

"We have openings tomorrow Mr. Goodwin. I promise it won't take long and everything is covered, you won't be out any expense at all."

How about driving two-hundred and fifty miles round trip and the expense of gas he thought to himself. It wasn't that Van was hurting for money, both his house and car were paid for and he had a good pension from the railroad. He just didn't like that drive. When his wife had been alive they made the drive to Lexington at least once a month just to get out of Prestonsburg for a day. They always ate someplace nice. Now the drive brought back memories of the way things used to be, namely the good times before his wife died. Maybe this trip would be good for him, he might even enjoy it.

"What time tomorrow?" He asked.

"I know it is quite a drive Mr. Goodwin but would nine o'clock be too early for you?" She asked.

"I'm an early riser, been that way since they put me on dialysis. Early doesn't bother me at all."

The nurse had Van's chart in front of her and something he had just said didn't make sense. "Did you say you are still on dialysis Mr. Goodwin?"

"Oh no, I only said I got used to getting up early because of dialysis. I've been off of dialysis ever since I had that bad spell a while back. No ma'am, everything is working just fine now. As a matter of fact I haven't felt this good in years. I've even started going back to the barber," Van said.

The nurse was now totally confused. "What do you mean you go to a barber Mr. Goodwin? I thought all men went to barbers?"

Van laughed. "Not if they're bald. I've been bald for at least ten years and it's just the damdest thing, my hair is coming back in as if I were a teenager again. I'm almost embarrassed to say this but I didn't even own a comb, haven't needed one in years. When I was doing a little grocery shopping a few weeks ago I had to buy me a comb and a bottle of shampoo. All my friends think I've started wearing a rug, you know one of those wigs for men. I think I liked it better when I didn't need to worry about hairstyle. It's been so long I couldn't even remember which side I parted my hair on. It's just the damdest thing."

It was all the nurse could do to keep from laughing. She didn't want to laugh at Van personally, it was just the way he said it. Most men would pay good money to get their hair back but here was a man who seemed to find it a burden. "Well, I expect to see you here tomorrow morning at nine o'clock and I better not see one hair out of place," she told Van.

This was too much for Van; he lost his breath laughing, the nurse laughed with him. When he finally recovered he told her he would be there and then said goodbye. After he hung up he had another laughing fit, it felt really good to laugh at himself again. It wasn't that many weeks ago that he had decided to stop dialysis and let death come after him. Now he had rallied and was enjoying life again with renewed gusto, new hair and all.

He stood and went to the closet where he kept his shirts and trousers. He felt like sprucing up a little for his trip tomorrow. He picked out a favorite shirt and a pair of pleated pants and headed for the ironing board. It took him nearly fifteen minutes to find the iron; he hadn't plugged that ornery thing in for at least three years. While he tried to iron, it seemed he had lost the touch; the shirt took him nearly fifteen minutes to iron and the pants another ten. He also burned a blister on his left thumb, a bad one. He didn't know it then but by six o'clock the next morning the blister would be completely healed, who would have imagined?

Van finished his ironing and then fixed himself a cup of coffee, decaffeinated, always decaffeinated after three in the evening. He added a little cream from the fridge and then headed to the swing on the front porch. As he sat and enjoyed the next to last day of October he thought about how close it was getting to November, where had this year gone?

At the Blood Center that Wednesday in Pikeville everything went as if it were just another day. The donors came and went. The staff joked and carried on a bit but did their jobs in a highly professional manner, they took their work seriously. The courier van came that evening to pick up the sealed boxes which contained the day's donations. It was the driver's second stop before heading toward Prestonsburg and then the Mountain Parkway. If the poor man knew how many people were watching and waiting he would have probably hidden under a desk.

The van pulled out at seven-o'clock sharp. He stopped at the local Speedway to fill up and also get a cup of coffee, he loved Speedway coffee. By seven-twenty he was back in the van and heading out of town, as he drove and sipped his coffee he wondered how long before the first frost. It was now November 1st and the first frost of the season usually came before the end of October, not this year. The closest it got was a week earlier when the temperature had gotten down to thirty-four degrees but there was a heavy fog that night and the frost just didn't show up.

Usually on November 15th of each year the Blood Center furnished him with an all-wheel drive SUV and he looked forward to driving something other than the van. Only two more weeks he told himself.

It was well past dark as he left Pikeville. The man driving the van was Hershel Rife and he had been driving for the Blood Center for seven years. In all that time he had never been involved in an accident, not even a fender bender. He had never gotten a speeding ticket or a parking ticket; it was a record he was proud of. Another reason to drive carefully was the bonus he got at the end of each year, fifteen-hundred dollars if his record stayed clean, one ticket or accident and no bonus. This late in the year he couldn't resist thoughts of spending the money, it was almost in hand.

Hershel was in Salyersville by eight-thirty and already starting to anticipate his stop at Slade. Drinking coffee made the stop necessary and the stop always made him crave more coffee, it was a vicious cycle that he enjoyed to the fullest, both needs helped to keep him awake as he drove. The Parkway had been undergoing extensive renovations for the last three years. The two lane portion was being upgraded to four lanes from Campton to Prestonsburg. The speed limit ranged from thirty-five to fifty-five miles an hour and the signs seemed to change from one speed limit to another as if by magic. The local cops in Salyersville liked nothing better than to ticket anyone going over the speed limit, which in a construction zone would double the fine.

Hershel knew every bump and curve on the Parkway; he drove it five days a week. A ticket would cost him not only the double fine but also his fifteen-hundred dollar bonus. Good luck catching Hershel, he drove no more than three miles over the posted speed limit and watched his speedometer religiously. Tonight would be the same as any other; he would make his shift and then be home by eleven-thirty, never later than midnight.

He didn't know it but he was being followed by two trail cars and led by another. There were three more cars at Slade along with the hidden box truck. A total of fourteen men were involved with the cars and the truck. Another two man team was positioned to take out the passenger side rear tire if the van didn't make the stop at Slade and sped on by. If that happened the operation would become more complicated. It was imperative that the contents of the van be acquired tonight.

Another reason for haste was the fact that Stu had identified the other company that had begun to snoop around the 'Ponce de Leon Project'. It was Steggman-Price, a notorious outfit noted for bad drugs and strong-arm tactics. Steggman-Price had connections with both the New York and Chicago crime families. They had always denied this and proof was never available but the shadows were there all the same.

Research and development at Steggman-Price was almost non-existent. Every spare dime of profit was used to fend off countless lawsuits and investigations. They used the same playbook as Beeler-Jordan, why invest in research when you can steal it. If Beeler-Jordan thought they were the only company that played hardball then they were sorely mistaken, Steggman-Price wrote the guidebook on dirty tricks.

The Steggman Group had clawed its way up from an obscure Pharmaceutical company to the number six spot, only two other companies stood between the two. Steggman knew more about its competition than any of the others knew about them. Corporate espionage was a mainstay at The Steggman Group.

Stu and Hells Bells assumed there was a mole somewhere in Beeler-Jordan but hadn't been able to find out who it was. Stu had been given the task of finding out how a competitor had found out about the 'Ponce de Leon Project' but so far had come up empty handed. About noon on Wednesday he managed to intercept something that startled both men and it was decided to inform PT. The fastest way was to just pick up the phone and call. Stu doubted he could actually secure the phone line because this new company had somehow managed to infiltrate the systems at New Circle. PT had to know regardless who was listening, the call would be made.

PT was in his office monitoring the situation that evening. When he got the call from HB earlier in the day he was astonished to hear that someone else had managed to breach the operation. "Do we know who is behind the breach?" He asked.

The question was asked of either man but HB felt compelled to answer. "There is a high probability that it is someone working for Steggman-Price."

PT thought a second as he considered all the worst case scenarios. "How serious is it?" He asked in an even voice.

HB and Stu were in the same office and each held a phone. HB nodded for Stu to take the question. "It's pretty bad sir. My security protocols noticed a shadow late yesterday afternoon. Nothing more than a few missing subtexts at first which could be mistaken for a system back-up which happens every sixty minutes throughout the day. I monitored all our programs throughout the night and really never had a reason to worry. The firewall was holding, no data was being taken. This morning, at precisely seven-fifty eight the entire program went into a system wide back-up and re-start. By the time all the monitors came back up someone was in but still not outwardly detectable. As the breach grew worse I had all the hard drives go into sleep mode until I could figure out if what was happening was something we had caused or if it was due to an outside event. Each time I isolated a hard drive and accessed it the situation had grown worse. Apparently whoever was attacking the firewall had managed to start some sort of sub-routine in the system. As of now I have a powerful program running to eliminate the alien software."

PT was disturbed by the breach but knew other companies had their own cyber-sleuths who were probably just as good as Stu. "How confident are you that your program can eliminate the breach?"

Stu answered, "It is very good sir. I have been working on it for years and the only copy is the one I developed. It is powerful and might even be able to ride the breach from our system back into the opposing computers. Even if they have the most sophisticated firewall available it shouldn't be able to stop my program. At the moment it is a hunter-gatherer so to speak. It is searching out the trail the other company used to invade our system."

"What happens when it discovers the trail?" PT asked.

"Once the opposing program is fully understood my Hunter-Gatherer software transitions into a Hunter-Killer, it will completely take down any computer that is associated with the breach. In the seconds before it destroys the other company's software it will steal every bit of information they have in those affected computers."

"I like the part about destroying the computers, what I don't like is the fact that this happened in the first place. What information have they gotten from us this morning?" PT asked.

Now HB decided to answer the question. "As far as we can tell they targeted the 'Ponce de Leon' Project. If they did intercept the files and manage to unlock the passwords then they could know everything."

"Even the operation that is to take place in a few hours?" PT asked.

"Assuming the worst and there is no reason to think otherwise, then I would say yes," HB said.

"How many field operatives do we have on this operation?" PT asked.

Stu answered, "Sixteen men sir. Two snipers if the van passes the Slade ramp to stop the van, two more in the box truck and six teams of two in six additional vehicles."

PT knew of Steggman-Price and he knew of their dirty tricks. He had been approached by Steggman a couple of years back but was afraid of their reputation. He would have gone to work for them anyway if Beeler-Jordan hadn't made him such a nice offer. "If they have had the files for twenty-four hours, and there is no reason to think otherwise, then how many men do you think they could field in Eastern Kentucky in that amount of time?"

HB wondered why PT would ask this question, he knew more about Steggman than anyone at New Circle. He felt compelled to give the answer he felt pertained to the situation. "With what is at stake I would say twenty maybe more. It's a logistical nightmare for them. They have operatives in the field in several states; we know this from our corporate research. But to pull them in on such short notice and put an operation together in such a short amount of time would be difficult if not damn near impossible."

PT looked at his watch; it was nearly two-o'clock. "Can we change the plan and do the pickup at any other place than Slade?"

HB had already run this through and didn't like what he came up with. "We can take the van anywhere on the Mountain Parkway but it could make things messy. We lose the safety that is built into the current plan. If we are spotted or if law enforcement is close by when we take down the van then people are going to die. We will still get the contents of the van but who knows how difficult it will be to get it safely away from the area."

PT knew he didn't want to quarterback this from his office in Chicago. He felt HB was better suited to run things from down there. "What do you suggest?" Was all he asked.

Without hesitation HB answered. "We proceed with the operation as planned. I have three more teams here and if you agree I want to send them down to help secure the area. Once the target van is loaded into the box we head it toward the drop point and have all the other teams run security just in case someone makes a try on the cargo. I strongly believe we can succeed given the sheer number of the personnel we have in the region."

PT didn't need long to think about it. "Proceed as planned and send the extra teams. Stu, what can you do to our competition?"

"Once the software transitions into Hunter-Killer then you will have your retribution, it will be fast and it will be severe," Stu said.

"Proceed as we have agreed," was all PT said as he hung up.

Little did the three men know but Steggman-Price had known about the plan for a little more than twenty-four hours. They had known about it for nearly a week thanks to the mole. The twenty man number HB thought Steggman could field in response to the computer breach was a pretty accurate number. It was eighteen and they had a plan of their own. The reason Steggman had such resources available for this operation wasn't totally because of the breach in Stu's computers but because of the woman who had supplied the files and then the three blood samples.

The Donor

If Cal was going to be so generous then why wouldn't someone else, Rachel Bevins thought. Being a nurse allowed her to hear a lot of gossip about drug companies. Steggman was notorious for stealing other company's information, all Rachel had to do was get online and ask a few questions, she had a deal with Steggman a full twenty four hours before Cal picked up the check for dinner.

When Cal had met with Rachel Bevins at the restaurant she didn't know it but Rachel was already working for the opposition. When Rachel acquired the three blood samples the previous Saturday she had taken two samples from each patient. The drop she made that same evening was the first of two, the second one payed a fifty-thousand dollar bonus. Rachel was very proud of her abilities to navigate through the layers of corporate greed that infested the pharmaceutical companies. She was proud of her abilities to work the second company into the plan. She was delighted; at least until the stun gun took away her awareness.

Rachel hadn't given any information about Beeler-Jordan or the attempt to steal the Blood Center van, she didn't have that information. Once she sold the other three blood samples, Steggman put all their resources into finding out everything they could about the project and the results were starting to pay off.

As darkness fell on the small town of Slade, Kentucky, two giant corporations were betting their futures, and the lives of many people, on who could snatch a small courier van away from an unknowing driver named Hershel Rife.

HB and Stu were confident that their plan would work. HB knew twenty-four hours wasn't enough time for Steggman to put together a plan and then find the people in the area to implement it.

The Steggman group hoped they had the upper hand; they weren't, as of yet, aware that Stu had discovered the breach in his systems. Steggman still had the advantage of being the underdog, Stu and HB didn't think Steggman could establish a counter operation in such short time. Both players were doing all they could but neither knew fully what the other was up to; Steggman might have a slight advantage. Tonight's operations would determine who would come out the winner and who would be the loser.

The box truck arrived at the predesignated location at eight-forty five. It was determined that the truck should be there at least twenty minutes before the courier van made it to Slade, any longer than that might invite trouble if someone spotted it in such a remote location. The two men inside were army veterans and knew how to take care of themselves. After about fifteen minutes the one who was in charge, Paul, got out of the truck to take care of some bladder work. As he walked to the rear and turned the corner he was jumped by a man wearing all black. In the darkness the only thing Paul could see was a glint of moonlight off the blade of a very sharp knife. As he brought his hands up in a defensive position the blade entered just below his chin and by the time it stopped it had pierced his chin, his tongue, and the roof of his mouth. As the blade sliced into his brain Paul went limp and fell straight to the ground, he never felt a thing.

The other man in the cab of the box truck never heard any noise as his accomplice was being killed. After a few minutes he stepped out to check on his friend. He never suspected any trouble, this was backwoods country and no one knew they were there. He too went around the rear of the truck and met the same fate as Paul. Both bodies were pulled into the timber and hidden with some tree branches. There were three men at the ambush site and two immediately put on the caps that Paul and his friend had worn. They also put on the two dead men's jackets, only one had a touch of blood on the sleeve but it was a dark colored jacket and the blood wasn't that noticeable. They checked and found neither man had a radio which was good news. They got inside the truck and found the keys still inserted in the ignition. A quick check in the back and the two ramps were found that would be used to drive the stolen courier van inside. Now all they had to do was wait, two in the cab and one hidden in the brush.

The Donor

All the trail cars followed Hershel from a distance as he approached the Slade exit. There was some apprehension as to whether the van would exit or drive on by. There was a collective sigh of relief as the right signal light came on and the van pulled off the Mountain Parkway. Hershel pulled the van into his usual spot at nine-twenty and went inside. There were already two cars there. Both had pulled in just seconds before Hershel and started pumping gas, very slowly. One man had gone into the bathroom and as soon as Hershel walked in he quickly went outside and headed straight for the van. Two more men had gone inside the restroom just before Hershel entered the front door. They had no intention of hurting Hershel; they just wanted to slow him down a bit. Hershel had to wait for the urinal to open up and then he had to wait to wash his hands, damn these guys were slow he thought.

The man tasked with the actual theft of the van had been practicing for almost a week. HB had rented a similar van and this was used for the practice. The key fob they had altered to match this van worked perfectly. It only took eight seconds to start the engine. As he backed away the two cars at the pumps started and began to pull out, they would assist in case the van was followed. It wasn't so they stayed to pick up the two men as they came from the bathroom. The van was well out of sight by the time the driver came from the restroom and headed for the coffee pot.

It had been determined that the stolen van would be driven and loaded into the box without being followed. Once the box was moving it would come back by the station and then enter the on ramp to the Mountain Parkway. At that point the two cars at the pumps would leave and drop in behind the box truck. It was estimated that it would take no more than ten minutes before the box would drive back by the station. In that amount of time the two men inside the convenient store would get coffee and snacks and pay with cash. The two men in the cars would wash windows and wait.

The man driving the stolen van turned into the small weeded road and then drove with his lights off. As he approached the box he saw that the back door was rolled up and the ramps were down and ready. He never stopped; he just eased the van inside, shut off the engine and set the emergency brake. He had to roll down a window to climb out of the van. As he did he never saw the man coming up behind him. Rather than kill him here in the box which would cause a lot of blood, he was stunned and then carried into the woods where his two dead accomplices were. Rather than kill him he was simply stunned again and left lying on the ground.

The door to the box truck was secured and locked. When the box made it back to the highway, instead of turning left, which would have taken it back by the convenient store where the other Beeler-Jordan cars were, they went right. Five miles away they turned off the road and into a field that was obscured from view by a tall stand of trees. There in the center of the field sat a helicopter. The courier van was opened and everything in the back was quickly loaded into the chopper. Less than twenty minutes after the van was stolen everything inside was airborne and heading due east away from the Mountain Parkway. No one would see the lights of the chopper as it took off; it was just too far away.

Hershel paid for his coffee, along with a couple of snacks, and headed for the door. Thirty seconds later he was back inside and told the lady working the register to call 911; his van had just been stolen. It took the police twenty-five minutes to get there and by that time the chopper carrying the stolen blood was nearly fifty miles away heading for a rendezvous point where a Cadillac Escalade waited to take the cargo to Bluegrass Field where a private jet was waiting. It had been deemed too risky to have the chopper land at the airport. It might give an investigator a lead.

The four Beeler-Jordan men at the station waited until the ten minutes were up. As each minute ticked by they grew nervous. At the fifteen minute mark they called Stu and let him know the box was late. He sent both cars in the direction of the box and told the men to report back immediately. Stu notified HB and they both waited. HB kept reassuring himself that there was no way The Steggman Group could have interfered with his plans.

The Donor

When the phone rang Stu answered and hoped it was just a bad battery or a flat tire, something that would explain the added time. Both Stu and HB were on the phone when they were told that two men were dead and another unconscious. The box was gone.

"Coordinate with all the units you have available. Start from the last known position of the box and search every road you come too. Call me back every fifteen minutes; I want that box truck found before the police get involved. Load the two bodies and bring them to New Circle. I'll figure out what to do with them after you get them here.

HB decided to wait at least an hour before calling PT. Maybe in that amount of time the box could be found. As HB waited Stu went into his systems and updated the virus he had planted into Steggman's systems that morning. HB gave him the go ahead to unleash hell on their mainframe. Within an hour Stu had managed to take down the entire operating system of the nation's sixth largest drug manufacture.

At ten forty-five HB got a call telling him that the box had been found. Eight men surrounded the vehicle with guns drawn. The courier van was in the back but it had been emptied. There were tracks where another vehicle had driven in and then left. There were also the unmistakable marks of landing gear where a helicopter had been sitting. It had knocked down the tall grass with its rotor wash when it had landed and then taken back off. There was no one there. The truck was taken away with the van still inside to be left for a chop shop, no need to give the authorities any clues about the theft.

PT was given the news, an hour after that he was on a plane heading to a meeting with Jason Freemont and Alex Trivett. The Steggman Group had managed to pull off a heist that a day earlier seemed impossible. They had the blood samples of the Primary. It wasn't known if they actually knew who the Primary was but it wouldn't take them long. They also had the three blood samples of the Reanimates, Stu had managed to pull that much out of the information his Hunter-Gatherer software had taken before crashing Steggman's systems. What had started out as a day of hope for Beeler-Jordan had now turned into a nightmare.

The corporate jet landed at a little after three in the morning. A car and driver were waiting. PT climbed in and thirty minutes later he was sitting in the austere offices of Jason Freemont. Alex was there in the office and there were three other men PT had never seen before waiting in the next room where they couldn't hear.

"Alright PT, tell us what happened," Jason said.

PT shifted nervously in his seat. "We had what we considered a solid plan. Extra people were in the area to oversee the operation and lend a hand if anything went wrong. We know it was Steggman but we don't have all the details yet. We lost some good people tonight, not to mention the total failure of the plan."

Freemont stood and walked to the front of his desk. "I don't care about the people you lost. What I care about is the samples you lost. And if that isn't bad enough you lost them to a competitor. Can you explain how Steggman found out about the operation?"

PT looked at Trivett. "Stu managed to install what he called a 'Lifter' in the Steggman mainframe just before the malware took down their entire database. He yanked volumes of information from them before his software disabled most of their systems. It will take time to go through and figure out how they knew so much so fast but he did get a name, the name of a mole."

Now Trivett spoke, "What was the name."

PT was on shaky ground here. He had called Stu just as his plane landed. The name Stu gave him seemed impossible at first but now it was starting to make sense. "It was you Mr. Trivett."

PT was giving a hard stare toward Alex. Freemont walked back behind his desk and sat down. "Stu is good PT. I wondered if he could figure out what was going on and it appears he has."

Alex Trivett never looked the least bit worried. "Jason is right; your man Stu is good. Jason and I got wind of another company snooping around the 'Ponce de Leon Project' a few months ago. Just a ghost, mind you, but the more we searched the more the ghost became real. We knew someone was selling us out, someone on the inside here at Beeler-Jordan.

We came up with a plan for me to make contact with the company we had good reason to believe was the ghost, Steggman.

"I had to give them something good in order to get their trust. They found it hard at first to believe the CFO of the third largest drug company in the United States would sell out his own company."

PT looked at Trivett with suspicion. "What did you give them?"

"It had to be something that was linked to 'Ponce de Leon' and it had to be verifiable. I gave them files on the Primary and the three Reanimates. Everything we have gathered so far," Trivett said.

PT clinched his fist, it was an involuntary reaction. Even if Freemont and Trivett were both in on this PT still found the need to strike out at someone. He looked at Trivett with his cold gray eyes and then shifted his gaze to Freemont. "Is this true, you gave away some of the most valuable information we have managed to acquire, information that has cost the lives of countless people." He was thinking of all the men at the security company he had killed, among others.

Freemont felt he was wasting time explaining something that wouldn't get back his samples. "The files Alex gave to Steggman were fakes, just a bunch of bogus information that wouldn't help anybody. The names we gave them are real people but not the right people. Our techs put together the files to make it look real. That, at the moment, is the only thing we've got going for us. Steggman will try to use the samples they have but they don't know which donors they came from. As far as we can tell they don't know the real names of the Primary or the three Reanimates. Also, that courier van carried the donations from two Blood Centers, Williamson, West Virginia and Pikeville, Kentucky. On a slow day that could be fifty donations. The donation containers go by a code, never is the name of a donor put on anything. The lab personnel at Steggman don't know which donations they are looking for."

PT exhaled and crossed his arms across his chest. "So where does this leave us?"

"Those three men in the other office are from The Steggman Group," Trivett said as he waved at the closed door.

Trivett then walked over, opened the door, and invited the three to join the conversation. PT rose from his seat. Those three might not have been the ones who killed his men tonight but they worked for the same people. PT took a step toward the three. He worked hard to control his emotions, emotions that, if released, would see these three men dead at his feet. PT was big and in reasonably good shape. Not as good as when he had been part of the Special Forces but still good enough to take down these three pinstriped suits. He held up a hand and pointed a finger at the three. "Why did you kill my men?"

The shortest of the three, a man who looked to be of Asian blood stepped forward, "I regret the loss of life. We at times need to hire outside contractors, the same as your company. In the short amount of time available to put together an operation we might have chosen a couple of men that took their jobs a little too seriously. I apologize."

PT managed to hold his rage, he turned back to Freemont. "Where does this leave us Jason? Out operation is in shambles and my men are dead." He turned back to the three strangers. "And these three are to blame."

Freemont asked PT to take his seat. Once PT was safely seated Freemont added. "You and Stu have managed to destroy a large portion of Steggman's data files. According to these three gentlemen we have successfully managed to stop them in their tracks and I don't just mean the 'Ponce de Leon Project.' You have affected almost all of their operations. I knew Stu was good but never knew just how much. These three contacted Alex within minutes after they realized their systems were compromised. They have agreed to share the contents of the van with us if Stu will disable his Hunter-Killer virus."

PT knew Stu had complete control of the Steggman operating systems. He could choose to destroy all the files remaining to them if he wanted. The only thing destroyed so far was anything remotely relating to the 'Ponce de Leon Project.' He had the bulk of their data held hostage. Steggman couldn't re-acquire the data without the help of Stu.

"Hell no, have Stu turn everything over to the FBI. I'm sure there is enough information available to put half their company behind bars." PT had been looking at the three as he said this and noticed the uneasiness in their faces.

Jason got up and went to his credenza. He opened a bottle of Kentucky Bourbon. He poured six glasses and then sat the tray on the conference table. "Gentlemen," he said as he took one of the glasses. He looked at the other five men in the room. "Please have a drink."

All five went to the conference table and took a glass. The three Steggman men made sure to keep a close eye on PT, they even stood on the opposite side of the table. Something about his eyes made each very nervous. PT didn't give a damn if anyone was nervous. He accepted his drink and knew he could use it.

Freemont pulled a chair from the conference table and sat down. "PT, I want you to listen and listen good. These three have agreed to share the contents of the van and I think we should at least consider their offer. Alex and I spoke about this alone and agreed it's the best way for everyone to get what they want."

PT wasn't convinced. "Six hours ago we had everything. Now these three thieves come here and offer to share something they have no right to even be a part of. I say we burn The Steggman Group to the ground."

Freemont knew he wasn't going to change PT's mind unless they could talk alone. He looked at the three Steggman men and asked if they could step out of the office for a minute. Once they were gone Freemont looked at PT. "Now I understand how you feel. Those men you lost tonight were my men too. When all looked lost these three showed up at our door. Now we have a chance to retrieve our samples."

There was something about this that PT couldn't quite wrap his brain around. "You say if we stop the malware they will share the samples they stole tonight. How is that such a good deal? If the 'Ponce de Leon Project' is successful then the amounts of money to be made are staggering. How can we share, or for that matter, how can we trust Steggman? We can get new samples and burn Steggman to the ground as a bonus with the malware."

Jason had known PT for years and knew he was a man of action. He was the type who wanted results and he wanted them now. This situation required a little diplomacy. "Let me try to explain. We can't attempt to get new samples from the three Reanimates because they are now afraid to let anyone even remotely resembling a nurse into their homes. The Primary will be just as hard. We can't start stealing a Blood Center van every other week. The main reason I'm telling you this is that I have other plans for Steggman."

PT, who had been looking at his empty glass, now looked up at Freemont. "Let me guess, once we have the blood samples back you are still going to run the virus?"

Freemont smiled. "That's right PT, and just for fun I want you to pin the theft of the van and all the murders on our friends out there in the hall."

PT thought for a second and then smiled. "We get back the samples and pin the crime on Steggman. I like it. What do you want me to do?"

"The jet is waiting. As far as this meeting is concerned we don't need you in attendance anymore. Now I want you to shake hands with the three when they come back in. I will tell them that I explained everything to you and you are now on board one hundred percent," Freemont said.

The three were invited back in after PT had managed to get his blood pressure back to something that resembled normal; the bourbon was starting to help a little too. Before leaving, PT shook hands with the three, he could sense their nervousness. He also shook with Freemont and Trivett. As he headed toward the elevator he made a quick stop at the restroom. He wanted to wash his hands after shaking with the three bastards from Steggman. He was anxious to get to the offices at New Circle and start his plans for the payback Freemont had promised. On the trip to Bluegrass Field he consumed two more bourbons. He also took a legal pad and started making his notes. PT had always operated in a methodical fashion and notes were just part of his preparation.

Once his jet landed at Bluegrass Field he went straight to the offices at New Circle where he shared the plan with Stu and HB, he was sure the details could be hammered out. PT didn't like going to New Circle but events demanded it. To show up unannounced in Lexington would surely be a surprise to HB. He doubted if anything surprised Stu.

The Donor

"Are you sure your friend there is onboard. He still seemed agitated?" The Asian asked.

Freemont felt like observing as Trivett spoke. "I can assure you Mr. Thorpe; Patterson Tingler is one-hundred percent on board." Thorpe might have looked Asian but he was half American. The name Thorpe had come from his American father, his mother though was South Korean.

"You say his name is Patterson Tingler, is that why you call him PT?" Thorpe asked.

"It is, he doesn't like the name Patterson and I don't like the name Tingler so I call him PT," Trivett said.

Thorpe looked at the door PT had just walked out of and asked another question. "He looks dangerous, is he?"

Freemont felt the need to answer and he wanted the answer to intimidate the three Steggman men. "He is. He and I served in the first Gulf War. I would say he's about as dangerous as they come."

"Why do you have a military man running your operation?" Thorpe asked as he continued to look at the door.

"He is ex-military, but now works for me. You ask this as if it's a problem?" Freemont said.

Thorpe finally took his eyes off the door. "It isn't a problem. We have a few men of military background working at Steggman as well but none of them hold a management position. Our ex-military men work on projects that require more than a little paperwork." Thorpe said this as he scanned the faces of both Freemont and Trivett. He had just sent a little message of his own and it wasn't lost on the two.

Freemont wondered if the men that had stolen the contents of the van were some of the people Thorpe had just alluded to. "Possibly in the future we can work together instead of against one another; maybe there will be less blood that way?" The less blood remark was not lost on Thorpe, less blood meaning less blood samples.

"Less blood is what I will suggest to my superiors," Thorpe said. Freemont and Trivett caught the hidden message and wondered if Thorpe would really veil a threat in such a flimsy way.

Freemont wanted to conclude the meeting in order to rid his office of the three Steggman men. "What do you propose concerning the blood samples you took this evening?" Freemont was blunt and didn't care.

Thorpe stepped forward. Freemont wondered what the other men were there for, they had yet to speak. Before Thorpe said anything he pulled a Walther PPKS from his pocket as did the other two men. Trivett saw the gun before Freemont and let out a gasp. The other two men's weapons were Walther PPKs as well. Freemont and Trivett were both frozen. As Thorpe screwed a small device onto the end of his gun he said. "The hijacking of the blood van and the killing of your men was only the first part our plan, you are now looking at the second part. As far as working together, this is what is going to happen, I pull the trigger and you will die."

"The bodies of Jason Freemont and Alex Trivett were discovered Thursday morning at a little after seven-o'clock by the cleaning crew, two women and one man. The first woman in actually made it to the big desk before she saw Freemont sprawled on the other side. Trivett's body was on the other side of the conference table. Both men had been shot once in the chest and for good measure a second shot was added to the forehead of each. Trivett must have been the second man shot because he had raised both hands in front of himself. The bullet had gone through his left hand before entering his chest.

The police were notified and were there in minutes. Funny how high profile people get a better response time to their murders than common folk. The murders were designated as a hit/assassination. It was determined that both men probably knew their killers and probably never knew what was about to happen until they saw the guns. Due to the high profile positions the two men held, and the fact that Beeler-Jordan had an international footprint, it was decided to contact the FBI.

The Donor

It took only thirty minutes for two agents to show up and completely take over the investigation. For the remainder of the day the building was sealed. Anyone that wanted to enter was allowed but were put through an interrogation before being allowed to leave again. The three people that discovered the bodies weren't allowed to leave until late that afternoon. Once it was determined that the three housekeepers, who had worked for Beeler-Jordan for a combined twenty seven years, hadn't killed the two men they were allowed to go home.

Security footage was pulled up and scanned. The camera in the lobby saw PT leaving at a little after five o'clock, 5:07 to be exact, in the morning. He was walking at a fast pace but not the pace of a man who might have just offed two men and wanted to get away. Three more men exited the building at 5:32. These men walked at a brisk pace themselves but also craned their necks after exiting the front doors.

The security guard stationed at the front foyer had admitted the three men hours earlier, 2:56 to be exact. They had been cleared through by Jason Freemont himself. The other man had arrived at 3:44 and had also been admitted by Mr. Freemont. The security guard had been on duty during the time the four men had entered the building and was still at his post when the four men left. PT was identified by some of the employees who looked at the security footage.

Special Agent Lonnie McCoy was assigned the task of finding Patterson Tingler. He found that Tingler worked out of Beeler-Jordan offices in Chicago. After a few calls it was determined that he wasn't in Chicago. Beeler-Jordan's main offices were in chaos; with both the CEO and CFO murdered it wasn't apparent who would now take over operations. An emergency meeting of the board was called and would be convened at three that evening. The board consisted of eleven men besides Freemont and Trivett. Seven of the members could be there by the three o'clock meeting and this was enough for a quorum.

By phone the other four absent members on the board had given a proxy vote for the leadership role to go to a man by the name of Elmond Frazier. He was trusted and at the moment knew more about ongoing operations than anybody else. It was assumed that once the other seven board members made it to town they would vote for Mr. Frazier also. Frazier would be assuming the position of interim CEO, once the other seven voted.

The highest ranking executive after the CEO and CFO was the head of operations. The pecking order at a pharmaceuticals company was different than other Fortune 500 Companies. This could be attributed to more federal regulation at pharmaceutical companies than other large corporations.

The head of operations was a man who had been at Beeler-Jordan since before Jason Freemont. His name was Elmond Frazier. Frazier had started with the company straight out of college. He was fifty-nine years old and in excellent shape; he ran 5K races as if he were twenty years old. In his running club he was known as the old man but never called this to his face. He was out of town at the moment but was reached by phone. When told that both Freemont and Trivett were dead he was devastated. How did it happen, he wanted to know. Frazier was in St. Louis, Missouri at the time and told to be at the airport in one hour. A company jet couldn't be there for at least five hours so a charter was reserved and waiting. Frazier was told he would most likely be assuming a temporary position as CEO and to get to New York as fast as possible. The board would be meeting at 3:00PM while he was in flight. He would be notified of their decision before he landed.

Frazier hung up and headed for his hotel. He needed to pack and then have the limo pick him up. The shock of having his two immediate bosses murdered was not only devastating, it was unexplainable. As he rode to the airport he made a list of the companies that might benefit the most from the murders. By the time he boarded the charter he had narrowed the list down to six companies that might have competing operations with Beeler-Jordan serious enough to have done something like this.

As he looked at the six names he thought he might be able to narrow down the list by looking at the company that might stoop low enough to have a corporate head eliminated. He started drawing lines through the companies that he held in higher esteem. When finished he had marked off five names, the only company still remaining was The Steggman

Group. The more he looked at the last name and thought about it, the more he felt certain that if it was a competitor that had Freemont and Trivett killed, then it had to be Steggman.

Frazier landed at seven o'clock and was immediately taken to corporate offices. When he entered the building he was met by Lonnie McCoy and told to follow him to an office that had been designated by the FBI as their turf during the investigation.

Frazier looked at McCoy and stated, "I am going upstairs to confer with the board that I was told would be waiting on me."

"Sorry Frazier, I need to see you first, come this way." McCoy took Frazier by the elbow and started to lead him in the direction he wanted.

Frazier, who was six foot four and weighed two hundred and ten pounds, only stood. McCoy lost his grip on Frazier's elbow and this made him angry. "Follow me so I can ask you some questions." This was said as a demand, not a request.

Frazier stepped forward. "If you touch me again I will call the police and let you explain yourself to them. I don't know how the FBI operates and don't really care. Unless you've got a warrant for my arrest then step aside and let me pass." Frazier knew what he was doing, he was an attorney and could hold his own with just about anybody. "I will answer your questions after I attend to business upstairs. This company has lost two very good men today and that is my first concern at the moment."

McCoy knew he was defeated. He stepped aside and let Frazier pass. "I expect to talk to you today. Don't try to leave the building unless you talk to me first.

This stopped Frazier in his tracks. He turned and walked back to the agent. He took out a pen and small spiral bound notebook. "What is the name of your supervisor and where would he be at this hour?" Frazier stood in front of McCoy, pen at the ready.

McCoy realized he was dealing with someone that wasn't intimidated by the letters FBI. He had always operated under the assumption that everyone was glad to talk, either truthfully or not, when he asked them to. The man who stood in front of him was arrogant and apparently knew what he was doing. McCoy had no authority to detain him in this situation and Frazier knew it.

"Tell me something Mr. Frazier. Have you ever dealt with the FBI before?" McCoy asked this in a cool monotone voice that he hoped would put a little fear into Frazier and get him to show a little respect.

Frazier again stepped toward the agent. He was at least four inches taller than McCoy and knew how to use his height to intimidate. "I am happy to say that this is the first time I have had the pleasure of talking to anyone even remotely associated with the FBI. You know, I once thought about working for your organization but when I interviewed and took the test I was informed that I was too smart. You see Mr. McCoy, I am an attorney and if you don't allow me to go upstairs and see to my duties then I will have no choice but to call some people I know in Washington. Now as to which people I know in Washington I will leave that for you to wonder." Frazier turned and headed toward the elevator. McCoy never said another word.

Once upstairs, Frazier went straight to Freemont's office. The bodies had been removed and a forensics team was there gathering evidence. Frazier stood at the door and could only look in. In those few seconds he thought about the first time he had ever met Jason Freemont. It was for an interview nearly twenty five years ago. Frazier already worked for Beeler-Jordan but as soon as Freemont was advanced to the position of CEO he wanted to meet all the senior staff. Freemont had hired a firm of headhunters to find him a man who could manage the far flung operations of Beeler-Jordan. Frazier's name had been at the top of the list and what was so odd was that he already worked for Beeler. Frazier was promoted that same day and went to work three weeks later as head of operations, only the second position below Freemont. He had never regretted a day of his service to Beeler-Jordan. This day might be the first.

The board had already finished their meeting and the vote was unanimous, Elmond Frazier would be appointed as interim CEO of Beeler-Jordan while a search committee was appointed to find a permanent successor. This suited Frazier just fine. He went into the boardroom where the seven members were waiting.

"What do we know Greg?" Frazier asked. Greg McKinney was president of a chain of banks that operated in the northeast. He was also head of the Board of Directors at Beeler-Jordan.

"Not much Elmond, what we do know is there was some sort of emergency meeting here late last night. It was actually around three or four o'clock this morning. Freemont and Trivett were here along with Patterson Tingler. From what we can gather there was an operation somewhere in Kentucky that went horribly wrong and some men got killed? Freemont summoned PT and once he got here there were already three other men waiting in Freemont's suite of offices. When the meeting concluded PT left and we believe the other three men shot both Freemont and Trivett. There is video footage of PT leaving a few minutes before the other three men exited the building."

"There is a security guard posted at the front entrance at all times. I know PT would have been allowed entrance but how did the other three men enter without alarming the security guard?" Frazier asked.

"Freemont allowed them to enter. The guard called up and Freemont said he was expecting the three and that PT would be along shortly." McKinney told Frazier.

"So were Jason and Alex shot before PT left or after?" Frazier asked.

"I know what you're thinking and as much as I hate to admit it the question crossed my mind as well. I know PT and Jason were friends from back in the service but you have to rule out every possibility. I am confident the two men were still alive when PT left," McKinney said.

Now the lawyer in Frazier came out. "I would never believe PT shot the two men but what proof do you have that they were still alive when he left the building?"

McKinney had the answer. "The NYPD figured that one out. There's a camera in the adjoining offices where Jason's secretary works. It doesn't point at her desk mind you, but at the waiting area in front of her desk. It allows Jason to see who might be waiting to see him. That footage was monitored by the forensics team and immediately after PT left the building there are four slight vibrations in the video. The forensics team said the wall mounted camera blurred four times when the concussion of the gunshots changed the air pressure in Jason's office. The building is fire-proof and soundproof and for that reason the walls are constructed using metal studs. The metal studs are great as far as fire proofing goes but lacking when it comes to vibration. The gunshots created a momentary increase in air pressure, it's called overpressure. This is what moved the wall ever so slightly but it was enough to momentarily jar the wall mounted camera. Two minutes and fourteen seconds after the last blur on the video the three men are seen on the lobby video walking out the front entrance. The security guard never suspected a thing, and there was really no reason to."

"I believe you Greg. The NYPD really know their stuff, I never would have thought of such things as air pressure and metal studs. Where do we stand as far as operations?" Frazier asked.

"There is something I wanted to tell you first, the board voted unanimously in your favor. I know the title will be 'interim' but don't allow that to bother you. There won't be a major push to find a permanent replacement for at least six months. The word interim might be hung around your neck for quite a while. In the meantime I want you to use Alex Trivett's office. I have been told by the head of forensics that they would like Jason's office sealed for a few weeks. The gathering of evidence is crucial and they don't want the carpets ripped out and the walls knocked down until they have everything they need. Before you move into Jason's office I can assure you that everything right down to the wallpaper will be replaced."

"What do you think was behind the murders Greg?"

"When the board met earlier this afternoon, it was the first thing that was brought up, a couple of the more finicky members wondered if they should hire bodyguards and I told them if a bodyguard would allow them to sleep better at night then by all means hire one. I will sleep fine; of course I keep a Springfield Model 1911 with a spare clip on the nightstand beside my bed which helps," Greg said with a smile.

"You know Greg that I am a lawyer by trade. My job at Beeler has always been head of operations. I have little knowledge on the pharmaceutical side. You and the other members of the board have thrust me into a job that I feel I am unqualified for."

"That was discussed in the meeting. What we need right now is someone to unite all the operations and you are best suited for that. As far as the drug side of the business let the PHDs handle it. You oversee operations, which is your true calling."

Elmond now asked the most important question of the day. "There must be a reason for the murders of both Jason and Alex. I need to know about any ongoing operations that might have led to this. What can the board tell me about that?"

"There is one operation in particular that comes to mind; it is ongoing and has been very secretive for the last year. Very few people at Beeler know of its existence. Have you ever heard of the 'Ponce de Leon Project'?"

Elmond thought for a second. "No Greg, I don't ever recall hearing that name other than in a high school history class."

Greg walked over to the door and closed it. He sat down with the other six board members that were present and said. "The 'Ponce de Leon Project' has been operative for eighteen months. Jason and Alex along with myself were the only ones at the corporate offices to know of the project. Not even the other members of the board were aware it existed." Greg looked at the other faces of the board members, just by appearances none of them had ever heard of it.

Greg picked up the phone and punched in a few numbers. "Yes, could you see to some coffee and possibly some sandwiches being sent to the conference room, we plan to be working for a while. And also I would like security to post a guard at the conference room door until we're finished." He listened for a moment and then said, "Thank you."

Greg continued. "The project was started by accident. One of our oldest drugs, a very successful blood thinner was being administered to a patient that was suffering from many illnesses. He already had two heart attacks and two open heart surgeries. Due to the scar tissue from the previous surgeries it would be impossible for him to have a third surgery. He suffered from high cholesterol, so high in fact his blood was nearly as thick as syrup and instead of a deep red color it really looked pink. I can't tell you the name of the patient because I don't know it but I can tell you where it happened, Eastern Kentucky.

"Anyway, the patient was given only a few weeks to live, the blockage was causing all sorts of problems but mainly he was dying of Congestive Heart Failure. His heart couldn't function to the capacity needed to allow his body to rid itself of excess fluid. Please understand that I am talking in terms as they were explained to me so as I could be made to understand.

"This patient continued to decline. When all looked hopeless he suddenly began a miraculous recovery. His heart became stronger, his blocked arteries began to clear, and the congestive heart failure was completely gone within three days. Within a week he was released from the hospital and sent home. Each consecutive two week appointment after that revealed improvement. The patient was eighty-four years old, eight weeks after he was released he was completely healed. Even his eyesight had improved to 20/20. The man wore glasses his entire life before that."

Elmond listened with great interest. He knew this story had something to do with Beeler-Jordan but didn't know why.

Greg continued. "The doctors decided to check all the medications that were administered while the man was hospitalized. We were contacted because of our blood thinner. Two of our lab staff were sent there and became involved in the research. All the drug companies involved had staff there; some of the smartest people in the business were trying to figure out what had caused such a miraculous recovery."

Elmond wondered why Greg had stopped. "What happened after that, what did the research turn up?"

"Nothing, such a recovery isn't just rare, it's Biblical. Our team was sent home along with the people from the other drug companies," Greg told the men and women seated around the conference table.

Elmond knew such research wouldn't have been stopped for any reason. "Why were the researchers sent home, why wasn't the research continued?"

"The patient died. We lost the man that had made the most miraculous recovery of all time."

Elmond knew there was still more to the story. "You're saying his illness killed him anyway?"

"Not at all, he was killed on his way to the hospital. It was his fourth appointment after his discharge and he was killed by a drunk driver. Seems a double cab pickup driven by a man who already had three arrests for driving under the influence ran a red light and t-boned the car the patient was a passenger in. He was killed instantly, it was a nasty wreck."

"A drunk driver with three priors," Elmond said as he thought. "Why wasn't a man like that in jail or had his license revoked?"

"I'll tell you why, that man was a state representative and had connections. He managed to wiggle out of each and every one of his convictions because he knew somebody. Anyway once the patient had been killed they lost the source of their research. After the accident the research teams were sent home." Greg told the group.

Just then there was a knock at the door and Greg said to come in. The door opened and a Beeler security guard opened it. "There are two ladies' here with a trolley containing coffee and sandwiches. Is it all right to allow them in?"

Greg was impressed with the security. Too bad it wasn't as efficient the night before. "Sure, have them roll the cart in."

Two women who worked in the Beeler-Jordan cafeteria rolled in a cart which contained two large silver coffee servers along with china cups and saucers. There were two large trays, also covered with silver lids. Under each were any number of sandwiches and confections. It was decided to allow the two women to prepare each of the coffees. This allowed the men to think over what Greg had just told them.

After the women had the coffee prepared and the two trays on the table they rolled the cart away. Elmond noticed the security guard was wearing a 9mm Beretta 92FS in a holster along with two leather holders that contained two additional mags each. This man was packing some serious ammunition. The Beretta he knew was the standard NATO weapon used after the military had retired the older 1911 model.

"Does the security personnel always carry guns here Greg?" Elmond asked.

"As of eight o'clock this morning they do. I took the liberty of contacting the contractor that furnishes security for the building and told him what we know so far about what happened last night. He is working on enhancing our video and audio in the building. The security personnel from this point forward will all be armed. The exterior doors in the foyer will be refitted with bullet proof glass and military grade locking mechanisms. These are just the quick fixes; more changes will be made once a detailed audit is conducted of the current security measures we have in place."

Elmond was impressed. He now realized why Greg was the chairman of the board of directors. "Sounds like the security issue will be fixed. Now back to the 'Ponce de Leon Project.' Do you think it has anything to do with the murders here last night?"

"I do. I spoke with Patterson several hours ago. He was in Lexington Kentucky this morning and he is now on his way here and should be landing momentarily. It was a good thing the corporate jet was still at Bluegrass Field. Anyway, he as much as guaranteed me that 'Ponce de Leon' played a part in the murders." After Greg said this he realized his phrasing left something to be desired. Ponce de Leon had been dead for hundreds of years.

"That's good; I want to talk to Patterson myself. Who is in charge of the 'Ponce de Leon Project'?"

"Patterson, he's been in charge since the beginning. I knew we needed to get him up here as soon as possible, the board and you need to find out what this project is all about and just how much it had to do with the deaths of Jason and Alex. I suggest we take a break and have something to eat. It has been a long day and none of us has had any lunch. Patterson should be here by the time we finish." The other members reached for a sandwich.

The Donor

The jet carrying PT landed and taxied to the private jet terminal. A car was waiting and within two minutes of the jet rolling to a stop PT was in the back seat of a black Lincoln Town Car and heading downtown. He had gotten the call around eleven-thirty that morning from Greg. When told that none other than the Chairman of the Board was holding for him he knew something was up, probably something bad. He had only been at the offices on New Circle for fifteen minutes when Hells Bells said he had a phone call from Greg McKinney. As PT went for the phone he had a knot in his stomach. For no reason in particular he thought of the three men he had left in the offices with Jason and Alex.

"This is Patterson."

"Hello Patterson, I'm afraid I have some bad news. Jason and Alex are dead. Both were found a few hours ago in Jason's office."

PT was silent for a minute as he thought of the Asian and the two men with him. "I was there last night Greg. I left around five this morning. There were three other men in the office when I arrived; they were from The Steggman Group."

This was the first Greg had heard of the meeting and who was there. He wasn't even aware that PT had been in New York. NYPD hadn't gotten that far with their investigation yet. "That is important stuff PT. If the jet is still in Kentucky I want you on it as soon as possible. If it has already taken off then get it back. I need you here immediately. As soon as you take off call me back with a brief summary of the meeting. NYPD is here and two agents from the FBI just came in. They will also want to include you in the investigation, be prepared to answer some tough questions." PT knew he was a suspect and this didn't worry him in the least. It was just part of police procedure and he would be cleared of any involvement soon after he got there.

PT was stunned by the news; he had served in the military with Freemont. PT had stayed in several more years but once he was discharged Freemont was there offering him a job. The two went way back and now he was dead, killed by three men that PT was standing right in front of just hours earlier. "I'll check on the plane as soon as we hang up. I should be in New York this afternoon." PT hung up and dialed the airport. The jet was still at Bluegrass Field. He told them to get it fueled and prepped; they would leave as soon as he got there.

Jacob Yates got a call late on Thursday November 2nd. It was a call he hadn't expected for at least two more years. When he answered the phone and heard the voice he knew something must have happened, probably something bad.

"Hello Jacob, can you talk?" The caller asked. The accent was unmistakable, leaning heavily toward Italian.

Jacob had only spoken to the caller once and that was a little over five years ago. "Yes, I hadn't expected to hear from you this soon." His voice was nervous.

"I'm afraid something has happened, we are forced to accelerate our timetable by at least two years. We won't be able to wait until the seven year cycle is complete."

Jacob was ready, he had been preparing for this day for years. "How bad is it?"

"We think it is pretty bad. He is safe for the moment but the next move is going to need to take place within days instead of years I'm afraid."

Jacob thought a minute before asking the next question. "Where will he go?"

"That hasn't been decided yet, maybe Spain, possibly even the Middle East."

Again Jacob thought, "He hasn't been to the Middle East in such a long time, are you sure that is wise?"

"We think so. We won't know his decision until we make the move. He never knows until he is brought out of the current cycle."

"How many people do you have?" Jacob asked.

"Enough, always enough," the man told him again in a heavily accented reply.

Jacob had only been with the organization for five years. He had been chosen because of his faith and his commitment. The committee that decided had thousands to choose from but Jacob was different somehow, he stood out from all the others. What he now had to do was going to be dangerous, it always had been. The committee always managed to lose men when the cycle ran out. This would be no different.

The main criteria, for anyone entrusted with what Jacob had to do now, was faith. He did not have to understand all that he was asked to do but he did have to believe. Above everything else he had to believe. This was why he was selected out of all the others. He was selected to assist the 'Chosen' at a critical time which was now drawing near.

Jacob lived in Eastern Kentucky. He had moved there five years ago and spent his days writing. Yes Jacob was a writer. He had no family and this was important. He had no job with a timeclock and this was also important. His home sat on seven acres of land, some flat, but mostly hillside. There were no other houses within sight of his property. Each morning deer could be seen from the front window of the cabin Jacob lived in, during the day wild turkeys could be seen in the yard.

As cabins go the one Jacob lived in was nice. It had five rooms with the most important being the one that faced the front. From Jacob's writing desk he could look up from time to time and be greeted by the sight of wildlife roaming the property. He had even seen Elk from time to time. Jacob hadn't been a writer until he moved here. It was decided that a man living alone needed a profession to help him pass the days and writing suited that need just fine. Writing is a very solitary profession.

Jacob hadn't been a writer before the move, he was an architect, he designed things to be built, this was something he had always wanted to do from the time he was a young child. At first he questioned the move and the new career, it was okay to question he was told. Blind faith wasn't as good as strong faith.

"You will be a writer and what you write will be very good. You will enjoy the solitude; you will enjoy the works you produce. But everything written by you must not draw attention to you. Maybe someday after you have passed from this life your works here will be recognized but not before. It is very important that no one know who you are or what you are about." He was told.

Jacob had always remembered those words. So he wrote, he wrote every day and to his surprise he enjoyed what he wrote. Sometimes as he sat at his writing desk and looked out over the seven acres he laughed at his previous doubt. He was told he would enjoy writing and he would be good at it. From the first paragraph five years ago he had been able to write volumes. He took each completed manuscript and each evening sat on his sprawling front porch and read. When he went over a previously written manuscript it was as if he were reading it for the first time.

When he wrote the ideas came to him as if he were watching a movie of the event. Words never failed to show up on the pages. His fingers worked the keyboard of his computer as if he had done this all his life. Jacob had never been good at typing during high school and also not much better in college. He was a hunt and peck kind of typist. From the very first day here five years ago he had placed his fingers on home row and typed as if he had been doing it for many years. That was the day he left any doubt behind. What he had been told was happening.

There was a book shelf in the front room. It was empty when he moved there but now, five years later, it was nearly full. Jacob estimated that by the end of the seven year cycle it would be completely full, it was as if his writings were being rationed as to exactly fill that bookshelf by the end of the cycle. Each completed volume was bound by a large butter-fly clamp at the top left hand corner. Each evening he would pick a volume and go to his ladder-back wooden rocker on the front porch and read. All of his works were fiction. Sometimes as he read of things that had happened long ago he wondered if it was fiction at all, it seemed so real. Jacob supposed the realness was because he had written it, but he still wondered.

Besides the cabin he had a car, a small car with nothing fancy except air conditioning. This was fine with Jacob. He only used the car once a week to go into town to check his mail and pick up the food he would need for the next week. He had a checking account which he used to pay his utilities and living expenses. He never knew how much was in the account; it was being managed by the Committee, as he referred to them. No one had ever visited the cabin, not even the census taker. Jacob felt since he had been omitted from the census that he didn't exist in the world. Jacob did exist in ways he could never imagine.

Part of Jacobs's life was spent making sure he didn't exist. He was warned about becoming too friendly on his weekly trips to town. "Never strike up a conversation with a store clerk or anyone at the post office. Don't linger at the gas pump when you fill your car's gas tank. Get the things you need in town and hurry back home, you have writing to do," he was told.

Something that bothered Jacob early on was his lack of health insurance and lack of a family doctor. As the weeks turned into months and the months into years he realized he didn't need healthcare, he never got sick. A dentist wasn't necessary either, he never got a cavity while he stayed at the cabin and daily brushing and flossing kept his teeth white, brilliant white. Before the Committee came into his life Jacob had experienced the usual medical problems a healthy adult might experience. A couple of colds a year, the flu every other year and the dreaded five-year cavity. Now those problems were happily absent from his life.

Jacob was also instructed to use different small towns to do his shopping, and to use different stores and filling stations to buy his gas and groceries in those towns. He was even told to use a hat on some days and not on others. As to these instructions he remembered mentioning that he hoped no one mistook him for the Unabomber. He was told that the Committee worked to expose people like the Unabomber, along with all other terrorists' organizations. They said organizations of terror had been around for thousands of years, it was a plague that held mankind hostage to fear. It was just part of civilization.

Jacob had always wondered about that. He hoped his doubts weren't an affront to the Committee. He was assured it was okay to ask questions. He was told that even a strong faith could and would be strengthened further by asking questions.

The cabin had a telephone but no television. The Committee considered television to be such a divisive form of communication that it had been abandoned years ago. Jacob had been instructed to purchase newspapers and two news magazines each week when he went into town.

Although he was cut off from the world it was still necessary for him to keep up with local and world events. Jacob read a little news each evening after he read a portion of one of the completed manuscripts. He enjoyed his evening time, he enjoyed all his other time as well. He would rise each morning and write the entire day only stopping to enjoy a simple meal for lunch. His lunch always consisted of a small piece of meat, usually cooked chicken, maybe a vegetable and always bread. This was all he needed. Breakfast and dinner varied little, a meat, a vegetable, and bread.

He usually stopped writing around five o'clock to prepare his supper, simple again, same as breakfast and lunch. His evenings were always spent on the front porch with his newspapers and magazines and a previously finished manuscript. He had done this for five years even in extreme heat and cold, the weather never seemed to chill or overheat him, it was all good. Twenty degrees and a coat or ninety-five and the porch ceiling fan were all he needed against the elements. Each night he prayed and at dawn he prayed again, it kept him balanced.

Now that Jacob had gotten the call his life was going to change. He began to organize his belongings. Everything would be left behind but he wanted to get things just right anyway. He arranged and then rearranged his manuscripts, after all it did represent five long years of work. Everything about the cabin was put in its proper place. He packed his shaving kit and a few changes of clothes. He had been told to leave his key on the kitchen table when he left, he would not be coming back.

Jacob took one last look inside before closing the front door. Once he had descended the front steps and was ready to get into his car he stood there for a while. He admired the way the cabin looked in the afternoon light. He looked over the seven acres; in the distance he saw a doe and her fawn. There were five turkeys not more than twenty feet from the two deer. It was as if they had come out of hiding to say goodbye. Jacob actually waved as he got into the car. As he drove away the deer and turkeys all went back into cover.

Jacob had been told to drive to Prestonsburg; a room had been reserved at the Comfort Inn just off the main road that led to the Mountain

Parkway. He made it there a little before seven o'clock. The check in was nearly effortless, the room had been reserved and paid for in full. The front desk was told to expect a Jacob Yates that evening.

The Committee which arranged all this had no permanent address; it had changed every seven years for as long as anyone associated with it could remember. There were seven permanent members and any number of others which, depending on world politics and world religions, could vary into the hundreds. All religions were included on the Committee with each being represented by a single designate. The designate was chosen by the religion and then his or her information was submitted to the Committee.

The seven permanent members were permanent because each of the seven religions had been in existence longer than the others. There were other criteria that came into account but longevity counted slightly more than the other considerations. None of the seven could be replaced unless a religion fell out of favor with God. That religion would be banished and then the next longest existing religion would become the seventh permanent member. The longest serving member of the Committee was of course the Catholic Church. The youngest being the Southern Baptist.

The Southern Baptist Church held the seventh spot on the Committee but by no means held this as a lesser position. There was a bit of jealousy on the part of the Catholics toward the Southern Baptists. All the religions represented had a vote in committee business but it seemed the Southern Baptists held more sway over more religions than any of the other six, even the Catholics. Most of the smaller religions of the world felt the Catholics held too much power and too large of a following. This didn't bother the Southern Baptists in the least, they did the work of the Lord and that was their only concern. Maybe that was why so many of the other religions leaned toward the Baptists.

All the religions of the world had only one common word that could be used in their description, worship. All religions worshiped something but if God wasn't at the heart of their worship then they would never be on the Committee. A few of the lesser known institutions held on to their Committee seats always with the fear that they could drop off the rolls at any time.

The Committee had been in existence for hundreds of years, some even thought it was thousands. The sole purpose of the Committee was to oversee the second coming of Christ. It had been argued that he was already here; it was argued that he had sent an angel to continue his work; it had been argued that a mortal had been chosen to continue his work, it had been argued that the second coming was in the future. This constant analysis only added to the seriousness of the business at hand, protect the Chosen.

The members of the Committee worked in silence among their respective religions. The Committee was the only organization that combined all the religions of the world. The work they oversaw was two-fold. Protect the Chosen and maintain total secrecy in doing so. This was the work that had gone on through the first and second millennia and would continue for possibly another. The world as a whole knew nothing of the Committee's existence; this was also to protect the Chosen.

Thorpe and his two associates walked out of the corporate offices of Beeler-Jordan in the early hours of Thursday November 2nd. The three men had successfully decapitated the top management of a major competitor. It wasn't actually a competitor of the three but it was for the company they worked for. They had done their jobs and were now expected to stay out of the country for at least two years at which time they would re-enter under different names. The paperwork would be perfect as was the paperwork they carried for this project. Four hours after walking out of the front lobby they boarded a plane at JFK headed for Atlanta. From there they could choose any destination they wanted but would most likely head for London to check on a three quarters of a million dollar wire transfer that was waiting for them, a quarter million apiece. So goes the price of corporate hitmen. The three wouldn't set idle during their two year banishment. They would take on a few other smaller foreign contracts but at the end of two years they would be back in the United States with brand new papers and ready for another job.

The FBI and the NYPD were already running the images of the three that were taken from the security cameras in the lobby but they would never get a hit. The three man team was meticulous about not leaving fingerprints and they didn't care about facial recognition software, their looks changed each time they entered the country. Only the top man at Steggman knew who they were. He had used them before and he would use them again.

Steggman now had in its possession the three blood samples of the Reanimates that Rachel Bevins had furnished and also the fifty-one samples that were taken from the Blood Center van theft. The Steggman labs were running countless tests on the Reanimate samples. So far no regenerative abilities had been isolated from those samples. It was a monumental discovery if only comparing the current blood samples against the files of the three. It was as if you were comparing the blood of the sick and dying to that of a teenager. This in itself proved the existence of a mythical recovery if only in their new biological make-up.

The key now was to identify the giver of this power. One of the fifty one samples would contain that person's blood; the problem was then to identify the person. To think that a man or woman was walking around out there with the ability to cure so much with as little as a few drops of their blood.

What The Steggman Group cared about more than the actual healing abilities of this unknown person were the financial gains to be had by controlling such a resource. Steggman had always said the strength of its products was a result of its people, now they really meant it. The Primary that the files alluded to never mentioned a name, he or she was only referred to as the Primary. All the Corporation's resources were now to be focused on locating this walking wonder, and if it was determined that another corporation had somehow managed to find him first and somehow start testing then it was decided that the Primary would need to disappear. It was this order that had thrown the Committee into action.

The Committee had been closely following the progress Beeler-Jordan had made in identifying the Chosen. Now they had information about the deaths of the two men at Beeler who were responsible for the 'Ponce de Leon Project,' Jason Freemont and Alex Trivett. It was determined that The Steggman Group was responsible for the murders and this information was extremely worrisome to the Committee, Steggman was a wildcard. As bad as Beeler-Jordan had been the Committee felt confident they wouldn't hurt the Chosen, assuming they could even find him. If that was the only worry then the Chosen would still be safe. They would never hurt someone so important. They might have killed a few people in their attempts to find out who he was but they were trusted to not do such a thing to the Chosen, or the Primary as Beeler called him.

The Committee hoped for at least five or six more months to leave the Chosen to his work, maybe even stretching it to the end of the seven-year cycle. Now with the events of the last twenty-four hours it was decided to make the transfer. Events were moving faster than during any previous cycle. What ever happened to the good old days when things only progressed at the speed of a tired old horse or a slow moving camel?

Members of the Committee had wondered for years, possibly even centuries, if the Chosen had ever been harmed in the past. It was rumored, but never verified, that a previous committee had allowed the unthinkable to happen. Was it blasphemy to think these thoughts? Whatever the Almighty had allowed to happen was for the good of all mankind, that point was never in doubt.

Samuel Edgemont completed his day of instruction and finished with his last office hours of the day, it was Thursday November 2nd. He checked his e-mail and realized it wasn't working. He wondered if Jillian had tried to message him. No worry, he could check from home later. Sam pulled the door shut to his office and headed for the Bronco. The drive to Prestonsburg took thirty minutes, time he liked to use for his audiobooks.

He was presently listening to spy novels. Good thing he had a supply of cassette audiobooks, they had stopped making them years ago.

When he got home there was a note taped to his front door. As he inserted his key into the lock he removed the note, it said to call Mrs. Potter. Sam folded the note and as he did he looked down the street toward her house. He turned the key in the door lock and as he opened the door the phone began to ring. He hurried to grab it.

"Hello," Sam said.

"Sam, it's Mrs. Potter, I have been watching for you and called as soon as I saw you pull in."

Sam could tell that she sounded worried. "Hi Mrs. Potter, it's good to hear from you."

"The reason I needed to talk to you was to let you know that some men have been parked on the street all day and they have been watching your house. You know this is a quiet street and I notice everything."

Sam eased to the window and looked out. He didn't see anything that looked suspicious. "What made you think they were watching my house Mrs. Potter?"

"A car came by the house a couple of times this morning. It wasn't a car I had seen before so I decided to keep an eye out. They left the neighborhood for about fifteen minutes and then they were back. I think they went to get coffee because both men were holding a Styrofoam cup when they came back. Anyway, when they came back they parked right in front of my house. I had my front door closed and I guess they thought it was okay to park there. They stayed until about thirty minutes ago and then left. That was when I walked over and put that note on your door."

"Well, thanks for the note Mrs. Potter; I'll keep my doors locked," Sam said.

"Sam, I think one of the men might have gone inside your house."

Sam was ready to hang up but this stopped him dead in his tracks. "What makes you think anyone could get inside my house Mrs. Potter?" Sam remembered the power company and how they had been able to get inside.

"One of the men got out of the car and walked up the street to your house. He first knocked on your front door and when no one answered he went around back. He was out of sight for several minutes and then he reappeared and came back down the street. I really don't know but I just felt he was inside."

As she was talking Sam was looking around his house. "Well thanks Mrs. Potter, I'm going to have a look around to see if your intuition is correct," he told her.

"Yes Sam please do and be careful." She hung up after that.

The words 'Do be careful' startled Sam. What did Mrs. Potter suspect? Sam first walked to the back door and looked at it. He unlocked the deadbolt and swung the door open. Everything looked alright; nothing appeared to have been moved. He closed the door and relocked it. He then proceeded to check every room in the house. Sam was a very neat person; he'd been that way for as long as he could remember. Everything in his house had a place and if he used something or moved anything he would put it back at least by the end of the day.

As he looked around he became more convinced that Mrs. Potter had nothing better to do than invent drama and now it appeared she was including him. As he came out of the hallway he noticed the living room coffee table. It sat on a thick imitation Persian Rug. It had sat there so long that the four legs had made permanent dimples in the deep fabric of the rug. Sam walked over and inspected the table. It had been moved and then put back but not exactly as it had been before, the rug was the proof. Sam looked around the room again and then he looked up at the ceiling. Beside the light fixture, one that hung down and was held in place by an ornamental chain he noticed something different. The fixture that attached the light to the ceilings electrical box had a small black device sticking out from the side and seemed to be pointed toward the front window and door. Sam went to the closet and pulled out his six foot stepladder.

HB and Stu watched that day as the man entered Samuel Edgemont's house, it wasn't a person that worked for Alterations. He had entered through the back door and was inside for less than ten minutes. They watched as he quickly took down the light fixture in the living room and installed a small device. Stu knew it could capture both audio and video. He then put a small transmitting device under the couch and left.

"Who would hide the transmitter under a couch?" Stu asked.

"They don't plan on gathering information for long, just a day or two or he would have hidden the transmitter a little better," HB said.

"Who do you think it is?" Stu asked.

PT had been there that morning but was called away for some sort of emergency. Hells Bells stepped into his small office and dialed up PT. "We got a problem in Prestonsburg," was all HB said.

PT was in New York at corporate headquarters. He had spent the little time he had been there talking to Elmond Frazier and Greg McKinney. When his cell phone vibrated he excused himself and went to the far end of the room. "What has happened?"

"Someone entered Samuel Edgemont's house a little while ago and installed a micro recorder, video and audio capabilities we suspect. Do you have anyone else working on this project that I should know about?" HB asked.

"No HB, there isn't anyone working that operation other than the people you have."

HB could tell his boss was stressed, his tone was harsh and his words were clipped. "What do you want us to do?"

PT had been startled at first but quickly regained his composure. "Jason Freemont and Alex Trivett were both killed last night. I think it was someone working for The Steggman Group, ever heard of them?"

Hells Bells was shocked, "Killed, how did it happen Patterson?"

PT knew his friend was as shocked as he was when he had found out. "Execution style, both shot in the torso and then a follow-up shot to the head. I was here last night just before it happened. When I left there were three men here from Steggman, they did it HB, I'm sure of it. The people who just bugged Edgemont's house must be working for Steggman too."

"There's something else you should know PT, the equipment they installed is extremely temporary. I would say whatever they are going to do will take place in twenty-four hours or less. Hell they even put the transmitter under the couch," HB told his boss.

PT had been in this business long enough to know that if you didn't take the time to completely hide your equipment then whatever was going to go down was going to happen quick, real quick. "It must be Steggman. They must have found out who the Primary is although I don't know how."

"What do you want done PT?" Hells Bells suspected the next part of the operation was going to be as messy as the box truck fiasco.

"They are a ruthless bunch of bastards. My guess is they are going to observe him for a few hours and once they get the go ahead they will take him, probably during the night. How many men do you have in the area."

"We have four teams. Everyone else is here at New Circle getting debriefed on what happened last night."

PT looked at his watch, it would be dark in minutes in that part of Eastern Kentucky. "Have everyone arm up with whatever they have. If it is Steggman, and we have no reason to believe otherwise, then you can expect casualties if everyone isn't on their toes. Pass the word and have all four teams near that house. I can't leave here for at least twenty-four hours, believe it or not I'm the prime suspect, along with the three Steggman men who were here last night. Word has it that I am about to be cleared but I can't leave town for at least twenty-four hours."

Before hanging up PT added, "My guess is Steggman is either going to kidnap the Primary or if that doesn't work out then they will kill him."

"You think they would really kill him PT?"

"If they can't somehow use him for their own experiments then yes, I think they would eliminate him so no other company can benefit from his biological make up."

"Then he is going to die Patterson. We can't watch him every second of every day, we're not the Secret Service."

"You're right HB. Other than thwarting Steggman's plans for the next twenty-four hours I don't know what we can do. It had been our plan all along to convince Edgemont to visit our labs in Hartford so we could run a few tests. It was going to all be kept confidential and he would have been compensated but now with a 'Capture or Kill' team on the way we are out of options. We can't protect him and he won't trust us."

HB thought about the options he had and asked one more question. "If Steggman kidnaps him and then starts their tests what will happen?"

"If Edgemont is truly some sort of walking biological miracle and Steggman somehow develops a cure-all drug using Edgemont's DNA then they will be the most sought after drug-maker in the world." PT thought a minute and then added, "I want Edgemont killed tonight and I want you to make sure the Steggman Group takes the fall, understood?"

HB thought it would end like this. "That is the safest course of action PT. I'll see that it's done and then pack everything up. All the teams will report back here once the job is finished. Within forty-eight hours New Circle will be shut down and vacated. All the operatives we have in Kentucky will disperse. By this time two days from now our whole operation will be nothing more than a ghost."

"I want hourly updates until Edgemont is eliminated."

"You got it boss." Both men hung up.

Steggman had found out who the primary was as easily as they had found out about the van heist the previous evening. Steggman had lots of people on the payroll and the gathering of information was as simple as picking up the phone. By cross referencing the two Blood Center's data and then correlating that information with the operatives who worked in Alterations it was determined that there was one man that had been watched more than any of the others, Samuel Edgemont.

Steggman had a mole in Alterations, he wasn't anything more than an IT man who had sold out the operation for a large chunk of money. Stu had hired the people he needed to run the operation and had done a good job, when all the staff was hired they were honest. When Steggman entered the picture it didn't take long to pin point where the offices for the Beeler-Jordan operation were located and then find someone who worked there and throw a bunch of money at him. The offices at New Circle had been compromised five days prior.

Steggman used the same contractors that had pulled off the operation the night before. There was even a role for the helicopter pilot and his flying machine. He would be used to haul away Samuel Edgemont, preferably alive and sedated but if that didn't work out then dead would just have to do. The team had been put together with the same efficiency as the one the previous day. The corporate culture at Steggman had a get the job done at all cost mentality. Tonight's operation would hopefully go off with the same sort of efficiency as the one the night before and this time it was doubted if any of the Beeler-Jordan team would be killed, it was doubted if they were even aware that Steggman was onto the name and location of the Primary. By the time anyone in Alterations figured out Samuel Edgemont was gone it would be too late.

As Sam climbed the ladder he had put under his living room light he looked around the rest of the room. There in the corner to the left of the front door was another weird looking device attached to the crown molding. What the hell was all this stuff he wondered. He looked at the thing attached to his ceiling light and again wondered why somebody had taken an interest in his life and he had no idea who it was. He couldn't take down whatever it was that was attached to the light but he could see enough of it to think it was some sort of video device. He climbed down and went to the kitchen. When he came back he was carrying a roll of duct tape. He tore off a small strip and completely wrapped it around whatever it was on the ceiling light. He then moved the ladder and did the same thing to the one in the corner. He got a good enough look at that one to see a small wire running into the loft through the tiniest of holes.

Sam wanted to check out the rest of the rooms but decided to climb into the attic first. He went to the hallway and pulled down the attic stairs. As he stuck his head through the opening he reached over and turned on the switch that worked the lights up there. When he was fully in the attic he looked around the junk that had piled up in the previous five years. He poked around and looked until he saw some insulation that stuck up a bit higher than the rest. When he pulled the piece back he found a funny looking box. Sam picked it up and noticed all the wires running from the damn thing. There was a cord coming from the box and it was plugged into an outlet that was installed in the attic, also there was a very small green light on what appeared to be the front of the box. He reached over and unplugged the cord and the light went off. He turned the box over and looked at all the lines coming out the back, they were all socketed into ports on the back. Sam started unplugging the wires and when finished he took the unit down the ladder and into his kitchen, but not before turning off the light and raising the attic stairs to their closed position.

A technician working for Steggman was looking through the camera when Sam came into the living room and started looking around. Sam looked directly at the Steggman camera mounted on the living room light. He left the room and came back with a ladder. As the duct tape was being applied the camera went dark and the audio became muffled. Steggman's dog and pony show had lasted exactly ten minutes after Sam got home.

At the New Circle offices Stu saw Sam put the ladder in his living room and start to climb. As Sam looked around and noticed the camera installed in the corner he was looking right at it and it almost freaked Stu out, it was as if Sam was looking right at him. When Sam went into the attic it wasn't long before the entire network went dead, Sam had found the main control box and unplugged it.

Stu rung HB in his office, "We just lost audio and video on Edgemont," he said.

"Is it Steggman?"

"No, Edgemont got suspicious and found the transmitter. He unplugged it." Stu told him.

HB marched out of his office and headed over to Stu's bank of monitors. "What do we have left?"

Stu had been running diagnostics on the outside receiver that was mounted to the telephone pole in front of Edgemont's house. "I've got the camera mounted to the receiver, it's still functioning and aimed at Edgemont's front door. Other than that we got nothing.

"When will all the teams be on location?" HB asked.

"We had one team following Edgemont from his offices at the college. They are in Prestonsburg now. One team is at the Pikeville Blood Center and another at the Williamson West Virginia Blood Center. The fourth team was rotating out of New Circle with a new vehicle and won't make it to town for at least ninety more minutes."

"That's not good enough. Steggman might be on site now with their people. They could be planning to make their move any minute. What kind of weapons does the Prestonsburg team have?" HB asked.

Stu switched screens and looked at the inventory the Prestonsburg team possessed. "Looks like a couple of 9mm Berettas and one Glock, also a nine. One 5.56 Daniel Defense assault rifle with a night vision scope, and the good news is it's silenced."

HB thought over his options, they were few. "Have the team in Prestonsburg go immediately and take up a kill position. They will need to park somewhere that the car won't draw attention and then find a suitable spot to observe Edgemont's house. When he walks out his door Friday morning I want them to take him down, one head shot and then two more after he hits the ground. We don't need verification of the death just verification of the three shots making contact with the target. Have the best shooter on the rifle and the other to observe with binos as his spotter."

Stu immediately dialed up the team on a secure phone and gave them the instructions. They gave the verification signal and then hung up. "All done HB; what should we do with the other teams?"

"Call back the other three teams. As far as I'm concerned this operation is over. Start shutting this place down, leave up the monitors and phone system until we get verification that the target is down." HB left

Stu and headed back to his office. It was going to be a long night and he was going to use the time to shut down New Circle. Once the hit was confirmed Stu could pack up his fancy equipment.

Elmond Frazier, Greg McKinney, and the rest of the board worked throughout the night. Elmond knew it was important to gather as much information as possible so new directives could be handed out first thing Friday morning. Once he had all the information that was available he had PT to exit the room while he and the board mulled over what to do next.

Greg McKinney knew Beeler-Jordan had exposed itself to immense litigation, both civil and criminal. He felt Jason Freemont and Alex Trivett had overstepped their bounds by even initiating the 'Ponce de Leon Project' in the first place. The team of people that worked under the Alterations heading had went even further by ordering the murders of several people, it was hard to say at this time how many bodies there were.

"Elmond, I think we should immediately shut down the 'Ponce de Leon Project' and turn over everything we have to the authorities. Since the project took place in several states the FBI should be notified first," Greg said. As he spoke the other members of the board were shaking their heads in agreement.

Elmond, who had been looking out one of the large windows at the New York skyline turned to face the group. "I agree, the sooner we get the FBI involved the sooner the killing will stop. I believe all of us here will be put under scrutiny just by the fact of our positions. I don't believe we will have a problem though. What took place was initiated by the two men who were killed here last night and the men who worked under them. We gather all the information available to us to assist in the investigation. After Jason and Alex who do you think is most directly involved?"

Everyone in the room knew the answer to that. "I believe the man standing in the adjoining office was in as deeply as Jason and Alex. Do you think he will cooperate?" Greg asked.

"I doubt it. If he was in charge of the 'Ponce de Leon Project' then he was giving the orders which resulted in the deaths of several people. Not Jason or Alex, mind you, they were killed by someone who wanted the research, or who already had the research and wanted to eliminate Beeler as a competitor. I think PT will cooperate to a point but he will hide everything that incriminates him. My guess is he's already done that," Elmond said.

"Alright then, get him back in here so we can tell him how things are going to work from now own," Greg told the group.

One of the board members, a man who hadn't been introduced to Elmond went to the door and summoned PT. Once he was back in the room Elmond stood and walked back to the window. Once there he turned to face PT.

"We have decided to shut down the 'Ponce de Leon Project.' I don't have all the particulars yet but I will very soon. I want you to turn over all the data and files on the project. I don't want anything destroyed or hidden. I will need a complete list from you of every person working directly or indirectly on the project from the beginning. And remember Patterson, we now have access to all of Jason and Alex's files and computers," Elmond said.

PT sat and listened without giving away any emotion one way or the other, he had assumed a poker face and Elmond and the members of the board were having a hard time reading him.

"I have had IT working on the computers in Jason and Alex's offices since I got here this morning. I also want you to turn over your laptop immediately. Is any of this going to be a problem?" Elmond waited for an answer.

PT absorbed everything without a hint of emotion on his face. If his face was placid his mind was racing. He knew there was enough information on the two private laptops used by Freemont and Trivett to probably have him sent away for a long time. He doubted there was any information about the numerous murders associated with the project to incriminate him but his personal laptop was bloated with information and passwords that probably wouldn't get him the death-penalty, but a life sentence was highly likely, maybe two or three. At this moment he felt Freemont and Trivett were probably the lucky ones. He also knew the two laptops the two top executives used were encrypted and password protected.

PT still sat stone faced, he really hadn't been asked a question yet. Elmond had saved the best part for last. "We are also going to fully cooperate with the FBI."

This last statement finally brought PT to life. He felt he needed to give the impression that he thought this was a very good idea and he intended to participate fully while behind the scenes he would do everything in his power to thwart the investigation. "I think under the circumstances that is an excellent idea. I will have everything gathered and sent here for examination. Shouldn't take more than a couple of days to box every file and computer up and then truck it here to corporate. How does that sound? As for my laptop, it is there also and will be sent along with everything else." PT was lying, he had rented a locker at the airport and put his laptop there before getting into the corporate limo for the ride into town.

Elmond knew PT was lying. He didn't like the man when he had met him earlier and he liked him even less now. That was why he had taken precautions. "That won't be necessary PT. I spoke to an FBI agent before you got here this afternoon. As we speak a search warrant is being served on your offices at New Circle. The FBI is good at such things you know. You will also be escorted to the locker where you stored your belongings before you got here. The laptop you possess is the main item of interest."

PT put his elbows on the conference table and then interlaced his fingers in front of him, he was thinking about his next move and everyone in the room knew it. His laptop was encrypted and password protected but if the FBI demanded him to unlock it and he refused he could be arrested for obstruction of justice and impeding a federal investigation. There was information in his computer that would implicate him along with HB and Stu. He just couldn't allow that to happen.

"That will be fine. When will this take place?" He asked.

"The FBI is here already. I was told that two agents will accompany you to the airport and take possession of the contents in the locker you rented. If you are ready I will ring downstairs for the two agents," Greg said.

PT smiled. "That's fine, after a quick stop at the restroom I will be ready to go." PT excused himself and went into the hall and down three doors to the men's restroom. Once inside he locked the door and took out his cellphone. He dialed a direct number to Hells Bells hoping the FBI wasn't already there with search warrants. He also hoped Stu and HB hadn't dismantled Stu's fancy equipment yet.

On the second ring HB answered. "HB, I need you to wipe my laptop clean, and then wipe every hard drive in the building. Do it now, the FBI is on their way with search warrants," PT said.

"That won't be a problem but I'm not sure about your laptop," HB said.

"Stu can do it. Tell him to log on remotely and crash the whole damn thing. Me and two FBI agents are going to the airport to pick it up now. I want it to be worth about fifty-cents by the time I hand it over, do you understand?"

"Has Stu got the ability to do that from here?" HB asked.

"We better damn well hope he does. The Wi-Fi on my laptop is on; plant the nastiest virus you got and hit go!" PT told him before he hung up.

PT flushed the urinal to hide any sounds he made as he took his cellphone apart and broke it into small pieces. He then dropped the pieces into the toilet and hit the flush lever. To his good fortune every piece of the phone disappeared down the drain. He washed his hands and then exited the restroom. Standing there to greet him were two men wearing dark sport coats and wearing Foster Grant sunglasses.

"Are you Patterson Tingler?" The shorter of the two agents asked.

PT looked at the two and wondered how long they had been in the hall and if either had heard him talking to HB. "I am."

"Mr. Tingler, you were supposed to wait in the conference room until we came to escort you to the airport," the second agent said.

"Sorry but there wasn't a restroom in the conference room. I didn't realize I needed permission to go to the bathroom."

"Consider as of right now you need to ask us permission to do anything other than breathe, you understand?" The shorter agent said.

"Did you use the phone in there Mr. Tingler?" The taller one asked.

PT decided he didn't like these two and he was going to give them a hard time. "There isn't a payphone in there, you can check for yourself if you like."

"Don't be a smartass, let me have your cellphone so I can see if you made a call and to whom!" Short Agent demanded.

"I don't have a cellphone; you two want to frisk me," PT said with a smirk on his face. He was really glad he had flushed his cell; the phone call to New Circle could have gotten him arrested on the spot.

One of the two agents did frisk PT and found him to not have a phone on him. The other agent, Short Agent, went into the restroom and had a look around. "Nothin in there," he said as he came out.

"We can check the phone records with your provider and find out if you called anyone," Tall Agent said.

PT thought that would be interesting if they could actually find his provider. He purchased a new phone every seven days and always paid cash. "Good luck gentlemen, I hope you find a dozen phones in my name."

The two agents realized they were truly dealing with a smartass who wasn't afraid of the FBI, at least not on the outside. They suspected PT was nervous as hell on the inside. "Come on, we got a trip to the airport."

PT and the two agents walked to the elevator and went down to the basement. That was where the parking garage was located. The two men went to a black Dodge Charger. Short Agent got behind the wheel and Tall Agent climbed in the back, "You sit up front Mr. Tingler." PT climbed in and closed the door.

"We would like to ask you a few questions on the way to the airport Mr. Tingler, if that is alright," Tall Agent said.

"You can do that if you like," PT said.

Tall Agent took out a small recorder and placed it on the front console between Short Agent and PT. "We would also like to record our conversation if you don't mind?"

"I don't mind at all," PT said.

As they pulled out of the parking garage and headed in the direction of the airport Tall Agent asked, "How long have you been in charge of the operation that has offices on New Circle Road in Lexington, Kentucky?"

PT looked out the window at the people on the sidewalks, but said nothing.

"Mr. Tingler, you agreed to answer a few questions on the way to the airport. Now how long have you been in charge of the operation that works out of the offices on New Circle Road in Lexington, Kentucky?"

PT continued to look out the window.

"This isn't going to help your case at all. You agreed to answer a few questions," Tall Agent said again.

'That isn't what I agreed to at all. I agreed that you could ask a few questions, I never said I would answer. Furthermore if I'm under arrest shouldn't you read me my rights, I think they're called Miranda Rights." PT knew exactly what they were called and had even had them read to him a few times in his younger days.

Short Agent looked back at Tall Agent and they both knew they were wasting their time; it was always worth a try though. The three men rode the rest of the trip in silence.

HB and Stu had the entire staff at New Circle shedding paperwork and erasing hard drives. Exactly eighteen minutes after PT had flushed his phone down the toilet six FBI agents in two black Tahoe's slid into the parking lot out front. They were accompanied by four cars from the Lexington Metro Police Department. After repeated attempts to raise someone at the front doors one of the LMPD officers produced a sledgehammer and a pair of safety glasses. After one mild tap on the glass the door was nothing more than a frame, the glass was lying shattered on the sidewalk. Another officer reached in and unlatched the lock.

The agents quickly went inside and noticed that all the offices were empty, it was a front. They then used the sledgehammer to smash through the back wall into the main offices of the 'Ponce de Leon Project' covered under the innocent sounding name of 'Alterations.'

The Donor

There were at least twenty people in the offices and they were all busy shredding paperwork. One of the agents, a man with a barrel chest stepped forward and shouted, "This is the FBI, everyone stop what you are doing and hold your hands in the air." By the volume it was assumed he was chosen for his ability to get everyone's attention without the use of a bullhorn.

Stu and HB stood and looked at the officers. "May I see some paperwork?" HB said calmly.

One of the agents stepped forward and reached a two page document to HB. "Have all your people walk outside. We don't have arrest warrants but we do need to take down everyone's names and addresses. After that you are allowed to leave."

HB looked over the paper work and found what he was looking for, a judge's signature at the bottom of the second page. He reached the document back to the agent and looked at Stu. "I think we should stay. After these boys get through with their search someone will need to lock up." Stu agreed.

The agent who handled the papers said, "If that's the case then I suggest you call a glass company." After he said this he left the two to absorb what had happened.

When HB and Stu were far enough away from the others HB asked in a very low voice, "How much did you get erased?"

Stu smiled and said, "Everything of course. I had a kill virus in a thumb drive ready for just such an occasion."

HB looked at him incredulously, "You mean you had a virus like that installed on the systems here the whole time? Wasn't that a little risky? What if it somehow got downloaded by accident?"

Stu reached inside his tee-shirt and pulled out a chain that hung around his neck. "Not risky at all. After I developed it I carried it on this thumb drive and simply downloaded it when you gave me the word. Another little surprise I installed, when the FBI or whoever tries to get into the system the virus will be waiting. It will instantly infect whatever software they are using to search with, just a little bomb that will cost them some software and quite a few days of work. Once they do get around my virus they won't find anything."

HB was impressed. Stu had told him he had a quick exit plan if the place had ever been compromised. "What about the laptop PT called about, were you able to infect it as well?" HB prayed that he had.

Stu looked at him and again smiled. "That is one laptop that will never give up any secrets. It also has the nasty little virus inside just waiting for some tech at the FBI to plug into. Again it will cost some software and several man-hours to find out nothing."

HB and Stu pulled a couple of office chairs near the back loading dock door and took a seat. They enjoyed the show.

Short Agent and Tall Agent walked into the airport with PT. They followed him to a section of the private terminal where lockers were stacked four high and twenty long. PT took a key from his pocket and reached it to Short Agent. "Here you go; it's the one on the bottom there, I figured you being closer to the ground and all."

Short Agent took the key and said, "Step back smartass."

"Be my pleasure." PT told him.

The two agents emptied the contents, one laptop bag and one carry-on.

PT reached for the carry-on, "I'll take that," he said.

"No you won't!" Short Agent said as he yanked the bag out of reach. "We'll need to have a look first. You will get it back in a couple of days. And by the way, you can take a cab back to your offices downtown."

As the two turned away PT couldn't resist the appeal of getting in a little barb of his own. "How's that lawsuit coming?" He asked Short Agent.

"What lawsuit would that be?" Short Agent asked.

"The one you filed against the city for building the sidewalks so close to your ass?" PT said as he started laughing.

Short Agent let it pass. He would get even before this little investigation was over. They walked away leaving a laughing PT standing by the lockers. As PT headed to the front of the terminal to grab a cab he really hoped Stu had been able to crash the hard drive on the laptop. If not then the FBI was going to hang him from a tall pole.

The two men that had been assigned to take up a position to observe Samuel Edgemont's house were in place. It was difficult but hadn't been anything the two couldn't handle. They both had done multiple tours in Afghanistan and Iraq and knew how to infiltrate a community without being seen. The problem was going to be getting out. If Edgemont never came out until the next morning then it would mean shooting him in broad daylight. The rifle shots wouldn't be heard but if someone saw him go down then law enforcement would be summoned and it would make the job of evasion quite a bit more difficult. The two assassins knew they could make it to where they had parked their car without being spotted. Time would tell.

Both men settled in for a long wait. They would have only one chance to complete the mission, and that would be when Edgemont exited his house and went to his big green Bronco which was parked on the street directly in front of the house. If someone saw him go down then they would assume it was an accident or a medical emergency, no rifle shot would be heard thanks to the silencer. By the time someone dialed 911 and an ambulance came it was hoped the two assassins would be nearing their car. Once it was discovered that he had been shot multiple times and a search was conducted for the assailants the two hoped to be at least twenty miles away. It was a good plan.

Steggman had a plan of their own! As the two Beeler-Jordan men hunkered near a small rise in a stand of small trees and brush a police car pulled up outside Samuel Edgemont's house. Steggman had done their homework and knew if a city car was used it would most likely be spotted by another Prestonsburg City Police Unit. They decided to use a car with the same markings as the Floyd County Sheriff's Department. Those cars were all over the county at all hours of the day and night. If it were spotted by a city unit it was doubtful if anything would be suspected.

The time was nine thirty-seven when the car pulled up behind the dark green Bronco. None of this was missed by the two Beeler men. One watched through binoculars and the other looked through the scope of his rifle. The sheriff's car had two men inside. They got out and looked around, the streets were deserted.

They both walked up to the front door and one rang the doorbell. Sam had been inside all evening hunting the wireless devices that seemed to be all over his house. He already found four and assumed there were more, he was correct. As he searched he wondered what was going on. There were just too many weird things happening to say it was just coincidence.

As he tried to convince himself that there had to be an explanation to everything, he found two reasons to think that might be possible. Number one was the thought that the devices might have been in the house all along and he was just now noticing them. Number two was maybe the previous owner had an elaborate security system and when he moved out and sold the place he just left everything behind. Actually it was one reason, number two supported number one.

Just as he found the fourth device his doorbell rang. He got down from the ladder and went to see who would be out on a cold November night. He answered the door and was surprised to see two Floyd County Deputies standing on his front porch. "Can I help you?" Sam asked.

It had been agreed to enter the house and cuff him there, on the porch might be more noticeable and that was something the two bogus cops didn't want.

"May we come in?" One of the deputies asked. How could any unsuspecting law abiding citizen turn down a request like that the deputy thought.

Sam looked confused as he stood back and invited the two inside. "What is this about?" He asked.

It had been suggested by the man in charge of this operation to snatch Edgemont fast and get him in the car. The longer the sheriff's car sat out front the more chance that a neighbor might become nosey or worse, another legitimate sheriff's or city police car happen by. The two men tasked with apprehending Edgemont were strong and fast, both were ex-military. It was amazing how many specialists both Beeler-Jordan and The Steggman Group had at their disposal to figure things like this out.

Once the front door was closed the two sprang into action. "Are you Samuel Edgemont?" One of the two asked.

Sam started to look worried. He wondered if there had been a car accident concerning one of his students or maybe a fire. "Yes, I'm Sam Edgemont. What has happened?"

One of the two men produced a set of handcuffs and said, "You're under arrest Mr. Edgemont. Put your hands behind your back and let's not make this difficult."

"Under arrest, what's the charge?" He asked.

"If you don't turn around right now and keep quiet it'll be for resisting arrest."

Sam wasn't a fool, hell he taught lawyers for a living. "What is the charge, I demand to know," he again asked.

The two bogus cops never had a charge, an arrest warrant, not even a parking ticket to present to the accused. "You'll be told once you are at the jail. Now turn around." If Sam resisted it had been decided they would Taser him and then put him in the car, again not a good situation for two men who wanted to get away without making a scene. If a Taser were used it would require both men to carry him to the car, this was a worst case scenario. Luckily for both, Sam relented, he assumed there was some sort of misunderstanding and it could be sorted out at the Justice Center once he and the two deputies got there.

Sam turned around and put both his hands behind his back. As they cuffed him he asked again. "I have never heard of something like this." It was then he realized something else that was strange, these two men were wearing deputy sheriff uniforms. "Why wasn't any of the city cops sent out with you. I know almost all of them and they would know that a mistake has been made."

"Shut up, we don't need to be lectured to by some smartass tonight. Now keep quiet before you get that resisting arrest upgrade I mentioned," one of the two said. Sam didn't know which one because he had his back to them.

Once he was properly cuffed they opened the front door and led him to the car. One opened the passenger side back door while the other one quickly shoved him in. Sam barely got his head down in time or he would have had a nasty bang against the top of the door frame. Now he knew something was wrong, he hadn't been read his rights and with all the cell phone cameras on every sidewalk no cop would ever handle a cuffed prisoner in such a flagrant way.

Whatever crime they were arresting him for, a crime he didn't commit, must have been really bad; he wished he knew what it was. The jail was only a mile away; maybe he would get some answers once they booked him in. Or maybe they would realize their mistake and he would be driven back home with an apology. Somehow he doubted it would end so pleasantly. Something had happened and they thought he had done it.

The one that had so roughly shoved Sam into the back of the cruiser walked around and got in on the opposite side. The second cop got behind the wheel and started the engine. Sam looked at the one sitting across from him; he was looking back at Sam and smiling.

"Will you please tell me what is going on?" Sam asked.

Neither cop spoke. As the car came out of May's Branch, Sam was counting the minutes until he would be at the jail and away from these two. He still couldn't place the two deputies; he had lived in Floyd County for five years and knew most of the city police. He doubted if he knew even two of the men who worked for the Sheriff's Department. The car got to the junction and turned left. One mile later and it turned right onto the road which led to the Mountain Parkway.

This wasn't the way to the Justice Center. "Where are you taking me?" Sam asked.

Neither of the two spoke.

"Where are you taking me? The courthouse and jail are in town," Sam asked with no small amount of worry in his voice.

Finally the one in the back seat decided to speak. "Just keep quiet and you'll be alright."

A terrifying thought just occurred to Sam; he looked at the one in the back seat and asked, "You're not deputies are you?"

"Maybe, maybe not, now as I told you, keep quiet."

Sam sat back in the seat as best as he could. He had been cuffed from behind; with both arms behind him he was very uncomfortable. The discomfort of the cuffs was nothing compared to the terror of being driven away by two men who were definitely not deputies. Sam thought of all the things that had happened in the last few weeks. The men watching his house, the men in the parking lot at the blood center, the devices he found in his house.

Maybe that was it. Whoever had installed the devices must have been watching him and when he started taking them down they sent these two goons to get him. But even if that were the reason why were the devices in his house and for that matter who would be watching him so closely? It was a clear case of breaking and entering and false arrest. Add that to kidnapping and false imprisonment and this was becoming a nightmare.

The Beeler-Jordan sniper and spotter were surprised to see a Floyd County Sheriff's patrol car pull up in front of Samuel Edgemont's house. They first thought they might have been seen and the cops were there to check it out. After some consideration they figured there was no way the two had been seen, they were just too well hidden. It was decided that rather than pulling out of their position they would just stay put and see where things went. If the cops started to head their way they would send a few rounds over their heads and while they were hunkered down calling in back-up the Beeler men could make their get-away.

One of the men watched through his binoculars and the other observed through the scope of his Daniel-Defense rifle. The two cops got out of the car and eased to the front door. They knocked and a few seconds later Edgemont opened the door. The two deputies went inside. Within minutes they exited the house and Edgemont was being led toward the car, he was cuffed. The Beeler man with the binoculars had a police band radio with an earpiece, he could listen but no one could hear the radio.

As Edgemont was placed in the backseat of the patrol car and then driven away there wasn't any radio traffic of the arrest, nothing. The two Beeler men suspected Edgemont had just been grabbed by someone other than the police. The man with the earpiece used his cell to call it in. The two were told to discontinue the surveillance and get back to their car. Instructions would follow.

Stu and HB had one more team positioned in Prestonsburg for back up in case the sniper and spotter got into trouble. Stu immediately called the second team.

"Pearson, what is your position?"

"Parking lot at Pizza Hut."

"Primary has been picked up by Sheriff's Department unit, heading your way now. Shadow and report."

"Roger that." The man named Pearson looked at his partner. "What the hell just happened?"

The other man in the car was named Binder. "What would the Sheriff's Department want with Edgemont? He is about the most boring person in Floyd County. I bet the man hasn't even got a traffic ticket."

"You said it. His idea of a wild night is to grade a boatload of exams and watch Jeopardy."

Just then a Floyd County Sheriff's Department car came out of May's Branch. It stopped at the junction and then turned left toward downtown. Pearson started his car and pulled out four cars back from the sheriff's car. Three more lights and the car should have gone straight but instead turned right onto the road that led to the Mountain Parkway. Pearson called it in and waited for instruction.

"Continue to follow but stay back. You got another unit on the way."

Pearson slowed a bit and allowed the distance to grow. He was afraid he would be spotted if he followed too closely. The second car with the sniper team quickly caught up. Both of the Beeler cars were now following the fake cop car.

Once it was determined the cop car was heading toward the Mountain Parkway Stu and HB sent three more teams from Lexington heading toward Prestonsburg. The main office at New Circle might have been raided and all the computers crashed by Stu but they were still able to coordinate with the teams.

Pearson called Stu and asked what he was supposed to do.

"Just continue to follow. Once they cross the county line the officers are out of their jurisdiction. If that happens then it is assumed they are bogus and Edgemont has been kidnapped." Stu told Pearson.

"Who do you think is involved if the car passes that boundary?" Pearson asked.

Stu and HB conferred for a few seconds and decided to let their teams in on what they thought. "If the car passes the county line then we think it's Steggman. Most likely the same men who killed our men in Slade." This was shared with the two pursuit teams to let them know how dangerous the situation could be. Knowing they might be following some of the men that had killed their friends the previous night would also add a level of anger that made sure the four men didn't lose the car they were following.

As they were traveling west, Edgemont was studying the car he was riding in. There wasn't a partition between the front and back seats. There wasn't a computer of the laptop variety mounted in the front seat, something that most cop cars were equipped with these days. There wasn't any fancy radio equipment in the car. Edgemont suddenly understood, this wasn't a police car and these two men weren't deputies.

Now in the back of the bogus cop car Samuel Edgemont was getting extremely nervous. The longer they drove the more terrified he got. He was afraid he was being taken away to be killed. Edgemont realized if he is going to survive he will need to use his head. First he must get the cuffs off and second he needs to get the car to stop. He came up with a plan and hoped he could keep his cool long enough to see if it would work.

"Would it be possible to get these cuffs off, my back is starting to spasm," Sam said.

The two Steggman men knew they had a long way to go and realized Edgemont probably had a legitimate request. Both men were armed and doubted Edgemont would be a problem if he wasn't wearing cuffs.

"Turn your back to me and I'll take the cuffs off but if you try anything I can't guarantee I won't shoot you."

Sam gladly turned his back so the cuffs could be removed. Once off, he straightened in his seat and rubbed his arms. When he finally got a little feeling back in his hands he reached up and grabbed his seatbelt and snapped it in place. Neither of the other two men in the car was wearing seatbelts. Sam figured if he was going to be killed then at least it wouldn't be because of a car wreck.

Sam didn't know it but that seatbelt was about to save his life, for real. As the bogus cop car raced toward the Mountain Parkway, which began at a town called Salyersville; a twelve point buck stepped from the tree line and nibbled on some late clover that grew beside the blacktop. Just as the car came around the curve at seventy miles an hour the buck decided he would rather be on the other side of the road, maybe the clover was tastier over there. When the big buck stepped across the white line he was met with a set of headlights and the sound of screeching tires on pavement. The buck went into high gear and made it to the other side without going nose to nose with the car. The buck climbed the opposite hill, none the worse for wear. It was a way better outcome than that of the speeding car.

No sooner had Samuel Edgemont gotten the cuffs off and his seat belt snapped into place than the driver shouted, "Oh shit!"

As soon as Sam heard those two words he felt the car braking hard. He grabbed the door handle and looked through the windshield. The blur he saw was a deer in high gear trying to grab some traction in order to keep from getting run over. The car was breaking left and at the speed it was going it started to spin. The big Ford clipped a guard rail and as the driver over corrected it came back across both lanes with enough force to sever the rail on that side of the road and then careen down an embankment, it landed nose first in Middle Creek. The water was only a foot deep due to a fall drought that had lasted seven full weeks. The impact was so severe that Edgemont was momentarily knocked unconscious. When he came to he noticed the car was standing almost straight up in the creek. He was still buckled in and realized the seatbelt had most likely saved his life.

Sam put his knees and his left hand against the front seat; with his right hand he unbuckled the seatbelt. He fell against the front seat but didn't go over it. The cop or whatever he was that was in the back seat with him was nowhere to be seen. Sam looked over the seat and saw both men piled under the steering wheel and dashboard. They were both wedged in the front floorboard. The windshield was completely shattered and there was blood everywhere.

Sam needed to get out of the car; his first thought was of the car catching fire and him being trapped inside. He reached for the door handle and then a terrible fear entered the picture, the rear handles in cop cars don't work. Criminals in the back of cop cars can't get out because the back door handles are either disabled or gone altogether. In a panic Sam grabbed the handle and gave it a mighty pull. It worked.

Sam eased through the door and fell into water; his fear of being burned alive was suddenly replaced with the fear of drowning. As soon as he hit the water he struggled to his feet, the water was only up to his knees and that was it. As he stood in the darkness he heard a car coming up the highway and it seemed to be going very fast. As he stood there trying to get his wits about him he saw the light of the cars headlights going by, the car never stopped, it didn't even seem to slow down. Sam turned and looked back inside the car he had just exited. There was no movement from the two men in the front. Sam looked and realized the two didn't even look to be breathing. He watched for the longest time, no movement at all.

It was time to get away before someone else came along wearing a policeman's uniform and holding an arrest warrant with Sam's name on it. He left the car and started up the embankment. Sam slid a time or two but was soon rewarded with the sight of the road right in front of him. He walked a few feet and sat down on the guardrail. As he sat he realized the fear of the wreck and the exertion of climbing back to the road had left him breathless. As bad as Sam wanted to go back down and help the two men trapped in the car he realized if they were alive and came to he didn't know what they would do. He couldn't help someone just to have them regain consciousness and possibly kill him. The two were on their own; someone would see the wreck and an ambulance would be called, that was the best he could hope for.

As Sam got his breathing under control he looked at his arms and legs in the dim light of a lazy moon. He saw no blood and he also knew there were no broken bones or he wouldn't have been able to climb back to the roadway. He stood as he heard the noise of another approaching car. It was on him before he could seek cover. The car slowed and eased over to the side of the road. Once to the spot where Sam stood the passenger side window came down. Sam could see there was a man in the car.

"You need some help Sam?" Was the voice Sam heard from inside the car.

Sam wasn't afraid, he actually felt this was someone he could trust. "There has been a wreck. Two men are trapped inside the car over the hill there. Can you call an ambulance?" Sam asked this even though these same two men had kidnapped him.

The man in the car looked in the direction Sam was pointing and said, "I wish an ambulance could help them Sam but they are both dead. Neither was wearing a seatbelt and the crash took their lives."

Sam took his eyes off the driver and looked in the direction of the wreck. The car couldn't be seen from the highway and he wondered how the man knew the two were dead. "How do you know they're dead?"

"I just know Sam. We need to leave."

Sam looked again at the wreck and realized himself that the two men actually were dead. He looked back at the driver, "How do you know my name?"

"This is the first time we have met but I've known you for five years Sam."

Sam looked one last time in the direction of the wreck and then for a reason he couldn't explain he opened the door to the car and got in, as soon as he was seated he put on the seatbelt. The car pulled away from the guardrail and headed in the direction of Salyersville. Sam wasn't afraid; he felt he could trust this person, maybe it was because he had been shaken up so badly in the wreck.

"Who are you?" Sam asked.

Without taking his eyes off the road the man said, "My name is Jacob."

Sam leaned back in his seat. He watched the road and then told the driver, "I feel as if I know you but I don't know how?"

"You do know me. We have never met but you certainly know me."

As each minute went by Sam was getting back some sort of awareness, he was stepping from one life toward another. "You weren't supposed to come for me for at least two more years, what happened?" Sam asked.

Jacob allowed the question to hang for a few minutes. "You're right Sam. I am two years ahead of the appointed time. Events have progressed faster than had been hoped. It became necessary to make the transition now rather than at the end of the seven year cycle."

As the cobwebs began to separate and Sam became more aware of what had happened he felt a sadness start to form.

"I wasn't finished Jacob, there was so much more for me to do."

"It will be like that for a while Sam. You always feel sad for what you leave behind but that will soon be replaced by happiness for what you were able to accomplish."

The two drove on for a few miles. "How many Jacob, how many did I help?"

"There were many Sam, almost three thousand. The lives you helped with your generosity will continue to spread that kindness to others, not physically as you have done, but by example."

Sam looked at Jacob. "I still don't understand why the two men in the car had to die, couldn't I have helped them?"

"No Sam. Sometimes good people are taken for bad reasons. Those two weren't good people. Sometimes bad people are taken for good reasons."

"A lot of hurt exists in the world today Jacob. Why?"

"It's the way of the world Sam. It's the way of God. He doesn't make bad things happen, people do that without any help. He watches us always and gives each of us the ability to do good; he also gives each of us the ability to do bad. The choice is a gift he gives us, we are allowed to take such a precious gift and then do with it as we choose. Many people waste what is given, bad choices. Many cherish what is given, good choices."

Sam thought about what he was being told. "Those people that knew me, what happens to the memory of me Jacob?" Sam was momentarily concerned by the way he had been taken away in the police car.

"As always your memory will be part of what you have given to those that knew you. In the next few days answers will come forth and the memory of you will be cleansed of the two men who just died and the way they treated you."

Sam smiled. It was as before, those who choose to believe would be rewarded with happiness, a happiness that was a direct result of his deeds. Those who choose to scoff would be allowed to stumble along in the darkness of their decision. That happens when you turn your back on what you know is real and choose to believe in something easy. Believing can be hard sometimes but that makes the results all the more worthwhile.

"What will happen to those two men back there in the car?" Sam asked. Even though he knew they both meant him harm he was still concerned.

"They chose their paths. The reasons are the same, always the same. Greed, excitement, hate, any number of other paths were available to them Sam. They will each be judged in due time. I, nor anyone else knows what the outcome will be, but it will be just." After a long pause Jacob added, "Forgiveness is possible but think how much easier it would have been if they had lived their lives differently."

Sam nodded his understanding. "I just needed to know Jacob, that's all."

"Your concern is part of who you are Sam."

Sam looked at Jacob. "Who am I?"

Jacob allowed a few miles to pass before answering. "You are the Chosen."

The first Beeler-Jordan car suddenly couldn't see the patrol car which carried Samuel Edgemont. They weren't more than thirty seconds behind and lost sight of the car at the end of a long straight stretch. They sped up in order to close the distance and by the time they finished the straight stretch and entered the curve they were doing eighty-five miles an hour. When they came out of the curve they were presented with another substantial straight stretch, no tail lights could be seen. The Beeler car sped up and proceeded at nearly a hundred miles an hour for three more miles. It was decided that the patrol car had either sped up or pulled off. Most likely they had pulled into someone's driveway in order to see if they were being followed.

The Beeler car slowed and turned around. As they headed back toward Prestonsburg they kept a lookout on all the driveways and side roads to see if the patrol car might be hiding in one, it wasn't. As they drove the only car they met was a Ford Fusion heading in the direction of Salyersville traveling the speed limit. When they got back to the curve where they had lost sight of the patrol car one of the two men saw the fresh dent in the guardrail on the right side of the road.

The Beeler car slowed and that was when they saw the marks on the highway. It looked like a car had decelerated hard and after clipping the guardrail went back across the road and ploughed completely through the guardrail on the other side and then disappeared into the creek. By now the second Beeler car had caught up, this was the car that contained the sniper and spotter. Both cars stopped beside the road. The four men got out and looked the situation over. Once they looked over the embankment they saw the patrol car standing on its nose in the creek. The car was smashed up really bad.

Two of the men raced down the hill with guns drawn as the other two stayed by the highway with the cars. One quick look in the car was all it took to find out the obvious, the two men piled in the front floorboard were most likely dead. The one in the back was still held in place by his seatbelt. He didn't look like he was injured. A quick check for a carotid pulse indicated that the man was dead; his neck was at a very extreme angle. The impact had been with such force that the shoulder strap of the seatbelt had broken the man's neck.

"Any survivors?" Shouted one of the men from the roadway.

A quick check of the two up front revealed they were both dead too. "No, all three are dead. The two up front are from impact trauma, the one in the back has a broken neck."

The four men knew they needed to leave the scene of the crash before another car came along. "Can you identify any of the victims?" The man up top yelled.

"Not the two in the front, both are wearing deputy's uniforms. The one in the back is Samuel Edgemont."

"Are you sure all three are dead?"

"They're dead, no doubt about it."

"Get back up here before another car comes along," the man on the road said.

All four men got in the two cars and sped away. They drove the speed limit all the way to Salyersville. There was a BP station on the right and both cars pulled in to fill up. As they pumped gas they considered their options.

"That was a hell of a wreck, looked like all three died on impact or seconds after. I don't think any of the three felt any pain," one of the two that went down the embankment said.

Once the cars were filled they pulled both away from the pumps and parked in front of the station. "You three go in and get some coffee while I call this in. Bring me back a large House Blend, lots of Half and Half. I like a lot of cream."

The three went inside as Pearson called Stu and HB. "Contact has crashed, all three occupants are dead," was all Pearson said.

"Hold Pearson," Stu said as he motioned for HB.

"What's up Stu?"

"Pearson says the Steggman car has crashed. It must have been bad, all three occupants are dead." Stu told HB.

"All dead, was one of the three Edgemont?" He asked.

Stu punched a button on the phone and asked Pearson, "Was one of the deceased Edgemont?"

"Affirmative," Pearson replied.

Stu put the call on hold again and turned back to HB, "Edgemont is dead."

HB knew the mission was now over. The sniper and spotter would have been at risk with the original plan but now, as it worked out, they were never needed. "Pull everybody back Stu. Have all the teams to come in."

Stu punched the button again, "All operations are suspended; you are to proceed to New Circle."

"Affirmative," Pearson answered.

Stu contacted the other teams and had them to cease operations and return to Lexington.

New Circle was nothing more than a location now. Everything that had once been known as Alterations was in a U-Haul Van being driven by two FBI agents on the way to a lab that specialized in such things as software forensics. Once the teams made it to town Stu and HB would have them diverted to the car rental shops to turn in the vehicles. By daylight the next morning everyone would be in another state, their fake identities destroyed at the state line.

At Slade the Steggman teams were waiting for the arrival of the patrol car which contained the two bogus deputies and Samuel Edgemont. The plan had gone so well on Wednesday night that it was decided to carry out the same plan again. A helicopter, the same one that was used before was sitting in wait. Once Edgemont was on board it would fly him to the same airport that was used for the transport of the blood samples stolen from the Blood Center van.

As they waited for the car carrying Edgemont they were unaware that an accident had taken place and all three men were dead. By midnight it was decided that something must have gone wrong, the car wasn't there and all attempts to reach them by phone had proven fruitless. Two cars were dispatched from the Slade pickup site and told to head toward Prestonsburg, the last place the two men escorting Edgemont had been heard from. The two cars unknowingly passed Jacob Yates and Samuel Edgemont at the Hazel Green exit.

As Yates and Edgemont headed west they were unaware the two cars they had just met were affiliated with the same men who had kidnapped Sam.

"What will happen when the authorities find the wrecked car with the two dead men inside. Will I be at risk of being captured again?" Sam asked.

"No Sam, you are safe now, but you can never go back. The police will find three bodies in the car, the two Steggman men and Samuel Edgemont," Jacob said.

Sam was at first startled and then he seemed too understood. "If they find my body there then what am I now?" Was all he could say.

"Sam, you were in Eastern Kentucky for nearly five years. What you accomplished, although extraordinary, was only one of the steps you have taken in your long journey. There have been lots of Eastern Kentucky's in your past and there are to be many more in your future."

Sam looked at the road ahead and tried to gather his thoughts. "A little while ago you referred to me as the 'Chosen.' What did you mean by that?"

"I can't answer that, not because I don't want to but because I really don't know. I myself was sent to a cabin five years ago and told to live there until the time came for me to intervene in your life. That is all the information I have for you, anything else would be only conjecture on my part."

The Donor

Sam rode in silence for another few miles and then asked, "You mentioned that they would find my body in the wrecked car. Am I dead Jacob?"

Jacob smiled, "You are alive Sam; you can hear your own voice and see with your own eyes. Your mind works and your heart beats. I can't say what exactly they will find in the wrecked car but one of the three bodies will be the man known as Samuel Edgemont."

"You said this has happened many times in the past and will happen many times in the future. What does that mean?" Sam asked.

Jacob wondered himself what the answer was, he would like to know. "I don't know Sam, you want my best guess?"

Sam smiled, "Yes, I want your best guess Jacob, what am I?"

Jacob felt he had known Sam for many years although the time the two men had spent since the wreck could be counted in hours, less than two actually. He looked at Sam and realized who he had in the car with him. "I think you are a spirit. I don't know anything other than that, you must be a spirit of some sort."

Sam continued to look out the windshield. As the miles clicked by he decided to press forward with his suspicions. "Are you saying I am an Angel?"

"That's exactly what I'm saying. I don't know for sure but I suspect you are."

"If that's true then the body they find in the car, will it really be me?" Sam asked.

"All I can tell you is what they find in the wrecked car will be the body of Samuel Edgemont, the same Samuel Edgemont that everyone in your circle of acquaintances has come to know and trust. There will be an autopsy to determine the exact cause of death, which by the way was a broken neck due to the shoulder strap snapping tight against your throat when the car impacted with the creek bed. After that the body will be sent back to Floyd County and the arrangements will be taken care of by one of the funeral homes there."

"That explains what happens to my body, what happens to the life I built there?" Sam asked.

"A will was prepared five years ago, you have never seen it but it is at your office at the college. It instructs that after a wake is held your body is to be cremated. Some think cremation isn't biblical but they are wrong; ashes to ashes, dust to dust. Your belongings are to be sold and the proceeds given to the church you have attended for the last five years. The money you have saved will be given as a charitable gift to the college where you worked," Jacob said.

"Why is my body to be cremated, wouldn't a simple burial be sufficient?" Sam wanted to know.

"A burial would have been more suitable to the members of your church which contains many of the people who consider cremation an affront to their beliefs. There is a slight fear that if your body is buried some of the people that have been after you for the last few months might attempt to rob the grave and confiscate the body. It's the physical make up of your body that the bad guys wanted; they wanted it so much they would commit murder to obtain it. Your gifts haven't gone unnoticed by the medical and pharmaceutical establishments of the world," Jacob said.

"Do you really think the body left behind could still be used for medical reasons?" Sam asked.

"Again, I can't answer with any degree of certainty, I can only tell you what I think." Jacob said this and then fell silent.

"Go ahead Jacob, tell me what you think."

"If your body were taken and sent to one of the labs these companies possess I'm afraid they would be one step closer to figuring out one of the secrets of God. Mankind isn't ready for that kind of information. I don't know that for sure Sam but it is the only answer I can come up with."

"There are two women I fear will be devastated by the news of my death," Sam said.

Jacob knew what he was thinking. "You're talking about Jillian Ward and Bertha Potter?"

Sam was astonished, Jacob knew everything. "That's right, how did you know?"

"It is our job to know. The transition from one seven year cycle to the next is attempted without undoing the good that the Chosen has accomplished. To have this cycle end and the memory of Samuel Edgemont tarnished would be a disservice to all you have accomplished.

"The two women you spoke of will be allowed to participate in your funeral and at the end they will know you were more than just an ordinary man," Jacob said. This made Sam feel better, he had known Mrs. Potter only vaguely and Jillian even less but still he couldn't cause them pain. Knowing they would be alright made the drive easier.

Sam looked out the windshield and felt secure that everything in his past had been taken care of. As they drove he started to feel as if he had done this before, many times before.

"That explains the past Jacob, what about the future?" Sam asked.

"The future will be no different than the past. When the next cycle starts you will remember nothing of this cycle. You will make new friends, you will teach again and after seven years you will move on to the next. It is the same, always the same."

Sam thought about this and wondered how many cycles, as Jacob had called them, he had been through. He let that question lapse away for another. "You say I will teach again, I like that."

"Yes, you will teach again, you are and always have been a teacher Sam."

Sam didn't know it as they drove onward but he would also start donating blood again. It was a miracle that was never apparent until enough people took notice and started to question all the miraculous recoveries that were occurring. Even then it would take the resources of a greedy corporation to possibly uncover the truth. This last cycle had been cut short by nearly two years because of the efforts of Beeler-Jordan and The Steggman Group. Efforts would be made to protect the next cycle. The work Sam was responsible for was just too important to be stopped by greed or jealousy. Humankind, with this ability to transfer blood from one person to another, allowed the Chosen to do his work without raising many suspicions. In times past the miracles were much more out in the open for all to see.

Bertha Potter had kept a close vigil on Sam's house after she called to warn him that someone had most likely entered while he was at work. She heated herself a cup of Earl Grey tea and sweetened it with honey. Cup in hand she decided to sit on her front porch swing for a while. As she sat and enjoyed the evening she kept glancing toward Sam's house. After about an hour she decided that everything was alright and went back inside, it was already past dark.

Bertha got a new John Grisham book she had purchased recently and sat in her favorite rocker intending to read a few minutes. The book was good, really good because by the time Bertha looked at the clock again she realized an hour and a half had elapsed. "Darn you Grisham," she said to herself as she stood and went to the front window.

When Bertha pulled back the drapes she saw a sheriff's car sitting in front of Sam's house. She was startled at first but figured Sam had caught someone in his house or maybe found the place to have been burglarized. Bertha turned off the living room lights and then went back to the window. She intended to watch until she figured out what was going on and it would be better to do that from the darkness.

It wasn't long before the front door opened and Sam was led out, he was wearing handcuffs. The way the deputy shoved him in the back of the car Bertha thought Sam had hit his head on the top of the door frame. This was a mistake, the police had shown up and thought Sam had broken into the house and arrested him by mistake. That was it, just a case of mistaken identity.

Bertha went to the phone and grabbed the directory. She thought about dialing 911 but decided to dial the Sheriff's Department number instead. When she found the number for the Sheriff's Department she dialed the number. After two rings a woman answered and Bertha began, "Hello, this is Bertha Potter and I want to report a case of mistaken identity."

The dispatcher was confused, "Did you say mistaken identity ma'am?"

"That's right dear. Two of your deputies just arrested Samuel Edgemont, he lives on May's Branch," Bertha said.

The dispatcher knew how many units were on patrol and where they all were. "Mrs. Potter, I don't have any officers in May's Branch, none are within five miles of there. Can you repeat what has happened?"

"Yes dear, my neighbor Samuel Edgemont was just put in the back of a Floyd County Sheriff's car, he was wearing handcuffs. The two officers were wearing deputy uniforms."

The dispatcher knew Mrs. Potter from church and knew her information was probably reliable. "Mrs. Potter, give me your phone number please." The dispatcher didn't need the address; all calls to the Sheriff's Office gave the address on the dispatchers screen. After she verified the phone number Bertha gave was the same as the one on her screen the dispatcher told her there would be a sheriff's unit sent to her house, expect it very shortly.

After Bertha gave her the number they both hung up. The dispatcher contacted a unit that had just left the detention center and was heading toward Lancer-Watergap Road, she had the car to turn around and head toward May's Branch and the home of Bertha Potter. The car went through the intersection to the Mountain Parkway not more than two minutes after the bogus sheriff's car had been there and made the turn.

Bertha stayed by the front window of her house hoping the sheriff's car wouldn't be long. She was worried about Sam for two different reasons, first she really didn't think Sam had broken the law but if he had she wanted to know what he had done, secondly if Sam hadn't broken the law then he had just been arrested for something he hadn't done and could be in danger. Bertha was extremely nervous as she stood at her big front window and waited. She wondered if she should call Jillian; she would wait until she talked to the deputy the dispatcher was sending, then she would decide whether to call Jillian or not.

Within ten minutes a car pulled in front of Bertha's house, it was a sheriff's car. Bertha felt easier knowing there would be someone who could answer a few of her questions. Then she realized that the car that had been in front of Samuel Edgemont's house had the same markings as this car, she started to worry even more. Bertha quickly redialed the sheriff's office and got the same dispatcher she had talked to earlier.

"Hello, this is Bertha Potter again; did you send a deputy to my house?" She asked.

The dispatcher recognized Bertha's voice as soon as she heard her say hello. "Yes Mrs. Potter, the unit just radioed in, it is in front of your house now."

"Thank you so much, a widow can't be too careful these days you know." Both women said goodbye and hung up.

Just as Bertha was putting the cordless phone back in its cradle there was a knock at her front door. Bertha opened the front door and was glad to see Billy Howard standing there, all six foot, two hundred and fifty pounds of him. Billy was a fat deputy. Bertha unlatched the storm door and pushed it open. "Why Billy Howard, you look so all grown up with your deputy uniform and all."

Billy laughed. He had grown up in the neighborhood and remembered all the candy Bertha had given the neighborhood kids at Halloween. "Hello Mrs. Potter, trick or treat." They both laughed.

"Oh Billy, that brings back so many memories, you and all those kids looked so scary in your costumes. That's not a costume you're wearing now I hope." Again they both laughed.

"Would you come in, I want to talk to you about something." Bertha stepped back and Billy walked in.

"Would you like something to drink Billy, how about a nice cup of coffee? You deputies stay out all night, some coffee might help you to stay awake."

"Why Mrs. Potter that would be fine but don't go to any trouble."

"Why it won't be any trouble at all, you come in the kitchen and sit down. The coffee won't take a minute and I got a big Styrofoam cup you can take with you when you leave."

"Thank you Mrs. Potter. What happened across the street?" Deputy Howard asked.

Bertha had been so pleased to see one of her little trick or treaters that Sam had slipped her mind. "Oh yes, I need to tell you about that." Bertha put a packet of coffee in her fancy little coffee machine and then added the water. "My neighbor across the street, Samuel Edgemont, he teaches at the college in Pikeville. Well, two deputies came to his house a little while ago and arrested him."

Deputy Howard knew who was working tonight. Floyd County isn't the biggest county in the state but it is substantial, there are also nearly fifty-five thousand people living there. The sheriff's department likes to have at least five cars out during the night in different parts of the county in order to have a quicker response time. He knew who was on duty tonight and approximately where each car was. He also knew that none of the other cars had been anywhere near May's Branch in the last three or four hours.

Bertha filled the cup for Billy and then put in a little cream and sugar. It was the way she drank her coffee and she just assumed everyone else drank their coffee the same way. "Here you go Billy; see if that is all right, I can add more cream and sugar if you like."

As Billy was thinking about where each of the other cars had been that evening he took a sip of the coffee, it was good. Bertha really knew how to fix coffee he thought.

"Are you sure it was a Sheriff's Department car Mrs. Potter. Lots of police cars look alike you know."

"Oh, it was a car just like yours Billy, one of them big Ford Crown Victoria's. I know it was because my husband loved the look of a Crown Victoria. He liked them so well that he drove one for years. I remember when they stopped making them, my husband was so mad. When it was time to trade again he switched to Chevrolet instead of buying another Ford," Bertha said.

Billy remembered Mr. Potter and his Crown Vic. It had been parked on the side of the street for years. He also remembered bumping into it with his bicycle one day. It had been an accident and he remembered how Mr. Potter ran off the front porch. He thought Mr. Potter was going to have a fit over the big scratch he put on the car but he didn't. Mr. Potter was scared that Billy might have gotten hurt. That big scratch on the side of the car never bothered Mr. Potter in the least.

"Why that's just a car Billy. That scratch don't hurt a thing, as a matter of fact I'll probably get better gas mileage now that I don't have to haul around all that extra paint," Mr. Potter said as he laughed. "The main thing is that you didn't get hurt. Now let's just keep this little scratch a secret, just between you and me. There's no need to let your mom or Bertha know anything about it, we'll both be better off."

Billy always remembered that little talk he and Mr. Potter had about the bike wreck. It had taught Billy two important childhood lessons. Use more caution when riding a bike and use more forgiveness when someone does something wrong. He was a deputy now and liked to consider himself a good one. He had seen men put on that uniform and gun and think they could rule over everyone they met in a high handed manner. Not Billy, he was kind but firm. He knew most people who made a mistake would probably never do it again.

"You said there were two police officers over there, what were they wearing Mrs. Potter?"

"They were both wearing uniforms just like the one you are wearing Billy."

He knew it was dark and the house in question was three doors away. "Are you sure Mrs. Potter? That is quite a distance in the dark to know what type of police car it was or what kind of uniforms the two men were wearing," Billy said.

"I saw the car and the uniforms plain as day Billy. I am positive of what I saw."

Billy got up and went into the living room; he looked up the street at the house. There was a street light nearby but still it was hard to make out any details from this far away. Just as Billy turned to explain to Mrs. Potter that an eyewitness account at night and from this distance left room for mistakes, she reached him a pair of binoculars that she had picked up from the coffee table.

"Here you go Billy, try looking through these." He almost laughed when she reached him the binoculars.

"Is this what you used to see what happened?"

"It certainly is. I can't see as well as I used to and those binoculars come in real handy at times."

The Donor

Billy raised the binos to his eyes and peered up the street. They were already adjusted to the distance. The view was crystal clear. "I guess that explains how you saw what you saw Mrs. Potter. Now if you could please explain the sequence that everything happened in."

Bertha explained everything that happened and then put the binoculars back on her table. Billy wrote everything down and knew he needed to get back in his car to call it in. He didn't want Mrs. Potter to overhear what he said over his radio. Anybody that peered out their front window with binoculars surely had a well-established network of busybodies and snoops to report to. "Thank you Mrs. Potter, I better get to work on this."

Bertha grabbed his coffee cup, "Not before I refill that foam cup of yours. You can't be working all night without some more coffee." Bertha headed for the kitchen and shortly returned with a full cup. She even had a plastic sippy lid on top. "Here you go Billy, now go and find out what happened over there tonight. I am so worried."

Billy again thanked Mrs. Potter for the coffee and headed to his car. Once inside he started the engine and then called dispatch, he gave the highlights of what he had learned from Mrs. Potter.

Just as the dispatcher, the same lady that Bertha had talked to, was ready to end the call with Billy she got another call, "Billy can you hold a minute?" With that the dispatcher took the call. Billy heard what she was saying and knew something had happened. While the dispatcher talked Billy turned his cruiser and headed out of May's Branch. He suspected he might be needed elsewhere.

"The dispatcher didn't use Billy's call number, she just asked if he was still there. "Got a report of a single car crash near the Floyd County line on route 114, didn't give which side of the line the crash is on. The caller was pretty excited. Caller reports multiple occupants in the car, serious injuries. And Billy, the caller said it's a sheriff's car."

Billy hit the lights and siren and sped away. He was told he was the nearest officer but others would be in route. Two ambulances were also dispatched. When Billy hit the road that led toward the Mountain Parkway he pushed his cruiser to ninety miles an hour. He would have gone faster but knew if he hit a deer at that speed he probably wouldn't live to tell about it. As he raced toward Salyersville he thought about the car Bertha had seen. He also thought about the two men dressed as deputies and the man they had arrested, Samuel Edgemont.

From the time Billy got the call until he reached the crash site thirteen minutes had elapsed, he pushed his cruiser as hard as he dared. There were four or five cars on either side of the road; thankfully this portion had a wide berm on both sides where a car could park completely off the highway. Billy killed the siren but left the lights blaring. He parked on the side of the road as near as he could to where several people stood looking over the embankment.

As Billy got out of his car he thought about putting on his hat but then decided if he was going to go down into the creek the hat should stay in the car. As he approached the bystander's one asked, "Are you Floyd County?"

"Yes sir, I'm a deputy with the Sheriff's Department." The bystanders could only see the police lights, not the type of car they belonged to.

"It's one of your cars deputy. I think the men inside are either unconscious or dead. I went down and checked, wanted to give aid but the car is standing on its nose and I was afraid it might turn over on me."

Billy had gotten out of his car with the powerful flashlight all deputies carried. He stood at the top of the hill and pointed the beam at the wreck. It was a Floyd County Sheriff's Department car alright. He grabbed the mic which was held in place on his shoulder by Velcro. He was ready to call it in when he noticed there wasn't a unit number on the back of the car. There weren't the standard Government Issue license plates on the back either.

Billy pressed the mic and said, "Got a single vehicle wreck, car appears to be a sheriff's patrol car but there isn't a unit number on the back. Got a standard issue license number WRJ-725."

As the dispatcher wrote down the information she thought about Bertha and her earlier call. "I'll run the plates. Two ambulances have been dispatched and are ten minutes out." The dispatchers name was Ermine and she had been working as a dispatcher for nearly twelve years. In all that time she had heard some strange things but this was taking it to a whole new level.

"You better get a wrecker or roll-back out here too, I don't think we can do much until we get the car stabilized," Billy said.

"One is on the way," Ermine said.

Ermine had the plates ran and within minutes called Billy back. "Plate number WRJ-725 is a stolen, reported four days ago out of Charleston, West Virginia."

"Roger that," Billy said.

Seven minutes after Billy got there another unit arrived on the scene. It was decided to block traffic in both directions until the injured men could be extricated, it still wasn't known as to the extent of their injuries. A few minutes later the first ambulance arrived. After the crew got a look at the extent of the crash and the position of the car it was decided to wait for the wrecker before entering the wreck.

Ten minutes went by before a wrecker pulled to the side of the road. It was directed to attach a cable to the rear of the car in order to stabilize it and then the ambulance crew could proceed.

Billy had already called dispatch again. "This is pretty bad. Roll the rescue squad."

Ermine called out the Floyd County Emergency and Rescue Squad, one of if not the best in the entire state. Forty-eight minutes after the twelve-point buck had sent the car into Middle Creek the rescue squad rolled onto the scene. Many of the team had been listening on their radios and had made their way to the squad building knowing they would most likely be called out. When the call came in enough men were there to load up and head out, these guys knew their stuff and were always anxious to mix it up. When the Captain's feet hit the pavement and he saw what had happened he was mad as hell. His crew should have been one of the first notified and now precious minutes had been wasted. A later review found no fault in the actions of any of the first responders. It had actually been determined that the response time was exceptional. This did little to soothe the feelings of the Captain, he always wanted better.

The rescue squad had the car secured nine minutes after they arrived. It was actually chained to the guardrail for safety. It couldn't tip over, it couldn't go left and it couldn't go right. The Rescue Squad sent one Paramedic and an EMT into the front of the car. The ambulance crew was allowed to check the man in the rear. Thirty seconds later they announced all three were dead. The men felt that if the Rescue Squad and the Ambulance had been parked within fifty feet of where the wreck occurred when they were notified, it wouldn't have mattered. Response time was not a factor. The autopsies of the men would later determine that all three had died on impact.

"Better get the coroner out here," Billy radioed in.

With three men still inside the car, but all three dead, it was felt the safest way to remove the bodies was to pull the car out first. The Captain didn't want to endanger anyone; the rescue had just turned into a recovery. The wrecker was attached and the chains removed. The car was slowly pulled from the creek bed and positioned on the shoulder of the road. The grizzly work went on for another hour; it took another two hours for the State Police to document the crash scene and take measurements and photos. Orange spray paint was used to highlight the skid marks and the spot where the car exited the highway. Finally, a little over three hours after the wreck had happened the road was reopened. Traffic was backed up over a mile in each direction.

The sheriff had been called once it was determined that a Floyd County Sheriff's Department vehicle had been involved. By the time the car was pulled from the creek no fewer than eight deputies were on the scene, some not even on duty.

"Billy, you were first on scene, what do you make of this?" The sheriff asked.

"I got a suspicion that those two men masquerading around in our uniforms kidnapped the man who died in the back seat of that car," Billy said.

The identification of all three men had been obtained by what they carried in their wallets. The two in the front carried fake papers and fake driver's licenses; this wouldn't be found out until the next day. The man in the back seat had been identified as Samuel Edgemont, and he lived in Prestonsburg.

"We know that isn't one of our cars, that's for sure. How do you know about the man in the back?" The sheriff asked.

"I was working on another call when this came in. The woman I talked to was a neighbor of Edgemont's and saw two deputies arrest him at his residence and put him in that car that is now on the roll-back. I got the call on this wreck just after I finished talking to Mrs. Potter," Billy said.

"I don't want anyone talking to the newspaper or the Hazard television station until we figure this out. The last thing we need is for someone to think we had anything to do with this wreck or the arrest of Edgemont," the sheriff said. Billy agreed. A large tarp was used to cover the car on the rollback.

Bertha Potter stayed up late, she didn't know why but she felt the events of the evening weren't quite over yet, she was right. At eleven twenty-five two deputies driving two different patrol cars parked on the street in front of Samuel Edgemont's house. Bertha went to the coffee table and picked up her binoculars. At the big picture window she saw the two deputies get out of their cars and look at the house. Finally one went to the front door and pushed the doorbell. No one came to the door so the deputy pushed the button again. Still no one answered. Now the deputy knocked and then knocked again. The door never opened.

Bertha knew Sam wasn't home, she knew two deputies that were wearing the same uniforms as the two over there now had come and taken him away. Bertha got the cordless phone and dialed the dispatcher at the sheriff's department.

"Hello, this is Bertha Potter again. I noticed there are two deputies at Sam Edgemont's house. I hoped when they pulled up they were bringing Sam home. I see now that they are knocking on his door but as I said before he isn't home. When will he be home?"

Ermine knew one of the bodies in the wrecked car was that of Samuel Edgemont, it wasn't her job to tell anyone. She could tell Mrs. Potter was concerned. "The deputies are just checking to see if anyone else is there. They will come back tomorrow and check again Mrs. Potter."

"Thank you and please let me know when you find him. I have been so worried." Both women hung up.

Bertha thought about calling Jillian but when she looked at the wall clock she decided against it, it was getting late. Bertha always watched the late news before going to bed. She sat in her favorite chair and with the remote she found the channel. There had been a car crash between Prestonsburg and Salyersville. There were no specifics yet, information was still coming in. It was known that a police car was involved. More details on the morning edition.

Bertha clicked the TV off. A police car had been involved in a crash. Sam was in a police car. Sam wasn't home either. Now Bertha changed her mind about calling Jillian.

Jillian had just finished getting ready for bed when she heard her phone ring. Now who could that be at such a late hour she wondered? She ran into her bedroom and picked up the phone. "Hello."

"Jillian, this is your Aunt Bertha, how are you dear?"

Jillian could tell by the late hour and the sound of her aunt's voice that something was wrong. "Aunt Bertha, why are you calling so late, is everything okay."

"No dear, everything isn't okay. I don't know where to start."

Jillian knew it must be terrible. "Go ahead Aunt Bertha, just start talking."

"I'm afraid Sam is in some sort of trouble. The police came to his house a few hours ago and they led him away in handcuffs." At this Bertha started crying.

Jillian was shocked, what kind of man had her aunt introduced her to? It didn't make sense though, Sam was such a nice man, and he was a teacher. "I'm sure there is an explanation Aunt Bertha."

"No dear, what kind of explanation can there be?"

Jillian couldn't think; this just didn't seem possible. "Let me do some checking Aunt Bertha, I'll call you back."

"Please do dear; I'm sure there is some kind of mistake. Call me as soon as you find out anything." Both women hung up.

Jillian called one of the partners in the firm she worked for. He was from Kentucky and maybe knew what to do. As it worked out the partner she called did the only criminal work the firm handled. He knew someone in Eastern Kentucky, another attorney that had a lot of friends down there. Attorneys might fight tooth and nail against each other in a courtroom but outside the courtroom they always try to do what they can for each other; it was just the way things worked.

Within an hour Jillian was told by the partner that none of the judges in Floyd County had signed a warrant for the arrest of one Samuel Edgemont, he hadn't committed a crime. The two men that picked him up weren't deputies either. This wasn't common knowledge but attorneys seemed to be able to find things out.

She was also told that Sam had been killed in a crash involving a Floyd County Sheriff's car. He said he was sorry to convey such bad news. Jillian thanked him and then sat down, she cried. How could this have happened, how could she ever tell her aunt?

The next day the news broke. A professor had been kidnapped the night before at his home by two men masquerading as deputies. In their attempt to leave the county there had been a wreck and all three men were killed. An attempt was being made to contact next of kin but as of yet none had been found. It seemed that all records for Samuel Edgemont only went back five years.

Jillian packed a bag and contacted her office; she needed to take a few days off for personal reasons. She filled her car with gas and headed for Floyd County. Her Aunt Bertha was sitting on the front porch when Jillian pulled up. Both hugged and then cried. When the crying stopped they were looking at Sam's house. There were police cars and crime scene tape everywhere.

"Has any of Sam's family been contacted yet?" Jillian asked.

"No dear, as far as they can tell he doesn't have any family. The college has no records of any in his file. It is as if he just dropped out of the heavens and landed here in Prestonsburg," Bertha said; if she only knew.

"If he has no family then who will make the arrangements for his funeral, who will see to his affairs?" Jillian asked.

Bertha stopped crying and looked at her niece. She stiffened her back and said, "We will, we are the only ones around that seem to have ever cared for Sam. We will see to a nice wake for him, I think he would have liked that."

Jillian smiled a sad smile. "I think that would be nice Aunt Bertha."

"We never really knew him but I don't think anyone else did either," Bertha said.

Helen Montgomery and her son made the trip back to Floyd County in a rented car. Her son had come straight to the nursing home as soon as his plane touched down at Bluegrass Airport. He rented a car and hurried to River Terrace. He and his mother hugged for at least five minutes. He was so glad to see her again. He was amazed, it was the mom he had known before the dementia had taken over, and she seemed completely healed. Her son couldn't believe how she sounded and looked. It was as if she were fifteen or twenty years younger.

Her bags were packed and the paperwork only needed her son's signature. Helen hugged her friends and promised to come back in a month or two to visit. As she left she wondered if they would all be there by the time she came back. Some of her dearest friends were so frail. As happy as it was to be going home it was just as sad to say goodbye to everyone, they had been so special these last few weeks, every one of them.

It took two and a half hours to make the drive from Lexington to Maytown. The fall colors had begun to wane; bright reds, oranges and yellows were giving way to dull browns. It didn't matter to Helen; the scenery of the mountains had never looked so beautiful. When they pulled off the four-lane road and took the two-lane that would lead them to her house Helen perked up considerably, if she had been excited during the trip now she could hardly contain herself.

When they rounded a curve and her house came into view she noticed the driveway was full of cars, there were even cars parked on the side of the road and a few in the yard. A place had been saved for the car she and her son drove. There in the front yard was a big handmade sign, "Welcome Home Helen" was written in big red letters. The porch and yard seemed to be full of people. Helen was laughing as she got out of the car.

With hugs and laughter all around Helen glanced toward the big window in the front of the house. Standing on the window sill on the inside was Blackie. The cat saw Helen and began to brush the glass pane with her front paws. Helen momentarily forgot everyone as she went inside. She picked up her beloved cat and when she came back outside carrying Blackie there were tears in her eyes, tears of joy. Along with the chatter of forty people could now be heard the loud purring of an extremely happy long haired cat. Helen Montgomery was home.

John and Nancy Oden were enjoying everything these days. John's new lease on life meant they could concentrate on putting the farm to rest for the winter. As the farm work got finished and there was less and less to do each day the two began thinking about a trip to Gatlinburg, Tennessee in the Great Smoky Mountains.

Nancy told John to plan on at least a week. He fussed about taking care of dogs and what other few livestock they had but Nancy told him to just smile and get over it. They hadn't been on a week's vacation in thirty years.

John had always been good to take care of other farmer's livestock when anyone was going to be out of town for a day or two, sometimes even longer. Water and feed the cattle, turn horses out at daylight and put them back up at night, he would even use a key to feed someone's house cat. He had done this for different people over the years just because he was a good neighbor. Now those same neighbors were glad to return the favor. His place would be looked after with all the care he had shown them over the years.

As the time grew near John actually began to look forward to a little getaway. He told his wife it would feel strange to not be wearing bib-overalls for a full week. He laughed when he told her he was still going to wear his muck boots the entire trip. She made a fist and asked him if he wanted to go back to the hospital. He left the muck boots at home.

John had a whole new outlook on life, now he enjoyed each minute of every day. Nothing was too small or trivial to be overlooked; he could find happiness in almost anything. He had been given a second chance and he was going to make the most of it.

Van Goodwin had felt better lately than he had in years. He had gotten so used to getting up at five-o'clock in the morning during the years he had been on dialysis that now he usually still got up at the same time. To sleep late for Van was to stay in bed until five-thirty. He was on his front porch each morning before six-o'clock drinking coffee and watching for the first lights of his neighbors to turn on, it always made him chuckle.

Van had enjoyed fishing when he was younger; he had an aluminum Bass Tracker boat that hadn't been on the water in years. That was about to change. He had taken the motor to a man in town that worked on such things and had it rebuilt. While the motor was being worked on Van cleaned the old boat and trailer up. He even bought a new trolling motor, a quieter more powerful version of the one he had used for years.

The boat trailer got two brand new tires and new tail lights. Van had gone out the previous Saturday morning and was on the water by seven. His favorite lake was only a few miles from home, Dewey Lake, or Jenny Wiley Lake as some people called it.

Dewey had a few good fish and Van knew how to catch 'em. Four hours was always enough to get at least two bass or maybe five or six crappie for his lunch. He could put the boat in the water, get to one of his favorite spots and then be back home before noon. By one-o'clock he was eating freshly caught and fried fish along with skillet fried potatoes. Now that his kidneys were fully functional he could enjoy all the iced tea he wanted. Not only was his kidney problem cured but his diabetes was under control without medication, it was actually non-existent.

Van's doctor never failed to tell him how lucky he was. Van knew how lucky he was; no one had to tell him twice. When the weather allowed he fished three or four days a week. Sunday was always worship day, he loved the morning service and since his health was no longer a concern he now had the energy to attend the evening services as well. He was even thinking about attending the Wednesday night service as he had done before he had gotten so sick. Van not only wanted to go for himself but also for the welfare of others too. Anyone who knew what kind of shape he had been in could look at him now and know it was the Lord's work. He was a living breathing walking miracle and he thanked God every day.

After the wreck that had taken the life of Samuel Edgemont, it seemed that both Beeler-Jordan and The Steggman group had fallen on hard times. Beeler-Jordan was under a federal investigation with a long list of charges filed against them, both civil and criminal. Steggman was in no better shape. The two dead men wearing deputy uniforms were traced back to Steggman and the FBI had gotten warrants and raided their corporate offices. They found a treasure trove of information and the list of charges was being amended almost daily.

With both companies on the defensive and management busy pointing fingers trying to save their own hides, any thought of corporate espionage and spying was now long forgotten. Both companies were in survival mode. The other drug companies that had competed with Beeler-Jordan and Steggman were relieved that they could now concentrate on what they did best; research and development of drugs that would help doctors and nurses heal patients. No more looking over their shoulders at two corporations with less than desirable ethics.

Of all the dirty tricks and devious behavior Beeler-Jordan and The Steggman Group had been involved in over the years it was their plans against Samuel Edgemont that had brought the two giant corporations to their knees.

Edgemont's time in Eastern Kentucky had helped so many; the numbers were in the thousands. He had managed to donate 126 times, mostly platelet donations. One donation doesn't help just one person, it helps several. Sam would never know the exact number; he would also never know how much he had done in straightening out the pharmaceutical industry. Although this seven year cycle had been cut short, it was still one of the most productive.

Jacob Yates and Samuel Edgemont traveled most of the night. It had been decided by the Committee that the airport in Lexington, Bluegrass Airport, was too risky. As of late, Beeler-Jordan and Steggman had used it on almost a daily basis. Edgemont was too important to take a chance of him being spotted.

Jacob had headed west on the Mountain Parkway to throw anyone off on where they were really headed, Atlanta. The quickest route to Atlanta from Prestonsburg wasn't through Lexington but that was the direction he wanted everyone to think, assuming anyone was following. At Lexington they would turn south on Interstate 75.

"Where are we heading Jacob?" Sam asked.

"For now, Lexington. We will grab a bite to eat and fill up the car. We head south from there once I get a phone call telling me that everything is okay."

"You think someone is following us?" Sam asked.

"Not really, this is just a precaution. We will have a different car waiting there along with new papers for you."

"If we are getting a different car then why are we filling this one up?"

"To make it look like this is the car we will be using when we leave Lexington. It won't be, but if anyone has been able to follow us then hopefully they will continue to follow this car. It will be driven by two men that look similar to the two of us but it will be heading toward Louisville. That is another eighty miles west, by the time anyone realizes the switch we will be that much farther south," Jacob explained.

Sam thought this over and decided he liked it. After being kidnapped and losing his life in a car crash, so to speak, he trusted Jacob and this Committee he spoke of. "You mentioned papers for me, what kind of papers?"

"New driver's license and a passport, you will also be given plane tickets and an itinerary."

"A passport, will I be leaving the country?" Sam asked.

"You always change countries after each cycle; your work takes you many places."

The two men rode along in silence for a while. As each mile passed Sam began to feel that he had done this before, as he really had. His mind was giving up the last cycle and preparing to move into the next. By the time they reached Atlanta he would be aware of many things but at the beginning of the next cycle he would forget everything again and his new memories would explain a life he had never lived, he would step into that life as if he had experienced everything his memories told him.

"How many times have I done this Jacob?" Sam asked.

Jacob didn't know the answer; he knew it was a lot. "I can't say for sure Sam. That was never important as far as my part in this goes. I would guess it has been many times, as much as to span a thousand years maybe even two thousand. You have walked this world longer than I myself can imagine."

"Two thousand years," Sam said. After the longest time he added. "I may have walked with Jesus; I may have even talked to him Jacob. Do you think that's possible?"

Again Jacob didn't have the answer. He only had his thoughts. "I don't know Sam but if I were to guess I would say the chances are high. I don't know how much information the Committee has but I do know how much they are willing to share. What I know now is all they are ever going to tell me. I do know there have been many others like me over the ages. My duty to the Committee, and you, will soon be over."

"What happens to you after I am gone Jacob?" Sam asked this with no small amount of concern.

"I don't know that part yet. I hope to be allowed to go back to the cabin I have called home for the last five years. If not I suspect I will just live a normal life from here on out. I will remember my contributions with great satisfaction though. To be able to take part in something like this is wonderful beyond description. There is one stipulation that was put in place the day I was told what my duties were, I was never to speak of this to anyone. I am only a participant in what you have done and are about to do again. The gift of being able to assist in something like this is my only reward, and it is a great reward. I will spend the remainder of my days believing, what more could a man desire?"

The body Samuel Edgemont occupied for the last five years was taken to Frankfort Kentucky for an autopsy the morning after the crash. Once that was finished it was sent back to a local Funeral Home in Martin Kentucky. He was to be buried three days after his death in a plot that had been purchased many years prior. All this had been explained in his Will. It was odd that the Will mentioned both cremation and burial.

The Will had been found in Sam's office with instructions for his arrangements. The Will was of such scope that no detail was left to chance. His belongings were to be sold and the funds dispersed equally between his church and the college where he had taught for the last five years.

The most amazing thing about his Will was that it named, as its Executor, a woman who he barely knew when he died, Bertha Potter. When Bertha found this out she was flattered that he trusted her to carry out such an important task. The Will was dated Sunday April 8th 2012. This was before Bertha had ever met Samuel Edgemont, as hard as she tried she never ever remembered hearing that name in her entire life, not until several months after he moved to May's Branch.

In the Will it was desired that the remains be cremated. Bertha would have nothing to do with that. He would receive a proper burial and that was final. It wasn't a problem, the man known as Samuel Edgemont had been buried as many times as he had been cremated.

On the day of the funeral there was to be no eulogy, if any words were spoken it would only attest to the fact that Sam was a teacher, he had taught for a very long time. This was stipulated in his burial arrangements. The body that had been placed in the casket three days prior needed no kind words, no tears, and no sadness.

The Donor

At one o'clock, under a cloudless sky, the hearse backed up to a freshly dug grave. The six men named as pall-bearers stepped to the back and removed the casket; it was a very light casket.

The End